HIGH PRAISE FOR HAGGAI CARMON'S
TRIPLE IDENTITY!

"An impressively authentic debut thriller."

—*Publishers Weekly*

"Riveting, full of imagination, unusual characters, and fantastic events."

—Shimon Peres, Nobel Peace Prize Laureate,
President of Israel

"All the intrigue and plot machinations you'd expect from an author with professional ties to the Department..."

—...*Post*

Carmon "has manage... ...d with his seamless weav... ...e wondering which is w...

...mber of Mossad's Directorate

"A thriller debut to rival the masters."

—*The Anniston Star*

"A new espionage thriller star is born."

—*The National Jewish Post and Opinion*

"Shows an unusual familiarity with the gritty reality of intel ops and has the feel and smell of authenticity in the dialogue and plot that will result in enthusiastic readers among our professional intel members. A number of tradecraft surprises, too."

—*Intelligencer*

"A fast-paced, compelling whodunnit...a worthy page-turner for spending a day at the beach."

—*New Jersey Jewish News*

"This book is terrific. Great characters, settings, and superb trade knowledge. I am eager to buy the first sequel."

—Jim Guy Tucker, former Governor of Arkansas

MORE PRAISE FOR HAGGAI CARMON!

"I find his book fascinating and as close to the truth as you could possibly do without infringing on confidentiality and issues of national security...."

—Daniel Ayalon, Ambassador of Israel
to the United States

"In *Triple Identity* first-time novelist Haggai Carmon gives Israel a spy worthy of James Bond...."

—*The Jewish Chronicle*

"Carmon gives you the feeling that he is letting you in on the spy's tricks of the trade....It's an exciting ride."

—*Hadassah Magazine*

Triple Identity "is a truly classic piece of spy novel fiction! I urge you to buy it, read it, and enjoy it."

—Hon. James J. Brown, U.S. Federal
Administrative Law Judge

"From the moment I began reading this extraordinary book, I could not put it down. Haggai Carmon takes us beyond the main plot and leads us on to several subplots, each as riveting as the principal one....As Israel's former Minister of Homeland Security, and mayor of Tel Aviv-Jaffa, I could identify some of Carmon's descriptions of Dan Gordon's adventures as very real, although Carmon in the introduction vehemently denies any resemblance. A must-read for anyone who likes to be riveted by an outstanding thriller."

—Roni Milo, Former Minister of Homeland
Security of Israel and Mayor of Tel Aviv

Carmon "molds into his first novel his professional experience and builds a rhythmic and captivating thriller that combines motifs favored by John Grisham with smooth nonchalant language."

—*Yedioth Acharonot*

UNDERCOVER TO IRAN

"Have you also done a risk assessment?" asked Casey.

"No. I was asked to deal with finding the Chameleon. Another team made the assessment. But since you asked, I agree that there are significant risks involved in penetration, even under our proposed plan and I understand them. If caught, whoever goes there has little or no chance of walking away from it alive."

I took a deep breath. "But if there's a good plan, I'm willing to volunteer for that mission." I knew that I'd fare better as a lone wolf in an operation designed for a single operative. During my military service I'd realized that many would volunteer for a mission until it was time to go. But not here; I was willing.

Benny, who sat next to me, said quietly, "Dan, you're crazy…"

Other *Leisure* books by Haggai Carmon:

THE RED SYNDROME
TRIPLE IDENTITY

HAGGAI
CARMON

THE
CHAMELEON
CONSPIRACY

LEISURE BOOKS   NEW YORK CITY

To Ella, whom I loved even before she was born.

A LEISURE BOOK®

April 2009

Published by

Dorchester Publishing Co., Inc.
200 Madison Avenue
New York, NY 10016

ISBN 10: 0-8439-6191-0
ISBN 13: 978-0-8439-6191-1
E-ISBN: 1-4285-0651-9

Visit us on the web at www.dorchesterpub.com.

THE
CHAMELEON
CONSPIRACY

INTRODUCTION

On this one-hundred-year anniversary of Ian Fleming's birth, Dan Gordon may become the new James Bond, to rid us of post–Cold War threats. Fleming's novels have created an image of the successful intelligence officer, who saves the world equipped with a Walther PPK and a martini shaken, not stirred. This tuxedo-clad hero seems to comprise the Empire's entire intelligence service. While both are masters at the game, Dan Gordon is closer to the reality I know. He is unarmed. He actually writes reports and worries about receipts. He operates within a professional structure where approvals are necessary. While he is mindful of the chain of command, Dan is an independent, self-sufficient, and smart risk taker. After discoursing on life in the CIA to a group of high school students, I was asked, "Yes, but tell us about the time you were surrounded by a bunch of bad guys all pointing their guns at you. How did you get away?" Dan Gordon understands that the essence of the profession is to take all the necessary risks to get the job done without ever allowing yourself to be surrounded by those bad guys, especially if they're armed. What he shares with the Bond character is his intelligence, his tenaciousness, and his love of good food, although Dan doesn't insist on five-star cuisine. And, so far, Dan hasn't run into the easy and beautiful women of the Fleming tales. And, in my long CIA career, neither have I.

Khomeini's 1979 overthrow of the Shah was the only successful religious revolution in modern times, helped by a confluence of factors, not the least of which was President Carter's pressure on a Shah dying of cancer to increase human rights.

More Iranians died at the hands of the new commissars than under the reviled SAVAK, the Iranian internal security service. Driven by nationalist and theological ambitions, Iranian military expansion was blunted by the long and bloody Iran-Iraq War. But its policies have not changed—only its tactics. Within easy reach of Iran's Shehab III missiles, Israel is only too aware of the threat. However, while the media focuses on Iran's nuclear, missile, and satellite-launcher programs, the regime of the mullahs has turned into a state mafia, a veritable criminal syndicate *sans frontières*. Under the radar, the Islamic Revolution's storm troopers, the Iranian Revolutionary Guard Corps, is involved in terrorism (according to the State Department), arms shipments and assassinations (according to the media), and illegal financial transactions (according to the Department of the Treasury).

Haggai Carmon convinced me of his intelligence bona fides in the first minute I spoke with him. He writes convincingly about the intricate world of intelligence. He understands the feeling of the intelligence officer's solitary walk to the lesser-used departure gates of international air terminals as he heads for nontouristic destinations. He brings to life the tension that characterizes the work of the clandestine operator in a hostile environment, where the opposition is not just the police, but the bloc *komites*, or Iranian moral police, and a citizenry cowed into submission into reporting all "suspicious" activities.

The vivid descriptions in *The Chameleon Conspiracy* bring the reader inside the story. A Haggai Carmon story requires an alert reader. Each page reveals new layers that the protagonist and the reader discover together. His use of suspense keeps the reader alert. Carmon succeeds in the first rule of the suspense writer, to have the reader wonder, *What would I do in that situation?* and compelling him to turn the page to find out how the fictional protagonist did it and survived to the end of the story. Whether he writes about Jaffa or Iran, it is like being there. And finally, as a longtime practitioner of clandestine tradecraft, I take my hat off to Haggai. Not all real intelligence officers have Dan Gordon's savvy or imagination, the author's gift to his brainchild.

Andre Le Gallo

Andre Le Gallo had a successful career with U.S. intelligence. As an operations officer with the CIA's clandestine-operations arm, he worked in collection, counterintelligence, and covert action, including special operations. His overseas assignments total twenty years, eleven of them as chief of station in four countries. Serving for thirteen years at CIA headquarters, he held senior positions in the Directorate of Operations, was the National Intelligence Officer for Counterterrorism (National Intelligence Council), and was a senior DO representative in the Inspector General Corps. Andre Le Gallo is the author of The Caliphate, *a thriller inspired by his long career as an intelligence operative.*

CHAPTER ONE

Sydney, Australia, August 17, 2004

"I'm not Albert C. Ward III. My name is Herbert Goldman! There must be a mistake." The man in the hospital bed was insistent.

I was amused.

"Look here," he tried again, when he saw my knowing smile. "I'm a sick man. The doctors say I shouldn't get overexcited. What you're doing to me is murder, you're killing me!" Seeing that I wouldn't budge, he rolled his eyes. He was dressed in a hospital gown that bared his backside, and a feeding tube crawled under the top part. Looking at him, I almost felt sympathy. Albert C. Ward III could have been any other patient in the ward: a slight, almost unnoticeable middle-aged man, lying there now like a deflated balloon. But that was Ward's greatest asset. Who'd be suspicious of a small man in his late forties, whose few remaining teeth weren't in such great shape? He had thinning hair that he combed sideways, applying the "savings and loan" comb-over: saving on the side where it still grew, and loaning it to the side where hair was long gone.

We had just met for the first time, but I knew who I was dealing with. Right there in his hospital bed, he might have seemed older than his years, and he might have seemed humble. Albert C. Ward III *was* humble; he wouldn't confront or cross you on anything, unless you were an investor or a banker sitting on some money, while he was thirsty for cash. The problem was that he was always thirsty. To quench that thirst, Ward would become a human chameleon and change from nobody to somebody in a heartbeat—a sneaky little devil, who'd siphon money from banks and walk silently away while the banks collapsed

into the receiving hands of federal regulators for being under-
capitalized, while investors lamented the loss of their uninsured
savings, and while American taxpayers picked up most of the
bill. Yes, that was Ward's expertise. He was a banker for a new
era: he banked on people's foolishness and greed. A con artist of
epic proportions.

Ward was the only patient in a small room at the internal-
medicine department of Macquarie Street Hospital in Sydney,
Australia. It was a public hospital in the city center, not far from
my hotel. Ward could have been mistaken for the man behind
the counter at the post office . . . the refrigerator repairman,
maybe. But that's not entirely fair to say. Those good people
never made history. Albert C. Ward III did.

One detail set Ward apart from the other patients in the hospital: a uniformed Australian policeman sat beside him, making
sure that Ward wouldn't vanish again. Ward lay there in a simple
metal-frame hospital bed, its white paint chipping around the
edges. The room was clean, almost sterile, but no one would
linger unless they had to. The unbroken view of cement wall,
the smell of antiseptic mixed with human urine, and the hollow
eyes of patients for whom this would be the last stop ensured
that.

For Albert C. Ward III, it was definitely not the last stop.
This was his usual route—feigning a critical illness, approaching death's door when he felt the law closing in on him. The
history Albert C. Ward III made wasn't an achievement to be
inscribed on his tombstone when the time came. He wouldn't
make the record books. But still, he was a champion of something. Otherwise, how could he have evaded law and justice for
nearly two decades, not to mention evading me for longer than
any other target I'd ever chased? Well, he had come close.

The only available pictures of him, dating back to high
school, were on my desk, at home, and even in my car. Ward was
a wanted man. Everyone was after him, including the FBI and
the Office of Asset Recovery and Money Laundering of the
U.S. Department of Justice (with me their senior investigative

attorney). All of my life—three years at the Mossad, Israel's foreign intelligence service, and the time spent earning my Israeli and American law degrees—had been leading up to this. As an investigative attorney at DOJ, I'd been finding the money launderers, the scammers, the con artists who made off with other people's money and stashed it away in sunny, far-off places and brought it back to the United States. Sometimes I also brought home the perpetrators. We called them absconders, targets, or defendants; the tax havens of the world called them investors. Obviously there was an ongoing conflict between me, the asset hunter, and these exotically located asset protectors. A better word would be *battle*, or even *war*. *Conflict* is a laundered word for stiff-upper-lip delegates at the UN.

We had long been at war with the money launderers and their guardians. And when you're at war, you enlist the finest. As for whether I fit into that category, well, you could ask any of the people who dealt with me professionally—that is, if you could get into prison to find them. So although I had pity for the chameleon that was in Albert C. Ward III's bed, I was still awed by how he had managed to pull it off. Not once, not twice, but eleven times. And those were only the cases in which the FBI had determined him to be the main suspect. Who knew how many others there had been?

"Mr. Ward," I said. "I'm quite impressed with your display. But would you kindly stop the drama and talk to me?" His resistance impelled me to try again.

"Here you go again," he sighed. "I'm not Ward, my name is Herbert Goldman." I noticed a slight accent when he pronounced the word *here*.

"I need to rest, I don't feel too well. You'll have to excuse me." He closed his eyes and turned his face to the wall. I stood there for five more minutes until a nurse came in.

"Please, you are disturbing our patient," she said, in a tone reserved for intruders aged ten and younger. I had thought Albert C. Ward III was disturbing my patience.

The policeman looked bored as he sat there apparently not listening. He never said a word.

The cafeteria outside was just about to close for the day. There was only one other diner, a man with a protruding nose hair noisily slurping a soup that even from a distance smelled like my socks after two weeks of basic training in the desert. I was hungry, and meat loaf with potato pancakes seemed safe. But one bite was enough. The meat loaf was probably made of the ass of an ass, and the potato pancakes tasted as if they had been fried in castor oil and lightly seasoned with sawdust. The plate smelled of ammonia. I pushed the tray away. Even my voracious appetite had its limits. Anyway, it was time to write my report on my meeting with Ward. My boss, David Stone, the director of the Office of Asset Recovery and Money Laundering, was going to love it.

Walking to my hotel, I thought about how long I had waited to face Ward, how long I had mentally prepared what I would say to him. But when the time had finally come, there had been no bombast, no fireworks. Just hollow emptiness. I wasn't recognizing yet that the battle wasn't over, it had just begun.

It wasn't just the anticlimax, I quickly realized. I was still disturbed by the meeting and didn't quite know why. Something just wasn't sitting well.

I pulled out my cell phone and called Peter Maxwell, the curly-haired, easygoing Australian Federal Police agent assigned to help me. I decided not to share with him the tinge of doubt I had.

"I think it's him all right," I told Peter. "Let's wait for the U.S. Department of Justice to prepare the request for provisional arrest with a view toward extradition. Meanwhile, just make sure he doesn't leave the hospital until the request arrives."

"He isn't going anywhere, might," said Peter.

"What do you mean, might?" I asked in a startled voice. "He could still leave?"

Peter, with his heavy Australian accent, had actually meant "mate."

"I mean, we've a court order for the next twelve days on

local Australian fraud offenses. Until then, you're safe, but the criminal division of the Justice Department better hurry."

"What did he do this time?" I asked.

"Sold the same real-estate property to three different people," said Maxwell, chuckling. "But the land wasn't even his in the first place."

The next call was to David Stone in Washington, DC.

"David, I just saw the Chameleon."

"Good. What's the latest color?" David never was much for emotion. He could be elated, but he'd speak with the same tone of a voice as if I'd told him it was sunny outside.

"Sick man, hospital bed. But David, it's going to be harder this time for him to change it up. He gave me a show that unfortunately won't be coming to a movie theater near you. The hot part is that the Australians have him on unrelated charges."

"We're sure it's him?"

"Pretty sure. The guy I saw matches Ward on seven points. Some physical, some circumstantial."

"Only pretty sure?" asked David.

I hesitated. "There are a few things that are still holding me back," I said. "He's been calling himself Herbert Goldman."

We talked over some procedural stuff, how the Australians would need to positively ID him before they'd extradite him.

"But that crap's not the problem," I said. "The Australian police can verify our ID information. Anyway, I'm after the money, not the body." I paused. "Any word on the U.S. request for his provisional arrest? We only have twelve days to get that provisional arrest request here."

He sighed. "Hold on. I need to take another call."

A few minutes later, David came back on the line and told me that the FBI had just received a memo from the Australian Federal Police that the suspect hadn't been fingerprinted yet, because he was in the hospital.

"They didn't?" I said. "Well, I think I can solve that problem."

I waited until evening visiting hours to return. The corridor and the nurses' station were empty, so it wasn't hard to borrow a plastic bag and a doctor's white coat from a nearby closet. Ward was sound asleep and snoring. A policewoman read a newspaper beside him. Nonchalantly, I slid one hand into the bag and, with my fingers protected by the plastic, picked up the empty water cup from his side table. With my other hand I peeled the bag off and over the cup, enclosing it in the bag without adding prints of my own, and walked away, returning the coat to its place. The policewoman didn't even blink.

Peter Maxwell was sitting at his desk, rubbing his eyes over a pile of papers, when I arrived. I held out the plastic bag. "Check the prints on the cup, and match it with the sample the FBI sent you. That'll convince you."

"Dan, I'm already convinced, but it may not be enough for the court. There could be an argument that this fingerprint evidence was compromised."

"That's not for the court," I said. "It's for law-enforcement purposes. I'm afraid if there's any doubt about his identity, he'll be let go even after the extradition request comes in. The prints on the cup will do for now."

After a pause, Peter agreed. I'd liked him from the moment we'd met. He was a tall, brown-eyed, well-built man in his midthirties. He was always smiling, willing to help, and never put bureaucratic obstacles where none were necessary. He also had that quirky, uniquely Australian sense of humor that can inject levity even into the most serious circumstances. So can I. During one of our conversations, somehow the subject of Jewish holidays came up. "Sounds mighty complicated, mate," he said.

I smiled. "Not really. It can be summed up easily: Our enemies tried to destroy us. They couldn't. We survived. Let's eat."

When I'd seen his toothy grin, I knew that he got it.

Back to Albert C. Ward III, now claiming to be Herbert Goldman. He had all the reasons in the world to fight extradition to the United States. In fact, he had eleven good and solid reasons, each of them a case bundled neatly into an indictment.

He was on the line for ninety-eight counts of bank fraud, money laundering, grand larceny, and more.

We were all lucky that con men who thought they could outsmart the world usually made one mistake too many. Albert C. Ward III's mistake was trying to scam someone who didn't deserve it. It was, indirectly, how I'd finally found him. I know I should never trade luck for skill, but there are exceptions.

Sheila Levi was forty-one, with no special attributes. She wasn't very pretty, or rich, or smart. But she was a nice woman, and she'd had the misfortune to fall in love with Ward. Sheila had worked as a secretary in a small Sydney law firm and had never married. Ward had charmed her, wined and dined her, and soon moved in with her to the one-bedroom apartment she'd bought after years of saving every penny, taking a big mortgage.

The rest of the story was sadly predictable, as I realized when she met me for lunch the day after my frustrating hospital interview with Ward. At his suggestion, she had taken a second mortgage on her apartment and given him the money to "invest in their future." She'd given him the jewelry she'd inherited from her grandmother, which he sold immediately. But Sheila still had faith in him. Why?

"I wanted so much to marry and have a family," she said, sobbing, sitting opposite me in the dining room of my Sydney hotel. "He proposed marriage, and I believed him. My dream collapsed just a few hours before the wedding ceremony. How could I have known that he was already married?"

I nodded sympathetically.

"I know it makes me sound stupid, but I really loved him and believed what he told me. That's where I went wrong. Now I don't have him, and I don't have my apartment. I couldn't make the payments, and the bank foreclosed."

"Where do you live now?"

"I share a rented room with a waitress I work with."

"A waitress?"

"Yes," she said faintly and apologetically, lowering her eyes. "I lost my job as well. My employers were sick of me being distracted, and the creditor phone calls got out of hand. I'm waitressing now in two different restaurants." She dried her eyes. "Today is my day off."

I felt mounting rage. Cheating banks out of their money was bad enough, but cheating a trusting woman who'd had almost nothing to begin with and was then left with even less was appalling. But more than just that, something didn't make sense. If Ward had scammed millions from U.S. banks and investors over the years, why was it worth his while to scam a secretary out of something as modest as her grandmother's jewelry? Where had all that money gone?

I flew back from Sydney to New York. After those three long days of travel, including a layover, I went to my office and read an e-mail from David that had just come in.

Your report that you found Albert C. Ward III in Australia is apparently inaccurate. The FBI compared the fingerprints of Albert C. Ward III maintained in its database with prints lifted from the cup you gave the Australian Federal Police, and against subsequent prints obtained by the Australian police after you left. They told me an hour ago that the prints don't match. The person you saw in the hospital bed is not Albert C. Ward III. The U.S. will not request his extradition. David.

The triumph I'd felt on the flight from Sydney had turned out to be fleeting, and was immediately replaced with bitter disappointment. How could this have happened? I'd followed my hunch as well as procedure, and still failed. I'd lost the round, but I didn't lose the lesson. I thought of a phrase from Samuel Taylor Coleridge's poem "The Rime of the Ancient Mariner." I wasn't ready to wear my failure like an albatross around my neck. How come when I managed to pull off a task, there was nobody around, but hey, when I failed, there were plenty of witnesses? When I fucked up an exercise during my Mossad training, my instructor had told me sarcastically, "You have to learn from the past experiences of others, although I'm sure you'll find new ways to err." It had hurt.

I shut the office door and collapsed into my chair, trying to figure out what to do next. I was facing a brick wall. I'd tried to scale it and failed.

Should I throw in the towel? How long do you keep digging before you concede that the well is dry? Not here, buddy.

My father had taught me that while a defeat is sometimes just a temporary setback, surrender makes it permanent. I wasn't there yet, far from it. I was determined to win, but how? I would have to start again from the beginning.

CHAPTER TWO

Manhattan, New York, November 2003

The sun wouldn't shine that morning, and the skies would only lighten to pencil gray. Glancing at the glowing red digits of the clock, I could already feel it. It was six forty-five A.M., and only the slowly fading darkness told me it was already morning. When I finally got out of bed, I instantly regretted it. There had to be a better way to start the day than waking up in the morning.

It was one of those days I dreaded. No pressing duties to perform at the office, just routine, snail-paced progress in the money-laundering cases I investigate for the U.S. Department of Justice. I forced myself not to return to bed, looking through the window at the cars passing through the Chelsea streets. New York City was unusually quiet. I felt strangely out of place. After twenty of years in the U.S., many of them right there in that apartment, I felt a pulling away. From the moment I'd landed in New York, I had considered it my home, and the U.S. my country and my future. But the dreary color outside made me long for the Israeli sun. Not the scorching rays of August that melt the asphalt, but the caressing sun of

May and June that wraps you like the warmth of loving arms.

Shaking myself out of memory lane, I went to the kitchen. I took a carton of orange juice from the half-empty refrigerator—extra pulp, the way I like it—and drank it directly from the spout, flooding my chin and neck with juice.

Damn whoever designed that stupid spout, I thought.

I wiped my chin, took a deep breath, and resigned myself to going to work. *Con men absconding from the U.S. beware,* I thought. I was cranky, and ready to take it out on whoever's file happened to be on my desk that day.

There has never been a shortage of new cases coming to my office from various U.S. government agencies. Major insurance fraud, telemarketing scams, banking fraud, and money laundering related to other white-collar crimes are the usual stuff. They expect us to find the perpetrator and recover the loot if either is located outside the United States. Once U.S. borders are crossed, foreign rules apply, leaving the U.S. government with little or no independent investigative and enforcement power. When a U.S. state or federal criminal case has foreign aspects, U.S. law-enforcement authorities can get police-to-police assistance from the more than 170 countries belonging to Interpol. Additionally, around forty-eight countries have bilateral MLAT, or Mutual Legal Assistance Treaties, with the U.S. for helping each other obtain evidence in criminal trials. That's the easy part.

Civil cases are even trickier than criminal cases. They are hamstrung by legal, bureaucratic, and political constraints that make it tougher for federal agents to pursue debtors for money outside the U.S. than it is for private creditors. The MLAT, limited to criminal cases, tends to be practically useless. Foreign courts take pride in their country's sovereignty and loathe attempts by foreign governments to twist their arms. And they aren't always eager to help the U.S. recover dirty money that might be bolstering their own country's economy.

That's how I got my office. The sign on the office door read

TAT INTERNATIONAL TRADE, INC., intended to mask our identity
as the New York extension of the Office of Asset Recovery
and Money Laundering of the U.S. Department of Justice. We
have the expertise and the budget to go after white-collar
crooks wherever in the world they are playing, and mostly winning, mind games designed by the culprits' lawyers, account-
ants, and investment consultants to keep us from getting their
clients or the money. Most of the time we outsmart them and
beat them at their own game. FinCEN, the Financial Crimes
Enforcement Network, is the much-larger U.S. Treasury intelligence agency that searches for assets within the United States.
But they do their job from behind a computer monitor, while
we go out to the streets of Geneva, Liechtenstein, the Cayman
Islands, and all the other locations favored by the money launderers of the world.

I like my job. It offers complete independence outside the
U.S., yet affords the entire might of the U.S. behind me. That
is, provided I conduct myself as a straight arrow. This only gets
tricky when dealing with what I'll call cultural differences.
David expects me to operate as legally and ethically as if I'm
operating within the U.S. But I'm not. I'm dealing with dubious and shady characters in off-shore tax shelters, far from the
reach of U.S. law enforcement. For them the phrases *comply
with the law* or *rules of ethics* are good for a laugh. They're over
there to avoid the law, so it's a bit far-fetched to expect us all to
abide by it.

Fairly early in the game, I saw the futility of convincing my
superiors that we couldn't win the war of minds against lawless
targets by behaving like nineteenth-century gentlemen. Fighting international crime and terrorism effectively, recovering
stolen money, and disrupting terror attacks against the U.S. can
mean resorting to Machiavelli. He put it best when he wrote
in *The Art of War*, "No enterprise is more likely to succeed than
one concealed from the enemy until it is ripe for execution."

"Do you expect us to apply Machiavellian methods or act like
the criminals you chase?" David had once asked, hearing me

air these frustrations. I'd known that he sympathized with what I was saying, but unlike me, he had clearly defined lines he would not cross.

"Of course not," I'd said.

But we both knew damn well that insisting that I comply with each and every U.S. rule fit for U.S. domestic cases, as well as with the foreign country's laws, was like sending a one-legged man to compete in an ass-kicking contest. Adhering to ethics is vital in intelligence gathering, because it constantly reminds you that your opponents can operate without any.

"What's the alternative?" David had said with a sigh.

It was a rhetorical question. We both knew the State Department would be knocking on David's door once some country started whining that I had bent the rules.

"David, there haven't been any complaints," I'd protested. He'd raised his eyebrows. "OK, just one. But I was exonerated, remember? I have a clean conscience."

"No, Dan, you have a bad memory."

But he hadn't continued, so I went on. "There must be some places where I can have some leeway. I'm not asking for permission to break foreign countries' laws, but this strictness is crippling me."

"You know we can't do that as a matter of policy," David had said calmly. "But . . ."

He'd let it hang in the air. "But you'll look the other way if it's not egregious, and if I don't get caught," I'd said.

He'd smiled, and that was enough for me. I've always been a deeply religious follower of the eleventh commandment as it applies to intelligence agents: Thou Shalt Not Get Caught.

CHAPTER THREE

That gray November day marked my introduction to the Chameleon case. Inside my Manhattan office were four newcomers that were impossible to ignore—battered brown cartons on the floor. A Post-it on the top carton read, "Dan, read these files and talk to me. David."

The FBI had decided to take a fresh look at a universe of high-dollar bank and other fraud cases that were committed within the past fifteen-or-so years, had seen indictment, involved scamming $15 million and up, and were never prosecuted, for lack of defendants.

Why now?

I suspected the FBI was dumping these cases on us because they thought terrorist financing might be turned up. The perpetrators of these stale high-dollar cases had similar MOs, had been out of the country for a while before the scams, and had all vanished afterwards.

A single page would keep me busy for six days reading bank statements and about other fraud cases.

The computer-generated sticker label with a bar code on the first file's front read "U.S. v. Albert C. Ward III, aka Harrington T. Whitney-Davis, case #86-981." I pulled out a fresh yellow pad and a sharp pencil. I would get the facts first. I started with the FBI report. On its front page was Albert C. Ward III's enlarged black-and-white photo and bio. Ward was born in Milwaukee, Wisconsin, on March 27, 1959. He attended the Milwaukee Trade and Technical High School's Evening School, and graduated in June 1977. Ward had worked at several minimum-wage jobs in the greater metropolitan area of Milwaukee until hired by a local security company. Following a two-week training session, Ward was given a patrolman's uniform and was assigned to the North Lake Drive area.

After two uneventful years as a patrolman, Ward was promoted and became a night-shift-duty manager. His supervisors described him as a highly motivated and effective employee who sought adventure. They also indicated in his job-evaluation report that there were a few instances when he had been too aggressive toward his fellow employees, including one incident in which he'd punched a coworker. Ward had been arrested, but was later released when the employee refused to press charges. No intracompany disciplinary recommendations were made.

In 1980 Ward left that employment and applied for a passport. He left the country in May 1980, on board a Panamanian-registered freighter sailing from Seattle to Hong Kong. Ward had filed no tax returns after 1980. A search for family members came up empty. There were no records of his reentry into the U.S. His name and Social Security number had nonetheless started reappearing on credit reports in 1985. A national-database search showed that Ward had lived in eighteen different locations throughout the U.S. since 1985, mostly in Michigan, Massachusetts, Wisconsin, New York, and Florida. An inquiry with landlords and neighbors at these addresses had yielded very little.

Those who remembered Ward described him as a reclusive, nonconfrontational, and quiet person who kept to himself. One neighbor mentioned that Ward listened to strange music. A landlord who lived close by described visitors to Ward's apartment as people who didn't fit in the neighborhood, and who'd come during odd hours of the night.

It was the one unusual detail in an otherwise routine and bland report, but there was nothing to substantiate a suspicion or lead me anywhere. Criminals flock with people of their own feather. And the music? My son listens to music I'm convinced was recorded with a knife grinder, a train on rusty rails, and an empty tin trash can dragged on the pavement. But that didn't prove anything other than odd taste in music.

The rest of the information detailed Ward's history of indictments, using and discarding aliases. His modus operandi was a good old hit-and-run. Amazing, but true. He had always slipped out of the hands of the law.

Ward's earliest recorded sting happened in a small town in South Dakota. Ward appeared there one day in 1985 as Harrington T. Whitney-Davis. He rented a nicely decorated office in a building housing a local savings bank and incorporated Fidelity Trustees of America, Inc. Ward came to the savings bank, introduced himself to the bank manager as manager of a new branch office of a national financial company, Fidelity Trustees of America, Inc., and suggested business cooperation. Of course, neither company had any connection whatsoever to the reputable Fidelity financial and securities companies.

It hadn't taken long to convince the bank manager to market "limited edition" treasury securities offered by the fancy-name, trust-inducing company of Ward, now Harrington T. Whitney-Davis. No hard sell was necessary. Ward had told the manager that the savings bank would act only as intermediary, selling the securities to its customers, assuming no risk, while collecting hefty commissions. Ward's business had come at the right time. The bank manager was being pressed by his board of directors to improve the bank's balance sheet and was looking for ways to expand its product line. The manager quickly agreed, and the savings bank started offering these supposed treasury securities to the bank's customers as a solid investment vehicle. The promised interest rate of 14 percent gave a significantly higher yield than the interest paid by the usual securities issued by the U.S. government, or deposits insured by the FDIC.

The problem was that the securities Ward offered were fictitious. There's no such thing as a limited-edition treasury security. It was a scam in the fullest meaning of the word. All that Ward had to do was use his pompously named corporation and generate official-looking stationery confirming that the bank had purchased Ward's bogus securities on behalf of a bank client, or even on behalf of the bank itself.

During the first three months, the bank sold $14.4 million worth of Ward's limited-edition treasury securities. In the beginning, when customers wanted to liquidate their holdings, Ward's company promptly paid the bank, which in turn credited the customers' accounts. There was no reason for anyone to suspect that anything was wrong. The bank had collected nice commissions. The manager and the board of directors were happy. So were the bank's customers. Through word of mouth, sales increased even further. To emphasize the exclusive nature of the investment, the bank manager had decided that the securities would be sold only in units of $10,000, and only to the bank's customers. If you were banking elsewhere, you had to first open an account at the savings bank to be allowed to purchase these wonderful securities.

Other banks in town, which saw their business volume shrinking, wondered why they couldn't offer the same securities to their own customers. Following a few phone calls by other bankers to the South Dakota Department of Commerce and Regulations' Division of Banking, which regulates financial institutions, and to the Federal Home Loan Bank Board, which at that time regulated federal savings banks, questions arose. A federal bank examiner called the bank manager for an interview without telling him why. The manager mentioned the call to Ward, whom he knew as Harrington Whitney-Davis.

Ward knew what the manager didn't: it was time to take off. He disappeared immediately, together with more than $20 million. Angry customers demanded their money back from the bank. But the bank couldn't help. In fact, the bank became one of the victims, having invested heavily in Ward's phony securities. The end was inevitable. The bank became insolvent and was seized by regulators.

Ward's next scam was more complex. He moved to Nebraska, assumed the name of Harold S. McClure, and incorporated Lincoln Premiere Equity, Inc., as an investment club for senior citizens. Of course, that name had no connection to any genuine, reputable business entity. "Harold" ran ads in the local newspapers claiming, confusingly but impressively, "Lincoln Premiere Equity's CDs are purchased from federally insured banks to secure the Certificate of Deposit Program of the FDIC."

Ward opened a bank account at a local bank and deposited the money he'd received from locals hungry for a high yield. A typical investor paid $100,000 and believed he was buying a federally-insured certificate of deposit. Ward used the money to purchase CDs, which to the bank manager's delight he left at the bank. But there was a subtle little detail to this scheme. Ward used the CDs as collateral for loans he personally took out. The bank enabled him to pull off the scam, because many investors were deceptively induced by the bank to sign a contract naming Harold S. McClure as the "trustee" of their money.

The result was obvious. The victims lost all their money when "Harold," now believed to be Ward, defaulted on the loans and disappeared.

The FBI believed that Ward then moved to Indiana, called himself Marshall Stuart Lennox, and incorporated Windsor, Hamilton & Pierce Investments, Inc. He rented a nice office and offered unsophisticated investors historical bonds, such as railway bonds. These were once-valid obligations of American corporations, but are now worthless as securities and only collected and traded as memorabilia. Ward marketed the bonds at prices ranging from $100,000 to $250,000—the same bonds that collectors buy for $25 to $100. Ward, or rather Marshall Stuart Lennox, described the bonds as "backed by the U.S. government" and "payable in gold." To add credibility to the genuine bonds' inflated prices, Ward attached valuations by "world-renowned experts," confirming that the bonds were worth significant amounts of money, far above the price the investors were asked to pay.

One investor became suspicious, contacted the Federal Reserve, and was told that the U.S. government was not backing these bonds. When confronted, Ward smoothly replied, "The Federal Reserve simply doesn't want you to cash it in, because if everyone did that, there'd be a run on the bank and the U.S. economy would collapse." But within the hour, Marshall Stuart Lennox had disappeared.

Similar sting operations in various forms followed in other unsuspecting small towns in the Midwest. Complaints to both state and federal authorities mounted, but the investigations led to indictments that went nowhere, because the defendant was nowhere to be found.

For more than a decade, Ward was an enigma. Nobody knew where he was, or could even accurately describe how he looked. He had shunned the ordinary business-publicity photos, and the descriptions his victims gave fit a million other men. All the FBI had concerning Ward's description was a high school photo more than twenty years old, and his fingerprints taken in 1979, when Ward had been arrested for assault. Ward's legacy ended abruptly in summer 2001. That was the last time there were complaints about scams fitting Ward's modus operandi. Had Ward died? No death certificate bearing his name or any of his aliases was issued anywhere in the U.S.

Had Ward left the U.S.? If so, how? His U.S. passport, issued in 1980, had expired in 1990. The State Department reported that this passport hadn't been renewed. Had a new passport been issued bearing any of the aliases the FBI said he used for his scams? The State Department said no. Was Ward in prison on an unrelated conviction? Again, the FBI said no.

The mantra *think outside the box* rang in my mind. They were the words of Alex, my Mossad Academy training instructor, repeated in his Canadian accent. "Your rivals aren't ordinary people. They operate differently, so why would you expect them to think like an average Joe? Put yourself in their skin. Then take one step forward." *Good,* I thought, *as long as we aren't on a cliff's edge.*

What did I do to deserve these damned stale cases? Suddenly angry, I tossed a heap of paper off my desk. It was useless—plenty more was still piling up on my desk. Why the hell was the FBI dumping these cases on us two years after the last scam and almost two decades since the first one, and where was the international connection? I silently cursed the anonymous FBI agent who had cleared his desk at my expense. I wished he'd drown in paper. I couldn't decide who to grumble to first—David or the FBI.

When I cooled off, I remembered what Alex had always told our class: "When you find yourself at a dead end, start from the beginning. One step back may not be enough, because it will lead you to the same brick wall. Revisit all assumptions, and recheck all facts. One or more could be flawed."

OK, Alex, I thought with a mental sigh, if you could only see how I apply your wisdom. I wondered what had happened to him. Ever since I'd left the Mossad, Benny Friedman, my classmate, had been the only lifeline to my professional past. For all I knew, Alex was still in the system, or maybe growing flowers in his village in northern Israel, enjoying retirement. I read the files again. Two hours later, I still couldn't find anything I'd missed the first time. The only mention of anything foreign was Ward's departure from the U.S. in 1980. But he returned sometime in 1985, as the credit reports showed. There went the international connection. I had no idea where to begin.

Think outside the box rang again.

The only thing left for me to do was go back and check the raw intelligence data the FBI was analyzing.

I was frustrated and intrigued at the same time. How could somebody evade the law for so long? It was clear that Ward knew well how to assume new names and identities. Was thinking that he had employed that skill to vanish, thinking within the box or outside it? I needed something to hang on to in this case, or the file would grow moss on my shelves, and I'd be getting polite but persistent reminders from David to report progress.

I called David Stone in Washington, DC, grimly bracing myself.

"David, how come you agreed to take Ward's cases? They're so stale that even the bookworms who lived in the reports died of old age."

"Dan, the FBI is fairly confident that Ward is outside the

United States," he said. "That makes the case ours, at least as it concerns the $311 million he stole."

I was startled for a moment. "$311 million? The amounts in the file don't even come close to that."

"Do the math again," said David. "Eleven known cases—he fared nicely."

"OK, I'll look again at the numbers. But what makes them think he's outside the U.S.? There's nothing in the file to indicate that. Or the FBI is holding an ace up their sleeve."

"The Bureau won't tell us. So I guess it's intelligence, not facts or evidence, and you know how zealously they protect their sources."

"What do you mean they won't tell us? Last time I checked we work for the same government."

"No need to be sarcastic," said David, trying to calm down my mounting temper, which he knew only too well. David himself could have a bit of a temper too, but he kept a much tighter lid on his than I did mine. "To the extent that any of it is grand-jury material, they can't share it with other sections of the government working on the civil side of the case."

That's bull, I thought. "Well, David, as an attorney for the government I can receive certain grand-jury material for use in performing my duty. Besides, this case appears to involve bank fraud, so there's an additional specific language allowing the disclosure. Let's chew the fat here."

I could almost hear David's silent and subtle smile over the phone.

"You're right," he finally agreed.

"And?" I asked hoping to get support here. "Why is U.S. law enforcement extra-interested nowadays in high-dollar cases, even if stale? Have they just remembered it has an international aspect, and the post–September eleventh public outcry made them resurrect paper cadavers?"

"Go figure," he said, joining in my despair.

I kept on pressing, "Unless someone at the FBI simply wanted to get rid of these cases to better his or her statistics, hoping we won't cry foul, they'd better tell us what they have, or they'll find these cases back on their desk in no time, dead and aging bookworms included."

"Dan," said David in his calm voice. "Think about how the Bureau handled the S-and-L cases in the eighties." I remembered it well. Neither the Bureau nor federal prosecutors went after the money looted in bank and savings-and-loan frauds. We went only after perpetrators. The statistics we tracked were numbers indicted and numbers convicted. The government wasn't going after the money.

"True enough," I said. "Back then we never went after the money. But I never understood why."

"One reason, I'd say," answered David, "was because going after the money would have required separate civil proceedings. Decision makers concluded that these would be resource-intensive cases, with little likelihood of recovering anything."

His point was that the U.S. government had been leaving millions of stolen dollars on the table, and U.S. taxpayers of course picked up much of the tab. Since that time, however, changes in federal criminal law have allowed us to get restitution, in criminal prosecutions, of ill-gotten gains resulting from crimes for which we got convictions. I'd been involved in many of these cases myself.

"But that doesn't explain why the Bureau waited so long," I said in frustration, David's compliment notwithstanding. "Maybe it landed on the table of this year's recipient of the phlegmatic agent award?"

"Let me make some calls, and I'll get back to you," concluded David.

CHAPTER FOUR

Getting David's help was the easy part. I had been working for him long enough to know he accepted reasoned arguments and never dug in his heels in a position proven wrong. But people change when they see retirement coming up. And in any case, David would still need to crack some bureaucratic walls. If you spend enough time in Washington, you know that sometimes it'd be easier to get a date with a reigning Miss America than to move things faster between government agencies. For sure, I knew that I had to get a breakthrough before David retired. With his clout and experience, he could back me up on almost anything. But when a new chief comes, things could be different, for better or—more likely—for worse, just because he'd be new on the job.

A week later I went to Washington for a routine staff meeting. After the pep talk, David asked me to stay.

"I thought it over and made some inquiries," said David. "The bottom line is that the FBI did have a reason to send us these files. But before we go over them, let me call in Bob Holliday. He's my new deputy."

"Who is he?"

"He's a Department of Justice veteran with many years of successful commercial-litigation experience, but with no international exposure. I hope you'll help him get acquainted with your work."

Bob Holliday had wide shoulders, smart brown eyes, and a thick mustache, and appeared to be in his early fifties. We shook hands when he walked into the office.

"Dan," said David, "I concluded that the Bureau has already

found common points. All of the names used during the scams were of white American males who one: were born within a few years of one another, but had no apparent connections among them; two: had obtained passports also within a few years of one another; three: left the U.S. and then disappeared; four: resurfaced years later just long enough to scam banks for millions with a reasonably consistent modus operandi—for example, never a bank insider, so never named on a list of persons barred from employment in financial institutions, but gets bank insiders to provide investor victims—and five: disappeared again without a trace."

"I see," I said with a mild tone of sarcasm. "What do we have here twenty years later?—millions gone, multiple names, one scam each, consistent MO, no investigative direction."

David smiled, and turned to Bob. "What do you think?"

Bob Holliday wasted no time in getting to the Bureau's motives. "At this point the Bureau sensibly concludes that it could spend scads of resources on these dogs and still come up with nothing re terrorist financing or anything else. Wanting at least to improve its statistical picture, and with money plus an international link such as the use of passports, albeit tenuous in the extreme, the Bureau thinks of David and off-loads eleven open cases. David thinks of you. Voila!"

Bob Holliday sounded as if he knew what he was talking about. Normally I didn't like it when someone came across as too self-assured, but I didn't mind it with Bob. He managed not to let confidence slide into arrogance the way a lot of people do.

He continued. "The Bureau came up with these cases when trying to look for terrorist financing where they'd never looked before. But it hit a dead end with them domestically."

"But why just now?" I queried. "And where is the international connection? Just the passports?"

"I know that the international angles are questionable," conceded David. "All I'm going to tell you is that the dollar amounts in these scams are so high, and it's so common for proceeds of large scams to leave the U.S., that it seemed worth

our taking them on, at least preliminarily. I don't want to tell
you any more about the Bureau's analysis, because I want you to
take a completely fresh look at them. I'm interested in whether
you see something in them that others haven't."

I returned to my office in New York and sat motionless behind my desk looking at the files, going back over each of the
eleven cases. Were there eleven perpetrators, or just one with
many aliases? There were conflicting assumptions in the FBI
reports. Apparently, I wasn't the only one confused.

I read each and every bit of testimony of the victims, the
bank managers, and the landlords. Their descriptions of each
perpetrator were very similar, except for one person who re-
called the con man speaking with a slight accent. I was intrigued by this detail and pulled out the FBI FD-302 interview
report from the file. Louis B. Romano, of 45–87 West Street,
Gary, Indiana, was interviewed at his home by an FBI special
agent. I looked up Romano's number and dialed.

An elderly woman answered. "I'm sorry," she said when I
asked for Romano. "My husband passed away two years ago.
Is there something I could help you with?"

I hesitated. "Well, ma'am, I'm sorry for your loss," I said.
"I'm Dan Gordon, an investigative attorney with the Justice
Department. Your late husband was interviewed a few years
ago about one of your tenants, and I wanted to ask him a few
more questions."

"Who was the tenant? Maybe I could help you. We've got
only two rental apartments, and I remember most of our tenants."

"The tenant was Marshall Stuart Lennox. Ring a bell?"

"Of course I remember him." She paused. "If you don't
mind me saying, I never really liked the guy."

"Why?"

"He was a real oddball. Never opened his mail."

"How'd you know?"

"I saw unopened envelopes in the garbage bin a few times.
Back then, we were living in an apartment we own in the
same building. And I never saw him use his mailbox to leave

letters for the mailman to collect." She let it sink in. "He also installed a telephone line under a different name."

"And how did you come across that?"

"After he left, a bill came to that address with a strange name on it. I opened it, and the telephone number was the same as Lennox's. I have no idea why he did it, but he never left a forwarding address—just took off."

I sat up in my chair. "Do you still have that phone bill?"

"Nope, I threw it out ages ago. The charge was for, like, $6, so I guess the phone company just wrote it off."

"So what name did he use for the bill?" I asked, trying to keep too much interest out of my voice.

She sighed. "It's been forever—I really couldn't tell you. But I think it was just a regular American name, nothing special. You know, Jones, Brown, Evans."

"Your husband mentioned that Lennox had an accent. Did you notice that too?"

"No, but Louis was always the one who dealt with him. I know he had one, though. Louis used to teach drama and English, so he always did notice accents. I did hear about it. Louis liked to identify people's origin and background by listening to them talking. After listening to a person's dialect, Louis could tell where the person grew up, and sometimes how educated he was. He loved doing that."

"Did he discuss Lennox's accent with you, or just mention it?"

"Well, he said Lennox definitely didn't grow up in Wisconsin, which is what he told us."

"What made him say that?"

"Louis used to go every summer to Wisconsin to teach drama to local kids in a summer camp. He could do that accent really well. So, one day he mentioned to Lennox that he'd been teaching in Oconomowoc, in the lake country. Lennox tried to change the subject, and he mispronounced *Oconomowoc*. Then Louis made a joke about people from Wisconsin saying 'cripes' a lot, but Lennox didn't seem to get it either. Louis thought it was really weird. But I told him, 'What do we know? Maybe

Lennox left Wisconsin when he was young. Anyway,' I said, 'why should we care? He pays rent on time and doesn't damage our property.' "

It wasn't much, but was at least something. "Did your husband continue to be suspicious of Lennox?"

She thought for a moment. "I don't know if I'd call it suspicious. He was just a little uneasy about him. He thought maybe Lennox had made it all up—had this crazy idea that maybe he was on the run from the police. Anyway, I don't know if it's important, but Louis said something once about how Lennox stretched his *a*'s and *h*'s."

"What, like a Southern drawl?"

"No, not like any American accent he knew. He'd taught speech for years, so Louis really knew his accents. Once he said he was sure that Lennox wasn't even American. But you know, that was before nine eleven. What did we know?" That was an attention-grabbing remark. I picked up on that.

"Why do you mention nine eleven?"

"Well, you know . . ." She sounded reluctant to pursue the point. "He had sort of dark skin. Not like he was black or Latino. Just a little darker than your typical Wisconsin dairy farmer, I guess, who's as white as his cows' milk."

I thanked her and hung up. I hadn't considered that direction. The yearbook's black-and-white photo wasn't high quality enough to set Ward—or Lennox?—apart from the other awkward teenagers on the page. I flipped through the file quickly. The FBI field office in Milwaukee reported on state records that showed that a Marshall Stuart Lennox was born in Meriter Hospital, Madison, Wisconsin, on June 11, 1960. His parents were Arthur James Lennox and Gretchen Melanie Lennox, née Schilling. Lennox attended local public schools and dropped out during the eleventh grade. He was issued a U.S. passport on May 1, 1980, and left the U.S. on a student charter flight to Athens, Greece. Both his parents died in a car accident two years later. Lennox had no siblings or any other known family members. A more recent report indicated that the neighborhood he grew up in had changed—people had moved out and small businesses and garages had moved in. From those who'd stayed behind, very few people who were interviewed remembered the family.

The first two aliases I'd randomly checked, Lennox and McClure, had some things in common: they both belonged to young men who grew up in the Midwest, had no known living relatives, and both had left the country in 1980.

I flipped through the pages of the FBI report and its attachments, pulling out the file on the first-reported savings-bank-fraud case in South Dakota. There, the con man had presented himself as Harrington T. Whitney-Davis. The FBI report went over the history of Harrington T. Whitney-Davis: born in Fargo, North Dakota, on April 6, 1959. Like a junkie looking for a fix, I quickly ran my eyes over the interesting, though now less relevant, stuff. All I wanted to know at that moment was whether Harrington T. Whitney-Davis had gotten a passport and left the country.

He hadn't, or at least the FBI report said nothing about it. My hopes deflated. The strange thing was, the name Harrington T. Whitney-Davis stopped appearing on mailing lists, credit reports, and IRS records in 1981. I opened the next file folder.

The con man in this one had appeared in a small town in Nebraska as Harold S. McClure. The FBI report gave his date of birth as March 1, 1958. I wasn't interested in the rest of the bio. Not just yet. Right now, all I needed to know was if he had disappeared from the U.S. like the others. It took just one glance to find out. Yes, Harold S. McClure had applied for a passport in July, 1980, and left shortly thereafter for Canada through a land-border crossing. Soon, his name stopped appearing in public records, until it resurfaced years later in the U.S. for a few months.

One thing was clear: we had ourselves a modus operandi. It was all too much to be a coincidence. Operating now with a solid lead, I decided to check the other eight names in the FBI file later. I had a direction. Three, maybe more, young American men in their early twenties left the United States in 1980, showing signs of life just long enough to carry out highly lucrative scams. Did Ward have anything to do with their disappearances? Did he know that they were absent from the U.S.? And if so, how? And then there was one more intriguing question. Without physical evidence, how did the FBI tie the eleven scams to Ward, despite the eleven different aliases? I couldn't answer the first two questions, but I could take a stab at the third by asking the FBI itself.

I called FBI Special Agent Kevin Lee, the last agent named in the topmost file. After the unavoidable cordialities, I asked him how they had connected Ward to all eleven scams.

"Well, our guys down at Quantico are pretty good at this type of analysis," he told me. "The physical descriptions of all the defendants made by all victims generally matched Ward's. We've a similar MO, and based upon that and other evidence we concluded that all the cases were perpetrated by one person."

"Other evidence? What evidence? I thought I had it all in the file."

"Let me look," he said. "This case is old."

You're damn right about that, I thought.

An hour later he called. "OK, we also discovered that each perpetrator used the same Delaware incorporation-service company to incorporate all the companies used in the scams."

"Did you interview the principals of the service company?"

"No. The company went out of business, and the directors disappeared without leaving a trace."

"Any additional evidence?" Based on what he'd told me, the FBI's backing seemed thin. "You know, as in, did you ever have the witnesses take a look at Ward's high school photo in a spread? Ask them to pick out the guy they gave their money to?" I tried not to sound like I was criticizing their work.

He sounded vaguely annoyed. "Well, I'll have to look up the file again. It was a long time ago. Anyway, all eleven aliases were of white males born between 1959 and 1962 in the Midwest."

"Did anyone check any passport applications of these people?"

"No. The State Department gets rid of routine passport applications after one year."

"So there's nothing on file?"

"The State Department may have something more. Why don't you ask them?" he said, having lost interest. I hung up, shaking my head at the apparent incompetence. It would be my job to pick up the slack.

I called the principal of the Milwaukee Trade and Technical High School's Evening School, from which Ward had graduated, identifying myself and my business. The secretary told me politely that the principal in the seventies and eighties, Donald Peterson, had retired to Arizona, but offered to give him my number. Within five minutes, my phone rang.

"Yes, I remember Ward well," said Peterson. "I hope he hasn't done anything foolish. Has he?"

"I don't think so," I said. "Please tell me about him."

"He was a decent young man. Very curious, loved geography and photography, and he said he wanted to be a photographer for *National Geographic Magazine* someday. I always wondered if he fulfilled that dream. He did manage to graduate in spite of his handicap."

"Handicap?"

"Yes, he was dyslexic, with serious learning disabilities. Until he graduated he had difficulty reading and writing. Now, compound that with his speech impairment, and you can understand why we really tried to help him."

"But what speech problem do you mean?

"He had a serious stutter."

My blood pressure went up. Stutter? None of the victims had mentioned that. In fact, most of them described a smooth-talking person. Although even a bad stutter can be cured, the hunter in me smelled blood.

"Thank you very much," I said. "I've got one last question. Do you happen to have Ward's picture?"

"You know, I must have it somewhere," said Peterson. "Ward loved photography, and he took many photos of class events. I'm pretty sure he sent me copies of several shots he made at graduation."

"If he was the photographer, doesn't that mean he isn't in those pictures?"

"No, I think he should be, actually, because he used a timer for the shutter, I guess. So he could run and be in the picture."

"Mr. Peterson, could I ask you a favor? Could you please send me those photos? I promise to send them back."

"Let me find them first."

Four days later, an envelope came in the mail with three color pictures of smiling high school kids at a party. In the attached note, Donald Peterson identified most of the students by name, apologizing that he couldn't remember them all. Ward looked like a nice kid, your neighbor's son. No especially distinctive features, overgrown light-brown hair, brown eyes, nice smile. They were a lot livelier than his formal high school graduation photo in the file. I wrote down the names of classmates Peterson had identified, and asked Esther Quinn, our office admin clerk, to run a check on them with their current addresses. I wondered, grumbling to myself a little, why Esther and I were stuck doing the legwork the FBI had neglected.

I called Donna Swanson, the first name on the high school principal's list, at her home in Los Angeles.

"Yes, I remember Albert, but I haven't heard from or seen him since we graduated," she said. "If you need current information, you should call his best friend, Tyrone Maloney. They must have stayed in contact. They were buddies."

Later, Esther handed me an address and phone number. "Tyrone Maloney has a bicycle store in New York," she said.

I decided to get some fresh air and see a face. I went to his store in SoHo, on the southern part of Manhattan. Maloney was a stocky fellow, with blond hair and a broad smile.

That smile disappeared when I told him who I was and asked him about Albert Ward.

"Bad news?" he asked. "Has he been found?"

I ducked the question. "What do you mean?"

"I mean, has he been found? The last time I heard from him was more than twenty years ago, and I haven't seen or heard from him since."

"When was that, the last time you heard from him?"

"Let me see," he said, frowning a bit. "That must have been 1982 or 1983."

"Can you tell me about it?"

"He left the United States at the end of 1980 after saving up some money. He wanted to travel the world, take photographs and sell them to travel magazines. He had no family left in the United States, so he figured he could do anything."

"Do you know where he went?"

"Yeah, I do. He went on a freighter to Hong Kong working as a cook's assistant. He liked jobs where he didn't have to talk a lot. Because of his stutter, you know."

"Did he stay in Hong Kong?"

"He did, but then he moved on. I received a few postcards from China, Thailand, and Pakistan."

"Which one came last?"

"I think the one from Pakistan. I haven't heard from him since."

"Did you try to find him?"

"I called a few of our mutual friends, but none of them had heard anything. None of his postcards carried a return address, so I could never write back. He didn't write much, just one or two lines saying he was having a great time, see you soon, stuff like that."

"Do you still have those postcards?"

"I'm sorry, no, I never kept them. Tell me, is he OK?"

"I don't know," I said candidly. "Not yet, at least."

It was getting dark. I decided that instead of returning to my office, I'd go home and walk Snap, my happy-go-lucky golden retriever. Though he had a tendency to overdo it with his licking and jumping on people with his long front legs that almost reached my shoulders, he was a loyal friend who always seemed able to put a smile on my face even when I was in a bad mood, which wasn't all that infrequent. He sure as heck deserved more attention than a bunch of stale files, now resurrected.

CHAPTER FIVE

I had to decide on a direction for my investigation. Shooting in the dark has its advantages, because sometimes you hit targets you didn't know were there. But on the other hand, the odds aren't great, and you waste time when you find out what you hit is irrelevant. I knew that Ward, for lack of a better name to call him, was already long off the U.S. radar. He wasn't going anywhere years after he'd vanished, if he hadn't done that thus far. So time wasn't of the essence—a reverse form of a phrase I had frequently used when I (briefly) practiced law and wanted to move lazy people into doing something. He couldn't get *more* lost. I thought of Alex, my Mossad Academy training instructor, who used to say that *urgent* is the legitimate son of *neglect*. But now, I was practicing futility. I needed to get a more current physical description of my man—or men. I called the OTS, the Office of Thrift Supervision, a federal agency that regulates the federal and some state savings banks and savings-and-loan associations. I was hoping that its examiners might have included identification information in their reports.

"That South Dakota case is a really old one, inherited from the Federal Home Loan Bank Board, our predecessor regulatory agency," said Brian DiLorenzo, an assistant general counsel. "The documents may be archived. Actually, they may even have been destroyed under our regular document retention schedule. Hold on." I heard him click on his computer keyboard. "Well, it seems that $20 million is a lot for just one in what looks like a series of scams. I see here that we still have these files open."

"Could I please have a copy of any investigation reports? I'm trying to figure out where the money is. Maybe we could recoup some of it."

A few days later a big envelope containing four inch-thick folders came by Federal Express. DiLorenzo's attached note said, "You're in luck. Enclosed are pertinent documents of the scams perpetrated by your con men against four regulated institutions. Please call me if you need further assistance."

I leafed through the files. They included the reports of four savings banks that had been had by a con man—or maybe con men?—and various regulatory steps that OTS's predecessor agency had taken when it seized the four failed institutions. One document attracted my attention. It was a letter written by Harrington T. Whitney-Davis on letterhead of Fidelity Trustees of America, Inc., the name of the firm he had misleadingly and fraudulently used to perpetrate his scam on the South Dakota savings bank. In the letter, Whitney-Davis confirmed that he had received $560,000 from the savings bank to purchase limited-edition treasury securities as an investment for the bank. There was an impressive looking signature by "Harrington T. Whitney-Davis," but there was also a handwritten note attached: "Tim, I'll call you later on today concerning dinner. HTWD."

So the manager of the defrauded savings bank was having dinner with fraud artist "Whitney-Davis." Maybe it meant nothing, but when you're a manager of a savings bank, meeting for dinner the person who later took off with $20 million belonging to the bank and its customers might not be that innocent.

"No," said the OTS attorney I called after reading that file. "There was no criminal investigation of the savings-bank manager. Why do you ask?"

"Did you try to figure out why he was such easy prey for Harrington T. Whitney-Davis's scam?"

"I wasn't working at the Federal Home Loan Bank Board at the time, and the only information I have is what I'm seeing in the file. Our examiners must have been satisfied that there was no criminal wrongdoing by anyone at the savings bank. They never made a criminal referral to the FBI about any bank insider."

"Do you know who the bank manager was during the scam and whether he still works there?"

"He was asked by the bank's board to resign after the scam was discovered. Being cleared of criminal charges doesn't mean he should be allowed to make more mistakes. So the bank let him go. If it hadn't, the regulatory agency would have done so when it took over the insolvent bank. His name is Timothy B. McHanna."

I called FBI Special Agent Kevin Lee. "Sorry, I haven't looked up the file yet," he said.

"I've got a different question. Did you interview Timothy B. McHanna, the manager of the defrauded savings bank in South Dakota?"

"Let me see," he said, clicking on his computer. "Yes, he was interviewed, but apparently he never became a subject of an FBI investigation."

"And?"

"That means we didn't establish that he might have been engaged in any criminal activity." He sounded so formal.

"I guess being gullible isn't a crime yet," I muttered. But it was lost on him. "Do you know where McHanna is now?"

"Let me look him up for you." A moment later he said, "He's an essential witness against Whitney-Davis, if that defendant ever shows up again. So we've kept track of him. McHanna now lives in New York City."

He lived on the posh Upper West Side of Manhattan, inside a prewar residential building, one of those sporting a royal name written in stylish lettering on a long green canopy, with a uniformed doorman who opens your car door. McHanna had certainly come a long way from his $37,000-a-year job as manager of a small savings bank in a small dusty town in South Dakota.

Additional inquiries brought me to his business: McHanna Associates, business consultants, located in the equally high-rent Financial District. A quick search of public records showed that the company had four employees and described its activities as "providing consulting services to foreign banks seeking correspondence and other business arrangements with U.S.-based banks, as well as providing other services to the banking industry." McHanna Associates also provided "consultancy services to charities in the United States for their international banking needs." *Nice niche with plenty of opportunities,* I thought. I decided to pay him a visit.

In a small and nicely decorated office, I introduced myself to the receptionist and mentioned the South Dakota savings bank and Whitney-Davis. "Mr. McHanna will see you now," he soon said.

"Tim McHanna," said a short, bald man in his late fifties, and gave me his hand for a firm shake as I walked into his office. His eyes were a dark brown. He was dressed in a tailored dark suit with a yellow tie. His initials were embroided on his button-down white shirt, and he wore golden cufflinks.

"I'm really ashamed that Whitney-Davis conned me," he said without my asking. He was eager to give me his version. Too eager, I thought. I went over the history of his relationship with "Whitney-Davis" with him. No great discoveries here—the same story already chewed up by savings-bank examiners and the FBI.

I decided to change course. "Please tell me about your business," I said in an interested tone. "I hear you're providing services to foreign banks."

Clearly relieved that I had changed the subject, McHanna launched into explaining his company. Due to increased U.S. trade with many foreign countries, overseas banks found it increasingly important to associate themselves with U.S. banks that could be their correspondents to collect on checks drawn on U.S.-based banks, and provide for all their other banking needs in the U.S. The relationship could be unidirectional or bidirectional, meaning that each bank at its discretion could decide whether to use the other bank for a given transaction. There was no exclusivity commitment by either bank.

"Do you provide additional services? I read someplace that you also assist charities."

He hesitated for a moment. "Yes, in fact we do, but it's not what we are promoting these days." There was a subtly reluctant tone in his answer.

"Is business good?" I didn't want to reveal that I had picked up on his lack of enthusiasm to elaborate.

"Can't complain," he replied.

Back at my office, I ran a quick check on McHanna. There was something about him that I didn't like. Maybe it was because he had the sweetness of a funeral-home director. A newspaper interview I found far back in the LexisNexis database service increased my interest. A small savings-industry newsletter had interviewed McHanna during the period that Whitney- Davis was perpetrating his scam, but before it was discovered. In the interview, McHanna boasted how innovative and resourceful thinking could increase the profit base of a small savings bank. "We are developing additional investment vehicles for our customers that will add an international aspect to our line of products. We will enable our customers to invest in foreign currencies through Tempelhof Bank in Zürich, Switzerland. That's why we hired the services of Mr. Harrington T. Whitney-Davis, a renowned financial advisor."

Hello, my friend, I said to myself. I thought of a verse from the Bible my father had liked to quote: "Do two walk together, unless they have agreed?" We would soon see how these men had conspired.

I checked the FBI report again—nothing about Switzerland. Same went for the bank examiners. I double-checked with their agencies. Nothing in the file. I went to see McHanna again, unannounced. If he was happy to see me, he was doing a good job of hiding it. Instead, he looked concerned.

"Mr. McHanna, I forgot to ask you one other question," I

said. "In the end, did your savings bank in South Dakota finally launch the idea, offering your customers some foreign-currency investment opportunities?"

He was stunned. After he recovered, he said slowly, "Well, actually, we didn't."

"Why not?"

"If I remember correctly, the board didn't think the product fit the needs of our customers. They were mostly farmers and small-business owners."

"So the program was abandoned?"

"Yes. And right after that we discovered the fraud, and I tendered my resignation."

Hmm. Brian DiLorenzo of the OTS told me that the savings bank had fired McHanna. What else might he have embellished?

"Have you seen or heard of Mr. Harrington T. Whitney-Davis since?"

McHanna turned his eyes to the window on his right and scratched his nose. "No."

My friend, I thought, *your mouth says no, but your body says yes.*

I remembered the course about body language taught by the Mossad psychologist.

Research has shown that many, but not all, people tell the truth when they look to the left trying to remember events. When they look to the right they rely more on their imagination, and therefore they're either intentionally lying or their answers cannot be relied upon. If a person questioned touches any part of his or her body, that indicates stress and the likelihood of a lie. Look at the person's pupils. They dilate when someone is lying. Same goes for a dry mouth that a person tries to moisten by licking his or her lips.

"And what about Tempelhof Bank? Do you still have any relationship with them?" I asked.

McHanna's smile disappeared. "I'm not sure. I would need to check on that. Anyway, I don't think it's relevant to your investigation, Mr. Gordon. This information is a trade secret of my company, and has nothing to do with my former employment."

He had a point, I thought, but I had plenty of them as well. He had just given me a reason to follow that lead and go to Switzerland.

CHAPTER SIX

David Stone refused outright when I reported my findings and asked for his authorization to go to Zürich. "You know the Swiss sensitivity when it comes to investigations by foreign agents," he said.

"Of course I know. Article 273," I said. The Swiss criminal code made it a criminal offense for anyone besides a Swiss official to question a witness within Switzerland, whether the case was criminal or civil.

"Right," said David. He then reminded me, though we both knew I needed no reminding, that this law includes agents of foreign governments who attempt to obtain information about a client of a Swiss bank. Even if a client authorizes the Swiss bank to disclose information to a foreign government, the bank cannot divulge any information on that basis.

"So?" I said when he had finished.

"I just wanted to make sure we're on the same page."

I knew David. Although he was content to hear me recite the Swiss law he had often suspected I overlooked, he also wanted to make sure I remembered Swiss law special restrictions regarding foreign governments. The Swiss legislature included that restriction to protect Swiss banks from pressure by foreign governments, which could make their life difficult if a Swiss bank also operated in that foreign country. We saw that when the Swiss refused for fifty years to give up any information on the bank accounts owned by Jewish victims of the Nazis. But, in that case, Congress and the U.S. courts made them finally talk and pay.

I waited for him to say more, but he did not. It was my turn. "It so happens that I have plans for a private visit to Switzerland," I said wickedly. "And I need to be on assignment in Germany. So I request your authorization to issue a round-trip ticket to Berlin, with a stopover at my own expense in Zürich."

"You're on your own," said David.

"I know that." It's the same old gambit: official refusal and a silent nod. It had worked fine thus far, because I'd been careful not to break Swiss law, laid low, and limited my activities to brain power. And I never broke the eleventh commandment of the trade: Though Shalt Not Get Caught.

The flight to Zürich was uneventful, except for the nosy and noisy lady beside me who insisted I meet her niece, who she swore had lost weight since the photo she flashed had been taken.

I checked into the Canton Park hotel, a cozy three-star hotel in the center of town. On the following morning I went to Tempelhof Bank near Bahnhofplatz in the heart of Zürich. The street-level entrance was palatial, framed by marble columns and lions. The inside was just as majestic, laid with Persian rugs, antique furniture, and a seven-foot flower arrangement. A uniformed blonde lady approached me.

"Grüezi," she said. She switched to English, seeing the puzzled look on my face. "Welcome, how can I help?"

"I need some information concerning investment in foreign currencies."

"Certainly," she said. "Please be seated. I'll have a specialist help you."

A moment later, we were joined by a slim young man with rimless glasses.

"Hello, I'm Manfred von Wilhelm," he said, and we shook hands.

"I'm Peter Wooten, an attorney from the United States," I told him. Two out of three accurate pieces of information wasn't bad. Peter Wooten was my frequent alias. The name, though, is an alias I use when I need to hide my identity from the opposition, and sometimes even from a foreign government as well.

"I'm exploring for my client—a major private U.S. investor—the option of investing in foreign currencies."

"You came to the right place," said Wilhelm. "Currency transactions have been our forte for many years. Swiss integrity, professionalism, and absolute discretion in protecting our customers are our bywords. May I ask who recommended us?"

"My client talked about Harrington T. Whitney-Davis, a consultant who had assisted a friend of his with satisfactory results."

"Many consultants recommend our services, and I'm sure Mr. Harrington T. Whitney-Davis did the right thing when he mentioned our name."

"Good, I hope to be associated with Mr. Whitney-Davis as well. Can you arrange that?"

He hesitated. "I'm not sure."

"Maybe I came to the wrong bank," I said cautiously. "I want to make sure about Mr. Harrington T. Whitney-Davis; I don't think it should be confidential. I'm asking about a business association, not about your bank's clients."

Slightly annoyed, he picked up his phone and dialed a three-digit number. He exchanged a few sentences in Swiss German, which I found difficult to follow, but the name Harrington T. Whitney-Davis was mentioned twice.

He hung up. "Well, my colleague just told me that years ago, Mr. Harrington T. Whitney-Davis was suggesting our services to his clients, as an outside consultant. I'm sorry I wasn't aware of it, since I came to work for the bank only last year. What is your client interested in? Speculative trading? Hedging against currency fluctuations to guarantee proceeds from an export transaction, or to safeguard against currency-exchange-rate hikes if he's importing goods?"

Forget about the transactions, I wanted to say, *let's talk about Whitney-Davis.* But recognizing that any additional reference to him would arouse suspicion, I reluctantly moved on. I could revisit the issue after Wilhelm invested more time and effort in trying to sell me on the bank's services. The more time he invested, the more effort he'd make not to alienate me.

"He wants to speculate," I said. "$10 to $20 million, for starters."

This didn't seem to impress Wilhelm. If he hadn't dealt with bigger fish, he certainly wanted to give that impression. Perhaps I should have mentioned a bigger amount.

"Would your client be giving the instructions? Or would he want us to trade for him?"

"Due to time differences, I think he'd prefer your experts to do it. Tell me how's it done."

He spent the next fifteen minutes explaining the investment mechanism. I gave him a gracious smile and a nod.

"Earlier you mentioned confidentiality. This is something that my client insists upon."

"Swiss law and our bank's rules assure that," he said.

"What about communication? How does he contact you?"

"On the phone, unless there's a problem for him in America," he said smoothly, looking at my face through his rimless glasses. "Or he could fax or e-mail us. We can also hold his mail until he comes to Switzerland to collect it."

"Do you have a U.S.-based correspondent bank? My client may want to use that link, rather than go through international communication lines."

"I understand, sir. In fact, we can use McHanna Associates in New York. They aren't a bank, but rather a service company, and I'm told they're very experienced."

"That sounds good," I said.

"With your client's written authorization, they could handle all matters for your client without any problem."

"Including receiving mail, like your monthly statements?"

"Of course."

"By the way," I said casually. "Where can I find Whitney-Davis? My client was so impressed with his professional abilities."

He frowned and dialed his phone again and exchanged a few sentences.

"We aren't sure," he said. "You may want to contact McHanna Associates in New York. They may know more about him."

Ah, but McHanna had already told me that he couldn't remember whether he'd heard from Whitney-Davis since his South Dakota scam in the mid 1980s.

I returned to my hotel with a briefcase full of glossy brochures and application forms. Discovering a current business relationship between the former manager of a savings bank victimized by Whitney-Davis and a Swiss bank that appeared to run a legitimate business was peculiar but not earthshaking. There were, however, two very interesting findings. First, McHanna hadn't only lied to me. He didn't seem to hold a grudge against Whitney-Davis and now, in fact, could be in contact with him. I was puzzled by that finding. I had just heard that Whitney-Davis continued to use that name years after the scam. But the FBI had told us that the name had disappeared from all credit-reporting agencies. And now it had surfaced again? It was highly unusual.

Second, McHanna Associates was apparently helping U.S. residents avoid the prying eyes of the U.S. government by accepting and keeping their Swiss banking correspondence. That could be considered aiding and abetting money laundering, if the proceeds deposited by the client were the fruit of a crime. But at that moment I was too frustrated, tired, and hungry to follow up on these promising leads or think about the resurrection of Whitney-Davis's name. The idea that man could live on bread alone turned out to be all wet. I was hungry and needed a beer. Unfortunately, the meal I ended up getting consisted of a tuna sandwich and a local beer that tasted as if it had gone through a horse first.

I hooked up my laptop to my room's high-speed Internet connection and sent Esther the efficient office admin an encrypted e-mail:

> Please check with the New York State Banking Department whether McHanna Associates need a license to act as a liaison for a Swiss bank in currency transactions for U.S. citizens. If such a license is necessary, please see if one was issued to McHanna. Also, ask the FBI field office in Manhattan whether there's an ongoing investigation regarding that company's possible involvement in money laundering. Finally, check if McHanna ever filed any tax returns listing Harrington T. Whitney-Davis as an employee, or engaged him as an independent contractor.

The latter two questions were legitimate, but the chances that the FBI would discuss the first question, even though we were both agencies of the U.S. government, were slim to none. As to the tax returns, the IRS could not, under federal law, share that information without a court order. Neither the FBI nor the IRS were the bad guys in this bureaucratic nightmare. They had to maintain a stringent procedure for information exchange. But maybe Esther, with her quiet demeanor, could achieve what I couldn't with my big mouth and aggressive attitude.

I had a free evening. But Zürich at night is as exciting as having a warm beer with an overly talkative blind date you agreed to meet during a temporary moment of insanity. Swiss TV isn't any better. I called my children and went to sleep.

In the morning, I had barely shaken myself awake when I turned on my laptop computer. There was an incoming encrypted e-mail from Esther:

There's no need for a license from the New York State Banking Department if the company isn't doing any banking activities in New York, such as taking deposits or making loans to the public. Providing liaison services alone requires no license. As for the FBI, I received an evasive answer regarding any investigation of McHanna Associates. The IRS says officially that they can't help us, but unofficially I was led to understand that Harrington T. Whitney-Davis's name never appeared on McHanna Associates' tax filings, although it's possible that an alias was used. Please let me know if you need anything else. Esther.

I returned to New York. Unenthusiastically, I pulled out the files again. I checked the names of the perpetrators in the remaining eight cases. By now, what I found didn't surprise me; it was all so obvious that I almost expected it. All eight men had left the U.S. in 1980 or 1981. Their respective names had resurfaced briefly, one with each of the banking or other scams perpetrated. Then each had vanished again. Since I discovered that the name of Whitney-Davis resurfaced, I ran a check on all other names to see if we had a wholesale revival. But the answer came as expected. No. No resurgence of any other name.

I had a hunch that the suspected perpetrators' disappearances weren't coincidental. There was a clear pattern. Since none of the men had any meaningful criminal record, or a troubled past, I didn't suspect that they had cooperated with the thefts of their identities, although I couldn't rule that out altogether. I had to decide on a direction. But I had no idea which way to turn.

Chapter Seven

There were additional questions I wanted to ask McHanna about his contacts with Whitney-Davis, but I decided against it. The information I had received in Switzerland was, at best, just raw intelligence, and confronting McHanna before I had hard evidence could be damaging.

I called David Stone. He had always been a good sounding board for my queries. David's physical appearance as a typical absentminded university professor with profuse white hair and eyeglasses slipping to the tip of his nose was misleading. Although nearing retirement, he was very alert, and all brain. He was always the first to come to the office and the last to leave, the exact opposite of a lot of guys in his position, who are just there to mark time until their pension kicks in. I tried to imagine what David would do in retirement, but it seemed so out of character for him that no clear picture materialized in my mind's eye.

"Let me put you on speaker," he said. "Bob Holliday is also here, and I want him to get involved."

"OK, I'm facing an interesting question. Who would know that a bunch of apparently unrelated young American men in their early twenties left the United States at about the same time, leaving no trace behind them?"

"There are many young men, Americans and other nationals, who take off and never return to their homelands. That's no news," David answered.

"I think there's at least one common denominator to all these cases," I continued, "but the FBI takes it even a step further. They think all the scams were perpetrated by the same person."

"I saw that. Their conclusion is based on paper-thin evidence. You know that from a false premise, any conclusion can be drawn. I tend to think that the FBI found itself in a cul-de-sac, or it wouldn't have off-loaded the file on us." David sounded tired. "I didn't get back to you on this because I had no answers either. So maybe you shouldn't follow their way of thinking, or you'll end up where they ended—facing a brick wall."

"This is strange, now that you mention it, David," I said. "Because it goes along with my line of thinking. If what I've discovered so far checks out, then the entire theoretical structure the FBI is working from will collapse. They had just one chink in the armor. Maybe we don't have Albert C. Ward III assuming eleven aliases. Maybe we've got ourselves a Mr. Anonymous with twelve aliases, including one as Albert C. Ward III."

"I hear you," said David, digesting my words. "Anything to support it?"

"Ward had a pronounced stutter. None of the imposters is described in the files as having that disability. On the contrary. The suspect in each of the eleven indicted cases actually has been pretty articulate," I said, gaining confidence with my theory.

"Go on," said David, sounding interested.

I picked up speed. "Let's establish, just for the sake of our little discussion here, that twenty-year-olds couldn't have pulled off the scams, because they weren't sophisticated enough, and because the little evidence we've gathered shows the perpetrators appeared to be much older. Therefore, let's suppose that whoever assumed the identity of four, and maybe even all twelve, young American men made a hit on a bank or on unsuspecting investors and ran with the money. Now, I don't even have this con artist's picture, if Ward's identity was also stolen. The yearbook picture and the photos that Donald Peterson, the retired school principal, sent me were definitely of Ward. But apparently the FBI never asked any of the victims whether the scam artist's photo was in a photo array that included that year-book photo of Ward. If my target wasn't Ward after all, then whom was I chasing? I'm back to square one, hunting a single ghost or a cemetery's worth."

"Dan, it's Bob. Didn't you just tell us that you think the FBI was wrong, and even the person calling himself Ward was an imposter who assumed Ward's identity, and not Ward himself? So if the FBI was wrong on that, why wouldn't they be wrong on the entire concept? Take your idea even further."

"How?"

"How do we know that the twelve cases are connected? Maybe just two or three or none at all," said Bob.

"The FBI said so."

"They could be wrong, you know. You've just suggested it," added David.

"Anyway, the FBI's conclusion isn't proof, but assumption," concluded Bob.

"OK," I said. "Although we've enough doubts concerning the FBI's conclusion, we also must make assumptions that could turn out to be just as baseless."

"Like what?" asked Bob.

"Like the one that seems most logical at this time, and take it from there."

"Fine," said David. "How about that? Assuming that all of the cases are connected, who could mastermind such an operation?"

"If it went beyond the one-person-crime-spree pattern we see in the usual identity thefts, I'd see a criminal organization with international activities, or some other structured body."

"Any basis for that?" Bob asked, more in curiosity than as a challenge.

"No proof, just my hunch."

"Why?" Clearly, like David, he wasn't the kind of guy who would settle for easy answers.

"Because it involves young American men, none of whom apparently knew any of the others, who first left the country at about the same time, each for reasons of his own. Only after they left the country did the common denominator kick in: their identities were stolen. The first step of the conspiracy didn't start here. It started somewhere, anywhere, wherever these guys lost their passports. Take Ward. He was traveling in Africa and Asia without known incident until he stopped writing his friends here. Since we don't know where the others went, it could have happened anywhere. But the fact remains—their passports were also taken. Therefore, my conclusion is that an organization that operates in more than one location could be behind it. Besides, why limit ourselves to thinking it was a criminal enterprise? Maybe there's a foreign power or a terrorist organization behind this."

"Any basis for that?" asked David.

"Not at this time, but need I remind you that we lost our innocence on nine eleven? Things that weren't plausible earlier are a reality now." I didn't want to elaborate, but in my mind was my Mossad training concerning planting sleeper agents in target countries. Those passports could now be used by foreign agents operating in any country that welcomes U.S. citizens. These could be used for far more dangerous purposes than money siphoning. I had no proof, just a hunch that I registered in my mind to develop later.

David brought me back to reality, which he was very good at. In fact, I sometimes felt as if he were my anchor, always keeping me tethered only to the facts at hand. Yet one more thing I was going to miss when he was gone. "Maybe the passports were taken in just one location by a sophisticated scam artist?"

"Sure," I agreed. "That's also a possibility." But I suspected that David's new theory was more farfetched than mine.

Bob developed the idea further. "Have you thought of the possibility that these young men simply sold their passports to finance their trips, claimed they were lost, and applied for new ones?"

"I did, and so did the FBI. The State Department told the Bureau that none of these men applied for a replacement passport. Besides, if all they did was sell their passport, why have they disappeared for good?"

"Did you investigate whether these guys had more than one citizenship? They could be selling their U.S. passports and continuing to travel with their foreign passports." Bob's tone was persistent. He seemed unwilling to consider my speculations unless I could prove that I'd considered every possibility. I realized he was only doing his job, and so far it hadn't reached the point where I found it to be irritating.

"No go. If any of them had a foreign passport, his entry into the U.S. with that passport would have been recorded, and it wasn't. Therefore, the genuine Ward left the U.S. only once and never returned. His passport and identity were given to someone already in the U.S., or who had initially entered the U.S. with a different passport under a different name, and then took Ward's identity. It is possible that either all the additional passports were delivered to that someone while he was already in the U.S., or they were brought into the U.S. with him. That is, if all these cases are connected."

"Yes, but . . ." said Bob continuing to be the devil's advocate. "To begin with, why does he need passports to steal identities? He just needs the bio details, Social Security numbers, and such."

I had an answer to that. "Because a U.S. passport is the best way of getting a copy of your old Social Security card, a driver's license, and many other personal documents. Once you have these documents, the passport becomes secondary in the identity-theft scheme, other than for leaving the U.S. with your loot."

Bob wasn't deterred. "Fine, but how do we know that Ward didn't have yet another passport with an alias that he used to exit the U.S.? It's not a big deal. If he managed to get eleven passports with aliases, he could get twelve."

"I still think there's some organization behind it," I said, but with less conviction.

After we got off the phone, I decided to explore that direction. Was Ward the only solid name I had to look at? What about the others? I decided to stick with him, because chronologically he was the first to disappear. But the age issue made me more confident in my earlier theory that we had ourselves a case of identity thefts. All victims described the perpetrators as men in their late twenties or early thirties, but the young men whose passports were used were in their early twenties at the time the scams began. Although a victim doesn't usually ask a purported business associate for a passport, in retrospect the discrepancy was too obvious to ignore.

I turned to my desktop. I wanted to see if there were any news items about Ward. Maybe he'd sold photographs to some magazine in India, or had been arrested after a bar brawl in Indonesia. With more than ten thousand daily newspapers published around the world, maybe he had done something nice, or not so nice, that had been reported. Ward had disappeared in the early 1980s, before most international news was routinely computerized, and had then resurfaced irregularly starting in the mid-1980s. Still, I might get lucky. Maybe Ward's irregular resurfacing was intended to establish a "clean" alias between scams? None of the other aliases turned up again for more than the one scam.

I first ran a Google search. Nothing relevant. Then I tried the Dogpile search engine. Still nothing. Next I tried legal retrieving services and limited the search to newspapers and magazines. After scrolling down over hundreds of items, and just as I was about to give up, I got a hit on *Albert C. Ward III.* It was in a newsletter issued by the Jewish community in Sydney, Australia.

A bigamous wedding was averted at the last moment last week, before Rabbi Applebaum was scheduled to celebrate the marriage of Mr. Herbert Goldman from the United States to Miss Sheila Levi, a member of our community. Just hours before the ceremony was to be held at our synagogue, Rabbi Applebaum received a facsimile from Loretta Otis, of Lexington, Kentucky, claiming that Mr. Herbert Goldman was still married to her. In the fax Ms. Otis said she had no objection to Mr. Goldman's marriage, provided that he divorces her first and that they settle "some outstanding financial matters." Rabbi Applebaum called Ms. Otis, who told him that Herbert Goldman's real name is Albert C. Ward III, and he is using the name of Herbert Goldman because he acquired a U.S. passport in that name while living in the U.S. Ms. Otis told Rabbi Applebaum that Goldman informed her that he was traveling to Australia for business. According to Ms. Otis, Goldman rang her weekly from Australia, but recently told her, "I'm marrying an Australian woman, Sheila Levi, because that way I can get permanent residence in Australia. You shouldn't worry, because it will only be a sham marriage, and I will always love you my sweet Loretta, my only true wife." When it dawned on Ms. Otis that Ward was not going to return to the U.S. or pay her father back the $34,000 he had borrowed from him, she faxed several rabbis in Sydney and the Sydney Registry of Births, Deaths, and Marriages, hoping to frustrate Goldman's marriage plans. Rabbi Applebaum commented that Ms. Otis's contact was timely, not just because the marriage would have been bigamous, but because he opposes people marrying out of their faith. According to Ms. Otis, Goldman, also known as Albert C. Ward III, is not Jewish.

"I'll be damned," I said in deep satisfaction. I looked for the date. It was only ten days old! I called David Stone.

"David, I need to do additional searching and verifications, but it seems that I might have a lead on Ward's trail."

"Where?"

"In Australia," I said, and gave David the details.

"How recent is the news item?"

"Ten days."

"Let me run it by the Office of International Affairs at the Criminal Division," said David. "Maybe they already have something on that."

Now it was time for *cherchez la femme*: look for the woman. If Loretta Otis had spilled the beans on Ward once, she'd do it twice. There's nothing more dangerous than a spurned woman. Maybe a spurned man.

I called the FBI field office in Lexington, Kentucky.

They called me back within the hour to give me the news: Loretta Otis had been found dead the night before in her apartment. Homicide.

"How did she die?" I asked, as if it mattered for my investigation. She was dead—I couldn't talk to her in any case.

"Gun shots, three times. Looks professional, and if we're not mistaken, she was the target. Doesn't look like a foiled robbery—nothing was taken from her house."

I told them about my initial finding in the media about the victim, and asked the Bureau to call me back as the police investigation developed. But I already knew why she had died, and feared I'd hit a dead end there anyway.

David called me later on that day. I told him about Otis's assassination.

He reflected for a moment and asked, "Do you think Ward is connected?"

"I can't rule it out. Look at the sequence of events. First she faxes the Rabbi to stop the wedding, then the Rabbi calls her to verify, then the Rabbi refuses to marry Ward and tells him why, and within days, bang bang bang, and Otis is dead. Probably silenced either as punishment or to keep her from spilling more. It seems that our case is not dead after all. It's very much in motion."

"OK. Let local law enforcement handle that—we're only after the money. Anyway, I've just got the authorizations. Start packing, you're going to Sydney. Your travel documents are on the way. We've received the cooperation of the Australian Federal Police. They have assigned an agent to assist you. His name

is . . . Hold on, let me get the cable. Peter Maxwell. I'll give
you his number. Call him directly to alert him of your arrival
time, and we'll take it from there."

"Peter Maxwell here," said a friendly voice with a heavy Australian accent, when I dialed his number.

"Hi, Mr. Maxwell, this is Dan Gordon of the U.S. Department of Justice."

"Hello, Dan, I've been expecting your call, and forget the
mister, just call me Peter." Peter Maxwell pronounced his name
Pita. He was warm and open as he brought me up to speed.
Goldman was still at large. Border records showed the entry of
a Herbert Goldman, a U.S. citizen, through Sydney's airport on
March 1, 2004. On the immigration form he'd indicated a hotel as place of stay.

"Which hotel?" I asked.

"No name, just 'a hotel.' "

"I'm planning to come over to see the Australian Federal
Police in action," I said.

"Please come, although I don't expect a lot of action on
this end. Hopefully we'll find him. But it's one hell of a big
country down here, mate."

Three days later I arrived at the Sydney airport. To my huge
surprise, all the red-eyed, weary passengers of my flight were
stopped in the terminal's hallway by uniformed policemen with
dogs on short leashes. Without much ado, we were told—or
rather ordered—to form two lines and put our hand luggage on
the floor. Nice welcome, I thought, but times being what they
were, it was reassuring in its own way. Policemen then walked
two dogs slowly along each passenger line, letting one dog, then
the other, sniff each piece of carry-on luggage. Ten minutes
later it was over and we were let go, without even one word of
explanation or apology.

There were ways to look for drugs or explosives, but that one
was the most unexpected. I knew they had to use at least two
dogs per line: one dog trained for explosives that sits stock still

and points if it finds them, the other trained to detect drugs by sniffing the luggage. Trainers had discovered that they couldn't cross-train the dogs, or the sniffing narcotics dogs might set off explosives. If using both types of dogs, you'd take the explosives dogs down the line first. Then, if no explosives were found, would come the drug dogs, which could snurfle to their hearts' content without setting anything off.

Peter Maxwell, a tall man with a rugged, tanned face and a firm handshake, waited for me in the customs hall.

"Welcome," he said as he walked me past customs into his unmarked police car. "Was it too tiring?"

"Somewhat," I answered, deciding not to rant about the sudden search. "Any developments?" I was eager to jump into it.

Peter smiled. "Yes, we found the lad at a Sydney hotel."

"Is he still there?"

"No. Ten minutes after we started questioning him, he said he was sick and fainted."

"He actually fainted?"

"You ask me, this bloke is full of shit, but just in case, we admitted him into a hospital."

"Is he under your watch? This guy can disappear in no time."

"We've got a warrant for his arrest on local fraud charges, so in fact he's a detainee in the hospital."

"When can I see him?"

Peter looked at his watch. "How's this afternoon sound? I'll drop you off at your hotel, and if you aren't too tired, you can walk to the hospital. It's very close to your hotel."

When we arrived at the hotel, I checked in, threw my luggage on the floor, and ran out the door. I was dog tired, but I hadn't come to Sydney to rest. I had to see Albert C. Ward III right away.

CHAPTER EIGHT

Manhattan, New York, September 11, 2004

Crushed by the fact that I had been wrong about Ward, I had to find a new bearing. I paced through the hallway outside my office. If the man in the hospital bed wasn't Albert Ward, then who was he? His denials didn't impress me. I'd seen con men in action, and wasn't about to be convinced by this guy. On the other hand, there was firm scientific proof that he wasn't Ward. Had I picked on an innocent person? I still had no idea of what the missing link could be. What about Otis's faxed letter connecting Ward with Goldman? Why wasn't that enough? But until the FBI and the Australian Federal Police cleared this matter up, I needed to move on. The solution had to be in the file. But where?

I sat down at my desk and opened the file for the umpteenth time. First, I read my notes taken during my conversation with the high school principal. Ward had wanted to be a photographer for *National Geographic Magazine*. Maybe I should see if he had ever made good on that dream.

"It'd take time to search the archives dating back to 1980," said a very polite woman when I called National Geographic. "Not all our freelance photographers are included in our computer database. If the person you're looking for sold us a photograph many years back, a manual search would have to be performed."

"Thanks, but can you please look to see whether his name appears on your computer database?" I asked. It was an absurdly long shot—lots of kids have dreams—but I had nothing to lose, and I could get lucky.

"Let me see. You said his name was Albert Ward?"

"Yes, the third. Albert C. Ward III."

I heard her clicking on her computer keyboard. "Yes," she said. "I think I found something. There's a series of photographs taken by a person with that name during a safari in South Africa in 1981."

"That's great. Is there an address listed for him?"

"Yes, we sent him a check to Comfort Student Hostel, Sandton Square, P.O. Box 97848, Johannesburg, South Africa."

Finally I was moving up in time, although just one year. At least I had an address overseas. "Thank you so much. Can you transfer me to accounting please?"

"Accounting, Lisa speaking," said a woman cordially.

"I would like to know how a freelance photographer named Albert C. Ward III cashed a check paid to him by your magazine in 1981."

"And you are?"

"Dan Gordon, U.S. Department of Justice."

"I'm sorry. You'll have to subpoena these records. I hope you understand," she said. "We must protect the privacy of our vendors."

"No problem," I said. "I'll get you a subpoena."

Two days later I sent her a subpoena, and a week later I had my response. Albert C. Ward III was paid $315 with a check. A copy of the check's front and back was attached. I looked at the back of the check. The check was deposited into account number AZ334465 at the First African Bank, Sandton Square, Johannesburg, South Africa.

The next step was to get my hands on that bank's records. But a U.S. subpoena would do no good in South Africa; I'd need a South African court order for that. Just the thought of going through the necessary bureaucratic maze made me dizzy. But first, I had to check if the account was still active. I called our accounting department and asked them to issue a check in the amount of $75 made out to Albert C. Ward III, drawn on "Department B's" bank account. That was our code name for the bank account of a limited liability company we had incorporated in Wyoming, whose shareholders or directors couldn't be traced.

In an accompanying letter printed on our dummy corporation's letterhead and addressed to the bank, I wrote, "Please deposit the attached royalty payment check into account AZ334465 of Mr. Albert C. Ward III. We've syndicated one-time reprint rights for Mr. Ward's photographs, which we acquired years ago, to a U.S.-based publishing company for use in a wildlife calendar. Our letter to Mr. Ward was returned by mail. We discovered this bank account through the details on the check we initially paid Mr. Ward. We trust this payment shall be promptly deposited into Mr. Ward's account." I scribbled a signature, put the check in an envelope, put a stamp on it instead of using our office postage machine, and sent it to the bank in South Africa.

Ten days later, I checked with accounting. Our check had just cleared. Accounting obtained a copy of both sides of our check. The stamp on the back of the check read, "Deposit to account," and a handwritten number was added: AZ334465.

I called the First African Bank branch manager in South Africa. "I'm the photography editor of *Wild Nature and Adventure* magazine, based in Denver, Colorado," I said. "A while ago we purchased several photographs from your customer, Mr. Albert C. Ward III, but we lost contact with him. We now have an important job assignment for him. Would you kindly let me have his address, or even better ask him to get in touch with us?"

Maybe banking secrecy laws didn't travel all the way to South Africa, I hoped.

"Let me look," he said. "We don't seem to have a current address either. I see that our statements were returned by the postal service."

"I have Comfort Student Hostel, Sandton Square, P.O. Box 97848, Johannesburg, South Africa," I said, trying to inject more credibility into my cover story.

"That's the address we also have," said the manager. "Well, it's a hostel. Obviously people don't stay there too long."

"Maybe you can help me in another way," I said, stretching his courtesy. "Maybe you can see if he continued to use his account by drawing checks or making deposits. We really love his work, and the job offer I'm about to make is very lucrative. I know he'd appreciate any help you could offer."

"Glad to help," said the manager. After a moment he said, "We have recent activity in the form of a check in a small amount that came from the U.S." That was our check.

"Anything other than that?"

"Well, nothing, in the account, but we did receive an inquiry from the Peninsula Bank branch in Islamabad, Pakistan, asking to authenticate Mr. Ward's signature."

He gave me the branch's address.

Although the lead was promising, I wasn't elated. It was almost twenty years old, and searching a nation of over 160 million for a tourist who had last visited it two decades ago was hardly a plausible proposal. Still, I had to try.

I knew how to hunt, but this prey's footsteps in Pakistan were long washed away by time. There had to be a way. I was hungry for the kill, but where could I start? I couldn't fail again. Usually the last place you look for something is where it was the whole time. I called my boss and took a deep breath. "David, on a strong hunch and a thin lead, I'm taking my investigation to Pakistan."

"How thin is the lead?"

"Like sliced salami, but it's the only thing I have. Nonetheless, maybe I can develop it further from there."

"You know the routine," said David, intuitively trusting my instincts, even after I'd told him how paper-thin my lead was. "Travel authorizations. The U.S. Embassy in Pakistan and the Pakistani government have to give you the go ahead."

Under the federal "Chief of Mission" statute, federal government employees could operate in a foreign country only with the U.S. ambassador's consent. Therefore, the U.S.

Embassy could assign an embassy control officer to be present during all my activities. Normally an embassy chaperone for my contacts with locals irritated me to no end—sources could be as silent as a house-trained husband in the presence of a foreign diplomat—but the deterioration of security in Pakistan made me less resistant.

"OK, let's do the routine."

David tried to hide his surprise.

"What's the matter?" he asked. "You usually grumble when I raise the bureaucracy involved in foreign travel."

"I've learned to live with it," I said. It was kind of awkward. David was right. I usually complained about that bureaucracy when trips to sunny locations and paradise islands were concerned, probably because it unnecessarily delayed my departure, but now I was compliant when a trip to Pakistan was concerned? Maybe I was happy to go to resort areas without any delay, but going to Pakistan nowadays isn't exactly a fun trip, particularly if you're an American. Usually it doesn't take much to make me professionally happy: catch an absconding con man with his multimillion-dollar loot in a sunny resort; find a cooperative bank manager in an offshore location who will spill on his clients for less than $1,000; or get a call from my boss telling me he got praises for my work, not just complaints I was cutting corners. But as always in life, miracles happen to others. I get reality.

Five days later, formalities were completed and Esther gave me the airline tickets. "Be careful out there," she said in her motherly voice. Esther was a very pleasant African-American woman in her early fifties with gray streaks in her black hair, which gave her a dignified appearance that perfectly matched her personality. I was constantly telling her she should go to law school, with her methodical and sharp mind.

"Don't buy any food from street vendors," she continued, knowing my penchant for food adventures. "We don't want you back here on a stretcher." I remembered the time I'd eaten nearly-raw hamburger in a remote town in Southeast Asia that gave me a five-foot-long tapeworm that took months to get rid of.

I looked at the ticket folder. I was leaving the following morning on American Airlines flight 132 to London Heathrow Airport, continuing on British Airways flight 6429 to Islamabad, arriving the day after at six A.M. I inserted into the folder my vaccination card showing I had received hepatitis A and typhoid vaccinations. Esther handed me a printed form. "That's the current travel advisory issued by the State Department," she said. I glanced at the memo.

The Department of State continues to warn U.S. citizens to defer nonessential travel to Pakistan due to ongoing concerns about the possibility of terrorist activity directed against American citizens and interests there.

The U.S. Embassy in Islamabad and the U.S. consulates in Karachi, Lahore, and Peshawar continue to operate at reduced staffing levels. Family members of official Americans assigned to all four posts in Pakistan were ordered to leave the country in March 2002, and have not been allowed to return. Al-Qaeda and Taliban elements continue to operate inside Pakistan, particularly along the porous border region. Their presence, coupled with that of indigenous sectarian and militant groups in Pakistan, requires that all Americans in or traveling through Pakistan take appropriate security measures.

Esther grinned. "Still wanna go?"

"Even more so," I said. I made quick arrangements for Snap, called my two children at their colleges just to let them know I'd be overseas for a while (they were quite used to it by now), and took a cab to JFK Airport.

CHAPTER NINE

I arrived in Islamabad together with the first rays of the rising sun. The streets were already bustling with cars, buses, taxicabs, and bicycle riders. The sidewalks were crammed with pedestrians, most of them dressed in the Pakistani traditional garb, men in *salwar kameez* and women in burkas.

"Mr. Gordon?" asked an overweight Pakistani man in his early forties wearing a khaki safari suit.

"And you are?"

"My name is Abdullah, sir. I'm a U.S. embassy driver. I've instructions to drive you."

"Where to?" I hadn't been expecting him.

"To your hotel first, sir. Your meeting at the embassy is not until noon."

"Can I see your embassy ID please?" You could never be too cautious, particularly considering where I was.

"Of course, sir," he said matter of factly, and showed me his embassy photo ID. I followed him to an unmarked embassy car, and we drove in silence to the Marriott Hotel on Aga Khan Road.

"I can get to the embassy by myself later on," I told him. "I need to get some rest first. I had a very long flight."

"I understand, sir, but my instructions are to drive you," said the driver. He explained that the RSO—regional security officer—had requested that no U.S. government officials use the city's transportation. "You know, sir, personal safety isn't what it used to be," he added with a sigh, wiping his forehead with a handkerchief. Although it was barely eight o'clock, the temperature was already 95°F, and the humidity high.

"Fine," I said. "I'll meet you at the hotel lobby at eleven thirty."

I freshened up and waited for Abdullah, who was twenty minutes late. "I'm sorry, sir," he said. "Bad traffic."

I entered the car. "Where are we going?"

"The American Embassy is on Ramna Street, in the diplomatic enclave of Islamabad."

After passing the security checks and passing through the lowered Delta barrier, I entered the embassy compound, which would be more accurately described as a fortress. But once inside, I felt as if I were in a country club. Beautiful gardens, an Olympic swimming pool, tennis courts, a restaurant, and a small baseball field. The embassy main building seemed to be rather empty. I saw only a few embassy staff. "The RSO is expecting you," said Abdullah. "He's on the third floor. I'm restricted from that floor."

"Ned Applebee," said the RSO, a well-built blond man in his early thirties, as he nearly crushed my fingers with his handshake. We sat in his small office. "Welcome to Islamabad. Sorry I can't offer you anything to drink. All nonessential staff has been sent home, and I haven't figured out how to restock that goddamned coffee machine. All we've got is soda. Anyway, the legal attaché wants to see you as well. He'll be joining us in a few minutes."

"That's all right, "I said. "Any diet soda will do." I followed Ned to the hallway and took two cans from the vending machine.

"Let's move to the bubble," suggested Ned Applebee. We walked over to a sealed and secure room, a must in any embassy where there are always ears on the other side of the wall. Such rooms are soundproof and windowless, with just a desk and chairs, where no electronic equipment such as computers or cell phones is allowed. They are mostly used for top-secret conversations, in the hope that no eavesdropping will be possible.

"I'm here on assignment looking for a U.S. citizen, Albert C. Ward III, whom we suspect of major bank fraud. His footsteps led me here. He could be using aliases."

"I saw the State Department's cable," said Applebee. "Did you ask for the Pakistani government's help?"

"Not at this time," I said. "It's too early. First I need to make sure I know who the players are."

He looked at me, surprised, but said nothing. There was no point in going into details, though luckily it didn't seem to bother him. "My first stop needs to be Peninsula Bank. Any contacts there?"

"Not officially," he said cryptically.

"And unofficially?"

"You could make new friends here easily," he said with a smile. "People like to be friends with rich Americans."

I gave him a quizzical look, but he just smiled and added nothing.

"Like all other Third World countries?" I pressed, trying to catch his drift.

"Only in some aspects," he said. "Just be careful. Anything else I could do for you before we start discussing my business?"

"No, thanks. Maybe I'll need more help as I develop my leads. What do you have in mind?"

"Security instructions," he said. "I don't have to remind you what's going on here, though I will. The place is crawling with Al-Qaeda and Taliban, no matter what the Pakistanis say or do. Out of all America's embassies, probably only Iraq and Afghanistan are more dangerous."

"Do they really try?"

"You mean the Pakistani government? Depends on whom you ask. They're very helpful, but only to an extent. They have tremendous pressures from all sides, particularly from within. We're not too popular here, so I suggest you exercise maximum caution and take prudent measures. That means a strong security posture, being aware of your surroundings, avoiding crowds and demonstrations, keeping a low profile. I'd also suggest changing around the times and routes you tend to travel. And lastly, call me immediately if you feel like you're in danger."

"I've fought wars," I said in a defensive tone.

"This is worse. In war you know who your enemy is and its general location. Here you don't know anything. They'd love to kidnap rather than kill you. You're worth much more if you're still breathing than as a motionless corpse."

My stomach moved.

"Are you planning a trip north?"

"I'll go anywhere I can find Ward."

"Well, if he's in the northwest provinces, then forget it. I suggest you don't go. We urge all American citizens to avoid travel to the tribal areas of Pakistan's Northwest Frontier Province. Anyway, the Pakistani government requires all persons, other than Pakistani and Afghani citizens, to obtain permission from the Home and Tribal Affairs Department before visiting these tribal areas. These regions lie outside the normal jurisdiction of the Pakistani government."

"I haven't got any plans now, but what does that mean?"

"It means you're prey," he said drily. "Even within its borders the Pakistani government can't guarantee your safety, but in these northern regions, you'll be walking into sure trouble. Just forget it."

I nodded, hoping Ward had taken the same advice.

"Next—no public transportation, no befriending of strangers who seek your company. The best thing that could happen to you is to have your money stolen." He paused, letting me figure out what the worst-case scenario would be.

There was a knock on the door, and a slight, darker man with a neatly clipped mustache walked in. "Hi, I'm Don Suarez," he said. "I'm the legat." I recognized the term. Legal attachés stationed in the U.S. embassies are in fact FBI special agents.

"I was just briefing Dan on the security requirements here," said Applebee.

"Pretty exciting, isn't it?" said Suarez wryly, sitting down next to me.

"I've been to worse places," I said.

"Just make sure you're not kidnapped," said Suarez, as if it were up to me.

"Anything happen lately?" I asked.

"All the time. But it gets the attention of the media only when foreigners are the victims. Stories about local fat cats that are herded at gunpoint until their family coughs up the money are a nonevent for the world media."

"Have there been any serious incidents against U.S. personnel lately?"

"Sure, there were several attempts against us," said Suarez calmly. "There was a church bombing that killed five, including an American woman from the embassy and her daughter, and a car bomb at the Karachi consulate that also killed fourteen Pakistanis. In Karachi, police arrested a Yemeni national, Waleed bin Attash, and five other alleged Al-Qaeda members, with three hundred pounds of explosives. The police told us he planned to bomb the consulate. Every morning we check our cars for bombs. In 2001, we found explosive devices attached by magnets to two cars of our diplomats."

"OK," I said.

He continued. "As for transportation, Abdullah has my instructions to drive you anywhere. We've had a ton of unmarked cars, ever since the evacuation of families and nonessential staff."

"Can I trust him?"

"He has been a loyal employee for almost ten years, but be careful even with him. You never know. One final thing," Don said. "We've got plenty of vacant apartments within the compound. We can host you here if you like."

"Thanks, but I may need to distance myself from the embassy, if I can," I said. "But I might change my mind later."

We exited the bubble and returned to Ned's office. Suarez handed me a mobile phone. "Here, use this. It's just another item left behind by departing embassy staff."

"Is the number traceable to the embassy?"

"No. You top it up with a card. It has no registration. I think it still has about three hours of local talk time. We'll call you only on that line, not at your hotel. Same goes with your calls to the embassy: don't use your room's phone to call us."

I was on my way to the men's room when a siren started wailing.

I heard shouts. "Secure all classified materials. Close all windows; all personnel must now evacuate."

I ran down the stairs, but the few others who joined me didn't seem to be in a particular hurry. SUVs were waiting outside the building with their doors open and engines running.

"Get in, get in," ordered a marine in uniform.

"Are we under attack?" I asked the person sitting next to me.

"I don't know," he said.

Then a bell sounded.

I saw Ned Applebee announcing loudly, "OK, the drill is over, you may now return to your positions."

I let out a deep breath and approached Applebee. "We are in the epicenter of terrorism," he told me. "We must be prepared. There are several threats or actual attempts every day. We live in a cage. See for yourself," he said, grimly pointing at the outside wall.

"I can see that," I said, looking around. The compound was surrounded by brick ramparts topped with razor wire, and reinforced by steel pillars to stop any car from breaking in.

"This place was built after the previous embassy building was burned to the ground by an angry mob in 1979," said Ned.

Once Abdullah drove me back to my hotel, I waited for him to leave, checked out, and took a cab. It was in clear violation of my security instructions, but following strict orders was never my forte. But now these instructions made me realize that I had to enhance my own security, not breach it. After driving around the city for two hours, I called my hotel from my mobile phone and made a room reservation for Peter Helmut van

Laufer, from Paramaribo, Dutch Guiana. An hour later I called the hotel again and asked at what time the front desk shift changed, because I needed to catch up with someone from the morning shift.

"At four P.M., sir," said the receptionist.

I continued touring Islamabad from within my cab. The city is in fact a nice town surrounded by hills. What struck me most was the abundance of trees, giving the city a calmer atmosphere. "This is a new city, sir," said my driver. "Only in 1959 this site was chosen to replace Karachi as the capital of Pakistan. Internationally known urban planners were commissioned to design the new city. In 1967 Islamabad was officially made the capital."

"What are the landmarks?"

"There aren't many," he said. "There's the National Assembly Building, and Quaid-i-Azam University."

I asked him to take me downtown. The change was significant. Hundreds of carts, bicycles, and peddlers were all over. Colors and smells were strong, giving the place a vibrant presence, as opposed to the too-planned wide streets of the other zones. I quickly became convinced that Islamabad drivers believe that traffic laws are informational only. The most-used instrument of their cars is the horn. If you learn to drive in New York City and live through it, with the delivery vans and the yellow taxicabs, then you may qualify to drive in Pakistan. I wouldn't be surprised if an Islamabad taxi driver told his passenger, *Take cover, I'm changing lanes.* I repeatedly looked around to see if I attracted any unwanted attention. Other than the children begging at traffic lights, I noticed nothing suspicious.

At four thirty P.M. I returned to my hotel with the cab, and checked in.

"Welcome, Mr. Van Laufer," said the smiling reception-desk employee when I told him my name. "How was your flight?"

"Too long," I said.

"Can I see your passport, please?"

"Sure," I said and gave him my Dutch Guiana passport. Dutch Guiana ceased to exist in 1975, when it gained independence from the Netherlands and became Suriname. For a nonexistent country, the passport I gave him was a work of art. It even had a registration number and an "official" seal, an authentic-looking cover embossed with gold lettering, and my genuine laminated photo. Its pages carried many visa and authentic-looking entry and exit stamps from very valid and existing countries. Unless you were a geography buff, you couldn't tell the passport and the stamps were faked. It looked like a real passport, but it wasn't.

Before going on assignment to Third World countries, or even to Western Europe, when my adversaries are no gentlemen, I assume a different identity. Due to political sensitivities, most of the time I cannot use a real passport issued by another country, unless I received it from that country's government. (If the assignment is for the CIA, it's a different ball game.) When crossing borders on routine Department of Justice cases, I always use a very genuine U.S. passport, almost always my standard dark-blue tourist passport. I have to carry my official U.S. government passport while overseas on official U.S. government business. But its distinctive dark-red cover is nothing to show when standing in a long line of strangers waiting to pass a foreign immigration agent. For other identification purposes, particularly when nongovernmental entities are involved, I resort to second best, passports "issued" by a service carrying names of countries that have changed, or even better, never existed. What's the chance that an average hotel receptionist or banker will know that British Honduras is now Belize, that Rhodesia became Zimbabwe, or that Zanzibar merged with Tanganyika to become Tanzania? With the declining popularity of Americans abroad, better to be a businessman from Dutch Guiana than a U.S. government agent.

During my Mossad days, the standards and practices were different regarding the use of passports. Admittedly, though, times were also different. Things that were acceptable in the early seventies may be no-no's now, and vice versa. I still remembered Alex, my Mossad academy instructor, lecturing on the various uses of passports:

We grade passports according to the security they afford the user—best, second, action, and disposable. The best passports, which are at the top of the list, are genuine passports with real people's names that could survive a police check in the country of origin. The second-quality passport is also a genuine passport. However, there's no real person to match the bio page. The third type is an action passport that could be used while performing a quick job—concluded in a matter of days—in a foreign country, but that's it. We can't use it to cross national borders, definitely not through airports. The least valuable is the disposable passport. This one's usually hot, meaning that it was either lost or stolen and therefore probably appears on most police watch lists. The best part of that passport is its cover, because it can serve its purpose when you need only to flash it. Obviously you can't use it as an ID, unless you opt to be stupid, depriving a village somewhere of an idiot.

Apparently, the hotel employee at the desk wasn't a geography maven, because he didn't even blink at my passport. I had already made up a "legend," a cover for why I don't speak Dutch, or why I was so much lighter than my supposed countrymen, not looking like the citizens of Dutch Guiana—now Suriname—who have much darker skin than mine. If asked, I could simply say that my father was a doctor, an eye specialist in tropical ailments, and I was born in Dutch Guiana when he was sent by the UN to help fight eye disease. Nationality? I don't really have one. At the age of four we moved to Switzerland. I studied in South Africa and Canada. My father was born in Germany to a Swedish father and a Czech mother; my mother was born in Hungary. Her father was Romanian and her mother Greek. My parents escaped their countries just when World War II started. That legend usually does it and has always satisfied people's curiosity.

I also knew that being born in Dutch Guiana didn't by itself confer citizenship. You needed one parent or grandparent with citizenship through whom you could claim it. If pressed, I'd have come up with a Dutch grandparent for the purpose. But I'd never needed to. In my wallet I also carried a Dutch Guiana driver's license and a genuine Visa credit card issued to Peter Helmut van Laufer by one of those offshore banks that don't ask too many questions about your true identity or the source of the money you're caching away, as long as you don't ask them why they charge an annual fee of $750 for the card. I also had another camouflage passport of another nonexistent country carrying my real name, as well as my genuine official U.S. government and tourist passports, just in case a suspicious banker called the local police.

If that happened, I could say, *Oops, sorry, wrong passport. It's my old name, legally changed. Here's my other passport.* I'd choose whether to flash my other camouflage passport, or, if push came to shove, and only as a last resort, my U.S. tourist passport, hoping I'd be allowed one phone call to the U.S. consul. The amount of explanation I'd have to offer the consul would probably exceed the amount of money suggested by a local policeman as contribution to shore up his personal finances and smooth things up. Never would I show my official passport. That could guarantee a free ride to jail in any country that regarded intelligence as the exclusive prerogative of that country's government. Violators go to jail, and the guaranteed result would be the size of the scandal, not whether it had actually erupted.

The hotel's lobby was half empty. I leafed through the local Yellow Pages and called Peninsula Bank, using my mobile phone.

"I'm the business manager of *Wild Nature and Adventure* magazine, based in South Africa," I said. "We plan to establish a small office in Islamabad. I'd like to open an account with your bank."

"Of course, sir. Please come to our branch. We'll be happy to assist you."

* * *

I took a cab and landed at the manager's desk in thirty minutes.

"I'm very pleased to meet you," said the manager, a heavy-set, middle-aged man with jumbo ears and piercing black eyes. He wore a three-piece wool suit with a chained gold watch tucked in the vest's pocket. Hell, I thought, this isn't London circa 1930, it's Islamabad in 2004, and it's hot in here.

He shook my hand. "My name is Rashid Khan." I looked at him thinking that for him, the happy hour is a nap.

I gave him my business card—Peter Helmut van Laufer, with an address in Amsterdam.

"This is our temporary European office, which we are closing next week. There isn't too much wildlife in Europe anymore," I said with a smile. "So, for the time being let me give you my number in Islamabad: 051 991 6687." He wrote it down on my business card. "We intend to open in Pakistan our regional office for Asia. Until I have Pakistani incorporation papers for our local company, perhaps I should open a temporary personal account."

"No need to wait, sir," said Rashid. "I can open an account for the magazine immediately. When you receive the certificate of incorporation, please send me a copy."

An hour later I had a bank account for *Wild Nature and Adventure Magazine*. I deposited $500 in cash.

It was time to chat. "I need a recommendation for a lawyer who can help us with our local Pakistani needs. Do you happen to know any lawyer who handles business and intellectual-property matters, and whom you can recommend?"

His eyes lit up. "Certainly, sir, you should call Ahmed Khan," he said, and pulled a business card out of a drawer. "He's very good," he said, and began praising the attorney's services.

The recommendation was too enthusiastic, I thought.

"Thank you, that's very helpful. By the way, we once employed a photographer in Islamabad, but have lost contact with him. How do you think I can trace him here? I may have a job for him."

"Ask Ahmed Khan. He'll arrange everything for you."

"Thanks," I said. As I got up to leave I added, "If you happen to hear the photographer's name, or, even better, meet him, give him my number."

"What is his name?"

"Albert C. Ward III."

"The name rings a bell," said Rashid. "Maybe he's a customer."

"Think so?" I said innocently. "Well, if so, I'm sure he'd be grateful if you gave me his address or phone number."

A few clicks and gazes into his computer monitor later, he said, "We did have him as a customer, but although the account is still open, there has been no activity for many years. We locked his credit balance in an interest-bearing account."

"Was it a big amount?" I tried my luck.

"I'm sorry, sir, I can't tell you that. But what I can say is that under our bank's rules we move inactive accounts to a long-term interest-bearing savings account only if the balance exceeds $500."

"Oh," I said. "So you believe he's no longer in Islamabad?"

"I've no idea, sir."

"OK. Just in case, can I have his address?"

"It will do you no good. Our mail to that address was returned."

There was no point in pressuring him for the address. It would only have aroused suspicion. Why would I be interested in searching for a person who no longer lived in Islamabad and hadn't for many years, just to offer him a job? Far more bothersome was the fact that Ward had left an amount of money in excess of $500 in his bank account, and never returned to claim it. He was a young man with limited resources. For him it was a substantial amount, so why had he abandoned it? I suggested all sorts of theories, some improbable, and some gruesome. But I let them rest until I could breathe some life into them.

* * *

I returned to my hotel, ignoring peddlers who tried to interest me in everything from souvenirs to dried food. I had dinner at the hotel's Thai restaurant, the Royal Elephant. I made
sure to ask the waiter for mild food. Although I like spicy food,
the Thai and Indian version of spicy is way out of my league.
If you ask for spicy, they give you their version of spicy food,
which burns you on the inside for days. I once ventured to ask
for spicy food in India. Three days later, the doctor finally let
me crawl out of bed.

I called Ahmed Khan. It was past seven P.M., but I hoped he
was still working. His phone answered after two rings. When
he heard my name, he became very interested, or rather eager.
"Yes, Rashid told me about you. I'll be glad to be of service."

I invited him to have a drink with me at the hotel.

"No alcohol, sir, I'm sorry. I'd be delighted to have tea,
though."

An hour later, a fat man dressed in a beige suit that was
about six months late for dry cleaning walked to my table at
the lobby lounge. "Hello, sir, I'm Ahmed Khan." He looked
to be about forty-five and was even heavier up close.

"I'm pleased to meet you," I said. For about an hour I told
him about the magazine, asking questions I thought would be
expected of a business manager coming to a new country to set
up operations. His answers were somewhat vague, and were
mostly characterized by the sentence, "Don't worry, I can
arrange it, I've got contacts." One would wonder why "contacts" were necessary for simple things such as incorporating a
company, renting an office, or leasing a car. The impression I received of Ahmed was that he was more a "fixer" than a lawyer.
I had no evidence, but I had the distinct feeling I could steal
horses with him, if the price were right. I realized of course that
such a quality could go in the opposite direction as well. I had
to make sure to play this right.

He then brought up the matter of Albert Ward. "I understand you're looking for him?" he asked.

"Yes, he was a very good photographer, and I've got an interesting assignment for him—that is, if I find him."

"I've got contacts," he said. "Would you be willing to pay for the information?"

"Well," I said, "what do you have in mind?"

"It may cost up to $1,000," he said, surveying my face for a reaction.

"That's too much," I said. "We don't need him that badly."

He wasn't about to let go, and I knew it. The bean counters in Washington would be all over me if I spent that much money on a tip that might be dry and covered with sixty generations of spider webs.

"What were you thinking, then?" he said.

"No more than $250," I said.

"Maybe $400?"

"No. $250. If the information is accurate and I find him, I'm willing to pay $100 more as a bonus."

The following morning I woke up by the ring of my mobile phone. "Good morning, Mr. Van Laufer. This is Ahmed Khan."

"Good morning," I said, rubbing my eyes and looking at my watch. It was almost nine. I had overslept.

"I've got information about Albert Ward. Can I meet you in my office?"

"Could you come to my hotel? I need to be here to meet some people." In fact I had no such plans, but I didn't trust Ahmed, and the idea of going into town just to meet him didn't seem right.

"Sure," he said. "I can meet you at twelve thirty."

"Good," I said. "Meet me at the Dynasty Restaurant at the hotel."

CHAPTER TEN

Ahmed Khan met me at twelve fifteen as I was crossing the lobby to buy a newspaper. We sat at a table in the corner. I looked at him, waiting for the news.

"Albert Ward left money in his bank account at the Peninsula Bank," he said. I was motionless.

"How much?"

"Around $2,000."

"So?"

"He never came back for it."

"I see," I said. Ahmed Khan was selling me recycled information he had probably received from Rashid.

"The last transaction he did at the bank was to buy Iranian rials; he used $200 to purchase them."

"So he went to Iran? Then I guess I'll have to give up on him." I was acting indifferent, but in fact this information made my heart go ballistic.

Ahmed wasn't deterred. "I think I know where he went."

That certainly aroused even more interest, but I wasn't about to show it, or the price would go up immediately.

"Where?"

"To Tehran."

"How do you know?"

"I've got sources."

I wasn't about to cross-examine him over that. He'd have to give me something better for my $250, and he knew that.

"Do you have an address in Tehran?"

"Yes."

"Current?"

He hesitated. "I don't know, it could be. Please remember, Mr. Van Laufer, that he went to Tehran twenty years ago. He may have moved since."

"So what good is it for me to have a twenty-year-old address? I need him now."

"I can make some phone calls," he said.

"OK, please go ahead. I'll be around."

Ahmed called me in the afternoon. "I have developments," he said. "But I'll have to pay my source $300, and that will leave nothing for me."

"What's the information?"

"I'll know more if you agree to pay the $300, and the $250 for me."

"OK," I said in feigned surrender. "Fine. Ward is really a great photographer."

"I'll come tonight for the money," he said.

"Well, you'll have to bring the information as well. It's not my personal money, it's the magazine's, and I must account for it."

At six thirty Ahmed appeared, unannounced. He was excited. "I think something strange has happened," he said.

"What?"

"Albert Ward arrived in Tehran on an invitation of Professor Manfred Krieger, who headed a German archaeological team for its excavation work in Tal-e Malyan. There were rumors of buried golden treasures of the Parthians and the Sasanians." He went on and on. A class in history is usually interesting, but not at that moment. However, it was no time to demonstrate my impatience.

"How long did he work for them?"

"They signed him up for three months and paid his first month's salary of $500 in advance."

"Why would they do that?"

"I don't know," he said candidly, and it was the first time I believed a sentence he said. "This was shortly after the Islamic

Revolution, and as an American he was probably afraid to go there, or at least to go and not be paid. So maybe this is how they made him come."

Again, it seemed to me that Ahmed's information had come from the same source: Peninsula Bank, and Rashid, its manager. I smelled a rat.

He brought his head closer to me, as if telling me a secret. "I think he was lured to Tehran for an entirely different reason."

"Oh?"

"The money he received from the German archaeologists didn't come from Germany."

"So? Why is it important?" I said casually. "They could have paid him from their account in Tehran."

"They could have. But the money came from Lugano, Switzerland."

"This is too much detective work," I said waving my hand in dismissal. "I'm just trying to help my magazine. Maybe I should let this thing go."

"As you wish," he said, clearly disappointed. "But if I were you, I'd look deeper into it. There might be a story behind it, although not for a magazine about wildlife, but for a news magazine. You could investigate it and end up with an interesting story."

"What do you mean?"

"I mean that after Ward left Islamabad, there were three attempts by the transferring bank in Switzerland to reverse the money transfer and get the money back, claiming that the transfer was made by mistake."

"Did the bank in Islamabad ever return the money?"

"No. Since it was already in Ward's account, there was no way of doing it without Ward's consent or a court order. And neither was obtained."

"I see," I said, trying to figure out how these bits of information fit into any of my theories. When I didn't respond, Ahmed tried to ignite further interest in me. "Do you know who the bank that made the transfer was?"

"No. How would I know?"

"Al Taqwa Management, a Lugano-based financial institution."

"Who are they?" I asked, although the name rang a bell.

"All I know is that they have ties to terrorist organizations."

"Oh," I said. "I should stay away from this matter then."

Ahmed gave me a long look. "OK, then can I have my money?"

I gave him $300. "Please sign a receipt,"

He quickly wrote down a receipt on a blank piece of paper. "I'm giving you only $300 because you didn't give me a current address, but still it's more than the $250 I promised you."

Obviously he didn't like that, but I threw in an incentive. "If you find him, I'll still be thankful. Anyway, we should talk about the main reason I came here, the incorporation of a company to publish our magazine. I'll call you this week."

Time to go back to the embassy. This matter was getting into areas outside my original assignment. I called Ned Applebee.

"Abdullah will come to your hotel to bring you over in thirty minutes," promised Ned.

Abdullah was as good as Ned's word. I was in Applebee's office in less than an hour.

"Any success?" he asked, though somehow he didn't sound too interested.

"The person I'm looking for left Pakistan twenty years ago with more than $500—probably around $2,000—deposited in his bank account, and never returned. Before leaving he bought $200 in Iranian currency. A source told me he was allegedly invited to Iran by a German archaeological team, which paid him $500 in advance for one month of photography work, and he vanished. Several years later, a bank attempted to reverse the transfer, saying that it had discovered during an audit that a predecessor bank made the transfer as a result of fraud and wanted the money back. The Pakistani bank refused."

"Interesting," he said, looking out his window. He couldn't have been less interested.

"I'm told that the institution that wanted the money back is located in Lugano, Switzerland."

"The fact that it's in Switzerland doesn't by itself guarantee integrity. Crooks are everywhere."

"I agree, but these guys are big-time."

"Who?"

"Al Taqwa."

Applebee sat up in his chair. At last I had his attention.

"Nada Management? Are you sure?"

"No, I said Al Taqwa."

"I know that. But they've been known as Nada Management since 2001."

"I'm sure I heard my man say Al Taqwa Management, but remember, it came from a single source, uncorroborated, and I didn't see any documents. Why? Do you know them?"

"They're backing terror organizations. If you missed reading the intelligence reports about their role, you may have read about them in newspapers."

Now I remembered where I'd heard the name.

"I need to get the Agency involved," he said, meaning the CIA. "The information you get here can be important."

I had been there before. When my findings had touched on matters of national security and I'd brought it to the attention of the CIA, they'd taken control over my case immediately, making my own job assignment secondary. I didn't mind, except it was time-consuming, and interfered with my own case. However, my job performance at the Department of Justice is measured by results; any distraction means fewer or delayed favorable results. Due to the ultrasecret nature of my time-consuming involvement with the CIA, it isn't reflected in my personnel file, which is brought up for periodic evaluation at the Department of Justice, so I risked looking like I was underperforming. But I had no choice. The result is that I appear to be performing less effectively than others in my department. Obviously, David Stone knew about my occasional side activities, and authorized them. A cautious man, David knew we both played for the same team, and therefore he was covering for me. But he was about to retire, so what was next? I'd have to explain to the new director. His name had already been announced—Robert Holliday, who had served as David's deputy for the past six months.

Half an hour later, a man in his early fifties came into Ned's office. He was of medium build, balding, with a goatee and piercing, ice blue eyes. "Hi, I'm Phil Boyd. Tell me what you have."

I repeated my story and Boyd took notes. "Are you planning to do anything with that information?" he asked.

"Well, I need to find Ward and the $300 million and change it looks like he stole. Seems like he had a string of aliases and stole from government-insured banks and private investors. Am I stepping on something?"

"Maybe. Nada Management, or Al Taqwa, is on the watch list of every intelligence service in the West."

"Why?"

"Terror financing. These guys were catering mostly to Muslim clients, and were known for their *hawala* exchange system. Small amounts, from $500 to $1,000, are transferred to other *hawala* in different locations."

"I know the custom," I said. "You meet one of their representatives in Europe, give him $500, and another person in the Middle East will deliver the money to the designated recipient. It's just like Western Union."

"Yes," he agreed. "But with one huge exception. Western Union isn't involved in money laundering for terror."

I knew what he meant. A few hundred dollars, multiplied by thousands, added up to significant amounts, without any written evidence. The Western world was unaware of the hidden potential in the *hawala* system. Rooted in deep religious convictions, the system provides services based on personal relationships and trust. Usually there's no collateral, and Western-style accounting is a luxury often done without. Not all the money transferred finances terror. Far from it.

The original intention of the founders of the custom was to collect money for legitimate Islamic religious and charitable purposes.

"And Nada?"

"How would you label an organization that takes money from Muslims in Europe, gives no receipt, creates no paper trail of its transactions—which are based on trust and the use of telephone messages—and sends money into the hands of terror organizations? Some of it might go into the hands of innocent people, but we have ample reason to believe that these transactions funnel millions of dollars to terrorist organizations to finance terror."

"I need to talk to my director at the Justice Department," I said. "Can I use a secure phone?"

Ned pointed to the room next door. "There, you can use that phone. Just dial the number as if you were in the U.S."

David picked up the phone. "Hi, Dan. How is Pakistan treating you?"

"Everything's fine. I'm at the embassy calling you on a secure phone." I reported my findings and asked permission to go to Lugano, to see what I could find about Nada Management's connection to my case.

"The operation was shut down a year or two ago," said David. Apparently he was more informed than I was. "What can you find there?"

"David, I went to Pakistan on a twenty-year-old lead and developed promising information, so maybe working on an organization that was recently closed won't be that difficult. Anyway, I want to stop by in Israel for a few days. Switzerland is just in the neighborhood."

"If you call countries two thousand miles apart 'in the neighborhood,'" said David amusedly. "Let me run it by some people first. Call me later."

Abdullah drove me back to my hotel. As I was looking aimlessly through the car windows, a motorcycle passed us on my right and the rider glanced through my window. I couldn't see his face through his helmet. A minute later, another motorcycle passed us on our left, and the rider also looked directly into our car.

"Turn the car back," I ordered Abdullah.

"What happened?"

"I forgot some papers at the embassy," I said, raising my voice just a tad. "Just turn back."

Abdullah turned the car around and headed back to the embassy compound. I saw the two motorcycles again. This was no coincidence; they didn't even make an effort to hide. It looked as though they were even trying to be visible.

I couldn't take any chances. I remembered well the story of Daniel Pearl, a *Wall Street Journal* reporter, who was murdered execution style after he was abducted in Karachi.

As we approached the main-compound wall, where I could already see the employee parking area at the corner of University Avenue, a truck blocked our way. I saw the driver just sitting there, with no attempt to turn or park.

"It's a trap," I yelled at Abdullah. "Turn around and go to the main gate!"

There was no need for my advice: Abdullah was already doing just that. With screeching tires, he backed up our car. I saw the two motorcycles again at our side, one cyclist holding a gun. I bent down on my seat to avoid an expected barrage of bullets. But none came. One motorcyclist tried to block our car from backing away, while the other, holding the gun, motioned to Abdullah to stop the car. "They're trying to kidnap us," I shouted. "Don't stop."

Abdullah stepped on the accelerator with might. The car jumped back, hitting the motorcycle riding behind us and throwing the rider up in the air. Abdullah managed to turn the car, and within ten seconds we were at the compound gate. The Delta barrier was lowered suddenly and we entered. I wiped drops of sweat off my forehead. "That was close," I said. "Thanks for the good work."

Abdullah nodded. "That's my job."

Applebee came running toward us. "What happened?"

"I think there was an attempt to kidnap us. How did you know we were returning?"

"There's a panic button in the car with a direction finder," said Applebee. "Abdullah must have pressed it. We saw that your car was actually around the corner."

We went inside to his office. I gave Applebee a full account of the events. He called someone in the building and sent him to check the scene.

"What do I do next?"

"Do you want to stay in Islamabad?"

"No. I'm done here, but I need to wait for instructions from Washington."

"Anyway, you'll have to stick around for a day or two until we complete the investigation and work with the local police on that." I went to the vending machine to get a soda and calm down. I sat on the couch in Applebee's office, trying to collect my thoughts.

The phone rang. Applebee listened, said, "OK, thanks," and hung up.

"Our Diplomatic Security Service agents on the scene reported that the motorcyclist disappeared together with his motorcycle. They just found pieces from a broken red tail light, and skid marks on the road. Nothing else. Did Abdullah hit him?"

"I'm sure of that," I said. "I saw him flying up in the air. Maybe he wasn't hurt badly, or he was picked up by a backup team."

"We're in touch with the Reporting Centre of the Pakistan Police Service. They'll investigate."

"Who are they?"

"Their criminal and political intelligence service. Who were you in contact with in Islamabad?"

"Just two men: a bank manager, Rashid Khan, and an attorney he recommended, Ahmed Khan."

"Same last name?"

"Yes. I suspect they're related, maybe even brothers. The lawyer was recommended by the banker, and he sold me information that most likely came from the bank."

"We'll get you a place to stay here," said Applebee. "I don't think it'd be wise for you to return to your hotel."

"I guess not," I said. "Could you send someone to my hotel to pick up my stuff and bring it over?"

I regretted it immediately. If anyone came to the hotel to pick up Dan Gordon's belongings, the hotel would tell him that I checked out few days ago. I couldn't tell Applebee that I'd checked in again under a different name. He'd have my neck for violating his security instructions. But it was too late. I needed to mitigate the potential damage.

"Who are you sending?"

"Probably Abdullah," he said.

"OK, I'll give him my room key." I went outside and approached Abdullah, who was sitting in his car, next to the entrance.

"I've been told to move into the compound," I said, handing him my room key. "Please go directly to my hotel room without stopping at the desk, and collect my things. I'll call the hotel to tell them my assistant is coming over with the room key to remove my belongings, and I'll settle the hotel bill over the phone."

Abdullah left, and as I turned to go upstairs, Applebee met me outside. "Let me show you to your new residence. We've got plenty of empty houses here. Since 2001, we've been singles only. Our staff goes home for family visits. There's the American Club in the compound, where you can meet other staff members, watch American TV, and have a beer."

"Thanks," I said, and followed him to a building nearby. He opened the door on the ground floor. "Here, you should find everything you need. Call me if you have any questions."

I sat on the sofa bed, glared at the walls and the small wall unit with family photos of smiling children, and thought of mine. I tried calling them using my mobile phone, and on the third attempt I reached Tom, my son, and Karen, my daughter, who was just about to go out the door. I didn't tell them about my narrow escape just an hour earlier, and we focused on family matters. Tom was just returning to his college, and Karen was about to graduate, but both of them had that vision of the world being at their feet that only the young can claim. Neither held back their enthusiasm, telling me of their plans and what was new in their lives. It always made me feel proud to see that they were growing into strong adults. Of course, we couldn't speak as freely as we would have liked to. Trained by experience as they are, they didn't even ask me where I was or when I would be returning.

"I'm going to be back home soon," I said. It was more wishful thinking than based on reality.

I decided to go to the club to socialize and get my mind off of things for a minute. There were four other men drinking beer and watching an American TV network. After an hour I was tired of watching stupid sitcoms with dubbed laughter even when they weren't remotely funny. I've often thought that when a sitcom producer's IQ reaches 50, he should sell. There was plenty about America I didn't miss. I returned to my new makeshift home.

Leaning my head on the soft, green pillow of the couch, I pondered my next move. Ward had left the United States in 1980 or 1981, gone to Hong Kong and South Africa, and finally left a trace in Pakistan. From Pakistan, he may have continued to Iran. Was it possible that just about the same time he returned to the U.S. without leaving a record with the Immigration and Naturalization Service, he'd made himself look years older, perpetrated bank fraud, and vanished again? That simply didn't make sense. The hunch that his identity had been stolen needed no further support, but it was still just an assumption, and I needed proof. Before falling asleep, I decided to discuss this matter with Don Suarez, the legat at the embassy.

The next morning, after recharging myself with fruit juice and a muffin for breakfast at the club, I called him. "Sure, come over," he replied.

As I sat down next to his desk, Suarez said, "I heard you had an experience yesterday."

"Yes," I said. "Any clues?"

"Not yet. The main direction in that kind of investigation is intelligence, not police work. The police couldn't find any witnesses to the attack, although Abdullah said the street was bustling."

"So are you working on intelligence?"

"Yes, together with the Agency, but that takes time."

The post–September eleventh era had finally seen a little more cooperation between the FBI and the CIA, with a little less time dedicated to turf wars.

"What do you think? Was it because I was snooping around Ward? Was I picked at random because they saw the embassy connection with the car and Abdullah?"

"Anything is possible," he said, shrugging, just when I needed a more concrete answer.

I told him about my suspicions about Ward, my unanswered questions about how he could be in two places at the same time.

"Maybe he wasn't," said Suarez. "In the sixties through the eighties, there were instances where young American men just disappeared. I guess some of them simply wanted to. I wouldn't be surprised if some of them are monks in a Buddhist monastery in Tibet, fishermen in New Zealand, or just basking on the beach in Goa."

"And you leave it at that?"

"Sure, if they're adults, and if there are no complaints from families about missing persons, and there's no evidence of foul play. Hey, there's a limit to the amount of babysitting the federal government can do with taxpayers' money."

"Do you have names of these people?"

"No, because if we had a name, that'd mean somebody was looking for him. We don't have a world chart with pins indicating where any American citizen is at any given moment. We aren't there yet."

I wouldn't get any answers from him, I thought. I lost interest in the conversation.

A cable from David Stone came in. "You are authorized a one-week vacation. No work is to be performed in any country other those included on the authorized list provided before your departure. David."

That was David's nice way of saying, "You can go wherever you want, but don't mess up things or you're on your own."

An armored embassy car drove me to the airport. I had changed my mind about Switzerland. I had started to think that the Al Taqwa link Khan was selling me was dubious. If necessary, I'd pursue it with the bank's receivers from New York. Instead, I took a British Airways flight to London. From London, I boarded an El Al flight to Ben Gurion Airport, Israel. When I arrived, it was already dark. I rented a car, listened to Israeli oldies, and drove to my hotel on the beach in Tel Aviv.

CHAPTER ELEVEN

The next morning I called Benny Friedman, my Mossad buddy. Friendship forged in military organizations lasts forever. Although we served together for only three years, we created a strong bond. Our friendship withstood the cultural gap between us. Benny came from an Orthodox family and adhered to all the tenets of the Jewish faith, while I considered myself nonreligious, only keeping the traditional rituals during holidays. Benny also had a wry sense of humor, but only those who knew him well could really "get it." I was one of the few who did, and I felt that if anybody could penetrate what was going on in his agile mind, I could. Well, maybe.

I'd left the Mossad when I was exposed to the enemy during an operation which effectively "burned" me from participating in any future field operations. But Benny had stayed on. He'd climbed through the ranks and made it to the top of

Tevel, the foreign-relations wing of the Mossad, which is charged with liaisons with foreign intelligence services, including with countries considered hostile to Israel.

When we'd first learned about this wing's functions during our training at the Mossad Academy, some eyebrows were raised. "What? Trade secrets with your rivals?" one asked. Alex, our training instructor, was very calm about it. "We are in the game of interests, and you don't let feelings and animosities get in your way," he had said. "If you need to exchange information with someone, you just do it. Politics may collide, but we do our work. Same goes for any intelligence service worldwide. We collect intelligence concerning our enemies' intentions and capabilities, and we'd get it from Satan if he were offering it at the right price."

Benny's secretary transferred the call.

"Dan, is that you? Where are you?"

"In Tel Aviv for a few days."

"Business?" Benny knew what I was doing, and in the past we had helped each other in matters of our work. I never felt I was abusing our friendship, and I don't think he felt any differently.

"Actually, I'm on a family visit. But you know me, I never stop working. Lunch?"

"Sure." Benny never said no to a good meal, and neither did I. The only difference was that he ate *only* kosher food, while I ate *also* kosher.

Two hours later we met on the fishermen's pier in Jaffa's old port. The city of Jaffa, now part of Tel Aviv, is one of the oldest port cities of the world, with a history dating back five thousand years. The pier is younger, only about a thousand years old, and is mainly used by fishing boats that bring their fresh catch to the restaurants lined along its outer walls. This was a place where restaurant decorators didn't need to fake authenticity—it was the authentic place. Weatherworn fishermen's boats bobbed nearby. Busy people were unloading crates of fish, and there was a strong mix of smells: sea air, fish, and burning wood coal from the open air grills barbecuing fish.

We sat at the table closest to the water. Benny hadn't changed much during the past year or so since I'd last seen him. But his mustache had grayed, he had gained a little weight, and he had lost much of his hair. He was starting to look older than his years. I knew why. He took his job more seriously than anybody I'd ever known. To him it wasn't just a job, it was almost some sort of sacred obligation.

"World travel is treating you well," I said, looking at his belly.

"Age has its indignities," he said wryly. "In 1975 I was interested in acid rock, and now I've got acid reflux. Besides," he added, "look who's talking. You don't exactly look like the slim serviceman you once were."

He had a point, of course, and I was quick to change the subject. After schmoozing for a while and catching up on our respective families, I moved on to business. I told Benny about my debacle in Sydney, without giving him any telltale details or mentioning Ward's name.

Somehow Benny wasn't surprised to hear my story, although he said nothing. I decided to whet his appetite.

"Ever heard of Nada Management?"

Benny left his fork stuck in the huge red snapper he was dissecting.

"Sure, why? Are you trying to dig dead corpses out of their graves?"

"What do you mean?"

"They went out of business and their principal figure committed suicide."

"How come I missed that information?"

"I'm surprised. It was all over the place."

"Do you have anything concrete on them?"

"I'm sure we do. I can send you some reading material later. Where are you staying?"

"The usual."

"Good."

★ ★ ★

At six P.M. there was a knock on my hotel-room door and a bellman brought me a yellow envelope. I opened it, and sat at the desk to read the printed document.

On the top it read "The Central Institute for Intelligence and Special Operations," the official name of the Mossad, Israel's foreign-intelligence service. Below that were today's date and a handwritten note.

Dan, I'm attaching the documents you have requested. Most of the information has already been made public. Some of it could be outdated or inaccurate, so treat it wisely and don't regard it as evidence, but as uncorroborated intelligence to develop further leads. I'm here for the rest of the week if you need me. Regards, Benny.

To the note was attached a thick, bound, printed document which seemed like a photocopied section of even a bigger document.

Nada Management aka Nada Management Organization SA, Switzerland, fka Al Taqwa Management Organization SA.

A financial institution in Lugano, located at Viale Stefano Franscini 22, Lugano CH-6900 TI, Switzerland, not far from the Italian border. The company was previously named Al Taqwa Management (*fear of God* in Arabic). Al Taqwa is believed to have played a major part in laundering money for Osama bin Laden. Swiss and Liechtenstein police raided Al Taqwa's offices in Switzerland and Liechtenstein, respectively, and Swiss police raided as well the home of its principal, Huber, in Rossimattstrasse 33, 3074 Muri, Bern (see more below), and the homes of Youssef Nada and Ali Ghaleb Himmat, two other Al Taqwa directors. Al Taqwa's accounts in Swiss banks were frozen. Separately, Italian police closed an Islamic cultural center in Milan used as Al-Qaeda's European logistical

center. The center was financed by Ahmed Idris Nasreddin, a Kuwaiti businessman who was also an Al Taqwa director. Three months later, Al Taqwa was shut down
permanently. The U.S. government's Office of the Coor-
dinator of Counterterrorism distributed a list of sixty-two
organizations and individuals suspected of involvement in
terrorist activities. Nada Management was included on
the list.

Al Taqwa was the financial arm of the Muslim Broth-
erhood. That organization was founded in Egypt in the
late 1920s and has fought for the formation of a pure
pan-Islamic theocratic state.

Obviously the document was sanitized, and anything meaningful had been redacted. What was left was history, not intelligence, I concluded, and just leafed through the rest of the
pages. Since Nada Management and Huber were all dead, it
was all very interesting, but what would I do with it? I pushed
the bulky document aside and called Benny.

"Thanks for the stuff, but the organization seems to be as
dead as its directors."

"Frankly, I don't know where it takes you," said Benny, reading my mind. "That's the only unclassified material we've got
on these guys. There's one thing you should know though, unless your friends at CIA have already told you."

"What?"

"We heard rumors that, immediately after the Islamic Revolution, the Iranians and their subsidiary terrorist organizations were looking for genuine travel documents issued by
the U.S. and other major Western countries."

"Why? Didn't they have their own version of Tibor who
could manufacture genuine-looking passports?" Benny and I
knew well the Mossad's Hungarian-born document artist.

"I'm sure they do. But why forge and risk detection, when
you can use the real thing? National passports are becoming
more and more difficult to forge, because they don't know

what hidden markers are included in the passport. Besides, maybe in this case whoever took the passport needed not only the passport, but the identity."

Benny had unwittingly just supported my earlier suspicion. And the real Ward—where was he? I had an idea, but wasn't in the mood to dwell on it just then. I wondered why he had brought up the passport issue when, on its face, it had no connection to Ward's case. Was he subtly trying to send me a message?

"Dan, let's meet tomorrow. I've got some ideas," said Benny, suddenly breaking my train of thought.

"Sure. Want to come to my hotel at one o'clock?"

The next day, Benny arrived unusually late. "You'll have to excuse me, I had a small emergency," he said as we sat at the restaurant downstairs.

"As always," I teased him.

Benny glared at me and got to the point. "I have more information on Nada Management. Although they were shut down, the money-laundering activity continues. Terror organizations need money, and if you dry up one swamp to keep the mosquitoes away, another one will pop up in no time.

"On April 19, 2002, the U.S. government blocked all assets of Youssef Nada and Bank Al Taqwa, both of which were designated as terrorist financiers by the Department of Treasury on November 7, 2001."

Benny pulled out a document from his briefcase and leafed through the pages. "Here it is."

On the same date, the U.S. Treasury also named four additional individuals as terrorist financiers connected to Al Taqwa: Zeinab Mansour-Fattouh, Mohamed Mansour, Albert Friedrich Armand Huber, and Ali Ghaleb Himmat. The Al Taqwa group has long acted as financial advisor to Al-Qaeda, with offices in the Caribbean, Italy, Liechtenstein, and Switzerland. Ahmed Idris Nasreddin and

Youssef Nada are both founders and directors of Bank Al
Taqwa. Osama bin Laden and his Al-Qaeda organization
received financial assistance from Youssef Nada. Al Taqwa
provides investment advice and cash-transfer mechanisms
for Al-Qaeda and other radical Islamic groups.

"Fine," I said. "So they're probably having a good time
somewhere in the Middle East, or they've dug in a hole in Afghanistan enjoying the company of seventy virgins, without
even having to blow themselves up."

Benny smiled. "Maybe. But they left a job half done."

"Meaning?" I was wondering why Benny, an Israeli Mossad
executive, was reading out U.S. government material to me.
"How does it help my case?" I asked pointedly.

"There's a need for their services. Now, when they go under,
who'll take care of the financially orphaned terrorist organizations? Where will they go?" he said in a mockingly sorrowful
voice. Then his tone changed. "Listen, unless we're ready for
them, we'll lose the war on terrorism, and our only option is
going to be choosing the magnitude of our humiliation."

Benny was telling me something, which I read loud and
clear. The Mossad seemed to be trying to fill the gap and provide financial services to the "needy" terrorist organizations.
But why was he telling me that? Friendship aside, in these matters you didn't share that kind of information with anyone, even
with a close friend. Benny had thrown a line with some juicy
bait. But was there also a sharp-edged hook?

Being direct seemed to be the best course. "Benny, why are
you telling me this?"

He smiled wryly. "Because I like you." He was as smooth
as they come when it came to playing it close to the vest.

"Right. But you want something. Now tell me what it is."

"I could use help," he said casually. He had anticipated my
reaction.

"What kind of help?"

"Your favorite kind. The exciting kind."

I sighed impatiently. "OK, I get it. Just tell me."

His story was intriguing. For the past few years, just after the 9/11 attacks, the four "financiers" had run a small but lucrative business in Europe, and over the last four years they'd slowly taken control of a family-owned bank. This bank had been in the business of providing financial services to rich Arabs for a long time. Until the midseventies, their clients had mostly been oil millionaires from the Persian Gulf States or corrupt politicians with dirty money. Last year, the bank actually made a profit of more than $70 million.

"I take it the Mossad finally put you on commission?"

Benny chuckled. "I wish. You know the drill—when you overspend five hundred dollars, accounting is all over you, but when you make seventy million a year, they don't even say thanks."

"Small business?"

"Well, you know, in proportion to other banks in Europe," he said with a grin.

"What bank is it?" I asked.

"Tempelhof Bank."

"Benny, are your guys following me?" Was it just a coincidence? I was annoyed.

"Not at all. You'll soon see that we have a common interest."

"OK, what's my interest?" I was getting tired of his slow game.

"You're looking for Albert Ward."

"How do you know that? Benny, let's cut to the chase. Have you been monitoring me?"

"No. I just know."

"How?"

"People talk."

"I didn't."

"You aren't people. Since when do you expect me to divulge my sources?" He smiled, enjoying the cat-and-mouse exchange.

"Benny! What the hell is going on here? You tell me about a serious and confidential operation the Mossad is running, but you don't tell me about a potential leak in my operation?"

"Pakistan is a sieve," he said, shrugging. "Rarely is information sold once. Three or four times is more likely."

"Well, U.S. government employees in Pakistan definitely told you nothing. That leaves one bank manager and one lawyer."

"Always knew you were a quick thinker," said Benny, his grin returning.

"Yeah, but how did that information reach you? Do they work for you too?"

"Dan, come on. Don't expect me to answer that. You know full well that in intelligence there aren't any loyalties. Just interests." Benny was toying with me again.

"Does that go for you and me too?"

He had talked himself into a corner. "You know that we go beyond that."

"Benny, don't play with me. I have to know whether the sleazeballs I was talking to in Islamabad knew who I really am. If they double-crossed me and sold you the information, then they could sell it again to people who aren't as nice as you are."

"They didn't double-cross you with me." This time there was no grin.

"So, you got it from a third party? They told someone else, who told you."

Benny lifted a hand in protest. "Please. This is beginning to sound like middle school gossip—who told whom what and when. I'll just tell you. We intercepted communications between Ahmed Khan and his handler in Tehran."

My heart raced. "Tehran? He's working for the Iranians?"

"Apparently. He didn't buy your story about the magazine. He was certain you were working for the CIA. He checked in with Iran about you."

"And the immediate result was an attempt to kidnap me in Islamabad. Did you intercept the Iranian response to Ahmed's query?"

"Well, you know what they had to say about it, don't you? They tried to kidnap you."

"That tells me a lot," I said. "That Ward's disappearance is probably connected to the Iranian intelligence services."

Benny nodded. "Nothing is coincidental with these people."

"So what are your plans?"

He paused. "Our bank could use additional business from Iran."

"And how do you encourage that?"

"Convince them that we are efficient, ask no unnecessary questions, and talk to no governments."

"There are plenty of banks with those qualifications in Europe."

"I know. But we have special persuasion techniques."

"Let me guess—from the department of dirty tricks?"

Benny smiled. "Dirty? That only refers to the people we target. I'm talking about intelligence-gathering techniques." He had the faintest sparkle in his eyes. He knew how serious all of this was and what the implications of it were for me, but that was part of what made him who he was. I'm sure he'd never let his own amusement put my safety or my goals in jeopardy, but this kind of banter had become an ingrained aspect of our relationship.

In fact, I knew all about Benny and his techniques. I could still remember that time when we were in the Academy and he'd pretended to be a police officer and convinced a bank teller to let him take his seat behind the counter because a con man—me!—was about to pass a bad check. That was years ago, of course, but my old friend hadn't changed one iota.

"OK," I said. "Let's get back to the point at hand."

"Fine by me," said Benny. "OK. In a sense, we're both looking for Ward."

Now that was a surprise. "Ward? What does he have to do with Israel that would make him interesting to the Mossad?"

"You already had one disappointment, when you jumped on that guy in Australia, right?"

"I get it. I fucked up again on something else," I said, a little testily.

Benny smiled. "Are you ready for this?" he asked. "We're after him too. So we know that the guy in the Sydney hospital bed isn't Albert Ward. And he's definitely not Herbert Goldman. We do, however, think he's an Iranian agent."

It was the bull's-eye of a target I'd been aiming at since I got the case, but hadn't yet had the proof to present conclusively. It was stunning to hear Benny sound so sure about my hunch.

"Why are you interested in him? Just because he's an Iranian agent? There are thousands of them."

"Because he's one of Iran's treasure hunters. A person who brought millions of dollars to their slush-fund coffers."

"Why is it your business?"

"When he steals money from American banks, it's your problem, but when that money starts financing Palestinian and other terrorist organizations, he becomes my problem too."

"If you're so sure it's him and can support it with facts to convince the Australians, then let's get him! He could still be in the hospital in Sydney."

"I wish. Immediately after you left, the Australian police received notification through Interpol about the FBI fingerprint comparison, and their conclusion was that your guy wasn't Albert C. Ward III."

"I think they were holding him on some local fraud charges," I said.

"Yes, land-sale fraud. Of the three complainants who said Ward sold them somebody else's land, not one is available to press charges. Two of them vanished, and the third one quickly withdrew his complaint. The Australian authorities had no choice but to dismiss the arrest warrant. So he walked into the sunset."

"Just like that?" I asked in disbelief.

"No basis to hold him," Benny said. He was right. The third witness had probably assessed his diminishing survival options after hearing that the two others had gone missing.

I was fuming. "I can't believe this bullshit," I grumbled. Even if he wasn't Ward, even if there hadn't been local fraud charges, they could have held him on immigration charges. He entered Australia with a false passport. What kind of idiots were running the force there?

"They dropped the ball," said Benny. He had had his time for rage and was merely calm. "By the time the Australian police rushed to get a new warrant, the guy was released."

I paused to rearrange my thoughts. It was too much of a revelation to digest immediately.

"Chameleon—that's what I've been calling this guy in my head. And I was right." I scanned through my trip to Pakistan, trying to reread things with the knowledge I had just acquired. "So Khan's agenda . . . He gave me those half-truths to get more money?"

Benny shook his head. "He did have an agenda, but not the one you think." Benny—good friend, or not—had a way of being cryptic that sometimes got on my nerves. It was as if he were Socrates, and I, one of his pupils. I wished he would get to the point more quickly, but I knew damn well that wasn't going to happen.

"What was it, then? It seemed pretty clear that his story about Al Taqwa trying to reverse the charge and get their money back from Ward's account was bogus," I said.

"What made you think that? You're right, by the way," asked Benny.

"This is home turf for me. It's just not the way banks work. They don't put in a lot of effort to get a measly $2,000 back three years later. Khan made it up because he thought I was losing interest."

"Or," said Benny, "he was trying to lure you to Iran, probably under instructions from Tehran. They told him they were sure you were an American agent. And they were interested in your Ward investigation."

"So if the guy in the hospital bed wasn't Ward or Goldman, who is he? Who's the Iranian agent?"

"We don't know yet," he admitted. "It's not going to be

easy. Even the wife he married in Kentucky believed he was Ward."

"I need to digest what you've just told me," I said. "Anyway, it occurs to me one good thing has come out of this conversation."

"What?"

"If you own Tempelhof Bank, can you tell me more about what kind of relationship McHanna has with it?" It wasn't too late to score some points at home by unveiling a money-laundering operation in New York.

"Who?"

"You mean you don't know him?" Benny shook his head. "He was a manager at the South Dakota bank that the Chameleon conned. Now he runs a financial-services company in New York, and I think he still is in contact with the Chameleon. I've got a piece of information linking him, using an alias, to Tempelhof Bank."

"Let me find out," said Benny. "But aside from that, I think we can agree to cooperate in finding the Chameleon."

"Helping you out is a decision made above my head."

"You never had to ask permission before."

"That's true. But working for you without getting my superiors' consent is a violation of my oath."

"Hey, I didn't say work for me," he said defensively. "I said work together."

"Like I said, I need to get permission."

"You'll get it." He sounded alarmingly sure of himself.

"What are you saying? That you already made a request through the proper channels?" His face confirmed that I was right. "Thanks for asking my opinion first," I grumbled.

"Don't give me that act, Dan. We both know that when we worked together the last couple of times, things worked out as they should have."

"You could have at least asked me."

"I was protecting you," he said. "An official request by the Mossad to the U.S. government to cooperate is standard procedure. Talking to you first before asking your government would have complicated things. You've just confirmed that."

I left it at that. "So what did my bosses have to say?" How odd that a foreign intelligence service would know about my forthcoming instructions before me. But pressing him further was not going to be fruitful; it would only make him dig in his heels that much more.

"We're still waiting. American bureaucracy, you know."

"Right. Well, let me see what my boss tells me. We've got a conference scheduled."

Later that day, after Benny and I had parted, I got a call from the U.S. Embassy. "A cable came in for you."

I was sure it was one of those routine memos circulated that the ever-helpful Esther kept sending me even when I was away.

"Can you deliver it to my hotel?" I had already taken off my shoes, stretched on the couch, and started reading the newspaper. The last thing I wanted to do was head to the embassy.

"Sorry, no. This is classified material that cannot leave this room."

Why would I get that sort of document? I was investigating money launderers and white-collar criminals. Communications about them are sensitive, but not secret. They're frequently called "sensitive but unclassified" (SBU), containing data that isn't related to national security, but where their disclosure to the public could cause damage. My curiosity exceeded my laziness.

"I'll be right over."

CHAPTER TWELVE

I left my hotel room and walked a few blocks to the embassy on 71 Hayarkon Street, right on Tel Aviv's shoreline on the Mediterranean Sea. I went directly to Pat, the secretary of COS—chief of station—CIA in Israel, who handed me an envelope. It contained a one-page document. I began reading immediately:

Central Intelligence Agency
Directorate of Operations
Washington, DC 20505
Memorandum
To: Dan Gordon, OFARML/DOJ
CC: David Stone, OFARML/DOJ
From: Pamela H. Grace
Date: October 7, 2004
Priority: Urgent
Classification: Secret
Subject: TDY
The Department of Justice has put you on a TDY to a CIA-led special task force on terrorist financing. A plenary meeting and briefing will be held for two days in France commencing on October 11, 2004. Travel arrangements have been made by the Tel Aviv embassy. Please confirm attendance. The scheduled meeting, its location, and its topic, as well as this memo, must be treated as secret.

An attached note informed me that I'd be met at the Paris airport by Matt Kilburn, an Agency representative. I returned the cable to Pat and signed a receipt that I'd read its contents. *TDY* meant temporary duty assignment. I was being put on an interagency transfer for a specific intelligence assignment.

Help was on the way from an unlikely source. The CIA had seldom been helpful in my efforts to retrieve money fraudulently obtained from criminal activities, which the U.S. government had to pursue under a federal statute. Usually the flow of information was unidirectional: from me to them. Maybe it would change now and, with their help, I could get moving on the Chameleon's case. I was surprised, though, that I hadn't received direct instructions from David or Bob telling me I was assigned to a CIA task force.

I went to the embassy's travel office on the second floor. Guy, a skinny staffer, gave me an envelope with an El Al ticket to Paris, departing Ben Gurion Airport on October 10. I used the secure phone to call David Stone.

After the initial pleasantries, David got to the point. "Have you met your friend Benny yet?"

"Yes, I always meet him while I'm in Israel. He's an old friend."

"While you were still in Pakistan a request from the Mossad came through channels suggesting cooperation in discovering the Chameleon."

"Did they say what their interest is?"

"They just said that we had a mutual interest, but didn't specify."

"Benny told me yesterday about their request. Israel has no direct connection, but he still wants to cooperate with us."

"What? Did he elaborate?" David sounded surprised.

"He told me that the Chameleon is an Iranian agent stealing money in the U.S. for a slush fund that finances terrorist organizations. The Mossad intercepted communications between Tehran and someone working for them in Pakistan mentioning Ward's names, and also mine. So this guy, whoever he is, is on the Mossad's radar as a terror financier. That made him a Mossad target."

"Be careful, Dan," said David in a fatherly tone. "One of these days questions could be raised. Just be careful."

"I am," I said. "I think my informal contact with the Mossad through Benny is invaluable for us. It has always been."

"I'm sure of that. But for the sake of transparency, why don't you make a written record of each of your meetings, and send me a copy for the file."

"David, would you have me fill out a report every time I meet up with a buddy? What is this, East Germany circa 1980?"

"Dan, don't take it to an extreme. You aren't meeting with your buddy. You're meeting with a high-ranking executive of a foreign-intelligence service. Although the Israelis are our close allies, still, any contact between a federal employee and foreign agents must be reported. These are the rules. Besides, believe me, it's also for your own good." I knew he was right, of course, and in the past, each time a meeting with Benny was more than just friendly and touched sensitive issues, I'd always written a memo to the file.

I asked David about my TDY to the CIA. I didn't even know whether the task force would be an internal CIA ad hoc group, or a multiagency group that included representatives from other government agencies. The distinction was critical, because in the latter case, each representative ranked equally with the others and took instructions from his or her own agency. However, in an internal CIA working group, I'd be subject to their directives, and David would remain in the background.

"You won't be working for me. It's for the CIA, as in the previous cases."

"You mean Eric Henderson again?" My tone must have revealed my reservations. Eric and I were never cuddle buddies; in fact our relationship was sulfurous at best.

"No. There's another guy, Casey Bauer. Try to be nice to him, for a change."

"I'm always nice!"

David laughed.

★ ★ ★

I returned to my hotel. Benny called me a few minutes after I entered my room. "Hi Dan. Any news?"

I felt a bit uncomfortable. Benny was always one step ahead of me. Or was it more than one? For a moment it flashed through my mind: *Good thing this guy is my friend, you sure wouldn't want him as your enemy.*

"Nothing yet," I said. "But you know how the fucking bureaucracy works. Give them time." I hadn't yet heard what my new CIA boss would have to say about cooperating with the Mossad. He might not be exactly thrilled about it.

Two days later, on a breezy morning with cloudy skies, I drove to Ben Gurion Airport just outside Tel Aviv, returned my rented car, and boarded flight LY 324 to Charles de Gaulle International Airport in France, twenty miles north of Paris. We landed at five thirty in the afternoon. A boyish, athletic-looking man in his early thirties approached me at the gate.

"Mr. Gordon?" I nodded. "I'm Matt Kilburn."

"Please show me an ID," I asked cordially, but firmly. He showed me his U.S. passport.

"OK," I said. "Where do we go?"

"First, please give me your passports."

"Why?" I asked.

"You're getting a new one. I'm sending your old passport back to your office in New York by diplomatic pouch." He handed me a sealed envelope with a new U.S. passport and an Arizona driver's license. Both carried my picture, with my new name, Anthony P. Blackthorn. I gave him my official government employee's passport and my personal passport, and walked with him through immigration and customs. Within twenty minutes we were outside the terminal building in a Peugeot 607 driven by a young blonde woman who couldn't have been a day older than twenty-six.

"Hi," she said as I sat in the back seat. "Welcome to Paris."

"Glad to be here. Where are we going?"

"To a nice place, I can assure you."

There was no point in asking any further questions.

Having been a frequent visitor to France, I couldn't help but notice that we weren't going to Paris. As we entered the A13 highway, the car turned north toward Rouen, instead of south.

Twenty minutes passed in complete silence while I looked at green fields and busy rush-hour traffic. I saw an Exit 14 sign to Vernon and Giverny, and the car took the exit. I remembered the name Giverny. This village, in the gateway to Normandy, was for many years the home of Claude Monet, the French Impressionist. We passed a bridge over the Seine and three miles later we entered the village. Many tourists were walking in the streets, particularly on rue Claude Monet, where a simple sign directed the visitors to Fondation Claude Monet, his home and garden. Approximately one hundred yards down the road, I saw the Musée d'Art Américain Giverny.

I could no longer hold back. "Is that where we are going?" I asked. "To these museums?"

"I wish," said the blonde female at the wheel. "But I'm sure you'll have an opportunity to visit these places. They are nothing short of magnificent." She pointed to the Musée d'Art Américain as we passed it. "This museum presents American Impressionist painters influenced by Claude Monet. I think they are affiliated with the Terra Museum, near Chicago."

"So where are we going?" I asked again.

"To a small, nearby chateau."

The car turned into a small village road, and ten minutes later I saw the castle. It was spectacular.

"This is it," said the woman. "An eighteenth-century chateau." The castle was surrounded by many acres of park, with a pond and trees. The landscape seemed taken out of the paintings of Watteau, the French rococo artist.

She stopped our car at the circular driveway. I got out and entered the chateau. On the right, connected to a spacious foyer on the ground floor, was a huge dining room with an ancient parquet floor and big windows looking out on the extensive gardens. An adjacent room was a winter garden, full of flower-pots and soft-colored couches.

"Hello, Mr. Blackthorn," said a prim, very proper sort of man in his early seventies. His white mustache was impeccably trimmed, and his black jacket beautifully tailored. "I'm M. Bellamy, and I'll be your host during the convention. Please let me show you to your room."

I followed him up the marble stairs to what Europeans call the first floor and into a large room that had an elegant mahogany bed, night table, easy chair, and small desk. Another door led to a small bathroom. There were no telephones or television in my room.

"If you need anything, please let me know," he said in French-accented English. "Dinner will be served at eight o'clock."

Nothing but envy crossed my mind when I saw the accommodations. That's what happens when your agency has a generous, nonpublic budget. Compared to my office's budget that is cut every year, while the workload increases. . . . David never stopped reminding me of that.

I went downstairs dressed casually for dinner. I opened the dining room door and was stunned. There were ten or twelve people seated, all dressed up—jackets, ties, the works. I stood shameful in my jeans and sneakers. I quickly turned around and returned to my room to change into my only blazer and white shirt, but I didn't even have a presentable tie. During a dinner in Tel Aviv I had stained the only one I'd packed. When I'd left the U.S. three weeks before for Pakistan, I'd brought nothing but light and casual clothes suitable for a hot climate. However, they were obviously inappropriate for a fancy chateau in Europe in October.

I seated myself at a table with a place card saying ANTHONY P. BLACKTHORN. Next to me, in a black evening dress, sat my blonde female driver. Her place card said NICOLE A. BLAIR.

"Hi, Ms. Blair," I said smiling. "Am I late for anything?"

"No. Call me Nicole. We're just having dinner." The setting was perfect.

A waiter came to our table and served us with *terrine maison*, a molded dish with smoothly ground meat and mushrooms. He poured Merlot into our crystal goblets.

A tall, distinguished-looking, gray-haired man in his mid-fifties rose from his chair, holding his wine goblet, while the waiters were clearing the table. The staff that served us in the dining room and later on in the winter garden could never have guessed that the attendees weren't gathered to hear lectures about art, but rather were (most of them) agents of the world's largest spy agency.

"Good evening, ladies and gentlemen. My name is Arnold Kyle, and I'm the chairman of this convention. Welcome to the annual meeting of the Arizona Chapter of the American Association of Impressionist Art Lovers. Cheers!" The men and women around the beautifully set tables raised their glasses and "cheered."

"One housekeeping notice before dinner. We start our day tomorrow at nine A.M. with a lecture on post-Monet French Impressionists given by Dr. Louise Guillaume, a lecturer at the Institut Français. At ten thirty, after a short coffee break, we'll have a general meeting of our chapter to elect a new board and president. I know you consider these matters boring, but we must go ahead with our agenda and approve a new budget, so I ask all of you to attend. After lunch we will continue with our deliberations concerning the future of our chapter. In the late afternoon we will tour the Fondation Monet and the Musée d'Art Américain and return here for dinner. After dinner we will have a closed meeting to discuss the proposed merger of our chapter with the California chapter."

I was appreciative of the idea—a disguised meeting in the heartland of Impressionism. The legend was perfect. It effectively masked the identities of a bunch of clean-shaven Americans in Europe. Bring one or two lecturers from town to talk about Monet, display a welcome banner, and we were in business. The rest of the time spent behind closed doors would be dedicated to far craftier, but less artistic, matters.

The main course was *gigot d'agneau rôti aux herbes gratin*

dauphinois, a roasted leg of lamb with herbs. For dessert we had *plateau de fromages*—a plate of French cheeses—and coffee. I skipped both.

I made small talk with Nicole. She was as much "Nicole" as I was "Anthony." She was rather attractive and friendly, but I had other things on my mind than getting friendlier, and I knew that the same went for her. So after a few drinks and nonrevealing conversations, we retired to our respective rooms.

CHAPTER THIRTEEN

The following morning we had an illuminating lecture about Monet, to satisfy the appearance of a convention. Immediately after the lecturer left, two young men went and sat outside the closed doors, while two others continued patrolling under the windows, all in a seemingly relaxed mode. When we returned, Arnold Kyle rose and addressed the small audience. I counted the participants. There were nine men and two women. Nobody looked younger than twenty-five or older than fifty-five. There was one African-American woman. Two of the men looked Hispanic.

"We are here in connection with our continued effort to combat terrorists by drying up their funding. This particular meeting focuses on Iran's role in terror financing. In addition to a new member from the FBI's Counterterrorism Unit, Matt Kilburn, we've another new member from the Justice Department's Office of Asset Recovery and Money Laundering, Anthony Blackthorn. Matt and Tony, please identify yourselves."

All eyes turned to me and to Kilburn, who sat across the room. Both of us nodded. Kyle continued.

"Matt has been working with us during the past two months in connection with our investigation of the affairs of Nada Management. Tony is a money-laundering expert who is currently investigating bank fraud perpetrated by an individual who may be helping finance Iran's clandestine terrorist activities. Iran continues, behind a curtain of strict confidentiality, to promote terror through proxies. You can find details in the notes we handed you earlier. Please read and return them to me before the conclusion of this meeting. No written material leaves this room." He paused to sip from his goblet. "Now, just as we sought cooperation with other nations to join a coalition to fight an overt war against Saddam, we are seeking collaboration in the covert war against terror. As you're well aware, terror is stateless, but its sponsors are not. Our role here"—he circled his hands as if to grasp us—"is to break the lifeline between terror and its sponsors. In one word, *money*."

He sipped again from his water goblet and continued. "Among the foreign intelligence organizations with which we've a history of mutual cooperation is the Israeli Mossad. Israel has a clear interest in joining our combat. This isn't only because we are close allies, but because Israel has been, and continues to be, victimized by terror. Some of it, and it is growing in frequency and severity, is Iranian backed. To make things worse from Israel's perspective, Iran is leveling direct threats against Israel by announcing that it is starting to enrich uranium, and that it has long-range missiles that could reach Europe. In case anyone missed the hint, Israel is situated halfway between Iran and Europe. So," he concluded, "we've asked the Israeli Mossad to send their representative to brief us and explore ways in which we can collaborate in combating terror financing as one battle of many against terrorism and its backers. Although much smaller than us, the Mossad is one of the big guys when we talk about Arab terrorism."

Kyle signaled a person at the door, and Benny Friedman walked in, escorted by a sleek young woman in her late twenties. Benny smiled at me when he sat next to Kyle. The woman who came with him sat near him.

"Let me introduce Mr. Benjamin Friedman, head of the Foreign Relations Division of the Mossad, and his assistant." Kyle then pointed at me. "And I'm sure you know Tony."

I nodded at Benny with a smile. He was too experienced to give any hint that *Tony* was an alias. Just for a moment I wondered why we would need to use aliases in a secret meeting, when all participants were government agents and the two foreign representatives were there to cooperate, not to snoop. But I knew the answer. The identities of U.S. covert agents and their relationship with the U.S. intelligence community are protected by a special federal statute, the Intelligence Identities Protection Act, enacted in 1982. If any of the participants in the meeting ever defected, or were captured and forced to talk, he or she would be unable to identify other agents by name, since no names are ever revealed, and aliases always change. Flies never visit an egg that has no crack.

Benny cleared his throat, drank soda water from a crystal goblet that had probably always been used before for wine, but not for Benny, who'd drink only kosher wine, and said, "Ladies and gentlemen. I'll be brief. The United States and Israel have a joint enemy: terror." He paused. "We've long realized that the battle against world terror cannot be complete or won unless we cut their lifeline—money to finance their operations."

Benny then commenced with a brief history of Iran's sponsorship of terrorism, saying that world terror is the Iranians' illegitimate son. He said that the Iranians make terror a strategy, not a tactic. They're the masters of implementing the slogan, "Hit and weep." They have managed always both to be the assassin and to claim to be the victim or assume the role of the good neighbor showing sympathy, and have reaped the benefits of all positions. He talked about Iran's nuclear aspiration to help them become the kings of the oil-rich region. He described the good relationship Israel once had with Iran, which had stopped when fanatic Islam took over and friends became foes.

"If you want to defeat terrorism, we've a unique joinder of interests here," Benny said.

Benny sipped from his goblet and continued. "The Mossad has recently learned of a link between Iran and financial institutions in the United States and Europe. That unholy alliance is one of the most closely guarded secrets of the Iranians. As you well know, since the Islamic Revolution of 1979, Iran has had a policy of exporting the revolution, first to Islamic countries that don't follow Iran's extreme interpretation of Islam, and then to other parts of the world. In their dictionary, 'exporting the revolution' means a reign of terror to undermine legitimate governments of other countries by wreaking havoc, fear, and uncertainty.

"The manner in which they export their doctrine is always through third parties, never directly. Look at the Hezbollah in Lebanon, or Hamas in the Gaza Strip and the West Bank. These organizations take money, weapons, and instructions from Iran. Of course, they all deny any such relationship, but nobody takes these denials seriously. We certainly don't. The facts are strong and clear. There are also indirect links that tie Iran with Al-Qaeda, the Gamaa Islamiya in Egypt, and Al Taqwa in Europe.

"I won't go into too many details here; you know the facts. There are also ties between the various organizations, not necessarily through Iran, but certainly with its blessing. Many foreign intelligence agencies, including your agencies, have evidence that after the nine eleven attacks, Al-Qaeda received financial assistance from Nada, which is Al Taqwa's new name. The terror they're financing has no borders, no territory, and no government. Therefore we must abandon conservative thinking, which has always been simplistic. If your enemy attacks you, you retaliate or conquer. But now? Your enemies could be in a bordering country, but they could also be five thousand miles away, planning how to send their tentacles to hurt you. They have no tanks and planes that you can match against yours to create a balance. All they need are explosives and good organization. They don't want to conquer your country. They want to wreak havoc so that your government will implode."

Benny continued with his presentation for another hour, overwhelming his listeners with the amount of information the Mossad had gathered on Iran's major role in terror financing. Benny paused dramatically to see how deeply his audience was concentrating. I looked around; it couldn't have been deeper. Benny had their complete attention.

"Any questions so far?"

None were asked.

"OK," said Benny. "Let's move to more current events. At the end of my presentation you will see how all the pieces fall into place in a current event."

Benny continued.

"I've my government's consent to cooperate with you in combating terror financing. Needless to say, the consent is general in nature. Before we take joint action Mossad must be convinced that any suggested plan is reasonably possible."

"Why do you need our cooperation? You've done fine so far. And more importantly, why does the U.S. need you in this matter?" asked Kyle.

"It's a valid question, and I'm happy it has been asked," said Benny. "The terror-fighting arena has become crowded. There were quite a few cases where we ran into American and other Western intelligence services. That has caused several problems. First, it took us—and probably you, also—time to realize that the other guy working on the same matter was a friend, not a foe. Obviously agents don't wear uniforms or carry other identifying credentials such as name tags with the name of their organization. The hairy guy with a week-old beard who reeks of tobacco may be one of us, rather than a conniving terrorist.

"Second, the law of supply and demand works here as well. If we compete with others on sources, the price goes up, and most likely the quality goes down, because the suppliers don't particularly care about after-sale service or warranty. These things create friction we want to avoid. We know that in the battle against terrorism, if you claim exclusivity and superiority, all other players are in your way and must leave the stage to you. But, as a sovereign nation with life-and-death interests in fighting terrorists, we can't outsource our national security. Therefore we aren't going anywhere. The conclusion is, let's work together."

"I see your point," said Kyle. "Thus far our achievements in the battle against global Islamic terrorism have been mainly through SIGINT, interception of radio and other electronic signals."

That was an understatement. No other nation in the world has capabilities in that area of electronic intelligence that come even close to those of the United States. In this field, size does matter. But America is sorely lacking in HUMINT, human intelligence, and inside Iran there are no longer any viable human assets. Therefore, cooperating with the Mossad made perfect sense.

Kyle turned to Benny. "You have made some notable achievements in gathering intelligence by recruiting sources."

Benny nodded in accord. "As I said, we don't outsource our defense," he proudly pointed out. "We continue to be active not only in drying up terrorist financing, but we vigorously toil to limit the number of terrorists to ease the burden on their financiers," he said with a chuckle. "Accidents happen—for example in Lebanon, which has always been a hub of terror."

I could understand why he chuckled. Although there were several such "events" each year, I thought of two that had attracted my attention. In 2002, two "accidents" happened in Lebanon: one to a drug dealer who provided intelligence to Hezbollah, and one several months later to an Al-Qaeda operative. The Lebanese media attributed these misfortunes to the Mossad.

"But who knows who is really responsible for these accidents? I hear that two Hezbollah operatives were sent to rest with their ancestors. In other news I heard that two Hamas men in Damascus, Syria, were killed. They should have been more careful," concluded Benny, and all smiled. What Benny did was a smart job of insinuation. It is quite possible the Mossad was behind those killings, but maybe some or all of the other eliminations had been a result of internal rifts and local rivalries. Benny left this open. It was nice to know he wasn't cryptic only with me.

Benny's tone of voice became serious. "The Iranians believe in tit for tat—*Aemaeli ya:t _e_ taela:fi ju:ya:neh*. After the capture of the U.S. Embassy and the taking hostage of sixty-six U.S. diplomats and embassy staff, President Carter froze all Iranian assets in the U.S., approximately $8 billion. The asset freeze and the other economic sanctions imposed by the U.S. had a devastating effect on Iran's economy. Most of Iran's foreign-currency reserves became unreachable, and that compounded the difficulties that the Iranian economy suffered as a result of the other sanctions imposed by the U.S. Therefore, getting back at the Americans by looting their economy seemed to be a legitimate and natural response to the Iranians, who believed that 'an eye for an eye' could also be interpreted in economic terms as 'a dollar for a dollar,' and whenever possible, even a better revenge-exchange rate.

"We discovered that the new Iranian government made a strategic decision soon after the seizure of its funds by the U.S.: recoup through unconventional means the money that the U.S. had frozen, plus interest and penalty," he added, smirking. "If additional goals could be achieved along the way, such as undermining the U.S. economy, then *tefadlu*, as they say in the Middle East—welcome!

"We don't know if the decision of the Iranian government was fully implemented. But we do know that as part of that decision, they earmarked money to be stolen from the U.S. to finance terror and clandestine activities. The slush fund created for that purpose was very beneficial, because terror funding didn't go through the regular Iranian government budget, which many eyes see.

"This is where U.S. and Israeli interests join. You want to get those bastards who collapsed some of your banks, and we both want to stop the money flow which finances terror organizations that murder our and your citizens. As nine eleven has shown the world, terror does not stop in the Middle East. May I remind you all," he said, just a touch theatrically, "that many people maybe haven't noticed, but World War III has already begun. It's the terrorists against the rest of the world." Benny sat down.

Kyle looked at his watch. "I'm sorry. I didn't realize it's already four thirty. Let's break now and meet at eight o'clock for dinner."

We went outside to get fresh air before dinner. "Come," Benny said. "Let's have coffee." We got in his car and went to Giverny. He stopped near Musée d'Art Américain and entered Terra Café. "Let's go outside," he said.

We walked to the beautiful porch and sat under a wooden pergola. I ordered a quiche, and Benny had just coffee. I knew Benny had something on his mind, so I just waited for him to start. When he didn't, I asked, "You just gave us a theory, but no evidence or even a direction. Where does it lead us? Where is the touch point to the money trail?"

"Our longtime clandestine cooperation with the Kurds in Iran and Iraq has yielded interesting results," said Benny with a smile like that of the cat that just ate the canary.

I knew what he meant. Israel had always thought it would be a fatal mistake not to extend its defense lines hundreds of miles away from its physical borders. It wanted to know when its enemy left its bases to attack Israel, rather than to be awakened when the enemy was at Israel's door. A close relationship with the Kurds in Iraq and Iran had given Israel an observation point and a human early-warning system. Since as early as 1965, Israel had been training and supporting Kurdish commandos fighting for Kurdish independence. That enabled Israel to run covert operations inside Kurdish areas of Iran, Iraq, and Syria, primarily for intelligence-gathering operations.

Benny continued. "Together with Kurdish commandos, our agents have entered Iran and installed sensors and other intelligence-gathering devices that, for the most part, target suspected Iranian nuclear facilities."

It had already been known for some time. Not all communications are transferred by the Internet, definitely not military and intelligence data, unless heavily encrypted. That is particularly true with respect to countries, such as Iran, which aren't there yet in terms of computer sophistication. So Benny's men were milking information from the Iranians by somehow listening to Iranian communication lines.

"As an observant Jew, I believe in the wisdom of our sages, which has taught us that we must study Torah not for a reward in the present or in the afterlife, but just for the sake of study. By studying Torah, a reward will come."

"So?" I asked impatiently, champing at the bit.

"Here is a present-day application of that wisdom. Our devices were meant to alert us to Iran's nuclear capabilities. But unexpectedly we benefited from these listening devices and unearthed loads of information about Iranian covert operations in support of terror organizations."

"Go ahead," I urged him. Of course, shrewd operator that he was, I fully realized that he would tell me only as much as he intended to tell me, but that didn't make me any less eager to hear what he had to say.

"We know that there were extensive top-secret communications in Iran in connection with the U.S. The word *Atashbon*, Farsi for *the guardians of fire*, was very frequently used. We assume it to be a code name." He gave me a clever look and started returning to his car, leaving me puzzled. But I knew Benny—more info was forthcoming. We returned to the chateau.

After dinner I joined Benny and Nicole Blair for a visit to Monet's gardens and the Musée d'Art Américain, but their gates were already closed.

On the following day, we convened again in the dining room. Kyle and Benny summed up the conference. We were divided into four working groups and were taken to separate smaller rooms to continue talking. We finally talked shop and specifics.

I had breakfast with Benny before he left. He ate only bread and yogurt, knowing that the food served there wasn't kosher.

"Do you know what's next?" I asked. "The conclusion of the evening last night was somewhat vague. Is the cooperation on Iran's terror financing between Israel and the U.S. across the board?" I asked.

Benny nodded. "I think we'll have an agreement to cooperate in the operations discussed. However, each operation will be independently approved. Intel gathering ops will be separate. In other operations, there will be no mixed teams. To avoid problems resulting from disparity in political cultures and translations, each organization will be assigned a different piece of the action, and there will be a coordination meeting every two weeks—or sooner, if developments warrant it. "One good thing happened last night," he concluded. "I wasn't preached to."

"What?" I didn't get it.

Benny glanced at me from above his eyeglasses. "Our agenda is to eliminate our worst enemies, while most of the Free World still wants to turn a blind eye—as long as their countries remain intact—and preach to us to see the good side of our enemies." He chuckled. "That is hypocrisy at its best, or rather, at its worst. Last night I was with people who think like me."

"Are you going back to Israel?"

"Shortly. I'll see you soon," he said.

"You never finished the story about *Atashbon*. Was it on purpose?"

"Yes."

"But do you know more than you told me?"

Benny looked at me with his intelligent brown eyes, studying my face. "Some."

"Then tell me," I said, taking the bait.

"Later," he promised. He was firm. There was no point in arguing.

Kyle approached my table. "Specific assignments to teams have been prepared. Here are your instructions." He handed me a piece of paper with a Paris address. "You can go there—it's a safe apartment."

CHAPTER FOURTEEN

After I packed my stuff, I joined Nicole for a ride to Paris. The journey was short, just about an hour. We were dropped off in the 16th arrondissement, the posh quarter on the west end of the French capital. I knew the area well. Whenever I'd come to Paris for more than two days, I would stroll in this quarter and behave like a tourist. We passed the commercial district of Passy, next to avenue Mozart in Auteuil, a small market community with a strong Provençal feel. Within minutes we stopped in front of a building on rue St. Didier. The building looked rather old and inconspicuous, but as all realtors say, what counts is location, location, location. Being in the 16th meant everything.

We lurched to the third floor in a squeaky elevator. But when Nicole opened the door of the apartment, I was in awe. It was massive. We entered a room with a twenty-foot-high ceiling and huge windows with wooden shades. Against one wall stood a long, upholstered sofa and an antique cocktail table. In the corner were two armchairs. On the other side of the living area, the dining area was set up with a simple, yet enormous, rectangular wooden table with carved wooden chairs. An additional sofa was placed in the alcove behind the dining area. Next to the dining area was a fully furnished kitchen that was modern in the fifties. A wooden stairway led us to the upper floor with its master bedroom and bathroom, two additional bedrooms, another bathroom, and a comfortable gallery designed around a balcony overlooking the living room. We looked inside the master bedroom: it had a king-size bed, a chest, and a vanity table. "That's my bedroom," announced Nicole, as if we were in the gold-rush era, when husky men were claiming property by the force of their guns.

She quickly backtracked with a smile. "Well, if you don't mind. It's just that it's perfect for my needs."

As a gentleman, I acquiesced, returning her smile. "Fine," I said.

The other bedrooms were smaller, but I found one with a king-size bed. The third room was empty but for two desks and office chairs, with a combined fax, copier, scanner, and printer and a digital telephone, both hooked up to a signal scrambler that made them secure.

"That will be our communication room," said Nicole. "I need to shower and change. I'll see you in a little while."

I wondered who watched the safe apartment while it was empty. Or was it ever empty? Obviously, the classified communication equipment could not be left there without security. I went outside. I'd always liked the area for its cultural attractions—the Bois de Boulogne, Champs Elysées, Arc de Triomphe, Musée d'Art Moderne de la Ville de Paris, and Musée Marmottan Monet were all within walking distance. There were many cafés and restaurants to explore. I strolled along the narrow rue St. Didier with its *boulangeries*, fruit and vegetable shops, and flower shops. I continued to Androuet, the famous cheese store.

I'll be back here soon, I promised myself, *once I'm done with my chores with Nicole.*

I returned to the apartment. Nicole sat on the sofa with her bare feet on the coffee table. In blue jeans, she looked miles away from her strictly business appearance at the convention.

"This is a great area," I said companionably. "Lots of interesting places to visit."

"We're here to crack a case," she said severely. "We aren't tourists." She wasn't kidding. I nodded. "Let's start by defining the perimeter," she said.

She's perfect, I thought—in other words, boring.

"I need to trace Ward's movements," I said, masking some anger.

"Right. Professor Manfred Krieger the archaeologist is our most solid anchor at this time."

"I agree."

"OK, we could start with him right now," said Nicole. "Shouldn't be hard to track him down, although we don't know if he's still alive."

"I sure hope he is," I said. Even in a world of hunters and targets, sometimes people aged and died of natural causes.

Nicole clicked at her laptop, briskly accessing the Net through encrypted wireless. "Here it is. Professor Krieger published an article on archaeology of the Orient in 2003, in *Archaeology and Heritage*, an academic journal published in London. So, unless the article was written a long time ago, then at least in 2003 he was still alive. It says here that he teaches at the University of Berlin."

It took only a few minutes to find Professor Krieger's address and phone number in Berlin.

"So what do we want from this guy?" she queried.

"I want to pick his memory, or even his records concerning his staff during his 1980 excavations in Iran."

"And do you think he'd still have them?"

"Nicole, archaeologists rummage through records left thousands of years ago. It's kind of against their religion for them to throw out their own papers, don't you think?" I was trying to reintroduce levity into the room.

Nicole allowed a smile. "OK. What's the suggested legend? We need to make it plausible and pitch it to Langley. We can't approach him without their authorization."

"Just for making a phone call you need Langley's approval?" I thought of the improvisational manner in which we operated at the Mossad, and the social-engineering methods I applied during my tenure as a lone wolf at the Department of Justice while hunting money launderers. We were working with totally different institutional cultures.

"We should bear in mind that the legend must hold water not only with the professor, but elsewhere. We don't know the types of connections the professor has in Iran. If there's a hole in our story and he suspects us, and tells the Iranians about our snooping, the doors will shut in our faces. And maybe some metal doors behind us, if they ever get us."

"On second thought, you're right," I conceded. "The source of information leading us to Krieger is a dubious character in Islamabad. We don't really know who he is, and why he was telling me this story for only the $300 I gave him. Definitely something rotten there. Getting me to contact Krieger could be one of his ulterior motives. Who knows, maybe he's more conniving than I thought." I decided not to tell Nicole about the information Benny gave me linking Ahmed Khan to the Iranian intelligence services. Not just yet.

For the next hour we raised and rejected several options, and finally came up with the one we thought would be reasonably plausible. Nicole e-mailed an encrypted message to Langley to get approval. She slammed shut her laptop computer, got up from her chair, and stretched her arms, revealing a flat, tanned stomach. "We're done here. It will be a day or so until we hear from them."

I went out to the street and walked straight to the *boulangerie*, bought two baguettes, and ended up in Androuet, the cheese shrine. The aroma was overwhelming.

"We sell 340 different kinds of cheese," said a friendly salesperson in a green apron, who realized I was besieged. I bought Camembert, Brie, and Fontainebleau cheese.

"Monsieur," he said, "may I suggest you take also Vacherin? We sell it only from October to March."

I stopped at the corner wine store and got a bottle of a promising Côtes du Rhone. I went back to the apartment, resisting an urge to start devouring the food en route. We feasted until I felt the wine pulling down my eyelids.

By the following morning, an encrypted message had come in: "Legend approved, mode of approach at your discretion."

"Do you think we should call him or pay a personal visit?" I asked Nicole.

"I think we should start with calling him. A personal visit

could be intimidating or suspicious. Why would an American come to Berlin to ask a few questions for a family memorial book for a person who's been missing for twenty-some years?"

I dialed.

"Krieger," announced a man's voice.

"Professor Krieger?"

"Ja." He answered in German.

"My name is Stanley Ward. I hope you speak English."

"Yes."

"I'm sorry to bother you on a small matter, but I wonder if you remember Albert Ward, a member of my family?"

"Remind me."

"He was a young photographer who worked for you in the excavations in Tal-e Malyan, Iran, in the early 1980s."

"I remember that name very vaguely."

"As I said earlier, I'm Stanley Ward, his cousin. We're preparing a family history pamphlet and want to dedicate a page to his memory." I paused upon mentioning that Ward had died, hoping he'd reveal something he might know about it. But he kept silent, and I continued.

"Since he mentioned your name in a postcard he sent my parents, I thought you might be able to tell me about his work. It'll take only a few minutes of your time."

"There isn't anything to tell," he said. "Dagmar Fischer, my assistant at the time, suggested bringing him over. If I'm not mistaken, she said she had met him some place in Africa. But at the end, he never came to work for us. The truth is, those volunteers are really good for nothing. Unless they are getting academic credit, lots of them don't show up, and some of those who do come behave like they're in a summer camp and forget we are involved in serious scientific research."

"Did he expect to be paid for his work?"

"Of course not, nobody did. We had a limited budget mostly spent on local diggers and food supplies for my staff and students. He was expected to be a volunteer like all others."

"Do you remember anything special about him?"

"Nothing. I never met him. I remember the name only because we had to sponsor an Iranian visa for him."

"Where can I find Ms. Dagmar Fischer?"

"She teaches at the University of London's Archaeology Department."

I thanked him and hung up the phone. Nicole, who had been recording the conversation, stopped the tape recorder. Next, we called Dagmar Fischer, who was found after a few tries and proved more pleasant than the grumpy Professor Krieger.

"Yes, I knew Al Ward pretty well. I remember him as a kind person."

"That's nice to hear," I said. "Have you been in contact?"

"No. I last saw him many years ago. While I was a student, I went on vacation to South Africa, where I met him in a youth hostel. We spent some time together, and I even went with him on a safari, where he took magnificent photos."

"I understand he had plans to follow you to Iran."

She laughed. "You make it sound romantic. It wasn't, at least not from my perspective. While still in South Africa I heard from my classmate that a German archaeology expedition was planning a dig in Iran and was looking for students willing to volunteer. I called the department and they agreed to take me. I flew from Johannesburg to Tehran and joined Professor Krieger's team. When the site of Anshan in Tal-e Malyan was discovered, we needed a professional photographer, but with a very small budget, we wanted a volunteer. I told Professor Krieger about Ward being a good photographer who was looking for adventure. Professor Krieger asked me to invite Ward. I had his next address in a youth hostel in Islamabad, Pakistan, and sent him a letter."

"Did he respond?"

"Yes, but it took some time, and his letter was very short, like one or two sentences—'Coming on that date,' or something like that. I was a bit surprised that he didn't even ask about the terms or anything else."

"Maybe he wanted to be in your company more than anything else?"

"Maybe," she giggled.

"Was anyone worried about bringing an American to Iran, considering it was after the revolution?"

"Well, we told the Iranians that we were planning to invite a young American photographer to join the group's excavations in return for room and board. Which for us meant, you know, a tent in the desert and canned food."

"So what'd they say?"

"You know, I have no idea. I was really just rank and file— I was helping Professor Krieger with some administrative chores. But I guess it wasn't OK, because Ward never actually showed up."

"Do you know who handled the visa matter for the Iranians? Perhaps he will know."

"I'm not sure I remember. It's been so long. But I think I saw the Iranian officer twice at the camp. Actually, I'm sure I did, because he came back about a month later. He told us they'd hold us responsible for attempting to bring Ward over. He said they'd discovered that Ward was a spy."

"He said Ward was a spy?" I tried to sound surprised. "That's shocking. And besides, even if that ridiculous story were true, why would you be responsible?"

"Because his visa application to Iran was sponsored by the expedition. Well, he said Ward was an American spy. We were pretty upset. Plus we were left without a photographer."

"Was Albert a spy?" I repeated in disbelief, sounding a complete novice.

"I hardly think so. He was too simple to be anything but what he was, just a kid wandering around. Why don't you ask Albert?"

"I can't," I said. "He disappeared. He never returned from wherever he was."

"Oh my god," she said. "I can't believe that!'

"Can you remember now the name of the officer? Maybe he could tell us if he knew where Albert went instead of coming to Iran after his entry was refused."

"Well, I guess I could look it up in my records. It's possible that maybe I wrote his name down in my log of the excavation."

"Thanks, that would be great. So while we're talking, what happened next?"

"What happened? Nothing, I guess. We completed the excavation and returned to Germany. Professor Krieger's paper on the excavation was very well received. I finished my studies, and the excavation site is now open to tourists."

"Have you seen or heard from Albert again?"

"No, and I did find it odd. I don't know why he would vanish like that. Though I suppose he could have been upset because . . ." She trailed off.

"Because . . . ?" I prompted, hoping I wasn't pushing her too far.

"It's kind of personal, but you know, I guess it doesn't matter. It's been twenty years. I . . . rebuffed his advances because I didn't find him attractive in a personal way."

A day later, when I called Dr. Fischer back, she had the officer's name: Bahman Hossein Rashtian. He was working in Iranian state security.

I consulted Nicole.

"What we should do is go to London," she said immediately, "to see what the NSA has to offer on the Iranian connection to our case."

"Why London?"

"Because their UK base is the largest outside the U.S. There's no point in asking the French station for broadscale assistance—they'll just send us to London, or even to Washington."

I called Bob Holliday, my new boss. David had just retired. To add to my other bones to pick with the Chameleon, he'd made me miss David's retirement party.

"Bob, we need NSA assistance."

"Why?"

"We need unrestricted international communications-intelligence reach, the kind of air sniffing that only NSA can provide." I gave him the details and answered his many questions. Each time we spoke I could see more clearly that working with him was going to be a world of difference from having David as my boss. He had a way of firing questions at me that sometimes made me feel as if I were performing under the baleful eye of a strict but very cordial schoolteacher.

After he exhaustively interrogated me, he agreed to see what he could do.

The following morning Bob called. "OK, an NSA connection is established. You'll be picked up tomorrow at nine A.M. from your London hotel." He gave me the details. "We expect a nice and sunny day."

The journey to London was fast. Bob was wrong on the weather. The next day brought us the typical English weather of rain and fog, and a new friend: a slim African-American woman in a black pantsuit. "Hi, I'm Pamela Johnson. I'll be taking you to Menwith Hill."

"What's in Menwith Hill?" I asked.

"That's the major station of NSA, operated jointly with the British Government Communications Headquarters, GCHQ."

"And what about the sunny weather you promised?" I asked.

"Well, you know. Weather forecasts are horoscopes with numbers."

After a three-hour drive ending amid the green meadows of Yorkshire, we arrived at a heavily fenced and guarded area. Following thorough security screening, we were brought to a round, windowless building.

"Welcome to NSA," said a man with an accent that smacked of the American South, as we entered his small office. "I'm Dr. Ted Feldman, and I'll do my best to help you. What's going on here?"

He and Pamela took notes as Nicole quickly explained.

"I see," Feldman said. "We'll try to do what we can, once formalities are satisfied."

The NSA picked up where others were bound by legal restrictions. As I well knew, they operated in cyberspace, where there were few rules, breaking encrypted communications and transferring the messages to linguists to analyze the messages in more than 110 languages.

"What do you have in mind?" I asked.

"We can engage Echelon, our global surveillance network," he said briskly. "It's the most comprehensive and sophisticated signals intelligence ever made. It can monitor every communication transmitted through satellite, microwave, cellular, and fiber optics. That includes communications to and from North America."

"How much does that all add up to?" I asked.

He shrugged. "We estimate it at five billion telephone calls, e-mail messages, faxes, and broadcasts daily."

"Any communication?" I asked with concern, thinking about some private conversations I'd held with several women I'd dated.

He smiled. "Not to worry." He must have heard that anxious question many times.

"How do you do it?"

"Echelon collects data through a variety of methods, including through radio antennae at listening stations located in key areas around the world. We scan the enormous amount of data through filtering software using a computer network hosted by the UK's GCHQ, Canada's CSE, Australia's DSD, and New Zealand's GCSB." The torrent of acronyms could make you dizzy. Only insiders knew and cared that they stood for Communications Security Establishment, the Defense Signals Directorate, and the Government Communications Security Bureau. We needed little explication.

"The filtering software flags messages containing any of a set of key words, such as *bomb* or *nuclear*," Feldman continued.

"How does the actual process of data sifting work?" asked Nicole.

"We've got word-pattern recognition technologies, plus advanced technology in speech recognition and optical character recognition. See, the computers convert sound gleaned from intercepted telephone conversations and text images from fax transmissions, and store them in a searchable database."

"What about foreign languages?"

"Translation software recognizes many languages and can translate them into English. Once text is stored in the database, our analysts engage data-mining software that searches data to identify relationships based on similarities and patterns."

"What about help in our operation, including getting access to enemy computers?"

"We've developed new tools to assist in covert-surveillance operations. One example is Tempest, a surveillance technology that captures data displayed on computer monitors by collecting electromagnetic emissions from the internal electron beams that create the images." Had he avoided answering my question on computer hacking?

"So much has changed since I last had contact with the NSA," said Nicole.

He smiled. "We've additional developments: Fluent and Oasis. Fluent does computer searches of documents written in various languages. Our analysts put in queries in English, just as if they were using any Internet search engine. Those results that come up in any foreign languages are translated." He paused. "Oasis picks up audio from television and radio broadcasts, and keeps them as text. The software is very sophisticated. It can identify the gender of the speaker, and if that audio has already been previously captured, our analysts can obtain a digital transcript of the data and compare. Oasis is limited to English, but the CIA is adapting it to understand additional languages."

"What about recordings from the past?" That's what I wanted to know.

"We occasionally have that, if what you're looking for was already captured for other purposes," he answered.

"It all sounds like omnipotence," I said.

"Hell no, far from it," he said. "Sure, we're the largest intelligence service in the world. We employ more mathematicians than anyone else, and we've got the strongest team of code makers and code breakers ever assembled. But the volume of information generated every day exceeds the capacity of our technologies to process it. Not to mention the encryption technologies that can give you a look at what turns out to be gibberish, without any possibility of breaking the code. We know, for example, that Osama bin Laden and other terrorists are using steganography: hiding data within a benign-looking file, such as a picture of a sunset in the South Pacific. Can you imagine the computing power necessary to detect it? And I'm not even talking about breaking it, which is even more complex.

"But why go that far? Even simple tricks can slow us down, and sometimes even derail us. That happens when messages are ciphered in a simple method that substitutes letters for other letters. Let's go to an even lower level of sophistication, to elementary school games, and create messages that substitute the word *football* for *bomb* and *baseball* for *American president*. Do you set the software to alert us each time it recognizes these words? We would drown under the sheer volume."

"I see," said Nicole.

"So you see why there's no assurance that any of these systems will be fail-safe and provide the kind of intelligence that you want."

I nodded. "I get it. Knowing those caveats, all I need to do is provide you with key words?"

"It's not that simple, but essentially, yes. Once a key word included in the Echelon dictionary is captured, it flags the entire message. After decryption, our analysts forward the data to the client intelligence agency that requested the intercept of the key word. We pass the signals through SILKWORTH, our supercomputer system where voice recognition, optical character recognition, and other analytical tools dissect the prey. Although five billion messages pass through the system every day, we actually transcribe and record only very few text messages and phone calls. Only those messages that produce keyword 'hits' are tagged for future analysis."

"Can I give you the key words now?"

"No. We must first start an IDP, an intercept deployment plan. I'll also need your agency's formal request. I was asked to give you only a presentation. But tell me more about the case."

I ran quickly by him the leads we had. The run was long, but the list of solid leads disturbingly short. We had a dozen aliases that the Chameleon had used.

"We don't know for sure if it's one person, or eleven, or twelve. So far Ward has been my prime target. He could be in the U.S., Australia . . . or back in Iran, although I'd be surprised if he were there."

"Why?"

"I hardly think he could adapt or would want to adapt to living in Iran again after living in the great satanic country for more than twenty years. No matter what the Iranians have to say about it, it still beats Tehran. So maybe he decided to be a sleeper for a few more years and live comfortably, hoping his handlers in Iran would forget about him. I thought I found him in Sydney, but there are conflicting reports about whether the person I saw there was indeed the person who assumed Ward's identity."

"You'll hear from us soon after we get the formalities in place," Dr. Feldman promised.

After we returned to Paris, I called Benny using his Belgian telephone number.

"Thank you for calling Marnix van der Guilder Trading Company," said the announcement. "Please press the extension number of the person with whom you wish to speak, or leave a message after the beep." I pressed Benny's code for this month, 8*890447**3#, heard a series of beeps, and recognized the familiar sound of an Israeli phone ringtone.

"Bonjour, comment est-ce que je peux vous aider?"—How can I help you?—I heard Benny's secretary ask in French. Whenever a forwarded call from Europe came in, although a complex code was necessary, the first voice identification was in French to hedge the remote chance that the code was correctly put in,

but the caller didn't know the call would end up in Mossad headquarters just north of Tel Aviv.

"Hi Dina," I said in Hebrew. "It's Dan Gordon. Benny back yet?"

"No. Still traveling," she answered, switching to Hebrew.

"OK, please ask him to call my U.S. mobile-phone number."

"Sure."

I went to get one of those crunchy baguette sandwiches, my diet ruiner for a week, and as I was about to take a bite, my mobile phone rang.

Damn. It had better be important.

"Dan?" I heard Benny's familiar voice. "What did I catch you doing?"

I stared down at the sandwich longingly. "Nothing but a baguette sandwich. Anyway, are you still around? I need to talk to you."

"Yes, I'm in Paris too. What's on your mind?"

"Can we meet?"

"Sure. How about you come to the George V hotel and meet me in the lobby at six P.M."

I took a cab to 31 avenue George V and entered La Galerie, a high-ceilinged lobby decorated with Flemish tapestries and excellent nineteenth-century paintings and furniture. A pianist was playing a quiet Chopin nocturne, while elegant waiters in the adjacent courtyard were serving tourists who had deep personal pockets or expense accounts not scrutinized by frugal bean counters.

"What happened? The office discovered the lost treasures of the Count of Monte Cristo? We never used to stay in these hotels." I looked around. A typical room probably cost more than $1,000 a night.

Benny glanced at me above his eyeglasses, which had slipped halfway down his nose. "Of course not. I just like these first-class places. Here money doesn't buy you friends, but it can get you a better class of rivals."

I felt that something was different with Benny, his cynical quip notwithstanding.

"What happened?" I asked, looking at his gloomy face.

"Nothing," his mouth said, but his expression gave a different answer.

"Is it something at home? Are Batya and the kids all right?"

"Yes, thank god, they're fine."

"Then what is it?" I persisted. I've known Benny for long enough to know that only a serious problem would affect his usual easygoing demeanor. "Something at work?" I tried again.

He nodded. "Things aren't the way they used to be."

"That's too general," I said. "Something must have hit you hard. What is it?"

"Changes," he said summarily. "Dagan is shaking up the house with the prime minister's backing." He was talking about the Mossad head.

"Isn't it time?" I asked. "Routine is the biggest enemy, right?"

"Well, Dagan has every right to install changes," said Benny, but his tone belied the statement. He sighed.

"Look around you. The old historic rivalry between states that require foreign intelligence service is decreasing, and, as a result, so is the need for classic intelligence gathering on enemies. We've had to redefine who the enemy is—and where he is."

"And the effect of that change on Mossad?" I said, pushing him to get to the point. I knew all that.

"Dagan says he wants to turn Mossad into a more operational body. Redefine Tsiach." The acronym stood for *Tsiyun yediot hiyuniot*, indicating the vital information priorities historically determined by Aman, Israeli's military intelligence. Benny said Dagan wanted to take advantage of Israel's known, and many more unknown, successes in recruiting human assets and informers and concentrate on three major targets: Arab and Palestinian terrorism, Islamic fundamentalism, and intelligence gathering on hostile forces' armament with nuclear, chemical, and biological weapons.

"So you are getting de-emphasized," I said succinctly.

"Probably," said Benny with a sigh. "But I'm not the issue

here. It's the importance of Tevel that's being questioned." By *Tevel* Benny was referring to the Mossad's former name for the now-renamed foreign-relations wing, responsible for liaison with foreign services among other clandestine activities.

"Is he breaking it up?" I found that hard to believe, given the wing's tremendous achievements, even though most of them were unknown to the public. Dagan was thought to scorn introspection, but encourage originality.

Benny shook his head. "No, but he made structural changes. The budget's been reduced and the resources for the research division and Tevel have been limited. Now we're divided into two 'directorates,' as he's calling them. The 'operational' one is responsible for all operational wings, divisions, departments, and units, such as Tsomet, Neviot, Tevel, Kesaria, Intelligence, and technological units. The other one is the 'general staff/head-quarters,' which runs everything else—strategic planning, human resources, internal security, logistics, communications, computers, counterintelligence, and so forth."

I remembered that Kesaria, after the old Roman city known in English as Caesarea, was in charge of operations and included an assassinations unit. *Kidon* was Hebrew for bayonet. Kesaria handles the "combatants," a euphemism for Israeli spies, Mossad employees who assume different identities to penetrate hostile Arab countries. Tsomet, from the Hebrew word for *junction*, was the main intelligence-gathering division, engaging "case officers"—KATSA, in its Hebrew acronym. It also controlled and handled non-Israeli agents on the Mossad payroll as "independent contractors." Neviot's agents infiltrated buildings and communication centers to install video and other digital listening and monitoring devices.

"Neviot," I said absentmindedly.

Benny brought me back from my silent reminiscing. "It needs a shake-up too, I suppose," he said. "You remember what happened in ninety-eight."

"Remind me."

"I can't believe you don't remember. On February 19, an agent from Neviot was caught in Switzerland trying to install surveillance equipment in an apartment building. It was in Bern, a building that contained the home office of a Hezbollah supporter. Anyway, the operation was botched when the neighbors got suspicious—strangers carrying suitcases into the building, et cetera. Some of our men got away, but one was caught and tried. Israel had to apologize. It was a complete humiliation, but if that wasn't bad enough, nine months later there was another fiasco. Two agents were caught spying on a military base in Cyprus where Russian-made S-300 missiles were to be deployed. The Cyprus government accused Israel of spying for the Turks, their archenemies, since the missiles were deployed aiming at Turkey. The Cypriots accused the Turks of spying on their defense plan. The Turks, according to the Cyprus government, wanted to know how Cyprus would defend itself in case the Turks decided to resolve the Cyprus problems between the local Turks and Greeks by walking onto the scene with their tanks and artillery."

"Yeah, I read about it in the paper. I was long out of the Mossad. But that's ancient history. What does it have to do with what you're talking about now?"

"He wants to avoid debacles like that. That means changing things around—and that's where it hurts."

"Does anything personally impact you?"

"It affects everybody. But it's all under the surface, because no one knows what's going to happen. There's an atmosphere of suspicion—who'll be promoted and who'll be passed over, whose department will be downsized. That's unhealthy in any organization, and particularly for us. Complete confidence and trust among the employees are an absolute must, because human lives are at stake. For us, internal rifts could be devastating."

"What's happened so far?"

"Several heads of divisions and units, and at least as many department heads resigned, and many line personnel."

"And you oppose it?"

"I think it's OK to make the changes and make Mossad more operational. But cutting our budget or ignoring our activities isn't helping that goal."

"I hope you're not planning to resign as well," I said. I knew Mossad was Benny's heart and soul.

"I haven't made any plans yet, but . . . I heard Dagan was saying that our unit doing political research is redundant. He thinks through the narrow prism of operational needs, and concluded that our foreign-relations wing isn't vital in supporting operations, and the political-research unit's role is secondary at best. He wants to downgrade us to a division and limit our intelligence-gathering activities."

"I'm sure he knows about your reputation and the benefits you bring from your close relationship with other intelligence organizations. Anyway, he must have his reasons."

"I hope so," said Benny. "You have to hope reality and good sense will prevail." A glimmer of his usual optimism was returning. "All he has to do is to go to the next prime-ministerial meeting on Israel's national security, and have to listen to Aman's military intelligence without having his own estimate, based on his own intelligence gathering. He'll be tacitly yielding to Aman seniority." Benny smiled. "In these meetings, Mossad, Aman, and SHABACH, the internal security service, present their opinions. Believe me, after the first session as a passive listener, he'll change his mind. There are no shortcuts here."

"To be the devil's advocate," I said, "even given the fact that your wing is the very best in what you're doing, what's wrong with increasing operational capabilities?"

"Dan, the intelligence-gathering world from human sources isn't limited to James Bond–like operations. You know that as well as I do. There is all the tedious work of identifying sources and recruiting them, with or without their knowledge. True, break-ins and eliminating rivals are vital elements of 'operations,' but only relatively small ones. We're less interested in Jordan and Egypt since the peace agreements. We've got enemies far from our borders, hosted by governments that ask no questions. To confront all that, you really need carefully planned operations."

"But Benny, don't you think you'd be better off using local intelligence services? Let's take for example friendly nations like Thailand or India, which are engaged in a daily battle against terrorists surreptitiously using their territories. You can send five case officers there, or even ten. They don't speak the local languages and have no local authority. So not only do they have to identify terrorists plotting against Israel, but at the same time they need to protect their backs from the wrath of the local governments that don't particularly like agents of foreign countries infringing on their sovereignty and playing cops and robbers on their land. Wouldn't it be simpler to cooperate with the domestic intelligence services and send just one or two case officers for liaison, and to inspect and taste the fruit that they're picking off their own trees and offering us?"

"Dan, that's my quibble with Dagan. The marketplace for terrorist-related intelligence is becoming crowded. Now we compete for the same information with the big guys. Why do you think I looked to the U.S. to join forces in Giverny? In order to survive in the newly created marketplace we need goods to trade with. Either we develop them independently or hook up with the bigger folks to broaden our capabilities."

Now the coin had dropped into the slot. I realized that there was another reason why Benny was seeking pointed cooperation in combating terror financing between his wing at Mossad and the CIA. A successful cooperation could give Benny a winning card in his efforts to keep his wing's central role, not to mention his own job.

"Dan, we must continue to regard as important the gathering of intelligence from sources you can identify, verify, and communicate with. That means operational capability. But maintaining our close contacts with foreign intelligence services is just as important, because of the volume. No operation brings us as much as a good contact with a foreign intelligence service.

"But your foreign-liaison activities buy secondhand or recycled intelligence that's always neutered to disguise its source. Foreign services trade or sell you stuff without a 'certificate of origin or authenticity.' You don't know the value of it. Foreign intelligence services aren't going to tell you how they obtained the information and from whom. It could be sanitized to protect sources—or worse, it could be disinformation. Anyway, the traded information is not of operational nature, but in the form of disseminated intelligence reports identified as such.

"That's one of the reasons Dagan wants raw intelligence harvested by our agents, not purchased in the marketplace," said Benny. "Therefore, we treat the information we receive through barter accordingly. Most of the time we use it as a lead, and nothing else. We never make a recommendation, or worse, plan an operation, based solely on that type of information. You know what happens in the end. Such an operation will take twice the time, will cost twice than what your plan said it would and, in the best-case scenario, will yield half of what we need. But," he concluded with a sigh, "these are my troubles, not yours. You said you wanted something?"

"Yes, your help with Iran. Can you run the name Bahman Hossein Rashtian and see what you can find in your database?"

"Is that all?" Benny knew me too well.

"Nope."

"Is the next request off the record?"

"Off the record, for now."

"Why?"

"I'm just checking things, and haven't got clearance for the idea yet. I'm developing a conviction that to crack this case we need to employ human intelligence, and I've got some ideas on that."

"And you say that you haven't asked the Agency about it yet?"

"Not yet, but I will very soon. They'll never answer anything without a gazillion procedures. Anyway, you heard during our conference a hint that they had lost their permanent station in Iran."

"How will human intelligence in that particular case help?" asked Benny. "And where?"

"I had some talks with the NSA. Even with all their gadgets

and sophistication, their help is potentially limited. Remember what Alex, our Mossad Academy instructor, said about recruiting human sources. 'Basically there are three ways to recruit an "asset"—a human source. Do it when your source is outside your target country, and you have a very limited selection to choose from, or you can travel to the lion's den and pick your prey. The third category are people who travel out for brief periods, to conferences, for example. They are often desirable targets.' In our case, the people with access to the information we want don't travel. We have to go to them. It's the logical thing to do. Computer surveillance and hacking are good, but nothing can substitute for personal presence."

Benny didn't answer at once. He just looked at me pensively, and said, "I think so too, hence my presentation at the conference. I think you should be ready to answer questions regarding the intelligence rationale of doing it. Show a raw plan, the risks, the probabilities, and the potential hunting field to recruit sources. Let's say that we have our respective agencies' consent to go ahead. Then what? Even after careful planning and logistics, we must have a head start while we are still here."

"Meaning?"

"Meaning that the first task will be to identify potential local sources before commencing with recruiting efforts. That takes time. But sending an agent cold turkey to Iran without preparatory groundwork will not only take much more time, it's significantly riskier."

"Granted," I said. "So we've identified potential targets of recruitment. Now we need to move in. Debriefing exiled Iranians in Europe is good, but your selection is limited, and you never know who you're talking to and what the guy's doing in Europe to begin with. Could be dangerous. Maybe he's after you to bilk you, or worse, to entrap you."

"Dan, bear in mind that with the kind of Iranian police supervision on every citizen and certainly on visiting foreigners, it's going to be difficult to return in one piece, even if we succeed in the intelligence-gathering effort. Unless there's a risk-free, maverick plan that will yield immediate results, I think we should concentrate on sources outside Iran."

"I agree," I said. "But doing nothing will get no results as well. I'm raising the issue so we can brainstorm the option and start looking for potential direction and resources. That's what I mean when I say penetration is unavoidable. Obviously, we need to jump through many hoops to get initial approvals and then do substantial preparatory work."

"Still, it's a suicide mission," said Benny. "If we're pressed for time."

I knew Benny wasn't hyping things, but I thought of the half-full glass. "The fact that twenty years have passed could, in an odd way, make it easier in some security aspects. The time passed makes it less risky."

"Dan, these people suspect even their own shadows. I hear that the diet in the Iranian prisons isn't something you would ask for a second serving of, even if you're very hungry. I don't even mention the Iranian treatment of spies or the thickness of the noose."

"Benny, if you don't want to go hunting, don't complain if we eat the catch without even offering you a dry bone. It's not as if we're gonna board a plane tomorrow or cross the border on a camel or a mule. If action is planned for next year, today is the time to talk about it."

"Dan, talk to me when you have something on your plate other than the urge to succeed."

He had been tough, but not unreasonable, and he hadn't dismissed my ideas out of hand.

I returned to the safe apartment. Nicole gave me that look reserved for a husband coming in late at night with a lipstick stain on his collar. "Where have you been?"

I shrugged. The days I'd had to report to anyone but my boss about my movements had passed the minute the judge signed the divorce decree. That was a long time ago, but sometimes it felt as though it were just last week.

"We've got results from Dr. Feldman at the NSA. He received the Agency's formal request for assistance, and here are the initial results."

Nicole held a one-page document. "We may be on to something," she said cautiously, and read from the document:

Bahman Hossein Rashtian, forty-four, is a senior officer of Department 81, an ultrasecret unit of Iranian security services in Tehran. He's a Shiite Muslim and a fanatic follower of Ayatollah Khomeini's doctrines. Soon after the Islamic Revolution in 1979, the Iranian ayatollah in charge of state security started Department 81 for several covert purposes, including training and sending agents to infiltrate the United States. Further information shall be provided as additional search is refined.

"So is Department 81 the enigmatic Atashbon?" I wondered.

"Could be," said Nicole. "Or maybe Department 81 was a provisional name indicating the year it was started? But no, not if it was started soon after the '79 Revolution. It's all guesswork."

I called Casey Bauer on the secure phone and reported the finding. "I've also asked Benny Friedman to run a check on that name. Can I share the information I've just received on Rashtian with Benny?"

Casey thought for a moment. "Yes, you may, but need I mention that you shouldn't disclose who provided us with the information?"

"No need. I know the rules."

I called Benny. "Are you still in Paris?"

"Yes, what's up?" Judging from his tone, he was no longer in a bad mood.

"I need to talk to you."

"Meet me in one hour at Café Rosebud, 11 rue Delambre, in the 14th arrondissement."

"Another fancy place?"

"Not at all. In fact, it's where Simone de Beauvoir and Jean-Paul Sartre escaped to for private conversations."

As I walked into the café, Benny was sipping coffee. We sat in the corner. "Anything new on Rashtian?"

"Yes, as a matter of fact, I was about to call you about that."

"Then tell me," I suggested.

"Bahman Hossein Rashtian is an Iranian security-services officer. We've information showing he was orchestrating penetration of his agents into the U.S. by using false identities stolen from young American tourists."

"Department 81," I muttered.

"So you already know," said Benny.

"I know very little about that," I conceded. "This is a big hunch based on small intelligence."

"Go ahead," said Benny eagerly.

"I believe that unsuspecting Americans were either lured into Tehran or were visiting neighboring states when their passports and other identification documents were taken."

"Right," said Benny, picking up the information flow. "And then they were videotaped by Bahman Hossein Rashtian's interrogators telling their life stories and giving minute details about their families, friends, places of study, and work. Thereafter, they were probably executed and buried in unmarked graves."

"So you support my speculation?" I asked curiously.

Benny nodded.

"That son of a bitch," I mumbled. "I know you'll never answer me in a million years, but just in case, how did you establish that?"

"Refugee interrogation," said Benny curtly. He didn't add other information, and I knew I shouldn't press the issue. He had told me what he could. Obviously, I wanted to know if he had any information on Rashtian's trained agents, and whether they were in fact successful in infiltrating the U.S., and why they were planted there in the first place. But knowing Benny, I was certain that if he had that information, he'd trade it with the CIA in exchange for information that Israel needed. The information was vital. Sleeper cells tend to wake up at one point and carry out a mission. It could be financial fraud, but more likely something more ominous and heinous than just stealing money. These days the writing was on the wall, and it said *terror*. When, where, and how? I had no clue, but I felt the urgency to find out.

I returned to the safe apartment and sent an encrypted message to Casey Bauer. Hours later a response came through the system: "Dan, I'm arriving in Paris tomorrow afternoon with Casey Bauer. Bob Holliday."

"Before they come, I think we need something more solid than the hunches and rumors we have," said Nicole.

"Like what?"

"Like stronger evidence on the identity of the Chameleon."

I stopped myself from asking her if she was nuts. The U.S. had been trying to find him for over twenty years, and now she wanted to solve the mystery in a day? Instead, I kept silent for a few minutes.

Then I stood up, grabbed my head with both hands, and exclaimed, "Of course. I think we can try that avenue."

"What avenue?

"We've got the Chameleon's fingerprints. I lifted them off his cup in Australia."

"No, you have the prints of one Herbert Goldman," she said defiantly.

"We already went over this," I said, without losing my temper. "The guy in Australia is the Chameleon. I have it on authority from Benny, and we've got his prints."

"And you're going to match them against what?" asked Nicole. I was at first defensive, but it was a valid question.

"I take it that the FBI had determined that the Chameleon wasn't Albert Ward, because they couldn't establish a match of the prints I lifted at the hospital with any prints in their database, including Ward's. So I suspect there's no point in asking them the same question again."

"And we suspect he isn't Herbert Goldman either, because his wife told that to the FBI," said Nicole.

"Right. I tend to believe her because she was the one to expose him in the first place. Why would she lie here?" I asked.

"So we're back at square one. Against what database are you going to match the prints you lifted?" Nicole demanded.

"The Iranians'," I snapped, without having any reason or basis to support what I'd said, nor any feasible plan on how to achieve it.

"Well," said Nicole. "We can ask NSA to do that." If she was joking, it didn't sound like she was. And when no cynical smile followed, I became convinced that I wasn't the only daydreamer in the room. There were officially two of us.

I called Dr. Ted Feldman in Menwith Hill, using the secure phone.

"Can you match fingerprints against the Iranian security service's database?"

His response was noncommittal. "Send me what you have. Make sure we receive it through your agency's liaison office, and we'll see what we can do."

"I'll ask the FBI to send you the samples I gave them. That, together with samples the Australian Federal Police took and sent separately."

"That's even better."

The following evening, Casey Bauer walked into the safe apartment with Bob Holliday.

"Any answer on the prints yet?" I asked Nicole, hoping to give my new boss a welcome gift.

"Let me check," said Nicole and went to the adjacent communication room. Ten minutes later she returned with a computer printout. "It's from the FBI," she said. "The encrypted message just came in."

She read the summary at the top of the page: "The prints received from Dan Gordon, as well as those received directly from the Australian Police, matched the prints received yesterday from NSA marked as taken from Kourosh Alireza Farhadi,

DOB August 19, 1960. All three sets of prints match each other. They were all taken from the same person."

"That's great!" said Casey, in an unexpected burst of joy. "Read out the whole thing!"

"That part of the report came from NSA through Langley," said Nicole, and read the text. "Top Secret/Eyes Only/Sensitive Compartmented Information." She raised her eyes and said, "Before any of you read this report, you must sign a Classified Information Nondisclosure Agreement, a Standard Form 312." She handed us copies.

I read the form. In it I acknowledged that I was aware that the unauthorized disclosure of classified information by me could cause irreparable injury to the United States or could be used to advantage by a foreign nation, and that I would never divulge classified information to an unauthorized person. I further acknowledged that I would never divulge classified information unless I had officially verified that the recipient was authorized by the United States to receive it. Additionally, I agreed that, were I to be uncertain about the classification status of information, I needed to confirm from an authorized official that the information was unclassified before I could disclose it.

I signed. So did the others.

Nicole continued reading it. "This report is based on documents contained in Farhadi's file, including a limited number of recently dated reports he had submitted."

Farhadi's file? Did NSA experts hack the Iranian security service's computer? My level of appreciation for Dr. Feldman and his team skyrocketed.

Nicole continued reading. "Please note that the most recent report Farhadi filed in Tehran was on December 13, 2003."

"Guys, look at the date," I intervened. "I saw the Chameleon in a Sydney hospital bed on August 17, 2004. Based on what we just heard, and provided that all the reports were kept in one place and intercepted by NSA, it could mean that the Chameleon was either infrequent in his reports to Tehran, or that he simply decided he had done enough for

Tehran, and now it was time to take care of himself. I guess from now on I'll have to use his real name of Farhadi," I said in feigned sorrow.

"Not so fast," said Holliday, making sure he retained command. "This isn't the end of it. He might have used additional identities, so for now, let's stick to the name Chameleon. Let Nicole read out the entire report, so we can all have it at the same time," he added, realizing how eager we all were. "Maybe there's an answer to that in the narrative."

Nicole read on:

Kourosh Alireza Farhadi, an ethnic Iranian, was born in Tabriz, in northern Iran, on August 9, 1953. His father, Ghorbanali, was a successful businessman in the rug trade; Kourosh Alireza Farhadi's mother, Fariba, was a homemaker. Kourosh had two siblings, Vahraz and Rad, born 1957 and 1959, respectively. In September 1959 Kourosh was sent to live with his paternal grandparents in Tehran so that he could study at the American School. One year after his graduation in 1978, Kourosh was drafted to join Department 81.

Nicole folded the paper and shredded it, but held on to the three additional pages of the report.

"Aha, we're getting closer to him," I said, realizing that this was independent confirmation of the info Benny had given me.

"And how exactly do you find Farhadi?" asked Bauer.

It was time to reclaim my lost face and my smeared reputation.

"At the time, I reported from Australia that I had found the Chameleon in a hospital bed. But I was called on the carpet by David when he got an FBI report refuting my finding. The truth of the matter is that I didn't make a mistake in identifying the Chameleon in the first place. I had found the right guy. The person I saw in Australia was the Chameleon," I said, and picked up the pages. "Now, now we have his name—Kourosh Alireza Farhadi. The FBI must have compared the fingerprints they had in their database of the genuine Albert Ward with the prints of the guy in the hospital bed."

"You mean the FBI's lab goofed?" asked Casey. "I'm lost here. And you still say you got the right Albert C. Ward III?" Casey was a very straightforward guy. He'd been in this business too long to be embarrassed when he didn't understand something. He wasn't the kind of man who saw asking questions as a sign of weakness, and I liked that about him.

"No, the FBI lab was right. The prints didn't match, because they were taken from two different people. When you steal the identity of a person, you can take almost everything he has, but not his fingerprints. The perpetrator of the eleven fraud cases was never Albert C. Ward III to begin with. That's why the prints didn't match—because they were compared with the prints of Albert C. Ward, an innocent young American. The fundamental reason that the FBI failed to make the connection is simple. He was an unremarkable young man who had no family to complain when he went missing, and unfortunately, there are an awful lot out there like him. The Iranian imposter apparently didn't use the Ward alias in committing any of the banking scams. The Iranian devised a double-tier buffer. First, steal the identity of Albert C. Ward. Then assume another alias to carry out the scam. That way, there's no reason for the FBI to know about him in the first place. But based on what we just heard, the identity of Albert C. Ward III was stolen and adopted by an imposter who conned banks using one or more stolen identities. The real Albert C. Ward III is still missing, probably dead in Iran, and so are the other individuals whose passports and identities were stolen by that imposter, or else by someone associated with him." I paused. "We should also leave the door open to the possibility that there could be a few imposters." There was silence in the room.

I continued. "This report confirms that I actually saw the Chameleon in Sydney. So instead of faded pictures from the late 1970s of people who aren't the Chameleon, we've got a positive identification and a recent location for him."

Casey was the first to react. "He may have slipped away from Australia, and he isn't stupid enough to return to the U.S. So where the hell is the slippery bastard?" I noticed he had a habit of clenching his jaw tightly when he was thinking intently about something.

"He could be back in Iran. Or the clue to where he is is there," I suggested.

"Hold on," said Nicole, breaking her silence. "There's an important item in the Chameleon's résumé. He graduated from the American School in Tehran."

"And why is it that significant?" asked Bauer, clearly engrossed in the affair.

"Because Iranian intelligence uses only ethnic Iranians who strictly adhere to the Ayatollah's interpretation of Islam. That means studying in their religious schools and undergoing the necessary indoctrination to guarantee blind loyalty. And here we see an agent who spent twelve years in the educational institute of the Great Satan, and still he was recruited for a sensitive assignment."

"So you could conclude that he was recruited not in spite of his American education, but probably because of it," I said. "After all he was assigned to perpetrate fraud in the U.S."

"We don't know that his mission was limited to defrauding banks," said Casey.

"I'm willing to bet those SOBs would be more ambitious than that."

"I wonder whether there could be additional graduates of the Tehran American School in Department 81," said Bob Holliday, touching his mustache.

"Well, first we discover that Rashtian recruited a team of agents to be infiltrated into the U.S.," said Casey. "Then at the same time we've got a shitload of unsolved cases of stolen identities of young Americans, and at least one of them ended up with a strong Iranian connection. Next we hear from NSA that Kourosh Alireza Farhadi, who was one of Rashtian's team, was a graduate of the American School in Tehran." He shook his head. "There's too much of a coincidence here. We've got to investigate if all other members of Rashtian's team were also graduates of that school."

"I need to set up another meeting with Benny Friedman," concluded Casey Bauer. "It may be time to talk shop." Casey knew when we'd gone as far as we could with our resources and was decisive when it came to taking additional action. He wasn't the type to second-guess himself.

As they both left, leaving me and Nicole to clean up the mess, she asked, "How do we find out if additional ethnic Iranians, graduates of the American School, were also recruited?"

"I have an idea that I need to check first." I locked myself in my room with my notebook computer. I emerged two hours later. Nicole was stretched on the couch reading a newspaper.

"Tell me what you think about this. I focused first on how to discover the individuals Iran sent to the U.S. Once we do that, we can move on to identifying their mission."

"Go on," she said, putting the paper down.

"If we follow the theory that Iran has planted a sleeper cell in the United States, then let's assume that what Casey Bauer suggested is true: Department 81 enlisted a whole bunch of young Iranian men who had two things in common—they were all ethnic Iranians, and they were graduates of the Tehran American School."

"OK."

"I did some research. Between 1950 and 1979 the American population in Tehran grew with the influx of many American companies to Iran, mostly connected to aeronautical, engineering, and oil businesses. Bear in mind that during that period Iran was a pleasant and hospitable place for Westerners to live, so the foreign employees brought along their families. The Tehran American School had almost two thousand students and was one of the largest American schools outside the United States. About a third of the school's students were Iranians whose families wanted them to have an American education and perfect command of English—families that could afford the hefty tuition."

"So if you were to follow that theory, the single most

important common denominator of all of the ethnic-Iranian graduates was their perfect command of American English," said Nicole.

"Exactly. After spending twelve, and sometimes fifteen years, if you count preschool classes, speaking and studying in English from American teachers, and with all your friends speaking American English to you, there's no wonder that all graduates spoke English at the same level as first-generation American students in Chicago or in San Diego do."

"Sounds right," said Nicole. "That characteristic must have proven to be invaluable for the Iranians. But why stop at stealing money from U.S. banks and investors? Is money all they cared about? What about old-fashioned espionage or modern-era terrorism?"

"I'm wondering about that too," I conceded. "It's more likely that if the Iranians picked up that idea, as the NSA report and Casey suggested, these young men were sent to the United States as Iranian undercover sleeper agents also to gather information or engage in sabotage when the order came from Tehran."

"Now I see how it all falls into place," said Nicole. "We may have two different cases here. We've got the case of the Chameleon and company, the money thieves as part of the Iranian government's strategic decision to siphon money from the United States. And we may have a case of Iranian sleeper cells in the U.S. waiting for an order to sabotage, or what have you. These two separate issues may or may not be related."

"Think about that," I said. "This is more than just a theory, if we adopt the idea that the Chameleon wasn't the sole perpetrator of the fraud, and that there were others, as the NSA report suggested. That theory, if substantiated, will deal another blow to the FBI's sole-perpetrator theory."

"We have no proof yet, just a presumption. And ours is as good as the FBI's," said Nicole, cooling off my enthusiasm. "We know that Kourosh Alireza Farhadi, a graduate of the American School, was a member of Department 81. But we don't know that other members of that department were also graduates of that school."

I wasn't deterred. "I agree. But let's move on in developing our theory. Let's assume for the moment that ethnic Iranians drafted by Rashtian to Department 81 were graduates of the American School intended for surreptitious operations within the U.S. We know that it was very difficult or actually impossible after 1979 to get U.S. visas on Iranian passports. Once the U.S. was declared an enemy, Iran needed an easy way to infiltrate them by getting agents into the U.S. The Iranians had to give their agents travel documents to make their stay in the U.S. look legal, so just sneaking them across the border was probably not an option."

Nicole contemplated this. "Of course, they could have used the visa stamps they captured at the embassy in Tehran, but in all likelihood these stamps were kept as souvenirs by the mob, or just thrown into the fire."

"Nicole, if what NSA tells us about Department 81 checks out, then it's quite possible that to this day there are Iranian sleeper cells in the U.S. waiting for an order to 'wake up.' That could come with instructions to sabotage American industry, shopping centers, power plants, airlines, trains. There could be orders to plant hazardous chemicals in areas likely to create panic and uncertainty—whatever you can imagine."

"I just said that," she said.

"But on the other hand, let's not forget we're building theories here, so let's get to work. We need facts to support them." Now it was the lawyer in me speaking. "We're looking for a group of Iranian graduates of the American School in Tehran. The school was shut down in January 1979 immediately after the Islamic Revolution, when the embassy finally admitted that something unusual was going on. The dependents were evacuated in early December just before Muharram, the first month of the Islamic calendar. So the youngest of the graduates must have been born around 1961. If we identify the Iranian graduates, we'll have something to start working on."

"If they graduated at eighteen," Nicole said, once again as meticulous as possible. "The upper perimeter is too thin. We should assume that some graduated at sixteen or seventeen; therefore their dates of birth could be 1962 or 1963. They would now be in their early forties. We should also look at the possibility that older alumni were used, a few years after their graduation. Let's put the mark on 1950 as year of birth and 1968 as year of graduation."

"Fine," I said. "But bear in mind that we've just increased the number of the potential members of the target group." I got up to open the window shade. "It's too dark in here."

"OK, since we've got a pool of fifty to one hundred graduates each year and a twelve-year range, that means that we've got to identify a group of twelve hundred to twenty-four hundred people," Nicole said.

"No, only about half, or perhaps a little more," I said. "The school was coed. I'd suspect that all the perpetrators were males."

"I suppose we can assume that," she said. "OK. Then we are left with approximately six to twelve hundred people, possibly all men. How do we identify them? The American School in Tehran no longer exists, but I'm sure there are records somewhere with a list of the students." Nicole paused for a moment and continued. "We can check that with the Office of Overseas Schools at the State Department. I'll place an inquiry."

A day later, Nicole logged into a remote site and downloaded an encrypted file.

"Here it is," she said. "The complete list of students who attended the school in the years 1960 through 1979. They didn't have records of students enrolled from 1954, the year the school was started, through 1959. But I think we've got more than what we currently need."

She projected the computer-screen image onto the opposite wall. It was a database sorted alphabetically, with 6,015 records. Each line included the student's first and last names, name of father or legal guardian, date of birth, sex, Social Security or other national identification number, address, year enrolled, and year left or graduated.

"That's fantastic," I said. "We could sort out the Iranian ethnics."

"How?" Nicole gave me a confused look.

"Iranians don't usually have American Social Security numbers."

"Nor would most other non-American students," she said. "There were many other foreigners in the school, children of non-American expats working for American and European companies such as Westinghouse, Phillips, or Standard Oil, or at their country's embassy."

I wasn't deterred. "I know that. But the lack of a Social Security number almost certainly flags out a non-American. That'd eliminate many from the list."

"I agree," she said. "Although there could be instances where an ethnic Iranian had an SSN because he was born in the U.S., say, or lived in the U.S. while his parents were diplomats or working there, if his parents applied for one."

"True," I conceded. "We'll simply have to work one by one."

With a few clicks on her laptop computer Nicole isolated all names that didn't specify an American SSN. From that shorter list, she eliminated all females. "OK," she said. "We now have 978 names of males who don't have SSNs listed."

I quickly looked at the list. Approximately a third had typical European names, as did their fathers. "Let's get them off the list too, just for now," I suggested. An hour later we had narrowed down the list to 294 names.

"What do you suggest we do now?" Nicole asked. "We're done with the easy part. Now how do we isolate from the list ethnic Iranians to be investigated, twenty years after they were recruited, without going to Iran?"

"Then go to Iran," I said. "Or better yet, ask your people in Iran to help us out. After all, this isn't guarded military or nuclear information. We're talking about a bunch of Iranian civilians."

"Too risky," said Nicole. "Some of the graduates are now potential suspects under our new theory, but we don't know which ones. We can make benign-sounding inquiries and hit on some of them. That will immediately trigger the attention of the Iranian security agencies, who'll wonder why people are asking questions about these men."

"Even with a perfect legend?" I asked.

"Making inquiries about one suspected individual could be a coincidence, but asking about two or three?"

"I agree that if we limit our inquiries to the suspected group, it will arouse suspicion. But we can broaden the inquiries to include women as well. That might lessen the suspicions." I paused for a moment and continued. "You've just given me an idea. We should have one of the alumni do the inquiries, ideally unwittingly. The end result will be a list of names of the ethnic-Iranian graduates provided by an innocent alumnus or alumna who, even if interrogated, will not be able to show any hidden agenda for the inquiries, just a 'legitimate' one. That person can be remotely controlled by your people in Tehran."

Nicole was quiet for a minute. "I think it's a good idea, but I'm afraid it can't be managed by our people in Iran."

"What does that mean? How can something so simple be beyond the reach of the omnipotent CIA?"

She hesitated. "We're a little short of assets in Iran these days, as I'm sure you heard during the Giverny conference. It's all been since the debacle of—" She stopped abruptly.

I raised my head. "What are you talking about?"

"A disaster," she said.

"Can you tell me what happened?"

"Well, the Iranians know, so I guess there shouldn't be any reason for you not to know. An officer at Langley mistakenly sent an encrypted secret data flow to one of the Iranian agents in the CIA's foreign-asset network directly to his high-speed personal communications device. The Iranian who received the download was a double agent. He immediately turned the data over to his handler at VEVAK—the Ministry of Intelligence and Security, the feared security police—and in no time most of our network in Iran collapsed. Several of our Iranian assets were arrested and jailed, and we still don't know what happened to some of the others. That left us virtually blind in Iran."

"My god," I said.

She nodded grimly. "Since then, and until we regroup, Iran is regarded as 'denied' territory for us. We've got no official station inside Iran and, insofar as human intelligence is concerned, until we redeploy and recruit new assets, we depend on sources outside that country."

"What about SDLure?" I asked. "I remember hearing from my Mossad buddies, years after I left, about the CIA successfully recruiting top Iranian government officials."

"Gone with the revolution. The mob discovered their names at the U.S. Embassy. SDLure/1 was Abolhassan Bani-Sadr, the first post–Islamic Revolution president. He fled the country. Another former prime minister, Mehdi Bazargan, was executed. And now this."

"On the bright side, for now we don't have to limit our search to Iran. Some of our sources could also be in the U.S.," I said.

"What do you mean?"

"Well, we're communicating with alums. The American Overseas Schools in China, Iran, and elsewhere created a special bond and affinity among their students, because they weren't just places of study, but also cultural and social centers for the children and their families. I'm sure if we interview the American alumni, we can cross-reference everybody in each of the classes. That will do, at least in the beginning."

"Do they have alumni associations?"

"I found several links. They keep photos, yearbooks, and other material that will make our job less tedious than we think. We'd still need to interview hundreds," I said, but she had already accepted the task.

"Maybe we'll get lucky and find information on more than one student from one alumnus or alumna."

We attached the list of all students without listed Social Security numbers to an encrypted file and sent it back to the State Department, asking them to locate any available information on the individuals on the list.

"So we're done," Nicole said breezily. "What should we do now?" There still wasn't a hint of *what do you suggest we do for the rest of the evening?* Thus far she hadn't used anything but coolly professional talk in our interactions. This was the most casual she'd been.

"Dinner?" asked Nicole, looking at me curiously. All of a sudden there was a personal tone to her question. Did that blonde iceberg have a personal life? Maybe there was lava brewing underneath the cold facade. I wasn't going to explore it, at least not yet. We went out to a nearby corner bistro to have dinner.

Still at the restaurant an hour later, I had a glass of 1990 Château Pétrus Merlot in my hand and was feeling pensive. "We shouldn't rule out the possibility that new aliases have been substituted for the ones adopted twenty-five years ago."

Nicole frowned. "Do I understand you correctly? Instead of looking for the Chameleon in a group of a few hundred graduates of the American School in Tehran, we'll be looking for an unknown number of people in a U.S. population of nearly three hundred million where, on an average day, more than one million people enter the United States legally and thousands more enter illegally?"

"I understand where you're coming from," I said, keeping calm. "But it's not our job to look for them in the U.S. We've got an assignment to find the Chameleon and whoever his comrades are. Now, I hope we get to solve the mystery of whether there are additional members of Department 81 in the U.S., but it's the FBI counterintelligence and counterterrorism sections' problem, not ours." I was starting to realize that maybe Nicole enjoyed being the sounding board for my crazy ideas. Her challenging questions were actually stimulants in what had become our mutual brainstorming.

As they placed our platters in front of us—juicy steak frites for me, buttered mussels for her—my mobile phone vibrated.

I glanced at its display. "There's a communication waiting for us at the apartment."

"It can wait," said Nicole, and I couldn't have agreed more.

CHAPTER FIFTEEN

When we'd finished our well-deserved dinner, we returned to the safe apartment. Nicole went to the communication room and minutes later handed me a memo from the State Department. It read, "We have cross-referenced all student names without listed SSNs against other databases. The number of individuals matching the criteria you set brought down the number of students whose whereabouts are unknown to thirty-four." The list was attached.

I quickly ran my eyes down the list. "We got him," I said slowly and decisively. Number twenty-one on the list was Kourosh Alireza Farhadi, an ethnic Iranian born in Tabriz, in northern Iran, on August 19, 1960. The short bio included additional background information. There were also passport-type photos of all but three men included in the list.

With mounting excitement, I inspected the photos. I didn't waste any time. In a photo marked as Kourosh Alireza Farhadi, I saw the Chameleon looking at me. I pulled out the photo of Albert C. Ward that I had received from his school's principal, and compared the two. Both showed their subject at eighteen. But there was no doubt that they were of two different people. I didn't have a photo of Kourosh Alireza Farhadi from when he assumed Ward's identity, or later, when he impersonated Herbert Goldman. But I was already convinced that Farhadi was Goldman too. I had identified the Chameleon.

"Nicole!" I cried, startling her. "We found him. Here's the bastard. We've got the evidence."

Nicole looked at the pictures. "Which one is he?"

"That's the one." I pointed at Farhadi's photo. "I can identify him anywhere. He's in my dreams."

Nicole wasn't budging until she saw some hard evidence. "We need a positive ID. Do you want to repeat the humiliation in Sydney?"

"What humiliation?" I responded. "I was right and they were wrong. Now the FBI owes me an apology. Big-time."

Nicole only raised an eyebrow.

Ice must run through icy liquid in her veins, I thought.

She inspected the photo, read the State Department's note, and said, "Why don't we e-mail the photo to Peter Maxwell in Sydney? He also met Goldman. Let's see what he thinks."

"Fine by me," I said. Her obsession with double-checking everything was starting to get to me, but there was little I could do. I waited as she went to her laptop and e-mailed the photo to Sydney.

An hour later, as I skimmed the bits of information the State Department file had on the graduates of the American School in Tehran, Nicole walked in from the communication room. "We've got an answer from Peter Maxwell," she said. "He cautiously believes the person they arrested and later hospitalized is the same person shown in the photo taken many years earlier of Kourosh Alireza Farhadi."

"What a surprise," I said drily.

Later, near midnight, a buzz at the apartment intercom heralded the unexpected arrival of Bob Holliday and Casey Bauer.

"Evening," said Bob. "We've got a few more questions."

"Before I answer you, let me bring you up to speed on the recent developments," I said, showing them the State Department report and Maxwell's e-mail.

Bob barely kept his composure when he exclaimed; "Hot damn, that's fantastic! Do you think Kourosh is still in Australia?"

"I'd be surprised if he was," said Nicole. "We now know he wasn't operating alone or independently, so we can safely assume that he has help outside and inside many countries."

"Australia may have become too hot for him," I agreed. "The Australian Federal Police told your office that there are no records showing that either Herbert Goldman or Albert Ward III, or any individual with any of the aliases we knew, had left the country. If we rule out swimming, then Kourosh must have used travel documents using another alias to leave Australia. Nicole has asked the Australian Federal Police for a computerized list of the names of all males leaving Australia during the five-day period after he was released from detention at the hospital.

"We expect to get the list in a few days, but the Australians have already cautioned us that the list would exceed fifty thousand names," I continued. "We'll provide the NSA with an electronic copy and ask them to match the names on the list against their various databases. We'll ask the FBI and the CIA to do the same. I don't have high hopes in that direction, but we must try. Kourosh knew that the U.S. government was after him. So he isn't likely to have used a passport that could be on somebody's watch list."

We all knew what that meant—a stolen passport, one whose theft would have been reported to Interpol, which would have notified police in all 177 or so member countries. Soon enough, border control in almost every country would have its details.

"So by what means do you think Kourosh has left Australia?" asked Casey.

"I tend to think that if he has indeed left, he used a freshly forged passport, one that had never been used," I said. "When you're exiting a country, passport inspection is rather lax. At most, the officer checks if your name appears on a wanted list, or more likely, if you overstayed your visit. So exiting is less of a problem. However, if you use a forged passport to travel, safe entry is the main problem. Therefore, your destination should be a country which you can easily enter, either because the ability of that country's passport control officers to detect forgery is limited, or because Iran can pull strings and get her agents to enter quickly with no questions asked."

"Other than Iran, which countries meet that requirement?" asked Bob.

"Syria," said Casey. "North Korea. A few more."

"Bear in mind that in many countries, particularly in the Third World, a $20 bill can go a long way," I added.

Bob smiled. "I hope you're not doing it." He was thinking about my work for DOJ, while I meant operating outside the rules, any rules.

"There could be a twist here," Nicole suggested. "For example. Kourosh could hold a ticket from Sydney to Italy with a stopover in Jakarta, Indonesia, and Cairo, Egypt. He could leave Australia using a forged passport and be met by an Iranian agent while in transit at the Jakarta airport. The agent would give him another passport to enter Italy, or a new airline ticket from Jakarta directly to Iran. So if an electronic monitoring of his movements is made, the airline computer will show he ended his trip in Jakarta, and searchers will focus their efforts on Indonesia, while in fact he continued his trip to another location such as Iran using a passport with a different name."

"I agree," I said. "I've been down that road myself to avoid FOE—forces of evil. There's no reason why a trained top Iranian agent who's been successfully avoiding the law for more than two decades wouldn't be capable of pulling it off." I shook my head. "I wish I could put my hands on him now!" I clenched my fists in rage.

"Dan, calm down," said Casey. "We want to preserve his ability to talk."

Was he referring to rough encounters I'd had with a few of my targets, who had required a convalescence period before they could be interrogated again? I decided not to raise the issue.

"Of course you do," I said, matter-of-factly, and quickly moved on to change the subject. "He seems to steal money to provide off-the-books slush financing, probably for Iran's web of terror. That makes him a prime target for us. When he's caught, we'll have to wrap him up in cotton wool to make sure he doesn't catch cold, get sick, or anything, so that he talks and lives through a lengthy prison term."

Casey and Bob were getting ready to leave. Bauer turned to us. "Dan and Nicole, we need your full written report, including case summary covering all events that took place before you received the case." He looked at me. "Start from the fraud perpetrated against that South Dakota savings bank in 1985, through your discovery in Australia, your visit to Pakistan, the most recent matching of the prints, and the NSA findings. End it with your recommendations, including suggested cooperation with the Israeli Mossad. Let me see it by Monday, then we'll talk."

"What do you think?" I asked Nicole as soon as Bob and Casey had left.

"I think Casey and Bob like the recent developments. It finally confines our case to a location. I have no idea how NSA got that information, and therefore we can't weigh its credibility."

"Recent developments?" I said. "Are you kidding? This is a major breakthrough. And you really don't know how NSA got it? Come on. Computer hacking perpetrated by a private individual sends him to jail. But when an NSA technician does it, he gets an award. We now have four different sources, with varying credibility, that are independent of one another. They all put the spotlight on Iran."

"Four?"

"Yes, my Pakistani source, Benny's information, the FBI fingerprints report, the State Department's file, and Maxwell's confirmation."

"That's five," said Nicole. "OK, let's see what value these clues carry."

We went back to the drawing board and reviewed most of what we had already learned. "The first clue came when I'd gone to Pakistan and bought information from that sleazy lawyer in Islamabad, Ahmed Khan. He'd told me that Ward was lured into coming to Iran with a promise to pay him $500 a month for three months. In fact, it was a kept promise, because he had actually received that money. When I'd first heard about that amount of money, it had flagged an ulterior motive immediately. Nobody pays a twenty-year-old photographer $500 a month in 1980 dollars for taking some pictures during an archaeological excavation, when most others volunteer their work. Dr. Fischer and Professor Krieger had told us that most of the diggers were either volunteer students working for food and university credits, or two-to-three-dollar-a-day Iranian peasants doing the actual digging," I said.

"And you don't know that the information Khan sold you actually came from Iran. Right?" Nicole pressed. "You said the lawyer was sleazy."

"Right. In fact, all the information he gave me might have come from his associate or relative, Rashid Khan, the bank manager. Ahmed Khan told me that Ward bought Iranian currency, and that there was a deposit exceeding $500 into his bank account, most of it still there. He also said that a successor in interest of the transferring bank, which we know was a center for distributing terror money, later tried to reverse the transfer. So the logical conclusion is that Ahmed Khan, the lawyer, was simply a conduit that Rashid Khan, the corrupt bank manager, used to sell me information, without compromising himself as breaching banking-secrecy law. I tend to cautiously believe it, except the part about the attempted reversal of the deposit at a later stage. That seems bogus." I thought Nicole would be satisfied with that.

"So why do you consider that an independent source of information?"

"Because it doesn't have to come from Iran to be genuine. These events took place before, or immediately after, Ward had left Pakistan. What supports the credibility of these pieces of information is that we learned about bits of them from different and independent sources. Then there's the attempted attack on me in Islamabad, when I was driven in an embassy car just outside the embassy's compound. Benny hinted it was connected to my search for the Chameleon. I've got no way of proving it, but I can't disprove it either."

"The other source of information is the FBI fingerprints report we saw today, with the State Department's photo that Maxwell confirmed to be of Herbert Goldman, formerly known as Kourosh Alireza Farhadi, who at a certain time assumed the identity of Albert Ward—and who is the Chameleon." She seemed to get closer to my way of thinking.

"We don't know if it was an NSA or an FBI work product," I said.

"More likely a combined effort," said Nicole.

"Right. But whatever it is, in some points it matches perfectly with the other sources we have."

"Such as the existence of Department 81," agreed Nicole.

"I tend to give the NSA/FBI report a much higher degree of credibility," I said.

"Why, because it's one of our own?" Her blue eyes were full of skepticism. "Don't fall into that pit. Always question the value and credibility of information." She sounded like some of my instructors at the Mossad Academy, although she was by far more attractive.

"No," I said. "Because of the fingerprint match. Remember, I lifted a set of prints from the Chameleon's cup next to his hospital bed." When I saw Nicole's brows rise again, I quickly added, "I know I'm not a qualified lab technician and might accidentally have contaminated the evidence. But apparently I didn't, because these prints matched the prints the Australian police later obtained independently. Now comes a U.S. intelligence agency, and, through means they don't tell us, it obtains another set of prints that match the two previous sets of prints. You can't get better than that."

"I agree," said Nicole. "Provided NSA got it from some files in Iran. If we can make a case for that, then I'm convinced."

"If you think NSA will tell you that they hacked into an Iranian government database and downloaded the personnel file of Farhadi, then good luck with this one. NSA didn't even confirm its own existence until a few years ago. You know what people used to say that *NSA* stood for—*no such agency*. If you believe that they'll tell us about their means and methods of gathering specific information, then there's a bridge in Brooklyn I want to sell you."

I was certain that NSA did talk about it with someone outside its walls of secrecy. Namely, the FISA—Foreign Intelligence Surveillance Act—court, while they were seeking a court order approving the use of "electronic surveillance" against foreign powers or their agents. I did have a hunch how NSA broke into the Iranian computers. Before the Islamic Revolution, some Iranian government agencies had used tailor-made software written by American companies. They'd left a trap door to allow them to service the computers from a remote location. Now, that concealed method of access could be used to hack into the computer without leaving a trace.

"Dan, there's no need to be sarcastic. We need to generate a report that is acceptable to both of us. Therefore, before I put my name on any such report I want to make sure I can live with the facts it describes. What good will our recommendations do, if some guy with average common sense can punch a hole in the tower of facts we're building?"

"Fine with me," I said. "Other than the prints, we have no facts, only a bunch of leads and pieces of information. The case isn't over. We aren't writing an autopsy report. We're summing up a case that has just gotten closer to breaking than at any time during the past twenty years. The report will set the path to go forward, not to bury a corpse."

"And it has characteristics of national security, rather than just catching a successful serial thief," she added. She'd finally jumped on the wagon of enthusiasm I had been single-handedly pushing uphill.

"By the way," I said. "We've got some indication that there's at least one sleeper agent in the U.S. other than the Chameleon."

"What indication?"

"Loretta Otis. She was murdered a few days after she reported to a rabbi in Sydney that Goldman was in fact Ward. The rabbi confronted the Chameleon, asking for his explanation. When no satisfactory responses came, the rabbi refused to marry the Chameleon. Now, knowing that his new identity as Goldman was in jeopardy, the Chameleon sealed Loretta Otis's fate. The Chameleon was still in Australia when Otis was killed. That means he must have arranged for her elimination in the U.S., either by calling Iran or directly calling another member of Department 81 in the U.S."

"So he's probably in trouble in Australia for that, and for the fraud."

"The Australian Federal Police is looking for him as well."

"OK. I think we should spend some time in making recommendations concerning our next move."

"We've a plenary meeting with the other working groups in a week. Do you think Casey set up Monday as our deadline to submit our report so that he could use our paper during the plenary meeting?" I asked.

"I think he's doing the same with the other groups—asking them for their reports. Since Bauer is acting as liaison, not as a decision maker, I think the real evaluation and decision making will be done at Langley."

"In Tel Aviv as well," I added. "One working group consists of Mossad guys."

Nicole yawned and stretched. "Right. Well, let's adjourn until the morning. I'm exhausted."

I looked at my watch. It was one thirty A.M. Based on my past experience, the bigger the operation, the shorter the time that management would give us to finish it. But at least because there were a few of us, we could always find someone to blame for any failure.

In the morning, it took four hours of debating and document review to write our report. The room was the worse for wear: empty beer cans, three half-empty bags of potato chips—a quarter of the chips on the floor and the rest in my stomach, giving me heartburn.

"Let's clean up the mess," said Nicole. "We can't have cleaners here." We spent the next hour sweeping the floor and removing garbage, not before making sure we didn't accidentally throw away any pieces of paper. Nicole went to the communication room and returned twenty minutes later.

"There has been a change of plans. There's a meeting in another safe apartment in northern Paris in two days. We should send our report immediately."

On the day of the meeting, we took Nicole's car from a nearby parking garage and drove to the outskirts of Paris, to a leafy residential area. More out of habit than as a result of any suspicion, I routinely checked our backs to make sure we had no unwanted company. I wondered whether there was any security backup. There was too much activity around our safe apartment, and if any of the visitors was unknowingly compromised to the opposition, they'd contaminate us as well. Opposition? I wondered who our opposition would be, here. There were too many contenders for the title. I decided to raise the issue with Casey. I was uncomfortable. We were too visible.

When we entered the meeting room, a large one with high ceilings, there were several other people already waiting. I recognized Casey, Arnold Kyle, and Benny. Four other men and one woman looked unfamiliar. In the center of the room was a big nineteenth-century-style dining table. We sat around it. I counted the participants. We were ten in all.

Arnold started. "The work of all the teams ended sooner than expected. That's a good sign. We're here today to review the various options following the recent developments in the Chameleon case, which now seems more than ever to be connected to Iran's terror financing."

"Chameleon?" I muttered to Benny, who sat next to me. "Since when is he using that name?"

"Dan, you're a lawyer. You know as well as anyone that

you haven't secured trademark protection for that name," he said, grinning.

"The purpose of this meeting is to explore whether a recommendation should be made to our respective governments to take additional measures. But before we begin, Jack Randolph, our security officer, will say a few words."

A man in his late fifties with a shaven head and dressed in a blue blazer addressed us. "Good intelligence is the best weapon in the battle against international terrorism. However, gathering intelligence about the identities, intentions, capabilities, and vulnerabilities of terrorists is extremely difficult. On top of that, we've realized that leaks of intelligence and law-enforcement information, some due to negligence and carelessness, but some intentionally stolen—or worse, secretly and illegally transferred—have endangered sources, alienated friendly nations, and inhibited their cooperation, thereby jeopardizing the U.S. government's ability to obtain further information. Therefore, I insist that each and every one of you understand the gravity of this issue. Particular security measures are undertaken concerning this meeting and the operation planned. Please respect these limitations, and protect all information received and treat it as top secret. I'll go over the security instructions before the conclusion of this session. Thank you."

Kyle proceeded to provide us with a brief history of the battle against terror financing. Then we went into specific cases, and finally, when I was about to lose interest, he discussed our case, mostly using the report Nicole and I had submitted earlier. "This report is an early-stage operational road map. I say early stage, because there's a lot of work to be done here. For starters, I need your input on two points: risk/benefit analysis of such an operation, and whether, how, and where to enter Iran—and once entered, the ways and means of achieving our ultimate goals."

He paused. "We're here to look at operational aspects. Any suggestions?"

"Dan, any ideas?" nudged Benny.

I spoke up. "If we want to crack the mystery of Atashbon or Department 81—if they are in fact separate entities—we just can't exclusively rely on ELINT/SIGINT. We must have HUMINT. We need someone with a pulse, an informer, or for one of us to get it independently."

"Not that I disagree with you," said Kyle, "but look at the results that NSA has brought. It's all ELINT based. They've just been intercepting electronic transmissions."

"Sure, but did they tell us where the Chameleon is? Did they tell us whether there are other sleeper cells in the U.S.? They just brought us the ladder. Now we need a person to climb it," I said. "We must have the human touch to bring in the smoking gun. If we can do it by remote control, then I'm all for it. But if we can't—and I do believe that to be the case here—then we should do the job ourselves, even if that means penetration into Iran." I was sounding more decisive than I actually was. I hoped I wasn't going too far.

"You do realize that such a mission could get you killed," said Bob Holliday. It was more of a statement than a question. "Is it worth it just to get even with someone who stole money?"

Though I was initially surprised, I realized with a quick flash of eye contact that he was handing me the ball to score. Maybe working for this guy wasn't going to be so stiff after all.

"It started as a case of stolen money," I said. "No longer. This is a case that concerns U.S. national security. For the first time we've got evidence to suggest that there could be Iranian sleeper cells in the U.S. If the suspicion is established as fact, do you think their hibernation will continue forever? We tentatively concluded that the Chameleon was assigned by his controllers to steal money. We know from the physical description of the other perpetrators of the banking fraud in the U.S. that there are probably other members of Department 81 in the U.S., because they didn't look like the Chameleon. Do we know, in case there are additional sleeper cells in the U.S., what their missions are? Do we even know that they were in fact asleep during the past twenty years? Maybe some of the unsolved mysteries during those two decades were connected to one or more of them. Remember, the U.S. is called the Great Satan by the Iranian ayatollahs, while Israel is the Small Satan. The Iranian message is, don't play with Satan—kill him."

"So you're suggesting we get the still-missing information regarding their identity directly in Iran," said Arnold.

I nodded. "Yes. But I want to make clear that my support for the recommendation for penetration is contingent upon identifying and finding a potential source, or a plan that could provide us with the necessary information or be a conduit to others who could give us that. I'm not suggesting we enter first and then start looking around. I hope you give me credit for not being that unprofessional and careless. We suggested a preliminary plan in our team's report."

"Have you also done a risk assessment?" asked Casey.

"No. I was asked to deal with finding the Chameleon. Another team made the assessment. But since you asked, I agree that there are significant risks involved in penetration, even under our proposed plan, and I understand them. If caught, whoever goes there has little or no chance of walking away from it alive. But a more accurate risk assessment must be made once a plan is in place. And we don't have an approved plan yet."

I took a deep breath. "But if there's a good plan, I'm willing to volunteer to be a singleton for that mission." I knew that I'd fare better as a lone wolf in an operation designed for a single operative. During my military service I'd realized that many would volunteer for a mission until it was time to go. But not here; I was willing.

Benny, who sat next to me, said quietly in Hebrew, "Dan, you're crazy."

Everyone else just silently stared at me. We continued discussing various options for three more hours until Kyle said, looking at his watch, "OK, I think we've accomplished something today. I ask for your summary operational suggestions by the end of the week. I'm going back to the U.S., and we'll review the options there. Benny, any suggestions?"

"Not at this time," said Benny. "I need to talk to the director of the Mossad before we continue. In general, I've got his blessing, but when concrete plans are drawn that assume our participation, we must revisit the entire matter."

When everyone was about to leave, Kyle asked Bob, Benny, Casey, Nicole, and me to stay behind.

"Let's talk shop," he said. "For the kind of detail I want to get into, we don't need the whole assembly. Under what guise do you think an entry into Iran could succeed?"

"There are two ways," I said. "The legal and the illegal. Well, both are illegal. What I call legal is an entry through the international airport of Tehran, with a cover story."

"And the illegal entry?"

"Through one of the extremely long borders Iran has with its seven neighbors. Preferably penetration through Turkey, or from Turkmenistan."

"If penetration isn't through the international airport, whoever we send has to be physically fit," said Nicole. "I'm sure you're aware of the distances, the heights, the lack of transportation, and the rivalry between various factions living in these areas that don't particularly like snooping strangers, regardless of their nationality."

"I know that. We submitted a general plan, which may or may not be plausible," I said. "But just two comments in that regard. One, we don't have to dwell on that now, because it's not our mandate to determine means of penetration. The operation departments of the CIA and Mossad are better qualified to recommend that. Also, the Mossad has an excellent long-term relationship with the Kurds, as we heard from Benny in Giverny, so maybe we could have a route here. But for the sake of our mock war game, and as suggested in our plan, let's assume entry through Tehran's airport. It has a lot of advantages."

"Such as what?" asked Bob.

"Such as support for the legend. Let's say, for example, that our men enter Iran posing as representatives of European companies selling pharmaceuticals to Iranian drug importers. Would their cover story make sense if they're stopped en route from the Turkish border on the back of a mule, or in a beat-up bus that travels twelve hours, seated among peasants carrying their goats? On top of these problems we must bear in mind that the border areas in the north are infested with informers and part-time spies in numbers greater than those operating in Berlin during the Cold War."

"I realize that illegal border crossing severely limits the options for a plausible legend," agreed Kyle.

"OK. That leaves a 'lawful' entry as a preferred option. Next, let's talk about a legend, just for the sake of our discussion, to see if we aren't too optimistic in the evaluation of risks," I said.

"Your report suggested several options, including posing as a European businessman. Why?" asked Bob.

"Because they're preferred as business partners by the Iranians. The idea can fly, provided we can show real links on both sides. A real company in Europe that upon inquiry will confirm that our men actually work for it, and an Iranian company that will confirm prior business contacts and scheduled meetings to discuss some business—can we show that?"

"Based on our problem in Iran regarding lack of human assets, the answer is probably no," said Kyle. "So we can't build a legend that will require bidirectional verifiable contacts."

"Or," I said, "we build the relationship from scratch with a genuine Iranian company seeking to do business with Europe. But that will take time, since a relationship with an Iranian company that has little past and no track record could be suspicious if you scratch the surface."

"How about another option we suggested?" said Nicole. "An independent German TV production company does a *Roots*-style program and sends a crew to Tehran, together with a European whose father, or rather grandfather, was born in

Tehran and later emigrated. Now the son or the grandson looks for the roots of his heritage."

"I guess you suggested a German company on purpose," said Benny.

"Right, because of all the European countries, the Germans have a history of good relationships with the Iranians."

Kyle intervened. "OK, we can work later on these aspects. Let's assume our men are in Tehran. Then what? How do they find traces of Farhadi and his comrades twenty years after the fact?" He looked at Nicole.

Nicole said, "Ask Dan, I think he's locked on one option."

"Dan?"

"We suspect that there could be additional graduates of the American School in Tehran who are members of Department 81. That's the single most identifying common denominator. So why go far? Other than the security services of Iran, nobody knows of that connection. Also, they don't know what we suspect. Twenty years went by, and we didn't catch any of them. There are several groups in the U.S., and maybe elsewhere, of former students of the school who like to communicate and reminisce. Why don't we build a legend around that?"

"You mean bring an American into Tehran to meet his classmates? It'd be tantamount to putting a small live animal in a snake pit," said Kyle.

"No, not an American necessarily. There were many students who came from other countries while their fathers worked in Iran—Germans, Swiss, French, Italian. Look at the list of students we have. They came from plenty of nationalities. We can recruit a German or a Japanese former student, send him or her to Iran to organize a reunion. Under that pretext, he or she could compile a list of the current addresses of the graduates. And if we narrow the list to the particular age group of the Chameleon, say those born from 1960 to 1962, for example, then we're likely to get current addresses of some. If we are still left with a group of unknowns, then we can compare that list to our existing list and come up with likely names of Department

81 members." The more I talked about it, the more I became convinced it might actually work.

"OK," said Bob. "Suppose you found 60 percent, or even 80 percent of the graduates. Then what?" As always, there was an edge of skepticism in his voice, but I now understood that this only meant he wanted me to talk him into agreeing with what I was saying.

"We get their pictures and vital statistics and ask the victims to identify them. Once we lock on an identified individual as a possible member of Department 81, we look for him in the U.S. We also put him on Interpol's alert list in case he ever travels outside Iran. Next comes the list of people who, according to their friends or family, no longer live in Iran. That list will be a hot list. If we get addresses from their families, we verify them. It's absolutely possible that these people emigrated to other countries and are law-abiding citizens. But at the end of the day, we'll end up with a list of unknowns, graduates of the school whose friends don't know where they are. That small and exclusive list will be our target for intensified and individualized search. At least we'll have twenty people on that list, not thousands. The State Department already gave us a short list of unknowns, but beyond that, we have no way of unveiling any other Atashbon members."

"So what do you suggest we do next?" asked Bob. I realized he took the initiative to ask leading questions to emphasize the initiative of his office in this matter—undoubtedly his first.

I took the bait. "As a first stage, I'd start the process while still in Europe and recruit a graduate of the school to be our unwitting spearhead. Then after a preparatory period, we send him or her for a visit to Tehran to prepare a successful reunion."

"OK," said Kyle. "We'll be in touch."

I returned to the U.S. two days later and went on vacation with my children for a week in the Caribbean islands. Especially since we don't get to spend as much time together as we'd like to, we crammed a lot of activity into that one week: scuba diving, sailing, swimming, and some great food. During one of several walks on the beach, my mind wandered back to my past. As I looked at my son Tom, nineteen years old, tall and strong, walking beside me, in my mind's eye I could see myself walking with my own father, long since deceased, on the warm beaches of Tel Aviv. I was a small child of maybe four or five, doing my best to put my tiny feet into his big footprints in the sand, because I looked up to that man as if he were a giant who could do no wrong. I wondered what my own kids thought of me. Were they proud? Had I been a good father to them? Maybe every father has these thoughts now and then. As for me, I rarely have enough time to dwell on such things as I spend my days chasing bad guys across the globe.

Back in my office with a suntan, I immersed myself in my routine work on other cases. The Chameleon had almost slipped out of my mind.

A year went by, and I was sure the plan was shelved, maybe to allow the next generations of moths to consume what was left of the twenty-plus-year-old case. I went to Panama on a routine assignment, and when I traveled to Washington, DC, to attend an office meeting, Esther welcomed me with her warm smile.

"I hope you won't mind traveling some more," she said.

"Why's that?"

"I guess you'll have to. This has just come in." She handed me a memo.

Top Secret. Interim decision has been made. Please report within four days to Apartment 6B, Margaretenstrasse 153A, Vienna, A-1050 Austria, for training. Be prepared to be away from the U.S. for at least thirty days. Casey Bauer.

Esther gave me a travel folder with a passport. "You're leaving in three days."

I opened the bio page. My new name was Anton Spitzer.

So, they hadn't given the moths or the maggots a chance. But what exactly was "training"? And for what? Had someone forgotten to copy me on the memo for some operation? I couldn't ask Bob—he was out of the country. I called Casey's secretary.

"I can't discuss it," she said cryptically. "Mr. Bauer has asked that you be there. Once you're TDY'ed to us for an assignment, I believe you're expected to take instructions from Mr. Bauer."

Formally she was right, but I wanted to be informal. What was going on? With imposed confidentiality, and with no one to call, I answered, "Please ask Mr. Bauer to call me. I need to make arrangements for my children and my dog. I also have pending matters in my office that need to be assigned to others while I'm gone."

The next day I received Bob Holliday's note, dictated over the phone to Esther. "Dan, please follow your instructions. It'll be clearer once you're out there. Bob."

I packed my bags and flew to London as originally scheduled. At the airport an Agency representative took my Anton Spitzer passport and gave me an airline ticket to Vienna and a Canadian passport carrying the name Ian Pour Laval. I opened the passport to look at Ian's photo. I saw some similarities between us, but I definitely didn't look exactly like him. I boarded an Austrian Airlines flight to Vienna. Was the lack of communication with me a result of bureaucratic apathy? Or maybe the nature of the assignment was so secretive that it couldn't be discussed over the phone, even the secure phone? On second thought, I concluded that both reasons were probably valid and could coexist. Nonetheless, from a simple human-relations point of view, this was an excellent way to alienate someone.

CHAPTER SIXTEEN

Vienna, Austria, December 2005

I arrived late in Vienna. I was tired, hungry, and particularly curious as to what was coming up next. My travel folder included a reservation confirmation slip at the Holiday Inn.

"*Guten Abend*, Herr Pour Laval," said the receptionist at the desk. "We've been expecting you." She quickly completed the formalities and handed me a room key card and an envelope. "This is a message for you."

I opened the envelope. The computer-printed message was short. "We're expecting you tomorrow at ten o'clock."

I looked up at the receptionist. "Could you help me get oriented here? What are we near?"

"We are close to the State Opera, St. Stephan's Cathedral, and the famous buildings along the Ringstrasse. We are also not far from the Messegelände, our fairgrounds," she answered.

I went up to my room and was asleep within minutes.

The harshly ringing phone woke me up. I thought it was the middle of the night. "Ian?" asked the voice. I was about to yell, *You've got the wrong idiot you number,* and slam the phone with an added variety of juicy expletives in select languages, when I suddenly remembered that I was in fact Ian Pour Laval.

"Yes," I mumbled.

"Welcome to Vienna," said the voice. "When you leave your room, don't leave anything behind."

"You mean I should pack up and leave with my luggage?" I wasn't quite awake.

"No. Just apply the usual field security."

For that he woke me up? I glanced at the clock on the night table. It was already seven thirty A.M.

I had a quick—meaning forty-minute—Austrian-style breakfast, and went outside. A cabby approached me.

"Herr Pour Laval, I've got instructions to drive you."

I bristled. "No thanks, I'll walk." Who the hell was he, and how did he know my name? "Please, Herr Pour Laval," he insisted. "Herr Casey Bauer told me to bring you over. Your meeting isn't at Margaretenstrasse, but at another location."

I hesitated only for a moment. It was cold outside; he knew my name, Casey's name, and the original location of my meeting.

What the hell, I said to myself. *I've got no opposition in this game.*

On second thought, I added, *For now.*

"Please give me the address," I said. I returned to the hotel and left through the rear exit to another street. I hailed a cab, which drove me through small streets of a residential area and stopped next to a three-story building. I went up to the second floor.

I checked the building and its vicinity. Other than a crying baby, there was no sound. I walked up worn, circular stairs to the second floor, rang the doorbell, and climbed ten stairs up, in case an unfriendly goon answered the door. Casey Bauer opened the heavy oak door. "Hi, Dan," he said in an apologetic tone. "We had a change of plans and I didn't want to call you or be seen with you. So I sent Johann to bring you over."

"Well, I'm here." I didn't tell him any more details.

"Good. Please come in."

I entered the apartment and followed him to a spacious living room. "You will soon meet Steve Corcoran, a graduate of the American School in Tehran, class of 1978. Currently he's employed by the State Department in Washington and has agreed to help us."

"To do what?" I asked.

"Spotting. During the past two months we've identified Steve as the most suitable person for the task."

"I'm listening." It had been a long time since I'd heard that term. *Spotter* was intelligence-community jargon for an individual who locates and assesses individuals suitable for potential recruitment. I was appreciative. Getting the State Department to agree to participate in this operation would have taken an unprecedented amount of cooperation. Or, more likely, intercession at the very top.

"We've been working on the plan and the graduate list you and Nicole obtained, and we came up with a potential candidate. Erikka Buhler. Steve will introduce you and withdraw. Bear in mind that Steve knows nothing about this case and shouldn't be told anything unrelated to the tactics of meeting Erikka."

"Who is she?"

"A Swiss woman, a graduate of the American School in Tehran, class of 1978. She lived in Tehran ages three through eighteen. At the time her father was a representative of a Swiss bank in Tehran. Erikka currently lives in Vienna and has just been through an ugly divorce that put her financially in the red. She's out of a job. We selected Erikka because we preferred a female. That gives us some assurance that we didn't stumble on a member of the men-only Department 81. And we selected Steve not only because he was her classmate, but because he was hired just weeks ago and has received security certification following substantial security checks before he started working for the State Department. None of his friends know about his new job."

Casey handed me three printed pages and as usual got straight to the point. "Read it—that's your legend."

I was a Canadian citizen and had lived most of my life in various locations, where my father, an agricultural expert, was employed by the United Nations helping farmers in poor countries to improve their crops. During my childhood we had lived in Uganda, Peru, Nepal, and Sri Lanka. Now I lived in Europe writing freelance articles for various magazines. My next big project was a novel.

"Should she know that I currently live in no special place in Europe?" I asked.

"Yes, a little in London, Paris, Oslo—no place is permanent for you. Just like when you were a child. We don't want your legend to fail a background investigation. If you only lived in a city for a short period, people aren't expected to remember you and you aren't expected to be familiar with small details every longtime resident would know."

We spent two more hours covering all contingencies.

A doorbell rang, and a minute later a clean-shaven man just on the edge of fifty, but still young looking, joined us. He was dressed in a button-down light blue shirt with a striped tie, khaki pants, and a blue blazer. Classic.

"Hi, Casey," he said. Turning to me he added, "I'm Steve Corcoran." We shook hands.

"Hi, Steve," said Casey, and led us to a dining table across the room. "Let's sit here. I've just discussed your agreement to introduce Erikka to Ian Pour Laval." He pointed at me. "Ian is a Canadian author who is writing a novel that takes place in Iran. He's interested in Iran, since his paternal grandfather—who was born in Iran—left Tehran when he was about twenty years old. Therefore, Ian needs help from a person who knows Tehran very well, speaks Farsi and English fluently." If he hadn't become a CIA case officer, Casey could have been an acting coach. He spouted off my cover story so convincingly that he almost had me believing that I really was Ian Pour Laval.

"A personal assistant to help find relatives?" asked Steve.

"Yes, exactly," said Casey. "As well as helping him with his book research."

"And who am I?" asked Steve, understanding the nature of his role.

"You're an executive of an international publishing house. You're assigned to their branch in India, which covers all of Asia. They signed Ian up for the publishing of his novel."

"Got you," said Steve. "That was in fact my job until a

month ago, so it'll be easy." Casey smiled knowingly and gave him additional details. It became clear to me that they built Steve's legend around his genuine résumé, leaving out only his new government job.

"How long has it been since you last saw Erikka?" I asked Steve.

"Fifteen years. I bumped into her on the street in Zürich once."

"Your next meeting will also look like it happened by chance," said Casey. "We know she frequents a certain café in central Vienna. Steve will just happen to bump into her." He handed us a printed sheet of paper with an attached photo. "Here are Erikka's details."

I viewed the photo. Erikka looked her age. She had blonde hair and gray eyes, and seemed a bit overweight. The text described her only briefly. "You'll have to get more details from her. I don't want you to know anything about her and slip in a conversation."

If he'd meant to offend me, it didn't show, and contrary to my infamous short fuse, I didn't react. Thirty minutes later, Casey said, "Let's move on. Go to Café Central this afternoon at five P.M." He handed me a note with an address scribbled. "Sit at a table toward the back. Our observations have shown that Erikka comes to that café on Mondays and Thursdays at about five fifteen P.M. after an hour of tutoring a twelve-year-old girl who lives in the neighborhood. Steve will enter the café five or ten minutes after our scout signals that Erikka has arrived and sat down. Steve, you walk inside and stop next to her table, as if trying to make sure you're recognizing your classmate. If she doesn't recognize you immediately, introduce yourself. If she asks you to join her, say that you've actually come to the café to meet someone, but you'll sit with her for five minutes. If she doesn't ask you to sit down, don't insist. You can try again when you pass by her table, saying that the person you expected to meet didn't show up yet. She may ask you to join her then."

"And if she doesn't?"

"Don't push her. Just wish her well and leave. We'll find another spotter to introduce Ian. Once you sit at her table, if you do, show genuine interest in her. Ask her what she has been doing through the years, ask about other classmates. If she tells you about her personal problems, show sympathy. Ask her how you can help. Conduct yourself as you'd behave without our intervention. Keep the conversation focused on her, but don't question her in a manner that makes her feel she's being interrogated. Just be nice to her.

"As you can see from the fact sheet I gave you, you're in Vienna to meet Ian for the first time and get a personal impression. The book Ian is writing that your company will publish is a novel about a love story between an Iranian man and an Austrian woman, against the backdrop of the cultural differences between people in Austria and post–Islamic Revolution Iran. When you have spent ten minutes with her, excuse yourself and say you think you've noticed the person you've come to meet. Go to Ian's table. Hold a conversation with him, order tea or coffee and cakes." He smiled. "They're actually very good."

"And then?" I asked.

"Then, Steve, you will go over to Erikka's table and suggest that she join you and meet Ian."

"If she refuses?" asked Steve.

"The only reason for her to refuse will be that she's waiting to meet someone else. However, I can tell you that in all likelihood she'll not refuse. She's very lonely and bitter. Most of her friends in Vienna sided with her husband during their divorce battle. He's a local guy, and she's Swiss. He has the money and the influence. She had nothing to offer him. Trust me, she'll gladly join your table."

"And then?" Steve asked.

"Leave the floor to Ian. Thirty minutes into the meeting with Erikka and Ian, I'll call your mobile phone and ask you to leave the café. Make up an excuse and ask for her phone number to call her later. If she hesitates, don't push. Give up. We have the number. Leave the café and return to your hotel. I'll call you there later."

Bauer got up. "OK, Steve, if you have no further questions, then we're done."

Steve left.

"Ian," said Bauer. "After Steve leaves the café, you stay and talk about yourself. Don't ask her any personal questions. Bear in mind that the purpose of the meeting is to recruit her to work for you as an assistant on your book project. But don't suggest it immediately. Mention casually the book and your need to do a lot of research regarding Iran. Ask her about her life experience in Iran. She lived there for fifteen years, which were her formative years. I'm sure she'd be happy to show you how much she knows about Iran for no particular reason—just to make conversation."

"I shouldn't offer her the job even if she says she could help me?"

"Right. Even if she does suggest helping you, smile and say that it sounds like an interesting idea to consider, and thank her for that. Don't commit. Get her phone number and promise to call. Leave twenty minutes later. You cannot appear to be too interested in her—just a bit, out of curiosity."

"No personal interest?"

"You mean becoming a honey trap and charming her pants off? Maybe later; definitely not now. Whatever the circumstances may be, she cannot—and I repeat, cannot—be recruited to work for you during your first meeting. Any questions?"

I shook my head. I thought of her picture. She was definitely not my idea of someone to spend a steamy Sunday afternoon with.

"OK. Then I'll see you this afternoon at the café."

"See me?"

"Well, metaphorically. I'll be listening in. Steve will carry a microphone."

At the time set, I entered the café.

"*Guten Tag,*" said the *Hauptkellner*, or headwaiter, who was wearing a tuxedo that badly needed dry cleaning.

"Table for one?"

"For two, please. I'm expecting someone"—so Steve would have a chair when he arrived. He nodded, took a menu, and I followed him to the back of the café. A strong aroma of coffee, foamed milk, and cigarette smoke filled the air.

I sat at a small table covered with a white tablecloth underneath a thick glass top. I looked around. Most of the guests were older men dressed in jackets and ties, or ladies of advanced age dressed to go out. I scoured the place but couldn't identify Erikka. I glanced at my watch; it was still five minutes short of her usual time. I went to the corner and took the day's newspaper, which was spread over a wooden frame—a European trick to prevent the guests from taking the newspaper when leaving. The frame made reading a bit clumsy. It felt like holding a placard in a picket line. I punched a small hole in the newspaper and pretended to be busy reading, but in fact I was peeping through the hole.

Ten minutes later Erikka entered the café and sat four tables away from me. She seemed to be a regular, because the waiter greeted her and they seemed to have a friendly conversation for a minute or two. Erikka was dressed in a brown skirt and a light-brown tweed jacket. Her wide, pale face looked like her picture, but her hair had been dyed since the photo was taken. She was medium height and about fifteen pounds overweight—nothing, compared to me. For me, fifteen pounds too heavy would be downright anorexic.

A few minutes later Steve walked in. He stopped next to her table, and from what I could gather they had a jovial conversation. I glanced over the framed newspaper and saw Steve sitting at her table.

OK, step one has been accomplished.

I put down the framed newspaper to allow Steve to locate me. As planned, a few minutes later Steve came over to my table. I got up and shook his hand in a formal manner, as if we were meeting for the first time. Steve sat down. We ordered coffee for him and tea for me. I didn't hesitate long before acquiescing to the waiter's suggestion to order *Apfelstrudel*, paper-thin dough filled with cooked apples. The portion was too big, and covered with rich, icy whipped cream.

"How was it?" I asked in a low voice.

"Not a problem," said Steve. "She was friendlier than I expected. I told her about our meeting and promised to talk to her again when I'm done talking business with you."

We just sat there talking about nothing for half an hour. Steve got up and said, "I'm going to the bathroom, and on my way back to our table, I'll stop at her table and suggest that she join us."

Moments later Steve returned to our table with Erikka. I got up. "Ian, I want to introduce my classmate. Erikka, this is Ian Pour Laval, a Canadian author whose novel my company is about to publish."

I shook her hand. It was small and tender. She smiled shyly. "Erikka and I were students at the American School in Tehran until the Islamic Revolution," he said.

"Really." I sounded interested. "I didn't know you had an Iranian past. Please, please sit down." Steve grabbed another chair and they sat at my table.

"Yes, I studied there for five years, but Erikka was a lifer— K through twelfth grade, wasn't it?"

She nodded. "Yes. All my childhood and adolescence was spent there."

"Have you seen each other since you left Tehran?"

Erikka tried to remember. "Yes, I think we met once in Zürich, right, Steve?"

"Yes," he said. "What a small world."

"Does the fact that you spent time in Iran have anything to do with your management's decision to send you to meet me?" I asked, as if I had just discovered America.

"A lot to do with it," answered Steve. And turning to Erikka he said, "Ian is writing a novel on an impossible love relationship between a Muslim Iranian man and a Catholic Austrian woman."

"Really," said Erikka with a spark of interest in her eyes. "Where does it take place?"

"Mostly in Tehran in the early 1980s."

"At the height of Khomeini's period," said Erikka. "That type of romance during that time was really problematic. Are you here also for the book?"

"Yes," I confirmed. "To do some research about Vienna and meet with Steve."

"Are you familiar with Iran? Have you ever been there?"

"No," I conceded. "But I've got Iranian roots."

"Now, this is a surprise," said Steve. "How?"

"My paternal grandfather was born in Iran, but left the country when he was nineteen or twenty years old and never returned."

"So, I'm sure you must have relatives in Iran. Do you know of them?"

"I think I've got a few second or third cousins, but I've got no idea what their names are or where they live."

Steve's mobile phone rang. Steve listened and said, "I'll be right over."

"I apologize," he said. "I must leave, but you should stay. Erikka, where can I get hold of you? I'd love to see you again sometime."

"How long will you be in Vienna?"

"Just one more day, but I intend to be back with my wife next spring."

Erikka wrote her number and gave it to Steve. "While I'm at it," she told me, writing again, "here is my number. I'll be happy to answer any of your questions regarding Iran."

"Thanks," I said and put the note in my pocket. "I may call you on your kind offer."

"Please do," she said in a friendly manner. "And I could help you regarding Vienna as well. I've been living here for the past nine years." There was a slight tone of despair in her voice, a yearning for human contact, or I was imagining things.

"Great, I'll certainly call you." We continued chatting for ten or fifteen more minutes. I paid for the drinks and cakes. "I need to leave. Thank you very much for your offer," I said, and left. She stayed behind.

Later on that night I was driven to meet Casey.

"It went smoothly," I said. "She sounded eager to talk to anyone about anything. I don't think we'll face major difficulties in recruiting her."

Two days later I called her.

"Hi, this is Ian Pour Laval. Steve Corcoran introduced us the other evening at the café."

"Of course I remember our meeting. How are you?"

"I'm fine, thanks; gaining weight on the Austrian food."

"Unfortunately I've experienced it too," she said in acceptance.

"Well, it looks nice on you and bad on me. Anyway, I've got a quick question for you concerning Iran. I hope you don't mind the short intrusion."

"Not at all, I'm actually happy you called. I like talking about Iran."

"I'm lucky I met you," I said. "My question concerns family customs in Iran, and how a traditional family would treat a Muslim member of the family who dates a Catholic woman."

"Just dating? No marriage plans are announced?"

"Well, at the beginning it was just a date—I need to fine-tune the dynamics of the reaction of people in the respective cultures when they see what develops between the two. Does the couple hear objections, or do people just talk behind their backs? Once I get a better feeling for that potential conflict, I'll move on to the issue of marriage, and how society and their respective families treat them."

"Generally speaking, Iranian society, like that of any other ethnic group, cannot be regarded as homogeneous," said Erikka. "For example, Iranian farmers in the south have different family values and religious beliefs from city people. So you'll have to tell me more about the familial background before I can attempt to answer your question."

"The man is a Shiite Muslim, born and educated in Iran. He works as a pharmacist in a pharmaceutical firm in Tehran. The woman is a Catholic Austrian who came to Tehran to teach German in a local school. Her parents are farmers in southern Austria. By Iranian standards, due to his education and exposure to Western values, the man is considered modern. His family follows the traditional Islamic customs of marrying within the religion and according men superiority in the family. He's torn between his love for her and his loyalty to his family and his upbringing and culture.

"These are the general parameters. But obviously there are nuances when they're faced with changing circumstances in Iran, and when her ideas on equal rights for women in the society clash with what she sees in his family and in Iran in general. Although I'm writing fiction, I want the book to be as accurate as possible as it concerns facts on Iran and its people's daily life."

"I think I can help you if you describe a particular event, and tell me from what perspective you want my answer— from the European woman's or the Iranian man's. I could do both."

"Well, it seems that you're more qualified to help me than I thought. Can we have dinner, at a place of your choosing, and we can chat?"

"Of course. When do you have in mind?"

I had the impression that she was available at any time I'd suggest. All I needed to do was set it up.

"How about tomorrow night?" I wanted to suggest tonight, but I didn't want to look too eager, or embarrass her by suggesting that I knew that she had no other things to do.

"Fine, I'll meet you at Figlmüller's at seven thirty. Is that a good time?"

"Yes, but where is it?"

"Just opposite St. Stephan's Cathedral. Any cabdriver will know the place. They serve genuine Viennese food, and there are even some Swiss dishes."

When I arrived at the restaurant at exactly seven thirty, Erikka was already waiting for me at the bar. The place had a beautiful decor of vaulted arches and wood-paneled walls. Erikka was dressed in a low-cut black dress and had put makeup on her rosy cheeks. She looked radiant, ready for a date, not the professional meeting I had in mind.

"Thanks for agreeing to help me," I said as I sat down. The smell of food made me almost drool.

"I'm happy to be needed." She smiled. "Look at the blackboard," she said. "This restaurant is famous for its old-style gigantic Wiener schnitzels."

My drooling stage went from potential to reality. These area rug–sized schnitzels are my favorite. Erikka ordered salad and local wine, and I ordered the biggest veal schnitzel they had.

"How long will you be in Vienna?"

"I've got no timetable. I want to spend enough time to feel the city and talk to people. Although the plot takes place in Tehran, I want to understand the culture that the woman in my novel brings with her."

"Does she already have a name?"

"Abelina. But that may change; I have only early drafts."

"I gave some thought to our conversation, particularly if the situation were reversed and the events took place in Vienna," she said. "Then one would expect that Austrians would be more tolerant of a Muslim trying to marry a local woman than Iranians in Iran would be when faced with your story line."

"Why?"

"Because Islam is the second-largest religion in Austria. Muslims amount to more than 5 percent of the Austrian population, 500,000 out of 8.1 million. I think Austrians would basically react in the exact same manner as the Iranians would react, though expressed differently, given the disparities in the respective cultures."

"You mean rejection and opposition, unless there's a complete assimilation into their culture?"

"Exactly."

We discussed in detail Austrian history and its relationship with Muslims until I felt we'd exhausted the subject. "I'm sorry," I said in an apologetic tone. "I meant to ask you questions about Iran, and yet I realize that you're so knowledgeable in Austrian matters as well. Can we talk about Iran? Do you speak Farsi?"

"Of course," she said proudly with a happy smile. "I grew up there. My father was the vice president of a Swiss bank's branch in Tehran. I came to Iran at the age of three and left when I became eighteen. At home we spoke Swiss German, of course. At the American school we spoke English, but anywhere else I spoke Farsi. Nobody can tell I'm not Iranian."

I grinned hearing that from a blonde-haired, gray-eyed, and pale-skinned woman with typical European features.

She caught up with me and smiled. "I mean by listening to me speak Farsi. There's nothing I can do about my Teutonic ancestors."

"Are your parents still living?" I asked.

"No, my father died two years after we left Tehran, and my mother died five years later."

I left it at that—no more personal questions, since I had to build some expectations in her for continued contact. If Erikka had other thoughts, she didn't mention them. Unprompted, she spoke about her childhood in northern Tehran and her friends. An hour later I felt it was time to stop, or I'd have to pose the question. But it was premature.

I looked at my watch. "It's getting late. I still need to make some calls."

"At this late hour? People here go to sleep pretty early," she said, signaling she wanted to keep talking.

"It's still early afternoon in the U.S.," I said briskly.

Back at the hotel, I wrote in my report, "Subject is already ripe for the move. I think I should suggest employment during our next contact. Since hiring her isn't expected to raise any suspicion or doubts, I see no forthcoming obstacles."

It was all déjà vu. In my Mossad years, my unit was sent to Austria to recruit a potential source spotted by a Mossad veteran skiing in Austria. Heinrich was a ski instructor on the slopes near Kitzbühel, popular among rich vacationing Arabs. We were supposedly Dutchmen and South Africans working for a large South African manufacturer of military equipment. Heinrich's students—Arab government officials, Arab military men, and Arab private-sector businessmen—were the ultimate targets.

We'd thought it would be a walk in the park, convincing a ski instructor who could work only a few months a year to introduce manufacturers of military equipment to his clients, thus earning a commission. The legend had been designed to give credence to our presentation. Since apartheid had led to an embargo on goods from South Africa during the late sixties and early seventies, personal contacts were key. Once introduced by Heinrich, we would "convince" the Arab officials to attend our sales presentation with a wad of cash just to listen. If these government officials agreed to take our cash, they would demonstrate their corruptibility. It would only take a few smaller, carefully planned steps for them to become ours for all intents and purposes.

After a few lessons with Heinrich, we asked him to join us for drinks, and a few rounds of beer later, Alon, my supervisor, made the first move and asked Heinrich about his other ski students. Heinrich was unexpectedly guarded; he didn't drop famous names, and, in fact, there were no names of Arab countries in the list of countries he mentioned whose citizens had hired him. On the other hand, it seemed that Heinrich was more interested in our background and in our business activities.

"There's something odd about this guy," said Alon later. And indeed, the following morning Alon told us to pack. "We are leaving," he said. "Heinrich is already contracted."

The office had just received a warning that Heinrich was on an alert list of BND, the German Federal Intelligence Service (*Bundesnachrichtendienst*), as working for a communist Eastern

Bloc country's intelligence service. He had perhaps been trying to recruit us.

That experience taught me an important lesson. In the intelligence world, there are no sure things. What seems like a slam dunk could turn up empty.

The next morning I called Erikka. If she was glad to hear my voice, she didn't sound like it.

"Are you OK?" I couldn't help but asking.

"I'll be fine," she said. "I'm going through a difficult time."

"Anything I can do to help?" She hesitated. "You can tell me," I said. "Maybe I can help."

"Well . . ." She paused again.

"Yes?"

"I need a job," she said abruptly, hesitation gone.

"Oh." I gave it time to sound surprised. "Well, that's funny. I was calling you about just that. I've been thinking about our conversation. I was really impressed with your knowledge of Austria and Iran, and I think I could use your talents."

"You mean hire me?"

"That's right. I consulted with Steve about it. I can offer you €2,500 a month, guaranteed for a period of six months." She was silent. "Are you still there?" I asked.

"Yes, yes," she said. "It's really a generous offer."

"Yeah, well, Steve also liked the idea, so the company's picking up the tab."

"What would I be doing?"

"You'd be assisting me, mostly in research. And traveling—I hope that'd be OK. Obviously, all travel expenses are covered."

"Travel where? To Iran?" Excitement suddenly entered her voice.

"Probably. Is that OK?"

"It's wonderful. I'd love to go back."

"Well, it's definitely an option. You know I want to find my Iranian roots—maybe write another book. Is there anything here that'd prevent you from traveling?"

"Only my cat. I have a grown daughter who lives in Zürich, and I can easily get another tutor to teach my only student."

"Good. So we're on. I need to leave Vienna for a few days, but as far as I'm concerned, it's a done deal. I'll put a letter to you in the mail with an advance for the first month. Is that OK?"

"Super."

The following morning, after a too-rich Austrian breakfast, the driver took me to a meeting at a modest-looking house in a residential area. The driver nodded towards the house and indicated he would wait.

I went through the gate and knocked on the heavy, dark, wooden door. A young man opened the door, and without saying anything, signaled me to follow him to a sitting room. I sat on the couch and waited. The wooden floor was clean, but worn out. There was hardly any furniture in the room and no personal items. Moments later Casey Bauer and Benny Friedman arrived.

They sat on the black leather couch opposite me, and Casey got right to it.

"I hear you've already successfully accomplished getting Erikka on board."

How did he know that? I hadn't reported it yet. Was her phone tapped, or maybe mine? Why was he revealing the fact that he knew?

"Yes. It wasn't difficult. She was very eager, as you said. We need to mail her a check." I gave Casey the details.

"Dan," said Casey in a serious tone. "We've got a tentative go-ahead for the plan that was discussed."

"Mossad is cooperating with the U.S. on that," added Benny.

"Dan," said Casey. "You will fly with Erikka from Vienna to Tehran."

I nodded. "When?"

"A date hasn't been set yet, because we need to train you in Iranian customs, get a designated contact to be ready for you, and make sure Erikka is ready to travel when the final approval is issued."

Casey opened a briefcase and pulled out a thick folder. "During your next meeting with Erikka, tell her that you have a pleasant surprise for her. While you were away from Vienna, you met Swiss bankers on a social occasion and told them about your forthcoming trip to Iran. When the language-barrier issue came up, you mentioned that you'd be accompanied by a European woman who graduated from the American School in Tehran and is fluent in Farsi. One of the bankers called you a few days later with an offer. He wanted to use your assistant's contact with the former graduates of the school as an opportunity to introduce his bank's services to Iranian businesses. He told you that he believed that graduates of that school will now be employed in high-ranking positions in the Iranian economy, and that he would finance efforts to locate alumni of the school who live in Tehran, and perhaps arrange a reunion to showcase the bank's services. Tell her that the bank's representative wants to interview her, and if she meets the bank's needs, they will pay her €1,500 a month, guaranteed for seven months, to locate the alumni and coordinate the reunion."

"Isn't €1,500 a month too little?"

"No. If she's paid too much, she might lose interest in your book project."

"Gotcha. By the way, she's gonna want to know the bank's name. She is, after all, Swiss."

"Tempelhof Bank."

I couldn't help but grin. Benny's bank. Benny kept a straight face, but the spark in his eyes said it all.

Casey turned to me. "We will provide you with a short family tree of your paternal grandfather's side to memorize and use in searching for your relatives." I would get a mission kit for review, he said, and would go to Iran as Ian Pour Laval.

I was told my new family history. My paternal grandfather was Ali Akbar Pour. He was born in Tehran and immigrated to Canada in the 1920s, where he owned a small candy and cigarettes store. He married a local woman, and they had one son, my purported father, Pierre Pour. Upon his marriage and my birth, my mother's maiden name was added to my father's family name, as is customary in many societies. I was the only living family member, making my legend airtight.

A local contact, Kurdish intelligence officer Padaş Acun, would be my weapon of last resort in case of emergency. Probably another Mossad contribution.

"Padaş's men will look after you as guardian angels, but from a distance," said Casey. "They don't know who you are, and shouldn't know, as well. The legend is that they're indirectly hired by an insurance company to protect you from kidnapping for ransom because you married a wealthy heiress. Your wife's family took out an insurance policy, and the insurance company hired a security consulting company to protect you, and they outsourced the job to Padaş. He thinks that he knows the 'real story,' that your wife's relatives are also important contributors to the ruling party in Canada, and therefore any harm threatened will immediately get the Canadian government to intervene. But that legend is really thin, so he may guess who you're working for. If he asks, deny. Although he's likely to suspect that you're more than just a writer and even guess that you're an intelligence officer, he has no idea about your allegiance or purpose of mission. By being at a distance his men will also be able to monitor and report if you have attracted the attention of any branch of VEVAK." The Iranian security service.

"So I'm married?" I tried to remember if I'd said anything to Erikka about my personal life.

"Only legally. You are separated, but until a divorce decree is entered, your wife's lawyers didn't want to take any chance, especially because you have children, so they had an insurance policy issued."

"If my Kurdish guardian angels establish the potential rivals to be Iranian security, what then?"

"They'll report any attention you might attract. They were told that kidnappers may use contacts within the Iranian security establishment to inform them of your movements. Therefore, they should regard any interest you're attracting as hostile, even if it comes from Iranian VEVAK."

I nodded. "How do I make contact with Padaş?"

"You don't initiate the contact. He'll introduce himself soon after you arrive and will tell you how to contact him in an emergency. Make sure that all your book-research contacts are made openly with people who would have no connection with government, military, defense, or anything strategic. Talk to shoemakers, bazaar merchants, teachers, farmers. Write down what they say, without attribution. If your notes are ever reviewed, they should show nothing but innocuous conversations on daily life and family customs of Iran. Same goes for your search for your roots. Try to get invited to homes, but wait for the second or third repetition of the invitation to accept. Keep in mind an Iranian proverb that may become handy: '*Bi aedisheh aez du:zaeh ya: behesht sa:degh ba:sh*'—'Be honest without the thought of heaven or hell.' "

"Why are you mentioning it?"

"Because we don't want you to do anything a regular tourist wouldn't. I'm sure you'll be rewarded."

"I didn't know you spoke Farsi," I said.

"I don't. I learned that proverb from a wise man." Funny, Casey didn't strike me as a proverb-quoting kind of guy. Maybe I wasn't as good at pegging people as I thought I was.

"What about Erikka?" I asked.

"What about her?"

"Any instructions?"

"Nothing that concerns the real reason why she's going to Iran. Obviously she should never learn who you are or what the real purpose of your visit is. Let her suggest ways she could help you in your book research and your search for your roots. If you can, escort her to her meetings with her alumni, but don't take center stage."

"Where will the reunion take place?"

"Europe would have been ideal, but since some of these people could be part of the current government or even the security establishment, they might become suspicious, or the government itself might. So we'll probably have it in Tehran."

"What about the American alumni who can't or won't return to Iran?"

"The American graduates came out squeaky clean in our check, so we don't need them. We'll say the reunion is regional—'Asian-European.' We can have alums from countries that have diplomatic relationships with Iran, so no one will think it's for ethnic Iranians only and get suspicious."

Three hours of instruction later, Benny said calmly, "I brought you a present." Casey Bauer smiled knowingly.

"What? A farewell gift? You don't expect to see me back?" I found myself sounding like the Jewish mother in all the jokes.

"Oh, stop," Benny said, signaling to Casey to open the door. A short, very thin, dark-skinned man in his sixties with wavy black hair walked in with a demure demeanor.

"Please meet Parviz Morad," said Benny. I looked at the stranger. He was wearing clothes that were about one or two sizes bigger than his frame. His dark eyes were sunken and his wrinkled cheeks fallen. His face was gloomy. He seemed so humble, looking at us as if he were waiting for instructions.

Benny touched the man's shoulder and said, "Please sit here with us." The man complied.

"Mr. Parviz Morad was born in Tehran in 1962 to an army colonel who had been the Iranian military attaché in London for two years during the reign of the Shah. Parviz attended the American School in Tehran from first grade through fourth, and from seventh through twelfth grades. He attended fifth and sixth grades in London."

Born in 1962? He was only forty-three, but looked decades older.

At Benny's prompting, Morad began to speak, in English with a slight British accent. "In late 1979 I was drafted into a highly selective unit of young Iranian men. We were sent to a heavily guarded location in northern Tehran, which before the revolution was used as a club for foreign military officers.

We were subjected to daily religious indoctrination and teaching of strict rules of Islamic behavior according to Ayatollah Khomeini's interpretation of Islam."

"Please tell my friend the name of that unit," said Benny.

"It was code-named Atashbon, Farsi for *the guardians of fire*," he answered, lowering his eyes.

I was staggered. So that's what Benny had meant. Parviz Morad was my farewell present.

CHAPTER SEVENTEEN

I hid my surprise. "How many of you were in Atashbon?" I asked.

"Eighteen or twenty, I don't remember exactly."

"Was it all religious indoctrination?" I asked.

"No. After the religious immersion that lasted six months, we were given military training and an additional six-month course in intelligence gathering and communications."

"Where were you located?"

"Department 81 maintained a top-secret center in the suburbs of Tehran, code-named Agdassieh Post, and another satellite office, Shiraz Post."

"Were you the only group to be trained there?"

He shook his head. "No. We discovered later that this place was used also for training combatants to carry out terrorist attacks, assassinations, and kidnappings outside Iran. We were also trained at Imam Hussein Post, usually used by a regional unit attached to the Revolutionary Guards—Pasdaran-e Enghelab-e Islami. That location was also used as a training center for sabotage and other terrorist activities in foreign countries."

"When you were selected, did you know why?" I asked.

He shook his head. "No."

"They never told you why you were assembled together, separated from your families and friends?" His soundtrack sounded untrustworthy.

"We immediately recognized that we were all graduates of the American School in Tehran. We speculated that we were sent there for reeducation to rid us of the satanic doctrines of America. When we asked why we were selected, we were told that we would soon find out. We then had military and clandestine-operation training. We realized they had specific tasks for us."

"Did you already know the other cadets?" I asked.

"Just two or three, and not even by name." He moved his eyes and looked toward the window. *We have a problem here,* I thought.

"What happened after the training ended?"

"We were taken to a meeting with an ayatollah, who told us how we should be proud to be chosen to fight for the Islamic Revolution," he answered. "He said that the Americans are infidel pigs and sons of monkeys who think that with the might of the Great Satan they can bring true believers down. 'They have no honor,' he said. 'You will give them a lesson they'll remember.'"

"And what was that lesson? Did he say?"

"No, he only said that our instructors would tell us. We returned to our base, and Bahman Hossein Rashtian, our commander, told us what was expected of us."

"And?" I said, struggling to keep the impatience out of my voice.

"Rashtian told us that the revolution was counting on us to destroy America. We were going to be sent to the United States using stolen identities and establish ourselves as regular U.S. citizens. Once we were immersed in a community, we were to receive instructions from Tehran."

"Did he tell you specifically how you would assume American identities?"

"Yes, we actually had training classes on that. They told us how they got the first American passport. Our instructor told us about the German archaeological team and its request to allow an American photographer to enter Iran. That request was brought to the attention of our commander, Bahman Hossein Rashtian. He boasted that he immediately identified the potential. Since the capture of the American Embassy and its diplomats, no American dared set foot in Iran. But if that photographer would agree to come to Iran, Atashbon's first project could be launched. He told us that since all the outgoing and incoming mail of foreigners in Iran was opened, he knew exactly what to do.

"Rashtian called the American photographer, posing as a member of the archaeological group, and offered Ward a job for $500 a month for three months. Rashtian told us that according to the visa application filed by the archaeological expedition, Ward's parents were no longer living. Rashtian then questioned Fischer about Albert's finances under the guise of investigating Albert's ability to support himself in Iran. Fischer told him that Albert was living on $5 a day. That, Rashtian told us, gave him the idea how to lure Albert into Iran."

"Wasn't Ward hesitant?" I asked.

"Yes, but when he heard that the first month's salary would be paid up front, directly into his bank account outside Iran, he gave in."

"Do you know what happened to Ward?"

"He was killed by Rashtian's men. We heard from Rashtian that before killing Ward they had extracted from him information about his life. It took some time, because he stuttered."

"And then?"

"Kourosh Alireza Farhadi, a member of Atashbon, with physical characteristics similar to Ward's, was chosen to step into Ward's identity."

"Tell us about Atashbon and Department 81," said Casey.

"Department 81 had several hundred staff members. Our unit of American School graduates was Atashbon. Both were operated under the overall command and supervision of Bahman Hossein Rashtian."

"Did Department 81 have other missions?"

"Yes, but I have no specific knowledge. We were kept apart from the others."

"How do you know all this about Ward?" I asked. It seemed suspicious that the Iranians hadn't compartmentalized the information, a must in any intelligence operation.

"Since it was the first case, we were all participating in the process to learn how to do it with the next American that was caught."

"Then what happened?" I asked.

"After viewing Ward's five-hour eight-millimeter film interview many times, and rehearsing his new role as Albert Ward, Kourosh Alireza Farhadi was given Ward's passport and other documents and was flown from Europe to Toronto, Canada."

"Do you know which country in Europe?"

"No. They didn't tell us. Later on, we were told that after a few days in Toronto, Farhadi, now posing as Albert Ward, boarded a bus and crossed the border to the U.S."

It had been that easy, I realized. In those days, there had been very little or no inspection at the U.S.-Canadian border. At many border crossings, there had been no immigration inspection, only customs officers interested if the passenger was bringing any fresh food from Canada. No entry stamps had been used for returning U.S. citizens, and no record of the entry had been made.

"Did they tell you how Kourosh immersed himself in the U.S.?" asked Casey.

Parviz nodded. "In our training class. Although he spoke perfect English, he'd never actually visited the U.S. They wanted us to learn from his mistakes and difficulties."

I immediately thought about the immersion training at Mossad. Those chosen to be sent into hostile countries were called "combatants," not agents, and were trained separately from the rest of us, who were intended to become case officers. During a period of preparation that lasted one to three years, most of the combatants were initially sent to a nonhostile third country to familiarize themselves with the country's daily routines—riding a bus, buying groceries, watching popular TV shows, and reading the sports columns. Only when the controllers were confident that a combatant was ready was he planted in the target country. From what Parviz was describing, it seems that the Iranians weren't that sophisticated, and had sent Kourosh Alireza Farhadi directly to the U.S. with only a brief stopover in Canada. I now understood why Louis Romano, the drama teacher from Gary, Indiana, had been surprised at the Chameleon's lack of familiarity with terms that any Wisconsin resident would know.

Still, I had to concede that the Iranians' mistakes hadn't harmed their mission much.

"Despite all that, they told us in the update meetings that Farhadi was able to pull off a series of scams, mostly against U.S. banks, eventually exceeding $100 million. The Iranian security-service officers in our camp were elated and said that they had awarded Farhadi with two medals that would be kept in his file until he returned to Tehran."

"Where were you all this time?"

"In Tehran, working at the headquarters of Atashbon. Rashtian said that my accent was too British."

I asked Parviz directly, "How did you end up here?"

He shrugged. "I came to think the new regime wasn't much better than the Shah's. When I talked about it with my friends, or people I thought were my friends, I was accused of being an infidel and a betrayer of the faith and was expelled from the unit. Within three days I was taken from the camp by military police, drafted into the Iranian army, and sent to the front lines to fight the Iraqis."

"When was that?"

"It was the end of the war, 1988. It took only two weeks for me to be captured. They held me until not long ago."

Benny spoke up. "Our agents heard about him from a released prisoner and managed to buy his freedom and smuggle him out of Iraq just before this most recent war. He received political asylum in Israel in return for his cooperation."

I excused myself and took Benny aside. "Why just now?" I asked Benny in Hebrew. "Where was he all this time?"

"We got him out only recently," he answered quietly in Hebrew. That meant he'd just finished squeezing out every bit of information available.

"Can he identify all other members of Atashbon?"

"He says he can't. He says he knew only two others by name. The rest were given code names, and he had never been in the same class with them at the American School."

I didn't buy that, but said nothing to Benny. Maybe Benny wanted that information fleshed out later and exchanged when he needed something from the CIA.

"And the two he knew?"

"We're working on it with Casey."

We returned to the sofa and joined Morad and Casey.

"How many Atashbon members were ultimately sent to the U.S.?" asked Casey. He'd saved the most important question for the end, always a good tactic.

"I was there about eight years," said Parviz. "I know for a fact that at least eight men were sent from Iran during that period."

"All to the U.S.?"

"I think so. All were gradually transferred to a third country, mostly in Europe, for a few days, and from there they were sent individually to the U.S."

"But you don't have their names?"

"No. Other than the two I remembered from school, the rest were strangers. It was all extremely secretive. We were forbidden to use our real names and were given new Iranian names. I got so used to my new name that I sometimes get confused and still use it, although it's been many years now."

"And do you remember any real names of the members?" asked Casey.

"Just one."

"And who was that?"

"Alec Simmons."

"Anything else about him?"

"I don't know. I've never seen Alec Simmons, I only heard of him. He was the second or the third catch of Rashtian."

"Do you know anything about the person who assumed his identity?"

"His new Iranian name was Ibrahim Soleimani. I have no idea what his real name is."

Casey intervened. "Do you know anything about him at all?" He was becoming impatient and dismissive.

"Very little. Although we lived together in the camp, we were forbidden to talk about our past. Once, one of us was overheard telling his friend about his grandfather. He was punished severely."

"Meaning . . . ?" Casey pressed harder.

"He was lashed, before all of us."

"What did Ibrahim Soleimani look like?" I resumed control of the questioning.

"Well, it has been eighteen years. But back then he was chubby. He was five foot eight and weighed, to my estimate, two hundred and fifty pounds. Black hair and eyes."

"Any special physical markings?"

"I don't remember anything special about him. He spoke very good English and had a nice sense of humor. We were lucky to be living in Tehran under reasonable conditions, while others our age were fighting the Iraqis in the desert trenches. So we kept our mouths shut and obeyed our superiors."

I continued interviewing Morad for two more hours until an aide to Benny arrived and took Morad with him.

"This is a transcript of his interrogation in Israel," said Benny as he handed me a bound copy. "It can't leave this place." He showed me to another room with a desk and a sofa. "Here you can read and take notes. Avoid copying telltale sentences."

"Do you trust him?" I asked Benny.

He gave me that look reserved for those born stupid who live to demonstrate it daily.

"Are you kidding? We use him as an intelligence source only, and not a very reliable one either. Read his story with a huge grain of salt."

Casey's mobile phone rang. Before moving to an adjacent

room to take the call he told me that a Mossad veteran named Reuven would instruct me on Iranian customs and daily life on the following day.

After Benny and Casey left the safe apartment, I spent most of the evening and some of the night reading the transcript of Morad's interrogation. I woke up on the sofa in the morning clutching the notebook, and gave it to a woman who'd politely asked me to return it to her.

I went back to my hotel for a change of clothes, and then walked in the chilly Vienna air to another safe apartment to meet Reuven. That safe apartment was located in a prewar building, just a few blocks from my hotel.

I rang the bell. A fifty-something woman with a sour face opened the door.

"Ja?"

"*Ich bin* Ian Pour Laval. *Ich werde erwartet hier.*" I'm Ian Pour Laval, I'm expected here.

She opened the door wider and let me in. I found myself in a big room with a high ceiling and a tall wooden door leading to other rooms. The apartment was sparsely decorated and had only minimal furniture. A long table with two computer monitors stood across the room, and an easel was next to the wall. I waited for the woman to say something, but she didn't. She opened the door to an adjoining room and left. I just stood there. A moment later the inside door opened and a dark-skinned man with white hair appeared.

"Shalom," he said. It sounded out of place here. "I'm Reuven Sofian. Pleased to meet you." Reuven looked like an old eagle, with dark sunken black eyes trapped in a face of wrinkled ashen rock, and thick overgrown eyebrows. He shook my hand.

"Same here," I answered in Hebrew.

"Sit down and relax," he suggested, pointing at the sofa.

"Relax? Why do you say that?" I asked in a mock surprise with a smile. But I knew he was reading my body language. He smiled at me genially.

"Because we'll be spending a few days together discussing Iranian customs and routines, and I want you to feel comfortable. We'll also work on the relevant portions of your legend."

"The legend looks rather straightforward," I said.

"True, but it needs to be embedded in your mind, since you're going into Iran, not to Norway. The Iranian security services treat suspects somewhat differently, so you'd better have a cover story that will seem logical, plausible, and consistent. Most of all we'll discuss how to stay out of trouble."

We should, I thought. After all, it was my neck.

Reuven gave me a very detailed description of daily life in Tehran. That lasted four hours. We broke for coffee and tea.

"I guess you were born there," I said, sensing he loved the country and the people but detested the regime. He nodded. "Have you ever been back since you left?" Reuven only smiled in answer.

We had to review the main cause for all of this conflict: the Iranian revolution itself. Reuven's presentation was straightforward. By welcoming foreign companies and culture to Iran, the Shah had disenfranchised two power bases—the bazaar merchants and the clerics. Once Khomeini seized power, those who had actually empowered him were pushed aside in favor of an unusual coalition of fanatic mullahs and bazaar merchants. The war with Iraq further quelled opposition, despite its terrible consequences for Iran. Reuven was thorough and precise. He concluded the political portion of his review within an hour, winding up with a gulp of coffee from his mug.

"What about Erikka?" I asked. "Any instructions?"

"Go over the rules with her, just in case, because she left Iran as the revolution started and may not be aware of the moral rules and dress code. Say you did some research. Tell her that you don't think it will be helpful if she gets in trouble in Iran, because it may reflect on you as well. She must cover her body, including her feet. No bright colors are allowed. If you leave Tehran, I'd recommend she stick to black. If Erikka wants to swim at the hotel's swimming pool, she must be covered completely. Women violating the dress code could be punished severely, even flogged."

He continued. "Don't offer a handshake to a woman, or touch a woman in public. Stay away from a religious debate—it can be dangerous. The Iranians are very fussy about their honor. What would be acceptable in Europe, or America, is forbidden in Iran."

"Such as what?"

"Such as giving a thumbs-up."

"Why?"

"Because that's the Iranian way of saying 'fuck you.' "

Definitely good to know.

"Crossing the street in Tehran is like swimming across a crocodile-infested river. Car drivers ignore all rules but their own, which change momentarily while they drive. Pedestrians are considered a nuisance by motorists. Be particularly wary of motorbikes. They take the liberty of riding on the sidewalks or against traffic. If you pass the former U.S. Embassy building, don't attempt to take pictures.

"Ask Erikka to teach you some basic words and expressions in Farsi. She will like that, and it's important in more than one manner. Not only will it become handy, since very few people speak English, but it will also endear you to them.

"Show interest in people, as an author is expected to. I repeat, in people, not installations or strategic points. Good places for you to meet people are the public parks. Go there on Thursday and Friday nights, at a late hour when many families and their young children assemble until after midnight. Summer nights are hot, and people escape the heat of their uninsulated homes."

"I'll be there in the winter, I presume, but just in case, any particular place in mind?"

"Yes. Park-e Mellat is located to the north of Vanak Square along Vali Asr Avenue, in northern Tehran. It's very popular among young families who bring food baskets and picnic. If you're hungry, cross the street; there are street vendors and also small coffee shops. Most people don't have money to go to fancy restaurants. Iran is a rich country, but the population is

Please return the items by the
due date(s) listed below, to
any Memphis Public Library
location.   For renewals:
Automated line: 452-2047
Highland Branch: 452-7341
Online: www.memphislibrary.org

Date due: 11/19/2010, 23:59
Item ID: 01152402169141
Title: The Chameleon Conspiracy
Author: Carmon, Haggai

Date due: 11/19/2010, 23:59
Item ID: 01152717523392
Title: Bone
Author: Gardner, Lisa.

Date due: 11/19/2010, 23:59
Item ID: 01152410003355
Title: Whirlpool
Author: Lowell, Elizabeth, 1944-

NO RENEWALS FOR:
Audio-visual material or
7-day Popular Library books

****
Go Green: Recycle Your Books
Today! Donate your books to
Friends of the Library.

poor. In 1977, the average personal income in Iran was $2,450, same as in Spain. However last year, Iran's per capita income was less than $1,640, same as the Gaza Strip.

"You will be given escape-route instructions separately, but you should know that there's a weekly train from Tehran to Damascus leaving Mondays at 18:35. A one-way ticket is 330,000 rials—about $40. The ride takes sixty-five hours, including long waits at each border crossing. One is while crossing from Iran to Turkey, and the second while crossing from Turkey to Syria."

"Syria? Why would I want to go there?"

"If you need to escape, a train to Syria may be a good idea. Of course you'll get off in Turkey, but buy the ticket all the way to Syria. The Agency personnel will discuss it with you in more detail. One more thing particular to Iran: Terminal 2 at Tehran Airport is the international departures terminal. It's easily confused with the domestic departures. Make sure Erikka goes through the female gate.

"There are a few more things you should bear in mind about Iranians. They're hospitable, but may not be candid with things they tell you. Concealment of facts and flexible definition of truth is a traditional way of life. Iranians trust only their family, no others, and definitely not *stranieri*—foreigners. Feel free to negotiate and bargain everywhere. That's acceptable, even expected."

Three detail-intensive hours later, Reuven looked at his watch. "John will join us in a few minutes."

I heard the doorbell ring, the main door opened and closed, and an elderly man with a sprightly gait entered our room escorted by the sour-faced woman.

"Hi Dan. I'm John Sheehan," he said as he shook my hand.

"John will bring you up to date on more recent political history," said Reuven while collecting his papers. "I'll see you tomorrow."

"Dan," said John as we sat down, "we will spend the next few hours discussing the darker side of Iran, something I've been doing for the Agency for more than thirty years."

"Shoot," I said.

He leaned back on the couch. "Let me give you an overview of Iranian security agencies, your potential adversaries. There are six key entities for your purposes. The most notorious is the Iranian Revolutionary Guard Corps or IRGC, also known as Pasdaran. They're entrusted with the responsibility of protecting the revolution, meaning being the muscle of the fanatic clerics to enforce their interpretation of Islamic rules."

I stretched on the couch as he continued. "They grew from a regular small police force to a whopping several hundred thousand, organized independently or attached to military units. They even have small planes and boats. The Pasdaran were very zealous in monitoring the regime's perceived inside enemies. To broaden their grasp over the lives of every Iranian, they recruited hundreds of thousands of volunteers, the Baseej. These volunteers report suspected behavior or activities of all citizens and arrest women who fail to follow the strict dress code that the revolution imposed."

"What happens to violators?"

"If you're lucky you get only an oral warning. Others receive written notices warning them of their 'social corruption.' Almost one hundred thousand people were actually arrested last year for violating the codes. Bear in mind that the Revolutionary Guards have other names for their units operating in foreign countries. That includes their subsidiary organizations, Hezbollah and Islamic Jihad. The names they use are the 'Committee on Foreign Intelligence Abroad' and the 'Committee on Implementation of Actions Abroad.' In essence, the Revolutionary Guards' foreign units operate like any other clandestine intelligence operation. They mask their foreign activities by using front companies and nongovernmental organizations, trading companies, and banks."

"I know the routine," I said patiently. "While outside Iran, some of their agents operate out of the Iranian embassies to enjoy diplomatic immunity." I remembered a case I'd been involved in earlier where Iranian agents in Europe had tried to shield themselves from arrest by using their diplomatic immunity. But they'd made one mistake: they'd worked at the embassy in Rome and operated in Munich. That transborder mistake had rendered their immunity worthless.

"Correct. They also started the 'Foundation of the Oppressed and Dispossessed,' or Bonyade-e- Mostafazan, used for infiltration into and then subsequent control of Islamic charities in many countries. Another clandestine unit of the Guards is the Qods—Jerusalem—Force. Our sources estimate that their size exceeds ten thousand men. They're assigned to foreign activities, which include terror. The Qods Force maintains training facilities in Iran and in Sudan for the terrorists of the next generation. In addition to training, they also gather intelligence on potential targets for terror attacks and monitor dissidents of the Iranian regime."

"Some of them sometimes mysteriously disappear," I added cynically.

John smiled. "And some not so mysteriously. Tehran continues to provide logistic support and training to Lebanese Hezbollah and a variety of Palestinian groups such as Hamas and Islamic Jihad. What we need to discuss is the Ministry of Intelligence and Security, or MOIS, also known as Vezarat-e Ettela'at va Amniat-e Keshvar, or VEVAK. It's the successor to SAVAK, the Shah's notorious internal-security agency. Religious leaders had recruited former SAVAK agents to help the regime eliminate domestic opposition. Consequently, some intelligence officers and low-ranking SAVAK and army-intelligence officials were asked to return to government service because of their specialized knowledge of the Iranian left, which emerged as the only opposition. VEVAK extends its hold outside Iran as well. Its agents are disguised as diplomats in Iranian embassies and consular offices, or as employees of the Ministry of Culture and Islamic Guidance representatives. Light covers include employees of Iran Air, students, or businessmen. We even saw Iranian agents holding themselves out as members of the opposition groups."

I could only imagine what happened to the poor souls

who believed them and talked against Iran or participated in any anti-Iranian activities.

John continued with a thorough lecture on the other military and security organizations for three more hours. He poured coffee from a large thermos into a white mug and waited for my reaction. I was tired and becoming restless, and John could tell.

"OK. You'll be picked up tomorrow morning for more Mossad briefing. At a later time I'll give you reading material."

I knew a fair amount of what they were telling me. But then again, knowledge was power, especially on these kinds of missions. It would up my odds of returning home alive.

CHAPTER EIGHTEEN

In the morning I returned to the safe apartment for an additional session with Reuven. The street next to the safe apartment was congested; a car with its hood open was idled in the middle of the road. That backed up traffic for the entire street. I entered the apartment. Reuven was wearing the same clothes as yesterday, and smelled of a good aftershave lotion.

"Let's begin," I said. I was alert and eager.

Reuven started. "The leaders of the Iranian Islamic Revolution set the agenda for state-sponsored terrorism, making Iran the world's most active sponsor of terrorism. Their strategy is first, to hit their political opponents—there were at least eighty assassinations of Iranian dissidents who fled Iran, mostly to Europe. Next, to expand their influence throughout the Gulf region and the Islamic world."

"And then?"

"The world. We have already heard the Iranian president saying that. The regime has planned or encouraged suicide bombings of American military targets. But recently they have changed course. Sensing the world's growing disgust with state-sponsored terrorism and an increased political pressure by foreign countries, Tehran's official new line is that they provide only humanitarian and cultural assistance to radical movements such as Islamic Jihad, Hezbollah, and Hamas."

"Do you believe them? I don't," I said.

"Of course not," said Reuven. "These are empty statements. In fact nothing has changed. Nonetheless, they vehemently deny any military or financial assistance to these organizations. They apply *Taqiyya* and *kitman*."

"You mean religious and historical concepts?" I asked, remembering learning about it at the Mossad Academy. *Taqiyya* is a precautionary dissimulation or deception and keeping one's beliefs secret, and *kitman* means more mental reservation and disguising malicious intentions. *Taqiyya* and *kitman*, or "holy hypocrisy," were used by Shiite Muslims centuries ago in their conflict with Sunni Muslims. Hundreds of years ago *Taqiyya* had been used by Persian warriors to confuse the enemy. One tactic was "deceptive triangulation": to make your enemies believe that jihad wasn't aimed at them, but at another enemy.

"Yes," he said. "The Iranian government has turned them into political tools. By applying it to their plan of plausible denial, present-day clerics resurrected a theological doctrine to make it a tactical political tool. We've found Al-Qaeda training manuals with instructions on the use of deception to achieve terrorist goals."

"I read in a brief I received last week that Iranian government spokesmen commonly use *Taqiyya* as a form of 'outwitting,' " I said. "The rule is, if you're faced with an unpleasant situation or with damaging facts, avoid the debate. You should 'outwit' your opponent through the use of *Taqiyya*, diverting your opponent and obfuscating the issue being discussed. Another form of distraction and 'outsmarting' is claiming to be the 'victim' of religious discrimination and intolerance during debate or discussion."

"Right," said Reuven. "You will see it in practice every-where you go in Iran, in the bazaar or in daily conversations, and of course by government officials."

"I already have," I said. "In previous cases when I had con-tacts with Iranian officials, it was abundantly clear that they were employing manipulative ambiguity tactics. Rather than admit that some of the things you say can be true, they adamantly de-nied it. They used double-talk that left me with no answer, even to the simplest of my questions," I concluded, remembering how frustrated I'd become.

We continued talking for two more hours. During lunch break I decided to walk to my hotel. The stranded car was gone, and traffic was flowing. I suddenly sensed that a late-model Japanese-made car was slowly following me. At the next street corner I "dry-cleaned" it, intel lingo for maneuvering tactically to shake off a follower, by entering a one-way street, and the car disappeared. To be on the safe side I changed my plans. Instead of returning directly to my hotel, I entered a café, ordered hot chocolate, left a €5 bill on the table, and went to the men's room before my order came in. I used the service entrance and went out to the street. When I arrived at my hotel, I entered through the service entrance at the back.

In the late afternoon I used the service entrance again and took a cab, telling the cabby to take me for an hour tour of Vi-enna, and when I was sure we weren't followed, I told him to take me to a street adjacent to the safe apartment. I walked a block and entered the building. I rang the doorbell, but nobody answered. I took out my mobile phone to call. The display showed that I had two missed calls. I dialed the most-recent number. It was John. "Ian, I'm glad you called back. Don't go to the safe apartment."

"Why?"

"It has been compromised."

"Meaning?"

"I'll explain later. Just don't go there."

"I'm already there. I tried the door, but there was no answer."

"Where are you now?"

"Next to the door."

"Have you noticed anyone surveying you?"

"I'm not sure."

"Anyone see you entering the building?"

"I don't know. The street was empty, but that means nothing." I told him about the car I'd thought was trailing me.

"You can't use the front door again," he said decisively. "Go down the stairs, pass the main entry door to the building, and continue to the basement. You'll see a big black metal door leading to the machine room. It's unlocked. Get inside and lock it behind you with the metal bar. Walk toward the back of the basement. There's a glass window behind the central heating burner. Climb to the window—it's only about seven feet from the floor—and exit the basement through that window. You'll find yourself in the backyard of the building. There's a low fence separating the building from the back of the adjacent building, which faces a parallel street. Cross that fence, pass through the backyard of the other building, exit to the street, and take a taxi. Don't return to your hotel. Call me when you're in the cab for more instructions."

I felt the adrenaline rush, just like in the old action-filled Mossad days. I went down to the basement. I had difficulty climbing up to the small window. I couldn't climb using the boiler as a step, because its surface was too hot, and the window was right behind it. I went to the adjacent laundry room, dragged out an old wooden table used for ironing, and climbed on it. As soon as I was halfway through the window, the table collapsed under my weight. *I should go on a diet again,* I promised myself, struggling to make it the rest of the way out. In five minutes I was on another street. I stopped a cab and called John.

"Now, take your cab on a twenty-minute ride around Vienna. After you have established that you aren't being followed, tell the cabby to take you to a nearby tram station. Take the tram to Stephansplatz. You will be about ten minutes from the city center. Get off and take a cab to your hotel, NH

Wien hotel at Mariahilfer Strasse 32–34. It is located on a very long shopping boulevard, at the Spittelberg area. I'll meet you there."

When I exited the tram I saw an empty cab approaching, but I ignored it. I waited for a few more to pass and stopped the fifth cab. Mossad Academy training. Never take a cab when the driver approaches you, and while in a street, never stop the first or second cabs that pass by you. They could be dispatched for you by the opposition. I perfected the rule and usually take only the fifth cab.

I checked into the hotel and went up to my room with John following. The room was small and decorated with light oak furniture.

"What happened?" I asked as soon as I closed my room door.

"We were riding shotgun. We placed a countersurveillance team in a building opposite the safe apartment to protect the rendezvous. They spotted suspicious activity. First a car that didn't have any mechanical problem was made to look like it did."

"How could they tell?"

"Simple. The driver stopped the car in the middle of the street, lifted the hood, and made himself appear as if he were fixing something. But he didn't touch anything. His hands were clean when he went back behind the wheel, purportedly to wait for help. Ten minutes later, he just closed the hood, started the engine, and left. That happened right across from the safe apartment."

"I saw that car too," I said, forgetting to mention that it looked odd to me, but didn't rise to the level of a suspicion, when it should have. "Is that all?"

"No. There was another car cruising the neighborhood repeatedly for no apparent reason. Then Benny reported he was spotted yesterday as he returned to his hotel."

"Is he still there?"

"No. He checked out. Finally, Parviz Morad was discovered making a call from a pay phone in the men's room of his hotel lobby."

"Was he unattended?" I was surprised at how that could have happened.

"No. He was under Mossad's supervision at all times, but during dinner he went to the men's room, and the Mossad agent waited behind the outside door. When Parviz didn't exit immediately, the agent entered and saw him on the phone. These hotels sometime install pay phones inside the bathrooms."

"Has Parviz been doubled?"

"I don't know. Mossad is interrogating him. I've just heard he swore that he only called his uncle in Hamburg, Germany. Parviz claimed the uncle was a known dissident of the Iranian government."

"What do we do now?"

"We wait for the result of the investigation and see if these incidents are directed at us or connected to Parviz's phone call. If he double-crossed us, we may have to conduct a thorough damage control. Anyway, you're not returning to the Holiday Inn. I'll go out and buy you some toiletries and overnight stuff," he said.

"Why don't you just send someone to remove my luggage from the Holiday Inn?"

"Because the hotel and your room are under our observation. I want to create the impression that you still live in that hotel. Maybe these guys will be stupid enough to go there and give us a better idea who they are. Anyway, I don't think you should leave this room until we assess the situation. Order room service," he said, reading my mind.

An hour later John returned with a shopping bag. "There's a change of underwear here"—he handed me the bag—"and shaving cream, disposable razors, a toothbrush, a comb, and toothpaste. That'll keep you for a few days." I looked at the bag; the underwear was oversized and looked ridiculous.

"Thanks," I said without sharing my thoughts on his taste in clothing.

"Let's continue with our original plan," suggested John.

"OK."

I sat on the bed, and John took a chair next to the small desk and dragged it to face me.

"Let me go into the political structure of Iran."

My mind was elsewhere, trying to analyze the unexpected turn of events. But John ignored my hollow look and continued. I had to listen—I was his captive audience.

"The Islamic Republic of Iran embodies Khomeini's doctrine of *Velayat-e Faqih*, or 'Islamic Rule.' He advocated exporting revolution to extend his absolute authority over all Muslims. Central to the concept is the doctrine that all Muslims, wherever they are, belong to the Islamic nation, the *Ummah*—and therefore must obey the authority of the religious leader. It's interesting to note that his followers attempted to broaden the definition of Islam. While most, if not all, Muslims consider Islam as their religion, while they belong to different nations, the Iranian doctrine tried to classify all Muslims as members of a nation."

"Because the Iranians aren't Arabs, and in fact are a minority in Islam," I said.

"Exactly," said John. "This is their sneaky way to install themselves as leaders of a group a billion people strong, rather than limiting their grip to only seventy million Iranians. They wrote a new constitution, which gives this immense power to one person to become the head of the *faqih*, the ruling council. Ayatollah Khomeini was the first head of the *faqih*. The supreme religious leader has almost unlimited powers. He appoints the chief judges of the judicial branch; the chief of staff of the armed forces; the commander of the Pasdaran; the personal representatives of the *faqih* to the Supreme Defense Council; and the commanders of the army, air force, and navy."

"Democracy is dead, long live theocracy."

"Obviously. The will of the individual has no meaning. For example, the *faqih* authorizes the candidates for presidential elections. If the supreme religious leader doesn't approve, then a candidate cannot run. There's no appeal."

"Did the Iranian people accept that?"

"Many of them didn't. Soon after the Islamic Revolution approximately fifty people were executed daily. On some days the number doubled. Many of the executions were public. We estimate that in two years the new regime executed seven to eight thousand people. Realizing that it would be only a question of time before a popular uprising would topple the new regime, they eased their grip a bit. But Iran continues to be a country where human rights—including women's rights, the way we understand them—mean nothing."

John's mobile phone rang. He exchanged a few sentences and flipped the phone's cover.

"OK. The number Parviz has called belongs to Mehrang Pahlbod, a sixty-year-old Iranian exile who has been a vocal opponent of the current Iranian regime. Parviz claimed that Mehrang Pahlbod is his uncle, and the pay-phone call he made was just to say hello."

"I don't trust this guy, and even if he's clean, and even if the relative checks out OK, his phone could be tapped by the opposition," I said.

"Right. We give zero weight to his explanation. But regardless, we had additional suspicious activities here that cannot be ignored. We'll have to keep low for a while until we determine if these events are connected with our plan, or were just a part of their general monitoring of the activities of the Agency and Mossad personnel, without knowing what is brewing. Security says this hotel is unmonitored, so your curfew is partially over, and you may leave your room, but not the hotel."

The next day, I was having a hearty breakfast in the dining room when a young man came to my table.

"Mr. Pour Laval?"

It took me only a second to respond to my new name. After all these years of using assumed names, I wondered why I had never become confused. My only fear was that I could one day bump into someone I had met while on assignment and forget what name I'd used then. What would I do? Ask him, *Excuse me, can you remind me of my name?* As a worst-case scenario he might think I was demented and suggest that I ask the nurse when I return to the institution for the feeble-minded.

"Casey asked that you please go out to a blue van parked near the service entrance." He gave me the security password verifying the instructions that had come from Casey.

I went outside through the back door and made sure, as much as I could, that nobody paid attention to the ten seconds it took me to get to the van. The driver drove me to a new safe apartment in a residential area in the outskirts of Vienna.

"Please go to the second floor. Ring the doorbell of the Kraus family."

Casey Bauer was waiting for me inside the apartment with John and another person.

"This is Tony DaSilva," he said, pointing at a middle-aged man with a dark complexion. "Reuven reported that you successfully passed the test on the Iranian way of life." Not a word about the sudden events of the past day.

"Test? I never took any test," I said instinctively.

DaSilva smiled. "Well, you did. Not all tests are identified by the person being tested. Think about your exchange with Reuven in retrospect, and you'll see what we mean." During the segments of my training when we were playing mock scenarios of me being confronted by Iranian security officers, I had suspected I was being videotaped and that my behavior was being analyzed by experts.

"Do you also have it on video?"

"Yes," he confirmed. "But for instructional purposes only, to learn from our mistakes, if something goes wrong," he answered unexpectedly.

What a bureaucratic way of thinking, I thought. *If I'm caught, they'll need the video to cover their asses and show to any investigating commission that there was nothing wrong in my training or in the instructions they had given me.*

Knowing that the present meeting was probably also video-taped, I kept my notorious big mouth shut. For now.

"Are you comfortable with the legend?" asked Tony.

"I'll tell you when I return alive. But from what I see now, I need to be convinced that Ian Pour Laval is a fail-safe identity. Can you confirm that?"

"I think we can," he said. "The passport you received is genuine. It was issued to Ian Pour Laval by Passport Canada, the government agency responsible for issuing Canadian passports. Canadian passports are valid for five years only, and a new passport must be obtained upon expiration. The one you're getting is valid for two more years. In 2002 Passport Canada introduced new passports with enhanced security, but we decided to use a version that predated the change, although we made no changes to the passport."

"What do you mean no changes?"

"The personal information page that carries the photo and signature is digitally printed and embedded in the page, and a thin security film displays an intricate pattern of images that are revealed as the page is moved."

"If no changes were made, then why did you mention that it had to be an old version?"

"Officially and publicly, the Canadians are saying that these are the only added security measures, but there could be additional hidden safety features that they didn't tell us about. Why take a chance? We simply used the available passport, which is an older version. Forgers need to worry about the new passports. You don't, because it wasn't forged or changed."

"Is there a real person by that name?"

"Yes."

"And where is he?"

"In the U.S."

I weighed the information. "People don't know that? I mean his friends and family?"

"No. In the last ten years everyone knew him under a different name. Prior to that he was a freelance journalist working in and out of Europe for European newspapers. That fits your new résumé and legend. He now has a different identity. For all intents and purposes, you're Ian Pour Laval."

"And what about the passport photo?"

"You two look very much alike," said DaSilva.

I was a bit angry. "Look alike?" I asked bitterly. "Have you looked at the passport?"

Tony didn't lose his temper. "I've seen it and I'm looking at you. I see a resemblance. Anyway, the process we applied was more scientific. Ian's photo was taken three years ago when the passport was issued. People change in three years. My ex-wife in particular," he added with a smile. "Then we took your photo from that period, and a computer measured the similarities and the disparities."

"Such as what?"

"Such as the distance between the eyes, or the skull structure."

"And the result?"

"Satisfactory," said Tony. "If a comparison is made by an expert at a lab, there could be a slight problem. But this isn't the issue here. There are no biometric identifiers on the passport, so the passport photo will survive a visual comparison."

"For both purposes?" I asked.

"What do you mean?"

I told them about my concerns. I knew that biometrics is used for two distinct purposes. First, to verify that the passport I carry is indeed mine. This is a "one-to-one match or verification." But the system can also identify or confirm my identity as it appears on the passport by searching a database of biometric records for a match. This is known as "one-to-many match or identification."

"We know for sure that the passport is clean and does not contain any additional information, such as biometrics, other than the printed personal data," said Casey in an assuring tone.

"How can you be so sure?"

"Because they'd have had to measure your biometrics and

record them. Ian has never undergone that procedure." Their answers confirmed that Ian Laval was cooperating with the CIA, and that the passport wasn't lost or stolen.

"OK, let's move on. Once we enter Iran safely, then what?"

"Once at the hotel, Erikka should look for her incoming mail to contact the alumni who answered our ad I told you about."

He handed me a printed page of an ad the bank placed in local Tehran newspapers. "This is the English translation. Erikka already knows about it, after the bank agreed to sponsor the reunion she's organizing. She knows it was the bank's idea to make her visit more efficient and fruitful."

I looked at the page.

Remember the good old times? The Iranian, Asian, and European students of the American School in Tehran have scheduled a reunion. Alumni, please send contact information to Erikka Buhler ('78) c/o Azadi Grand Hotel on Chamran, Evin Cross Road Expressway, Tehran 19837. And let your fellow alums know about the reunion!

"Let Erikka communicate with those who respond. You can volunteer to help her find and meet her classmates, but don't make it appear as if you're in it as well. Deliberately miss one or two meetings she holds, and show only a passing interest in what she's doing. The same rule applies to how interested you'll appear to the alums. But watch, because they're the principal targets. You're going to increase how interested you are in Erikka's activities, but first have her suggest that you get more involved. You're her handler, but don't make her feel pushed or controlled. She might get suspicious—or worse, others might."

"Right, so I'm just manipulating her." It seemed so patently obvious, I wondered why it was being repeated.

"I know you know this, but you know I need to repeat it so

there's no misunderstanding. The immediate goal is to identify and locate the names and whereabouts of all ethnic-Iranian males born between 1954 and 1962 who graduated from the American School in Tehran before it was shut down in 1979. The delimiters make them seventeen to twenty-five years old during the Islamic Revolution and their subsequent recruitment. Therefore, their current ages range between forty-two and fifty. From that list we will try to identify the members of Atashbon."

"Right."

"We, or rather Erikka, will ask each of the alumni she locates to fill out a short questionnaire with current contact information, year of graduation, current occupation, marital status, children, hobbies, and a short résumé telling everyone what they have been doing since graduation. The pretext will be that the information is needed for a brochure that will be distributed to all participants, like a present-day yearbook."

I objected, "Isn't it a bit simplistic to assume that alums in Iran right now weren't Atashbon sleeper agents in the U.S.? They could have just returned to Iran."

He nodded. "We've got to account for all eighteen or so original members whose locations we don't know. But in principle you're right. We want to use the initially traced graduates as a conduit to identify and find the others. Anyway, even the ones who lived in the United States and came back will probably put that down on the biographical profile."

"How do we make the initial contact?" I asked.

"I think you should encourage Erikka to set up individual meetings and manage the entire matter the way she sees fit. Don't make her suspect you of having an ulterior motive. If she feels lost and asks for your advice, you can direct her subtly by asking questions."

"Such as, *Are you preparing a questionnaire?*" I stopped for a moment to arrange my thoughts. "We could prepare a courtesy folder for all graduates who respond. Make it a fancy leather-bound folder—a calculator, a nice pen, whatever—all embossed with the bank's logo."

"We can also include one or two brochures about the international services of the bank," said John, warming to the idea.

"And Erikka will tell everyone who contacts her that they'll get a free gift," I finished.

"Good call," said Casey. "I'll get it going."

I still had some questions about the operational wisdom behind their planning. "What's the reason for not sending Erikka by herself?"

"We discussed that, but it was scrapped for several reasons. First and foremost, since Erikka doesn't know the real reason for your and her visit, she's likely to miss things that you'd never overlook as her controller. From the Iranians' perspective, she's your research assistant. She also has a side job of organizing the reunion. Besides, sending a blonde Western woman by herself to Iran isn't a good idea. She'd be limited in her movements in a conservative society, which believes that the place of the woman is at home with her children, not in a five-star hotel talking to strange men."

"OK," I said moving on. "Do I need an Iranian visa?"

"Yes," said Tony. "Your first option will be at the Iranian Embassy in Vienna." He handed me a visa application form already filled out. "Please read it carefully, and if you're interviewed, don't make comments on the application form's poor English or its spelling mistakes."

Had my bigmouthed reputation preceded me?

"Let's talk about formalities," continued John. "You'll arrive on a commercial airline. Lucky for you, Iran's got a "Commercially Important Persons" clubroom that only costs $50. They meet you on the tarmac and drive you to a lounge while all the formalities are completed. Unluckily for you, you're not using that service."

"Great. I love bureaucracy."

"Because it'd immediately identify you as a businessman or a VIP. We need you to pass as an ordinary tourist. Before you arrive in Tehran, the airline will give the passengers an immigration landing card, customs-clearance form, and foreign-currency declaration form to fill out. Here are the forms already filled in. Keep a carbon copy of the landing-card form and surrender it when leaving Iran. We'll inspect your luggage before you leave, but at any rate don't buy alcohol, or any magazines at the airport. They might contain pictures that the Iranians consider offensive. Don't bring playing cards; gambling is forbidden. Make sure that the customs officers register your camera in your passport. When you leave, show them the camera, and insist that the record be deleted from your passport, as any tourist would."

"Gotcha. Where are we staying?"

"The Azadi Grand Hotel in Tehran. The details are in the folder. You'll get two separate rooms, of course. Let's keep it professional. The hotel should have a courtesy van, but if it doesn't come through, take a taxi from the station that has a dispatcher. Erikka will help you communicate with them. But don't look as if you're taking instructions from a woman—you'll attract attention. And Erikka left Iran when the Islamic Revolution started and might not fully appreciate the radical changes since then."

"What about communication?" I asked.

"There will be two methods. One for Ian and Erikka the tourists, and the second for your reporting and distress. As tourists, go occasionally to Internet cafés and use their voice-over-Internet service to call numbers we are providing you with to chitchat with your friends—Agency personnel. Tell them how much you're thrilled with Iran. No criticism. You can talk about the food, weather, whatever. Use your hotel room's phone to call your publisher in India, or to look for your Iranian roots. But let's be clear: no calling anyone else, not even your kids. We can't control what they might say or who listens in."

"OK. What about money?" I asked.

"We've opened an account for you at the Frankfurt, Germany, branch of Bank Melli, the Iranian bank. Your travel folder includes an ATM card that you can freely use throughout Iran, charging the withdrawals to your German bank account. Every two days you must visit an ATM to withdraw money. Additionally, whenever you move outside Tehran, the first thing you do is look for the nearest ATM and withdraw more money."

"Even if I don't need to?"

"Yes, just withdraw a minimal amount. But it has to be an amount that does not include the number five, like fifty, a hundred and fifty, fifteen hundred, and so on. If the number five appears it will signal to us that your ATM card—or, even worse, you—has been captured. All other number amounts will signal that you're OK, and where you are at that moment. Also, every fifth withdrawal, make a small cash deposit with an envelope through the machine. Look at that," he said, and handed me a sheet of paper. "Learn it by heart."

I glanced at the one-page document. It instructed me on how to deliver messages by making innocuous-looking cash deposits through an ATM.

He continued. "The withdrawals and deposits and all other ATM activities will immediately appear on your German branch account, which we'll be monitoring all the time. We'll replenish the account by wire-transfer deposits."

"From where? I lost you."

"From your publisher's bank account in India, of course. If for any reason you cannot make a cash deposit through the machine, but still need to send a message, here are the instructions." He handed me another one-page document with short messages and instructions for how to use the ATM keypad to instruct the bank to carry out routine banking activities, which included an alphanumeric conversion table.

"How do I get instructions while in Iran?"

"We will convey only emergency messages, such as if you need to leave immediately. We'll use Padaş. If he's unavailable, we'll call your hotel, and a person with an Indian accent will give you a message on behalf of your publisher in India. For example, if the message is that your publisher wants to discuss copyright issues of translated editions, and he asks if that night will be a good time to call, that will mean 'leave immediately.'

It's all in here," he said, and handed me another printed page. "Memorize it; your life may depend on it."

We spent the next two days rehearsing communication methods, escape routes, and various contingencies. You always hope things will go smoothly, yet plan for the worst.

CHAPTER NINETEEN

I traveled to the United States for a family visit and additional briefing. When I returned to Vienna I went to the Iranian Embassy at Jauresgasse 9, a nineteenth-century three-story building across the street from the British Embassy. Three stern, unshaved security personnel were standing near the entrance. After telling them I needed a visa, I was led to the consular section. I handed my Canadian passport with my visa application form to the consular officer, a young man dressed in black pants and a collarless white shirt. Like the other men I saw in the building, he also had a three- or four-day-old beard. He looked like he should still be in college.

"What's the purpose of your visit?" he asked politely with a strong Iranian accent, as he sifted through my passport and glimpsed the attached application form.

"Tourism, mainly. I'm writing a novel and I need more inspiration."

"A book?"

I nodded.

"What kind of book?"

"A fiction. A love story between an Iranian man and an Austrian woman."

"Whom will you be meeting?"

"Nobody in particular, just people on the street, everyday people who could tell me about your culture and heritage. Maybe do a little shopping, visit some monuments."

"Where will you stay?"

"I've made reservations at the Azadi Grand Hotel in Tehran."

"How do you intend to pay for your stay?"

"I have sufficient means, and my publisher covers all costs associated with this visit." I showed him a letter with an attached bank letter confirming the publisher's ability to bear all costs of my travel.

"How long do you intend to stay?"

"Just a few weeks, two to four."

"Do you have a round-trip ticket?"

I showed him my ticket.

What the hell, I thought, *do they suspect any Westerner would want to remain in present-day Iran voluntarily? Last I heard it was more like a penal colony for foreigners who like to feel safe in a democracy. Not to mention having a drink at a bar with a local woman.*

"I see you have an Iranian name," he said in a tone I couldn't immediately decipher.

"Yes, my grandfather emigrated from Iran to Canada more than eighty years ago."

"So you have family in Iran?"

"I'm not aware of any, but I might have distant relatives. I thought of maybe trying to find them."

"We'll transfer your visa application to Tehran to receive an authorization letter from the Ministry of Foreign Affairs."

"How long will that take?" I asked, expecting him to say *two to three days*.

But he was noncommittal. "I don't know. It could take three weeks, or even three months. It's up to them."

"Why does it take so long?"

"I see a problem," said the consular officer. "You're a Canadian applying out of your country."

"I'm embarrassed to say that I didn't know about this requirement. I've already made hotel and airline reservations, and there could be a penalty for changing them. Is there a way to overcome this problem?" I recited the apology my briefers had suggested I use in case such a question arose.

I considered, then rejected, offering him a €100 bill as my

modest contribution to his personal financial needs. There was too much at stake, and I couldn't risk a refusal.

He gave me a long look. "Wait here," he said and entered into a back office. I was left wondering under the video camera mounted on the opposite wall and the prying eyes of a fat guard who stood silently nearby.

He returned fifteen minutes later. "The consul will see you now."

I was led by the consular officer through a narrow staircase to the second floor.

The consular officer knocked respectfully on the door, opened it gingerly after a moment. On the far end of a majestic room, behind a king-size desk, sat a man in his midforties with gray hair, a beard, and clever eyes behind rimless eyeglasses. We crossed the room walking on a soft Persian carpet.

"Please sit down," he said, pointing at a chair, and signaled to the consular officer to leave.

"What can I do for you?"

I told him briefly why I needed the visa soon and couldn't wait a few months for an authorization to come from Tehran.

"Why don't you return to Canada and apply for a visa there?" he asked. It was the most logical question, the one I'd feared he would ask. Luckily, I had prepared an answer.

"Well . . ." I said hesitantly. "I'm reluctant to do it. I have a dispute with my ex-wife over support payments, and I'm afraid she'll attempt to ask the court to keep me in Canada until the matter settles. I hope maybe there could be a way to spare me the unnecessary cost and legal risk of flying to Canada just for the visa."

"If Tehran approves your visa," he said. "I'm sure that after your visit you will be able to describe our country in a favorable manner, as opposed to the hateful propaganda that the politicians and the media are so fond of."

"While of course I will offer my honest impressions, I assure you that politics isn't my field. I would like to get to know your country's traditions and culture, to make my novel more realistic."

"I see," he said, giving me a pensive look. "Maybe I could expedite the visa matter. I could explain to the Ministry of Foreign Affairs how important for Iran your visit is." He wrote something on the application form. "Leave your passport here and come back in a week." Although I was happy to hear his comment, I felt uncomfortable. Nothing I'd said indicated that this would be favorable for Iran. Why would the consul put himself out there for me so quickly? The little suspicious devil in me woke up.

He handed me his card and shook my hand. His card gave me his name and title: BEHROOZ MESBAH, COUNSELOR.

"Mot'sha'keram," I said, thanking him.

He raised his eyes and gave me a surprised smile.

"I've learned a few words in Farsi," I explained. "My grandfather was born in Iran, and I'm really excited to visit the land of my ancestors."

I left the embassy feeling odd. Counselor? My foot. That only enhanced my earlier suspicion. I decided to talk to John Sheehan about it.

I went on a long cab ride, changed cabs several times, and when I was sure I wasn't trailed, I went back to the safe apartment.

"How was it?" asked John.

"I can't really tell. I'm sure the walls had ears and eyes. The visa consul was mildly suspicious when I wanted the visa expedited. I had to meet another higher-ranking person. Although his card said he was a 'counselor,' my hunch says an 'intelligence officer'; there's no question he was sizing me up. We'll probably know more about the visa in a week."

"Getting a visa for Iran can be a difficult matter," said John. "But if they've given you a hard time, we've made a contingency plan to fly you to Dushanbe, in Tajikistan, where the process is simpler for us." He didn't elaborate.

"OK."

During the following three days, I met Erikka several times, making sure she understood the rules of conduct in present-day

Iran. We discussed traditions, cultures, and the American School. I also broke the news about the Swiss bank's deal.

"That's wonderful," she exclaimed.

Contrary to my earlier expectations she didn't ask too many questions.

I flew to the U.S. to see my children and receive more CIA briefing. Ten days later when I returned, I met Erikka and she showed me her Swiss passport. "They gave me a visa in no time," she boasted. "I spoke Farsi and my visa was issued."

Four days after my visit to the Iranian Embassy I called Behrooz Mesbah, the "counselor."

"Mr. Pour Laval, how are you?" He was exceedingly friendly. "I've got good news. Your passport is stamped with a visa. You may come anytime during business hours to pick it up. Iran welcomes you."

"Thank you so much," I said. "I'll come by today."

I alerted Casey and took a cab to the embassy. The consular officer gave me my passport. "You have a sixty-day visa," he said. "That's double the time we usually grant to tourists." He sounded as if he had just announced a winning lottery ticket.

"I've got more good news. The Iranian Ministry of Culture and Islamic Guidance has given you an invitation to call them with any of your questions. You may find it useful. Their telephone number and address are in the envelope with your passport."

I thanked him and left. I had gotten what I wanted, and yet I felt like live prey pushed into the lion's den. I took a cab, made the usual circle around the city for an hour, and when I felt safe to return to my hotel, I reported to Casey and John from a pay phone located a block away. After completing the calls, I dialed a random number and hung up.

Three days later Casey called my mobile phone. "Take a cab immediately to Café Vienna. Enter the main entrance, but leave right away through the back door past the men's room.

A white Mercedes taxi will wait for you. Ask the driver if he can take you to the train station. If he says he's waiting for Herr Zauber, tell him you're Mr. Zauber and ask him to drive you to 98 Porzellengasse. Once there, get out of the taxi, pay him, and wait for him to drive away. Then walk to 106, repeat, 106 Porzellengasse, second floor. Take extreme precautions."

That address was new to me. Casey was signaling that it was a safe house.

When I arrived, I saw Benny Friedman, Reuven Sofian, Casey Bauer, Tony DaSilva, and John Sheehan. The attendance was too broad to be just another briefing.

"Is it happy hour?" I asked. "Where are the drinks?"

Casey smiled at first but then changed his expression to dead serious. "Dan, you're leaving tomorrow morning. You're staying here tonight. Your luggage will be here momentarily."

My stomach moved nervously. "What about Erikka?" I asked.

"We sent her tickets by messenger from the travel agency and attached a note asking to confirm. She called the travel agent to confirm and asked if you'd be on the same flight. I suggest you call her now."

He handed me a cell phone. I called Erikka, and we agreed to meet at the airport.

"You should also know that she met our men posing as the bank's representatives. She signed a contract and received an advance." He gave me a travel folder with my airline tickets, five million Iranian rials, €8,000, and $5,000.

"Why American dollars, when I'm a Canadian?"

"Because the U.S. currency is more popular. Many Iranians have probably never seen a Canadian dollar. Everyone, even people who've never been to the U.S., carries U.S. dollars."

"Yeah, but isn't this a lot? It could get people suspicious."

"No. There are the two of you for a month or two. You are engaged by a well-known publishing house, and Erikka is under a contract with a Swiss bank, so you can account for the money if asked. That money could help you out of Iran in case of an emergency." He also gave me a Visa credit card, an ATM card, and pocket debris. "The rials are worth only $500; use them to pay your initial expenses." I looked at the stack of bills that filled up a big bag. In the bag was also a receipt from Melli Bank.

"Keep the receipt. It's proof that you bought the rials at a bank, and didn't exchange your dollars on the Iranian black market."

Benny shook my hand. "Dan, I trust you. Return safely." He hugged me. For a minute I felt he was saying good-bye for good. It didn't help my mood.

If I had doubts whether what I'd got myself into was the right thing to do, certainly it was too late to air them. I knew I was assuming a huge risk. If the khans in Islamabad got my photo and transmitted it to Iran, I'd be toast. Iran wanted them to lure me in, and now I was going there voluntarily? Did this entire operation make sense? Knowing that only mediocrity makes sense, because then you don't invade anybody's turf, didn't make me feel more relaxed. It sounds great as a proverb, but now how was I supposed to feel in reality when I had doubts? I sat down on the couch and took control of my mental hesitation.

I suppressed that hesitant devil in me. *Hey, you live only once. I don't smoke, don't do drugs, don't gamble or drink excessively, so what am I to do for that little extra excitement and fun? Not that— I still get a chance for that here and there. I mean what this job gives me. The thrill of the hunter focusing on his prey when it's close, when there's nothing in the world that you want more than the kill, the score, the success . . . although recognizing that after basking in it for a while, you return to mediocre life, to another low . . . until you start looking to get that fix again.*

I thought of my father, who had always told me, "Bravery is being the only one who knows you're afraid." I kept on a brave face as everybody hugged me and left.

In the morning I was driven to the airport by a driver who apparently had taken a vow of silence. At eleven A.M. I took a deep breath and checked into Lufthansa flight LH6334/LH6447 coming from Frankfurt to Vienna, continuing to Tehran. Erikka was waiting for me at the airline counter. She looked and sounded really excited, though for a different reason. The plane was only half-full. Some of the passengers seemed to be European businessmen, but most were probably Iranians dressed in European attire. Only a few wore collarless, buttoned white shirts. We were scheduled to arrive at three A.M. on the following day. Two hours before landing, I saw the cabin crew collect all liquor bottles, full or empty, and lock them in the galley.

The flight service manager announced on the PA, "Under the law of Iran, all female passengers must have their hair covered." About a dozen fashionably dressed women with makeup went to the bathroom holding plastic garment bags, emerging later dressed in black chadors, the one-piece cloak. They had their hair covered, nail polish removed, and faces clean of makeup. They were transformed to black, nearly indistinguishable masses. I overheard Erikka talk with a European-looking woman sitting next to her about the dress code.

"Don't worry," said Erikka to the woman, who had also noticed that several Iranian women had changed their clothes in the bathroom. "Foreign women aren't expected to wear the chador. Just make sure that you cover all parts of your body except your hands, feet, and face. As for your head, remember the rule, 'from hairline to neckline.' I'd also make sure," added Erikka as she saw that the woman was dressed in a tight skirt, "that your clothes don't reveal the shape of your body."

The woman rushed to the bathroom with a fashionable handbag. Moments later she emerged wearing a long dress.

"My friend gave it to me before leaving and suggested I carry it on board. I thought she was teasing me, I thought the cover-all dresses were only for Iranian women."

"No, she wasn't joking," said Erikka. "What you're wearing is a manteau, a dress many Iranian women use instead of the chador."

From the aircraft's window I saw Tehran approaching through the haze, a city of nine million located in the foothills of the Alborz Mountains, with elevations increasing towards the north and sloping lower to the south. Pollution was bad during that afternoon hour of early winter, with yellow-gray clouds of smog.

I thought of the rule I'd discovered. *In an underdeveloped country I can't drink the water, and in a developed country I can't breathe the air. With that thick smog, can I still drink the water here?*

At touchdown, I felt my tension rise again. Erikka, who had slept most of the flight, didn't leave me with much time to be concerned. "I'm so glad to be back," she said. "I haven't been here for twenty-five years!"

I couldn't say I exactly shared her enthusiasm. But at least the time had come to get things started.

CHAPTER TWENTY

Tehran, February 5, 2006

As we taxied bumpily to the terminal on the worn-out tarmac, I saw through the cabin's windows the sign MEHRABAD INTER-NATIONAL AIRPORT. The terminal's building looked small, unfit for a nation of seventy million. Since the capture of the U.S. Embassy staff in 1979 and the sanctions imposed on Iran by many countries, there weren't many incoming flights to Iran. I saw only a few planes of Iran Air, Gulf Air, and Air France.

I walked with Erikka toward the passport-control booths with my heart pounding hard. Erikka walked toward the booths reserved for women. I thought of my instructions.

When you arrive, the passport-control officer might ask you questions concerning the purpose of your visit and the length of your stay. Give him the routine tourist an-swers. Look him in the eye and don't avoid his. Give short answers, and don't smile or act as if you're hiding some-thing. These guys are very experienced in detecting suspicious behavior and maneuvering tactics employed by people who hope to avoid a thorough inspection.

I looked around. A big mural of Ayatollah Khomeini was displayed on the wall. The immigration officer, in a uniform that seemed as if he'd slept in it for a week, gave a very quick glance at my face and keyed a few strokes into his computer. I waited for him to stamp my passport and ease my accelerated heartbeat, but instead two men in plainclothes entered the booth. He gave them my passport, and they exchanged a few sentences in Farsi. The man holding my passport flipped through the pages and returned it to the officer and nodded. The officer stamped my passport without giving me a second look. I wanted to let out a deep breath, but I waited until I was out of his sight.

That's it? I thought. Were these all the security checks? I guess the Iranians didn't expect terrorism. I didn't have to wonder why.

After Erikka and I met again in the customs hall, spent almost an hour waiting for our luggage, and went through customs and currency control, we were finally outside the terminal building—three hours after landing. When we exited the arrival terminal we were hassled by endless numbers of people offering to change money and sell us stuff. Self-appointed tour guides and unauthorized taxi drivers told us that the last bus had already left the terminal and suggested they drive us to town. We ignored them. A courtesy van sent by the hotel was waiting for us and within less than an hour delivered us to the Azadi Grand Hotel, a five-star hotel.

When I exited the van, I looked up at the tall building. To my estimate it had several hundred rooms. But the empty lobby during the early-evening hour signaled that the hotel wasn't fully occupied. After a quick check-in we were taken to our rooms. Mine was on the third floor and Erikka's on the fourth.

"I'll see you in two hours for dinner," she said before I got off the elevator.

I opened my room's window curtains to view the Alborz Mountains, to the north of Tehran, and waited. Erikka tapped on the door of my room two hours later dressed in black pants, with a white manteau over them. She wore a black scarf that covered her hair and neck. The black and white combination was dominolike.

"Has anyone seen you coming here?" I asked. I didn't need unnecessary attention.

"Don't worry, I was careful," she said with a smile, sounding like a high school student escaping through her bedroom window to meet a boyfriend. I joined her in the hall, wary that she not enter my room.

"It's beautiful out there," I said, nodding back toward the window as I closed the door behind me.

"The view? I agree. Did you know that the name *Tehran* means 'warm slopes' in Farsi? Maybe they meant these slopes."

"Where are we going to have dinner?" I asked.

"I'd love to have Persian food," said Erikka. "How about you?"

"Fine with me." Usually, I blame jet lag for confusing me after a ten-hour flight. When I go to dinner I feel sexy, and when I go to bed I'm hungry. But not now. I was neither. I was too tense and focused.

We went outside and the doorman hailed a cab. "Please ask him to take us to a good restaurant," I said.

Erikka spoke with the driver in Farsi. The driver's face lighted up, and they continued with what sounded to me like a friendly conversation.

"He suggests Sofreh Khaneh Aban, a Persian dining room, on Aban Street," she translated. "He says they have a live band playing traditional Persian music, although the price may be high."

"How much is high?" I asked thinking about my per diem, forgetting that there are completely different rules in these situations.

"A meal for two might cost as much as 200,000 rials."

As I made a quick calculation, I smiled. "It's about $20. What are we waiting for? Let's go."

Half an hour into the ride, the driver said with a smug expression, "This is where we gave the Americans a lesson," and pointed the building that housed the U.S. Embassy until 1979. Erikka was translating. "This was the den of spies." I had no reaction. I glanced at Erikka, who held a deadpan expression and gazed at the people on the street. We played the part of tourists to perfection.

The restaurant was packed with families, some with young children, and the noise was almost unbearable. My eyes were burning immediately. Most men were smoking cigarettes; others were using a hookah, a "narghile" in Farsi, with a water-pipe filter that flavors the smoke with cool water. But only the smoker enjoys it. What he exhales to the neighborhood is churning smog mixed with his CO_2, not recommended.

A courteous waiter offered us a table near the string orchestra. Erikka shouted into my ear, "He recognized us as tourists and gave us the best table in the house."

The noise was excruciating. I smiled at him with a virtual thank-you, and with my eyes tearing from the smoke I said, "Please thank him, and ask him for a table where we can talk without using a PA system or oxygen masks." We were moved to a corner table near an open window and away from the orchestra.

The waiter gave me a menu in Farsi. I could read most of the Arabic script and even understand some words, but there were additional letters I couldn't identify. I gave up.

"He says they serve the best *chello* kebab. Do you want to try it?" suggested Erikka.

"Just order anything good. I put my faith in you," I said, realizing I could contribute nothing to the meal choice.

"Well . . . there are these superlong skewers of chicken kebab with fresh chilies—they're really succulent, and they're for real kebab lovers. Or the *baghali-polo*, an oven-baked lamb shank in sauce, served with basmati rice; or *sabzi-polo-ba-mahi*, a fish grilled on a skewer, served with basmati rice, Persian herbs, dill, broccoli, and almonds."

"Can't decide—let's order a couple and share," I suggested.

Two waiters brought trays with huge amounts of food.

"I don't think we can eat that much," I said.

"Let's take our time, eat slowly, and enjoy the music," she said. It was clear that Erikka was captivated by memories and was enjoying talking about them and reliving her Iranian experience. My mind was somewhere else. I was curious to know whether there were any responses to our ads in the paper. We'd have to wait until tomorrow when the hotel's business office opened to find out.

I looked around us. People were having good meals and conversation. There were no alcoholic beverages of any kind on the tables. All waiters, and most male guests, looked unshaven, with two- to three-day beards.

How do they do it? I wondered. *For a three-day beard, you must shave every three days. Then how come I don't see many clean-shaven men?* I looked around and saw one clean-shaven man. He was wearing a Western-style suit and an outdated black tie. He was wearing dark sunglasses. But it was nighttime.

Maybe he's blind, I thought for a second, but then he appeared to read the menu as he spoke with the waiter.

For dessert we had *falude*, a tasteless dish that looks like white noodles, served with *bastani sonnati*, a Persian traditional ice cream with rose syrup and cherry and lime juices. When we were done with dinner, it was almost midnight, but the restaurant was still packed, and many more people kept coming in.

So not everyone in Tehran is poor, I thought. We returned to our hotel.

The following morning we went to the hotel's business center. A surprise was waiting for us. There were forty-two letters responding to the newspaper ads.

"Ian, care to help me sort them out?" Erikka asked.

"Sure, I'd be glad to."

We sat at a desk at the business center and opened the envelopes. After an hour we had a better picture. Twenty-two letters came from alumni of the American School living in Iran. Two letters came from alumni living in the Gulf States. Three letters came from former teachers, who were elated to hear about the reunion and wanted to participate. Fourteen letters were from companies offering us services such as live music or catering for the event, and one letter came from a Shiraz man asking us to find him a suitable American woman to marry. He attached his photo.

Erikka went quickly over the names of the responding alumni. "I think I recognize some names," she said. "But I'm afraid the group is too small for the Swiss bank to be interested in. I wonder where the others are."

"Don't jump to early conclusions," I said smoothly. "Why don't you call those who answered and get additional names of their classmates? I'm sure many alumni just missed your ad. If I were you, I'd get on the phone and start networking. Your schmoozing skills will get them all together in no time."

Erikka smiled. "You already know me," she said. "What are you going to do in the meantime?"

"I think I'll take a tour of Tehran, just to get a feel for it. I'll meet you here tonight." I wanted to leave my room available for the Iranian security services to do anything they wanted. I needed to know whether I had indeed attracted their attention. Who had the man with sunglasses at the restaurant been? A routine counterintelligence measure? Evaluating me as a potential recruit? Was I a conduit to lead them to a target? The answer wasn't likely to change my conduct—I remained Ian Pour Laval, an innocent author. It would help me plan ahead—but plan what? Here my thoughts hit a brick wall. I had no idea. But I had to figure it out.

I went outside through the lobby and asked the dispatcher to find me a cabdriver who spoke some English. He returned a few minutes later. "Sorry, nobody speaks English, but there's one who speaks a little German."

"That will do," I said. When the nightingale is too busy to sing, even a crow will do.

"Take me to see the city," I told the driver as I got into his Mercedes taxi. "Let's start with Golestan Palace." He started the engine and we left the hotel.

I looked at the guidebook. "During the reign of the Safavid Shah Abbas the First, a vast garden called Chahar Bagh (Four Gardens), a governmental residence, and a Chenarestan (a grove) were created on the present site of the Golestan Palace and its surroundings," it read. I looked through the cab's side mirror to see if we had company. Not a big surprise. There was a car just behind us at all times, with two men. Why were they so close? It seemed too obvious, rather unprofessional. Maybe they wanted me to know I was being watched. But why? Obviously, they didn't know who I was, because if they'd had just a shred of suspicion, I would have been in prison with mice and cockroaches as my cellmates. I continued to play along, taking several pictures of the palace with my camera.

"Please take me to the bazaar—I've heard so much about it." Situated in the heart of southern Tehran, built under a roof, the bazaar is a city within the city, at once beautiful and chaotic. When the Shah razed old but precious traditional buildings during the oil boom in the seventies and replaced them with ugly high-rise buildings, the bazaar had been spared.

After getting dropped off, I walked slowly, mindful of the crowds and the slippery pavement. There were unwritten traffic rules, I noticed: people kept to the right to avoid porters of merchandise, who sped through the crowd. I was overwhelmed by the different faces I saw. Iranians and Arabs, Mongols and Azeri, a very colorful and exciting mix of colors, smells, and cultures.

There were two types of people in the bazaar: oglers and hagglers. I crossed the definition line and bought a few pieces of bric-a-brac, and bargained on the prices like a typical tourist, using sign language or the little English a few merchants knew.

"These things are from Abadan," said one merchant. "My family came from there. Believe me, they're special."

A well-built young man in jeans and sunglasses stood next to me watching me haggle with the shopkeeper. Not wanting to lose another customer, the merchant interrupted our conversation and asked the man something in Farsi, and he responded in two or three words. I picked up one word, but that was enough. *"Adadish,"* he said—police.

I took a deep breath, turned my back to the young man, showed particular interest in a backgammon set, and left the store. From the corner of my eye I could see him following me. I was still just an innocent tourist returning to his hotel.

Erikka was standing near the reception desk in the lobby. "Good timing," she said. "I'm expecting a classmate. Want to join us?"

As a well-dressed man walked into the lobby, Erikka whispered, "Here he is. Farshad Shahab!" she exclaimed and ran toward him with her arms stretched to embrace him.

Visibly uncomfortable, the man stepped back. "Sorry," he said quickly. "It's not allowed in public."

"I'm sorry," said Erikka. "It's just that I'm so glad to see you."

I was uneasy. How could she be so heedless?

"Same here," he said. "But things have changed."

"Farshad," said Erikka. "I want you to meet Ian Pour Laval. Ian is an author who is currently writing a novel on a romance between an Iranian Muslim man and an Austrian Catholic woman. I'm helping him with his cultural research." We sat in the lobby and ordered cherry juice. Erikka excused herself and went to the ladies' room.

"Difficult subject," said Farshad, looking at me with interest.

"Why?" I asked.

"Because of the cultural gap and the religious clash. Where does the romance take place?" he asked.

"In Tehran," I answered.

"That makes it particularly complex," he said. "The love must be very strong and the couple very persistent for the relationship to survive."

"The Iranian society, as a whole, will not accept a European woman marrying an Iranian man?"

"Many will accept, to an extent," he said. "But the price for the woman will be high. She'll have to convert and adopt all tenets of our religion and culture. That means she'll have to give up her past and become a Muslim woman, not only by adopting our traditions and religion, but also in the way she conducts herself and raises her children. She'll have to forego many of her values, her culture, and—most of all—her beliefs on women's place in the society."

"Will there ever be a change?" I asked. "I mean, will Iranian women ever be treated as we treat women in Canada . . . equally?"

He shook his head. "The Muslim Revolution gave us pride, but it also took us back in time, as far as human rights and women's rights are concerned. Religions don't change."

That was a bold statement, I thought. The little devil in me took notice. "Back in time?"

"Yes. I'm not criticizing it, of course. The so-called 'modernity' that the Shah and his corrupt followers brought exposed the Iranian society to Western-style 'values,' but the Iranian people much prefer the old style." He uttered the word *values* with visible disgust. I sensed it was an overkill gesture, as if he knew somebody was watching.

Erikka returned, and she and Farshad commenced with their conversation reminiscing about old times. I didn't want to interrupt. I excused myself and returned to my room.

An hour later I went back to the lobby. Farshad and Erikka were still chatting.

"Ian," said Erikka. "Farshad just started telling me about what it was like to be here during the Islamic Revolution. Why don't you come listen? Could be interesting background for your book."

With a serious face Farshad said, "Please don't mention you've met me, and don't use my name in your book."

The request was odd, given that they had been chatting publicly in a hotel lobby for more than an hour. I was sure the Iranian security services already knew about his contact with foreigners.

"Of course, you have my word," I said. "I just need background information to understand the political and social atmosphere at the time. My novel starts about a year after the revolution."

Farshad relented. "It was exciting and frightening at the same time," he said. "As a young Iranian I was proud that there was a popular uprising hoping to topple the crooked regime of the Shah, but as a moderate Muslim I was concerned at hatred I saw in the extremists. Instead of promoting a political change, which most Iranians supported, the mullahs took over, and instituted a theocracy intolerant of any other opinion."

I registered surprise, in my suspicious mind, to hear that.

"Where were you when the unrest began?" asked Erikka.

"That whole period is so blurred in my memory, but I remember well the beginning. It was on 'Black Friday,' September 8, 1978. I was a senior at our high school and had plans to go to the U.S. for college."

"Yes, I think you told me about that plan at the time," said Erikka.

"I was in my room at home and heard noises—gunfire and shouting. My parents didn't allow me to leave the house; I was under a family-imposed curfew. So I climbed to our rooftop and saw flames. Parts of southern Tehran were on fire. The student-led revolution against the Shah had begun, but I didn't know it then. The Shah had declared martial law, and a citywide curfew was enforced by armed soldiers. Just to make sure he'd maintain control, the Shah also turned off the power every evening to the entire city of Tehran. That made the nights very quiet, except for bursts of gunfire."

"I remember that," said Erikka. "I was so frightened."

"The uprising was spreading," continued Farshad. "Other citizens joined the students. Most people were staying home and obeying the curfew. But many others climbed on their rooftops chanting and praying. Angry soldiers loyal to the Shah interpreted that as defiance and were shooting anyone seen on the roofs. I heard people chanting 'Allaahu Akbar'—'God is

Great.' Those incidents spread from southern Tehran, which is heavily populated by poor people, to the northern parts, where the rich and powerful live. My father was an ethnic Iranian, but he was fearful for our safety, because my mother is Italian. So two weeks later he sent me with my mother to Rome to stay with my maternal grandparents."

"That means you weren't here when the revolution toppled the Shah?" I asked.

"I returned to Tehran six months later when his regime was already doomed."

"From what I know, the hatred was directed against the U.S." I said.

Farshad nodded. "But those who captured the U.S. Embassy weren't the real fanatics."

You can say that again, I thought. *Even he doesn't believe it. I saw their hatred on TV. If that mob wasn't fanatic, then I'd like to see who are fanatics, in his opinion.*

"They were protesting against the U.S. for agreeing to let the Shah undergo cancer treatment in the U.S."

"What happened to your plans to go to college in the U.S.? Did they ever materialize?"

"Yes, I was lucky. I went to the University of Nebraska in Lincoln."

I smiled. "Not too many people like to leave that beautiful state, unless they have to. But you returned to Iran."

I regretted that statement immediately. It was too sarcastic. But he didn't seem to mind.

"I agree," he said. "It was difficult, but my family needed me here, so after spending just two more years in Nebraska after my graduation, I returned home."

"Was it hard? I mean shifting from the Western-style society in Nebraska to a different culture in Iran?" I chose my words carefully to make them as benign as possible.

"Only for a short period. After all, I'm Iranian, and I was returning home."

"Farshad is a mechanical engineer and works for an oil company," said Erikka, looking at me. Turning her head toward him, she added, "You'll prepare the list for me, won't you?"

"Sure," he said. "But I know only a handful of graduates who are in Iran. Many who were brought up in a school such as ours couldn't cope with the changing atmosphere in Iran and left."

"Where to?" I was really curious.

"Some went to the Gulf States, some to India and Pakistan, and some went to the U.S." A boxing-ring bell rang in my head. However, I decided not to press the issue at this time. In that kind of subtle questioning, less is more. I hoped that Erikka wouldn't pose the follow-up question, *Who went to the U.S.?*

"Who is sponsoring the reunion?" he asked. "Seems that you're spending money on that project."

"A Swiss bank," said Erikka. "They want to be able to sell their services to the alumni and their businesses, and besides, the expenses are really low so far. My trip here was paid for by Ian's publisher."

There was a moment of silence, and then he said in a friendly tone of voice, "I've always wanted to visit Canada, but never managed to do it, although I lived in Nebraska. Where did you grow up?"

I had my script meticulously rehearsed, so I was able to answer the questions that followed without missing a beat. Still, I had the feeling that I wasn't being questioned, but rather subtly interrogated. I was becoming even more suspicious. Why was he so openly critical of the regime, daring to talk about it with a complete stranger in public? Hoping to provoke me to jump on the bandwagon and say something negative? And those questions about my background . . . I would have to remember his name.

I excused myself again to go to my room. I'd be wiser when I saw the list he promised. When I crossed the lobby on my way to the elevator I had that funny feeling that I was being watched. I entered the gift shop and walked around, pretending to look at the merchandise. There was no mistake; a man was standing outside the store looking at me, making no effort to disguise his interest. I had to react contrary to my training, which said, *Dry-clean him*. But if I did that, I'd expose myself as a trained intelligence officer, rather than remaining Ian Pour Laval, a bona fide author. So I continued with the normal behavior expected of a tourist. I bought a local English-language newspaper and went up to my room.

It was clear that if a follower had been assigned to monitor my movements, there could also be electronic devices planted in my room. The author wouldn't care less, but the intelligence expert under my skin was on the alert. However, with no countermeasures to discover any hidden microphones or cameras, and with no suspicious activity or material to conceal, I crawled into bed, acting out the "I couldn't care less" attitude. Good thing they couldn't read my mind.

CHAPTER TWENTY-ONE

The next day, we had to run errands. First, a visit to the Ministry of Culture and Islamic Guidance to see if the note I received at the Iranian Embassy in Vienna was sufficient to conduct book interviews in Iran. They told me that legally, if I wanted to travel outside Tehran or visit any university or museum, among other sites, I first had to obtain a permit. I had to undergo a one-hour interview by a stern-looking bureaucrat about the content of my book, and supply a list of people I wanted to interview.

"We will let you know," he said at the end.

Next, I suggested that Erikka help me trace my roots in Iran. We went to the Civil Registration Department, which manages Iran's data related to births, deaths, marriages, and divorces.

"You'd have to be more specific," the skinny and short

clerk behind the counter said with Erikka translating. " 'Pour' is a very common Iranian name, and if your grandfather left Iran in the 1920s, I don't believe we can help you, unless you remember names of other family members."

I rolled up my eyes, pretending that I was trying to remember. I thought about using the information I memorized from the brief "family tree" with which the Agency had equipped me, but I thought I should first try showing him that I was unprepared, as not to arouse suspicion.

"I remember my mother telling me, from stories she heard from my father, that my grandfather was a shoemaker in southern Tehran. Will that help?"

"No, I'm sorry, we don't record professions. Do you know any cousins on your father's side?"

"I only heard of one cousin, who went to France. I think his name was Javad Yaghmaie," I ventured, hoping my earlier research was accurate.

"Now, that's a beginning," said the clerk, who turned out to be a fairly friendly fellow. "I'll try to find this person. Do you know how old he should be now?"

I hesitated. "I know he was related to my father somehow, but I'm not sure how. Can we search his name first?"

The clerk went through a side door to the archive. Ten minutes later he returned holding a dusty carton file. "I may have found something," he said joyfully. He opened the file. "This is the file of Javad Yaghmaie." He leafed through the thin file and said, "Javad Yaghmaie was born on 16 Azar 1309 in Neyshābūr, in northeastern Iran."

"It's not far from Mashhad, the second largest city in the country," volunteered Erikka.

I gave the clerk a puzzled look. "1309?"

"That's December 7, 1930," he said. "His father was Ibrahim, and his mother Fatima. That's all we have."

I wrote down the information, thanked him and left. Now, I'd at least satisfied the initial appearance of a person genuinely seeking his roots.

"We may have to go there," I told Erikka.

"I'd like that," she said. I made a half turn, and from the corner of my eye I could see my shadow staring at me. I said nothing to Erikka.

"There's a rally that is starting in about an hour," said Erikka. "President Mahmoud Ahmadinejad is speaking. I think we should attend."

We had the cabdriver let us off about a mile from Freedom Square, and then walked along with the huge crowd heading into the square. The sound was insistent: people chanting *"Marg bar Amrika"*—death to America—and to make sure that any non-Farsi speakers wouldn't miss the message, the protesters also carried banners in English cursing George W. Bush, the United States, and Israel.

"That's for the television cameras," said Erikka when she saw me looking at the banners. "This is all choreographed." From the looks of the crowd—tens of thousands strong—this was quite the show to stage-manage.

"That square is where the 22nd of Bahman march was, where they declared the Islamic Republic in '79," said Erikka. "I don't think we should get too close."

Looking at the red-faced, bearded men punch the air with their fists and scream about death to America and *Allaahu Akbar*, it seemed a fairly unorchestrated hatred. I saw women in black chadors, clerics with turbans, and bearded religious students—many people who didn't look particularly well-off. In a makeshift parking lot, buses and trucks were bringing in additional demonstrators.

"Marg bar Amrika," they chanted, sending chills down my spine. In the eyes of some there was a fiery hatred. Passing my eyes over the crowd, I saw a few indifferent or gloomy faces. But most were in an ecstatic state of anger. The crowd was closing in on us. Uniformed police emerged, and probably double their number of plainclothes security men. Children stomped on images of Uncle Sam. A big placard said, BUSH IS SATAN. A crowd of chanting Iranians were burning

an American flag and stomping on its ashes. A colorful, paper, distorted picture of George W. Bush hovered above the crowd. Enterprising street vendors were selling everything and loudly announcing their merchandise. I continued hearing the crowds chanting, "America cannot do anything. Iran is full of Baseejis!"

I saw a big effigy of George W. Bush as a mouse, *mush* in Farsi, swallowing up Afghanistan. I tried to blend in with the flood of people around us. I couldn't move. I was cramped between bearded men there after a day's work, who had no time to take a shower and no money to buy deodorant. There was nothing I could say or do. Worse, the crowd had seeped between Erikka and me, and I was having trouble getting closer to her. Definitely not a good idea for her, so obviously foreign, to be let loose in this crowd.

"Marg Bar Amrika!" It wouldn't end. Then the leader yelled *"Marg bar Israel!"* and the crowd followed suit. I looked at the people around me and couldn't avoid wondering what their role, if any, had been in burning the American Embassy in Tehran, or in sponsoring and financing terrorism. It was enough that their collective hatred was fueling those actions.

Reunited in a small clearing, Erikka and I loosed ourselves from the suffocating grip. We stepped back, more safely out of the action. Even from there, we could see President Mahmoud Ahmadinejad, wearing a light, tieless suit, ascend the podium.

"Can you translate?" I said, glancing at Erikka.

She shrugged. "Same as ever. America, Bush," she said quietly. "He says Iranians should join in the battle against America and defend Islam and the revolution."

"He's inflaming the crowd." I concluded the obvious.

Still listening, Erikka continued, "He's now talking about rooting out corruption. Ahmadinejad is promising to support the private sector and reduce the size of the public sector to help growth. That theme is likely to be accepted by the bazaar merchants."

As the president closed, the crowd let out a massive shriek of affirmation. We had seen enough; it was time to go.

Back at the hotel, Erikka told me she was planning on meeting some school friends at their home. "I hope you don't mind if I go by myself—it will probably all be in Farsi," said Erikka apologetically. "They're classmates, so I'll be able to get more names tonight."

"Not to worry," I said quickly. "I'm exhausted, and it'll be a good chance to catch up on my writing." It had been awhile since I'd had a night to myself.

The next thing I knew, I was in bed and heavy knocks on my door were jerking me awake. I looked at the clock on the night table: four thirty A.M. Gingerly, I went to the door and peeped through the viewer. I saw Erikka. I opened the door and found her crying and shaking.

"Come in," I said instantly. Under the circumstances, I'd risk it. She entered my room and sat on the couch. I didn't know what to do or say. I didn't really know Erikka, and there was no user's manual to consult. I gave her a glass of water. "Please stop crying and tell me what happened."

She sobbed. "I'd heard about it—the Komiteh, the moral police—and the way they harass people in the streets, or round up and jail them. I read how lucky people were just to pay a fine and avoid being lashed. But that's just not how I remembered Iran. That's why I wanted to come back. I didn't think it would really affect me."

"Please tell me what happened," I repeated.

"I left my friend's house at around three in the morning. She begged me to stay overnight, but I was too foolhardy to accept, thinking everything would be OK. So she called me a cab. Next thing I knew, the cabdriver looked in his rearview mirror, and said, 'They're following us.' So I turned around, and there was a car right there. He said it was Komiteh. I didn't know what to think. I was alone, it was three A.M., but that would have been fine anywhere else. I thought maybe they were targeting him, not me. We got pulled over, and a guy—he didn't have a uniform—wanted the cabdriver's papers. That was it, and then he told us to move on. But I'd barely started breathing again when he changed his mind. He told me to step outside."

"Did you?"

"Yes. I stepped out of the car and walked up to their Jeep."

"Why? You could have stayed next to the cabby, at least until you were sure they were indeed police." I knew it wasn't exactly the most supportive thing to say, second-guessing a decision that was too late to change. But even at the risk of making me seem like kind of a jerk, I had to be sure that her story was true and that the incident was not related to my mission.

"Well, the cabdriver said they were Komiteh. And I figured he would know."

"Did the cabby do anything?"

"He was trying to protect me. He stepped out of his cab and walked toward them, but they yelled at him to step back."

"What happened then?"

"Two men sat in the Jeep, and I was standing next to them. I asked them in Farsi what the problem was."

"Were they surprised to hear you speak Farsi?"

"I think so, because they changed their tone a bit, but then they interrogated me about where I'd been at that time of night and why I was traveling alone without the supervision of a man." She paused to wipe her eyes. "One of them was really aggressive. I told him about my meeting with my classmates. He asked, if he went to my friend's house, would she verify my story? I told him yes, of course. But had I done anything wrong? He told me that Islamic law forbade an unchaperoned woman to be alone with a man who isn't a close relative.

"The whole encounter was surreal. I was standing in the middle of the street answering questions about my private life to two strangers. They said nothing. I wasn't sure what to do or say. Then it dawned on me—maybe they were expecting payment. But I wasn't going to bribe them and risk serious trouble. I just wouldn't do that anyway. They copied my name from my passport and suddenly said, 'You can go.' And that was it. They drove off, and I got back in the cab. The cabdriver was really nice. And he said it wasn't my fault, that I was dressed modestly enough, but that the police had been looking for a brothel that was supposed to be around there."

Erikka broke into tears again. "I was so humiliated."

My suspicious nature came into gear again. Was the encounter incidental or, given the fact that I had a permanent shadow, was it now Erikka's turn to be harassed? I knew that when the Iranian government established the moral police, they'd justified it by quoting the Islamic concept of *amr bil ma'rouf nahi anil munkar*, "join the right, and forbid the wrong." That was also used to encourage people to report the suspicious activities of others. The result was a seventy-million-strong intelligence force. Even the Stasi, East Germany's feared Ministry for State Security, wasn't that successful in its heyday. For the average Iranian, mutual trust had all but disappeared. You now suspected your neighbor, your friend, and your grocer of being informers. And you were probably right.

"I'm so sorry that happened to you," I said gently. "It sounds awful. But I guess there's a whole set of rules here that we need to learn. . . ."

She nodded, sighing. "It's nothing like I remember," she said softly. "Anyway. I should get some sleep."

"Do you want me to walk you back to your room?" I offered.

She grimaced. "Normally I would, but who knows? The morality police might still be watching." She held my hand for a minute. "Sorry to barge in on you like this." I shook my head, signaling that it was nothing, and with that she was gone.

I returned to my bed, restless and unable to sleep. I couldn't shake the suspicion that this was all tied together somehow. To distract myself, I pulled out "my" novel, *Dead End Love: An Impossible Love Affair*, courtesy of some particularly creative CIA employee turned ghostwriter.

"Not bad," I mumbled, "not bad at all. I didn't know I could write that well . . ." and fell asleep.

I met Erikka in the dining room for a late breakfast. Other than slightly red eyes, she looked fine.

"How are you feeling?" She smiled wanly and nodded to say everything was OK.

"If you don't mind me bringing up a little business," I began, "did you accomplish anything last night? I mean getting new names and addresses?"

She seemed happy to be back at a task. "Yes. I already have a total of ninety-five names of people still living in Iran, with addresses and phone numbers."

"That's great," I said eagerly. "How did you manage to get so many?"

"The news spread," she said. "Everybody's very excited about the reunion."

"So are they all ethnic Iranians? I read that everyone else left here, right? After the revolution, I mean."

"Yes, all of the alums responding are ethnic Iranians. I also have a list of thirty-one alumni who live in Europe, Japan, and the U.S. I found out last night that one of them just died in the U.S. So awful—I remember him."

I paused for a moment to let her compose herself. "How do you intend to manage it?"

"What do you mean?"

"I mean administratively. Did you create a table with all the names?"

"I haven't thought of that yet," she said, embarrassed. "Everything happened so quickly. Do you have any suggestions?"

"Not particularly." I paused to show I hadn't thought about it earlier. "Why don't you just draw up a table to include all personal details, such as current address and year of graduation? Then you can ask the bank to send the people on the list an invitation to the reunion and ask them to confirm and attach their short résumé. You know, tell in a few sentences what they've been doing since they graduated."

"Good idea," said Erikka. "I'll do that after breakfast."

"I have another idea," I said. "Why don't you prepare a separate list of all the alums you located that live outside Iran? Maybe the bank would want to use their connections in their respective countries. Didn't they say in the briefing, part of their marketing strategy is to get a piece of the Iranian overseas business, because they want to set it up bilaterally?"

"I'm one step ahead of you," she said. "Look." She handed me two handwritten pages with many names.

Next to the name Reza Nazeri, in the space left for a current address, she'd written "deceased." Although his name rang a bell, I couldn't remember if he was on the list of students we had received from the State Department. Obviously, I hadn't brought the list to Iran. It'd have to wait until I returned to Europe.

"Maybe you should send a copy to the bank."

"But it's incomplete, isn't it?"

"I know, but it would be good to show them that you're already getting results."

"Good idea."

"Are you going to contact any of the people on that foreign list?"

"No, not right now anyway. There's no point in my calling long-distance from Iran to other countries. It can wait until I return to Europe. The reunion is a few months away. We have time."

"You're right," I conceded. "What about the deceased alumnus, do you know what happened to him?"

"I heard he had an accident."

"Did you know him?"

"Yes. He was a really good friend. We used to have playdates when we were young. I also knew his mother very well. He grew up without a father, so he spent a lot of time at our house."

"I see," I said contemplatively. I needed time to plot.

"Will you need me today?" she asked.

"I was thinking of going to Mashhad to search for my roots. Maybe stopping in Neyshābūr, where I think I might have family. It says in the guide that Hakim Omar Khayyám was born there—you know, the poet. Could be interesting."

"Ian, it's almost six hundred miles away," she said in surprise. "We need to make travel arrangements and hotel reservations. Do you want to take a train or drive?"

"Well, don't be alarmed, and I'm sorry that I didn't consult you, but I sort of planned it yesterday when you were out. I've actually already rented a car, and made a hotel reservation at"—I stopped to look at the note I'd prepared—"Homa Hotel on Taleghani Square in Ahmad Abad Street."

"How long do you want us to stay there?"

"Two or three days. Is it OK with you?"

"I guess so." She didn't sound too enthusiastic. "When do you want to leave?

"Well . . . whenever you're ready?"

She hesitated, "I scheduled six meetings with alums, but I can cancel. My work for you comes first."

"No, please don't cancel," I said quickly. "Keep the meetings; we'll go on another day." After a quick glance at the list Erikka had prepared, I no longer wanted to make that trip that day. But I had to at least pretend that I was sticking to my original idea to search for my roots. We would have to go soon.

I went outside the main entrance. A white Peugeot Persia was parked in the hotel's driveway. A rental agreement was left on the driver's seat. I drove the car to the parking lot and entered the gift shop in the hotel lobby.

As I was pulling out a copy of *Tehran Times* in English from the display rack, I felt a man brushing his arm against my right arm. "I'm sorry," I said, and moved to the left. He brushed against my arm again. I turned around to look at him. He was a well-built man in his early forties with intense black eyes and a black mustache.

"Mr. Ian, please go outside," he said in a low voice.

I froze. "Who are you?"

"Padaş sent me."

"Padaş? I don't know any Padaş," I said. I needed to hear the passwords.

"I know where to find nice carpets made by hand in Kāshān. Very cheap."

It was the right code at the right time. "Oh, I'd like that," I said innocently. "Where are they?"

"I can take you now." He walked slowly to the exit.

I paid for the newspaper and followed him outside.

"You must be careful," I said quietly. "I think I'm being followed."

"No, you are not."

"But I detected followers," I insisted.

"They were my men watching you," he said calmly.

"I saw one at the restaurant, and another one in a car that followed me."

He smiled mischievously. "You missed the others. We are always behind you. Unless the Iranian VEVAK is smarter than us, we didn't notice any interest in you."

"How do I contact you? I mean in case of emergency?"

"For one, we'll see any emergency and will come to your help. But if we lose contact for any reason, call this number and say that you'd like to purchase Kāshān carpets." He handed me a piece of paper.

"Who gave me that number, in case someone asks?"

"An Iranian you met on the plane coming here. You don't know his name."

"Do I identify myself on the phone?"

"No."

"What about Erikka?"

"We aren't following or protecting her, unless she's with you." He opened the car's trunk, and I saw three rolled carpets. "I'll show you these carpets now. Look as if you're interested."

"I thought you said I'm not being watched."

"Just in case." He pulled the carpets out and laid them on the pavement.

The carpets were magnificent. For a moment I even entertained the idea of actually purchasing them. *Bad timing for shopping,* I told myself. I stood there for a few more minutes admiring their beauty.

"Kāshān is a city in north-central Iran that was producing Persian carpets at royal workshops at least since the seventeenth century," he said. "But the best Kāshāns come from Ardistān. These carpets came from Yazd, but they're almost as good." He rolled up the carpets and put them back in the trunk. He shook my hand and drove away.

In the afternoon, I got hold of Erikka in the lobby.

"I have two cancellations," she said. "They postponed our meetings until tomorrow."

"In that case, I've got an idea," I said. Why don't we visit the family of Reza Nazeri? They'll probably hear about the reunion you've got coming up, and it might hurt them to be left out. The right thing to do is pay them a personal visit."

"You mean right now?" asked Erikka.

"Yes, why not? We have time. I'm sure they and the rest of the alumni will appreciate the gesture."

"Yeah, you're right. You know, I'd love to see his mom again. She was always so kind to me."

"Visiting an Iranian family at home will be a good experience for me—it'd help me understand a lot for my book," I added.

"I still remember where he lived, after all these years. It was on Darband Street, in northern Tehran," said Erikka. She called information for the telephone number. It was unlisted. "Do you want to take the chance they're still living at the same address?" she asked hesitantly.

"Let's do it," I said. "Cab?"

It took us through Imam Khomeini Boulevard, past the National Archaeological Museum of Iran, and arrived at a pleasant residential area. Erikka buzzed the intercom and a woman answered. Erikka said something in Farsi, and after a pause, the door opened.

CHAPTER TWENTY-TWO

Inside the spacious, well-appointed apartment, Mrs. Nazeri stood alongside her maid. She appeared to be nearly seventy, and was clad in a black dress without a head covering. Her eyes were puffy and lined. When she saw Erikka they both burst into tears and embraced, murmuring in Farsi.

After a moment, they seemed to remember I was there, and stepped apart politely.

"It's very nice to meet you," said Mrs. Nazeri, in English.

Erikka smiled. "I forgot how good your English was."

"You haven't changed a bit," Mrs. Nazeri told Erikka.

Erikka smiled again. "I'm not that young anymore. My daughter is already nineteen years old."

"You're lucky," said Mrs. Nazeri.

They continued talking, shifting from Farsi to English and back, until the maid brought a tray with silverware, a teapot, and delicious-looking cookies sprinkled with white powdered sugar.

Many long minutes later, during which they talked in both languages about personal things, Erikka said, "As I was saying, I'm using a professional visit to Iran to help Mr. Pour Laval in his book research, to organize a school reunion."

"It's a nice idea," said Mrs. Nazeri, turning to me.

"I only heard yesterday about Reza," said Erikka delicately. "I wanted to come and see how you were, and to offer my condolences."

"That's so kind of you."

"Perhaps you'd like to include some information about Reza in the brochure they'll be making," I suggested. "They have a

Swiss bank sponsoring the event, and one of the ideas is to collect pictures of alumni taken during their school years, include a short résumé, and publish it in a bound format, like a yearbook. It might be a good opportunity to commemorate the memory of Reza."

Erikka looked at me, surprised. I had again broken the rule of not leading the direction in the alumni matter, but I just couldn't resist that opportunity.

"I'd love that," said Mrs. Nazeri. "Let me see, just one moment . . ." She went to the other room and returned carrying two photo albums. "It's all here. I've been left only with memories."

I leafed through the pages of the albums and saw Reza, a skinny, light-complexioned young man, at family events, smiling and happy.

"What happened to him?" asked Erikka in a soft voice.

"Last month he was killed in an accident in New York."

"Did he live in America?" asked Erikka.

"He left Iran soon after the revolution. He said he was hired by a company to do business in Switzerland and America. I didn't understand much of it."

"It's so sad. Careless drivers are everywhere," I said.

She looked at me with sad dark eyes. "It wasn't a car accident. Some crazy person pushed him off the subway platform while Reza was waiting for the train."

There was a shocked silence. "How awful," I said after a moment. "Did they catch the lunatic?"

"No, he escaped."

I didn't know what to say.

"Was Reza married?" asked Erikka.

"No. He told me it was difficult having a family with his lifestyle."

"You mean traveling a lot?"

"Yes, between Switzerland and the U.S., but he used to come to visit me every few months." She looked at me. "He was my only son. His father died when Reza was just a young child. Now I have nothing."

Erikka wiped a tear away.

"Take any photos that you like, but please return them, as I have no copies," Mrs. Nazeri said.

Erikka began poring over the photos. I suggested that she take photos depicting Reza when he was in his twenties and thirties.

"This is how I'd think people will remember him," I said. When I saw a picture that looked recent, I added, "And show his friends who haven't seen him in many years how he looked just before he died."

"Mr. Pour Laval . . ." said Mrs. Nazeri hesitantly. "I need some help in the United States; perhaps you can help me. It is very difficult for us to get information from the United States. Because of the animosity between the countries, communications are slow and unreliable. Here they open many letters sent from foreign countries, and it delays delivery for days or even weeks."

"Well, I'm Canadian, but I visit New York frequently, and I'll be happy to help you."

"I need a lawyer in New York to handle Reza's estate. Can you recommend a good one?"

This was a golden opportunity I wasn't going to miss. This was my entry card into Reza's life and activities in the U.S.

"Of course—you mean a wills-and-estates lawyer? I know a very good one who doesn't charge a lot."

"Can I trust him?"

"I do," I said. "He handles all my American friends' estate matters. I know he's very reliable. I intend to be in New York soon and can call him."

"In that case, let me give you some information the lawyer may need." She opened a black leather folder with documents. "Reza lived at 45 East 78th Street in Manhattan. He owned the apartment. He had at least one bank account that I know about in Chase Bank, but there could be others. Apart from that, I know very little about his business affairs."

"Did he leave a will?" I asked.

"I don't know, but I hardly think so. He didn't expect to die so soon, and other than me he had no family."

"Did he leave any papers with you, such as business correspondence or letters that may help locate his assets?"

She thought for a minute and said, "Yes, in fact he did." She went to the other room and returned with a big brown envelope. "That's all I have," she said, and handed me the envelope. I went through its contents. Inside were a few handwritten letters in Arabic script, business cards, used airline tickets, and the like. Nothing looked immediately important. As I was casually going through the papers I saw a business card with the logo of Al Taqwa. I looked at it indifferently but put it aside with trembling hands.

"I don't see anything particularly important here. Maybe just in case, I'll copy some business cards to give the lawyer. Maybe these people did business with Reza and they owe him money."

"No need to copy," she said. "You can just take them." I put the cards in my pocket.

"What are these letters?"

"Oh, letters he had written asking me to do a few things for him. I don't know why I put them in that envelope." She excused herself and went to the other room. Erikka went to the bathroom. They returned a few minutes later.

"What about Switzerland? You mentioned he was working there?" I asked Mrs. Nazeri.

"Yes, for some bank or something, but he never actually lived in Switzerland. He just visited it for long periods."

"If the lawyer asks me about any property in Switzerland, what should I say?"

"I don't know. Maybe the lawyer will find things in Reza's apartment that will give him more information."

"OK, I think I could do that." I paused. "I have an idea. I'll simply call the lawyer and tell him to expect your letter. And I'll ask him what he needs from you to start working."

"Good," she said. "What's his name?"

"Dan Gordon," I said, and regretted it immediately. I just couldn't think fast enough of any other name. It was a bad answer, but I couldn't take it back. I'd have to make arrangements.

"I'll have him write you. He'll probably need a power of attorney to be appointed as administrator of the estate of Reza."

"There's one thing I need to add," said Mrs. Nazeri. "Reza had to change his name. He told me it was better for business. In fact he changed it twice. His first new name was Christopher Gonda."

I felt heart palpitations and hoped Mrs. Nazeri and Erikka wouldn't notice my excitement. In my mind I vividly saw the picture of Christopher Gonda, a good-looking young American man who disappeared in the early 1980s without a trace. Now I was having tea with the mother of an Atashbon member.

"And then he changed it again?" I queried, praying that my voice wouldn't betray me.

"Yes, he told me that there was another person with that name who ran into trouble, so he decided to change it again, this time to Philip Montreau."

When we returned to our hotel, Erikka noticed I was behaving differently. "What happened?" she asked. "Are you OK?"

"Of course I'm OK," I quickly answered. "I was deeply touched by Mrs. Nazeri's grief. Losing her only son in such a ghastly accident. I sympathize with her."

Erikka gave me one of those "I don't know if I should believe that" looks. When we arrived at the hotel's driveway, she said, "I'm going to meet another graduate, Hasan Lotfi. You're welcome to join us."

I was going to politely reject the offer, but when I saw a chauffeured black Mercedes just behind us and a distinguished looking man exit, I changed my mind. Erikka looked back and said, "My God, it's Hasan." She walked over to him and held out her hand in excitement to shake his. But he pulled away from her without touching. I was afraid that Erikka was going to get in trouble—all that touching. He nonetheless smiled at her. I just stood there. They came over to me, and Erikka made the introduction.

"Why don't you join us?" he asked. "As a matter of fact, I insist."

There was a slight tone of command in his voice. His demeanor was that of a man of authority. He was of medium height and build, with a trimmed beard, dressed in a mix of Iranian and Western-style clothing. I looked at his shoes and wristwatch. They looked expensive. I remembered one of my Mossad instructor's comments: "If you want to quickly assess a person's financials, look at his watch and shoes. Wealthy people don't scrimp on these items."

"Thanks, I'd be happy to," I said.

We sat in the lobby and Hasan and Erikka spoke in a combination of English and Farsi about the school and their mutual friends. I felt like a fifth wheel, and quietly sipped my cherry juice and listened.

Erikka sensed my boredom. She switched back to English and said, "Hasan made it big. He's now a high-ranking officer in the Revolutionary Guards."

I breathed deep to mask the immediate change in my vital signs. Hasan didn't smile when he said, "They agreed to ignore the fact that I was educated by infidels."

Erikka smiled guilelessly, although to me it wasn't funny at all. I wasn't going to ask him any questions and instead let him speak. But Erikka was the one to ask him directly what he was doing at the Revolutionary Guards.

"I started as a supervisor at the Intelligence Department of the Revolutionary Guards. Then I moved to the Security Ministry and became in charge of the Secretariat, and then returned to the Revolutionary Guards as its chief of intelligence."

"That's very interesting," said Erikka, as if Hasan just told her he was working at the local zoo training birds to sing. She had no idea how important this man was or how dangerous and treacherous his organization was. We were sitting and drinking juice in a fancy hotel with a man whose organization was responsible for catching, marinating, and frying guys like me.

"Do you get to travel?"

"Unfortunately not," he said. "I used to, but now I'm a bureaucrat in an organization that enforces the rule of Islamic law and exports the Islamic Revolution, among other things," he said, looking at me enigmatically. I tried not to break under his glare. The only comparison that came to my mind was of a cannibal ogling and drooling at a fat tourist lost in the jungle. Had he insisted I participate in his meeting with Erikka only because he didn't want to be seen with a woman at a hotel? Or did it have to do with his ministry's instruction to Khan in Islamabad to lure me into Iran—and now I had walked into his trap willingly? I kept to my training: cool and relaxed, not revealing my thoughts and fears.

"Mr. Pour Laval, please tell me about your book. Erikka mentioned it's romantic and dramatic at the same time."

"Yes, in a way," I said.

"Have you started writing it?"

Now that was a direct question that an interrogator asks, not a polite curious bystander. I decided to pick up on that.

"As a matter of fact I've gotten a lot of writing done lately. Are you interested in literature?" I asked.

"Sometimes. It's sometimes interesting to see what people from other countries think of our country and our culture."

"Well, this person," I said, pointing a finger at my chest, "thinks very highly of your country." Kissing up never hurt anyone.

"I'd like to read what you've written," he said, and softening the tone of command, he added, "If you don't mind, of course."

"Well, it's just a rough draft, and I wrote a lot before coming here. I expect to make many changes. I've learned so much since I came to Iran."

He tightened the screws. "Good. When can I see it?"

"Can you wait for the book to come out? It will be edited and updated after I conclude my visit."

"Only if you force me," he said lightly with a smile, exposing perfect white teeth. I let him lead the direction of the conversation. "You'll be making good changes after your visit, I hope?"

"Certainly," I confirmed. "The manuscript is here, in my room. If you promise to return it to me by the end of the week, with your sincere and critical comments, I can let you read it. I could use an early critical review."

"I'd like that," he said.

"Let's go to my room then," I said and got up.

Erikka remained sitting. "I don't think it'd be a good idea for me to go to a room with two men."

"Don't worry," said Hasan calmly. "You have nothing to worry about when I'm here." This was his subtle way of showing us how powerful his position was.

There was a moment of silence. Erikka didn't respond. Apparently the wee-hours encounter with the moral police had left its mark on her.

"OK," I said easily. "I'll just go upstairs and bring it here."

I went up to my room and took the bound manuscript the ghostwriters of the CIA had prepared for me. There were many handwritten comments on the text that I'd inserted to make it look like it had been worked on at different times with different pens.

"Here it is," I said as I handed him the bound copy.

"I have additional copies at home and on my computer, but that copy is the only one with my comments. Some of them were made during this visit, so please return it."

"No problem," he said, and I sensed that he was somewhat surprised that I had met his challenge.

After awhile, I excused myself, saying I thought they would like some time to catch up, and that I could use some rest. An hour later, my room phone rang. "Ian," said Erikka. "I didn't realize you already finished your book. You never told me."

"It's just a first draft," I said, wondering whether she suspected anything. "In fact I've just written another page which isn't included in the printed draft."

"I'm so curious—can I see it?"

"Sure, meet me in the lobby."

I quickly copied longhand from a printed page the CIA had prepared for such a contingency. I tore the printed page to pieces and flushed it in the toilet. I couldn't give her a printed page I said I'd just written.

A few minutes later we sat on the soft couches in the lobby and I gave her the text.

"Razak, can I ask you a personal question?" she asked shyly, ignoring the staring looks of guests at the restaurant. Abelina felt encouraged that Razak had agreed to meet her publicly.

"I think so, but I don't promise an answer."

"Have you ever loved a woman that you wanted to spend the rest of your life with?"

"I thought I did, but I was wrong."

"Do you think it could ever happen again? I mean, falling in love?" Abelina clenched her fists in anticipation.

"I hope so, but it hasn't happened yet. . . ." Razak thought of the too-many introductions his family made to eligible young females. He was tired of the futile efforts and the not-so-subtle pressure of his family to marry. They had to realize that times had changed.

"What would she have to be like?"

Razak hesitated. The questions were too direct. Iranian women didn't discuss these matters with men who are not family, but he felt mysteriously drawn to this fair-skinned woman with the soft voice, making him forego custom.

"It's difficult," he said, looking at her blue eyes, resisting the urge to hold her hand. "Because there are rules I set for myself that I must follow before I bind myself forever."

"Rules? What rules?" asked Abelina as she looked him in the eye. She bent over the table and he smelled her perfume.

Razak took a deep breath. "I must love her with all

my heart so that I will never make her cry from sorrow. God counts her tears."

"That is so nice," said Abelina softly. "Any other rules?

"Yes, equality," he said. "I read in the Bible you gave me that Eve was created from Adam's rib, not from his feet, nor from his head. Therefore my loved one, who loves the Bible so much, cannot be below me or superior to me, but at my side to be my equal. She'll be under my arm to be protected, and next to my heart to be loved. But she'll always have to remember my tradition and follow my lead through it."

Abelina sent her hand under the table and held his hand.

Erikka gave me back the page. "You're so talented," she exclaimed. "It's so romantic. I can't wait to read the rest of the novel."

"This piece is also just a first draft."

If Erikka had had any suspicion of me, I think reading that page shelved it.

CHAPTER TWENTY-THREE

The jangling telephone woke me up. The sunrise was just beginning to send rays through my window.

"Hello, Ian. This is Hasan. Remember me?" His tone was unnaturally friendly. "I read most of your book last night, and enjoyed it immensely." I felt proud until I remembered I hadn't written it, and that in fact I didn't believe he'd read it, maybe just flipped through it.

"Thank you, it's very kind of you. I need every bit of criticism to fine-tune it, but people seem just to compliment me rather than criticize."

"Of course there's always room for change," he quickly agreed. "Although I'm not a professional writer or reviewer, I think that as an Iranian I could draw your attention to a few points that could be better explained."

"I'd like that," I said.

"Good, then we'll have lunch and talk about it." A Revolutionary Guard top executive moonlights as a literary critic? Hello? Add the sense that he was too eager, though in a polite and subtle way, and the conclusion could be ominous. Was I the mouse in Aesop's fable about the lion and the mouse? I didn't care to think what usually happens in these rendezvous. In the fable they live together in friendship and in harmony forever after, but in reality I knew who got devoured. Never the lion.

Hasan, all smiles, came to my hotel at noon. He drove me to Shandiz Jordan Persian Restaurant on Jordan Street. Where was his driver? I wondered. Hasan was warmly and enthusiastically welcomed by the owner, who practically bowed and danced around him. I felt embarrassed. We sat at a corner table without ordering anything, and a school of waiters started loading our table with delicious Iranian *chello* kebab and *shishlik*. Contrary to a rule of thumb I'd coined after eating in fancy restaurants in Europe and the U.S., where the bigger the plate was, the smaller the portion, here both the plates and the portions were huge.

"What I like about your book . . . ," said Hasan, as he dipped *naneh sangak*, the Iranian flat bread, in a plate containing a white sauce and placed a small piece of *shishlik* on the bread. I waited for him to continue, but his mouth was full. He swallowed and said, "As I was saying, I like the candor and the realism with which the novel describes present-day Iran. It doesn't criticize our culture and the Islamic direction the Iranian people have decided to take, but rather tries to understand it and yet bridge the differences between the man's and the woman's respective cultures. I hope many people read your book and that more people will come here to see the real Iran, rather than listen to political propaganda."

"Like what?"

"I hear false accusations distributed by the Zionists and America that Iran is sponsoring terrorist organizations. I can tell you that these rumors are baseless."

Why was he kissing up, talking about "my" novel? Why was he mentioning terror when it wasn't even in the book? This person didn't strike me as a man who wasted words for no purpose. What was going on?

"I didn't get the impression that Iran was encouraging tourism," I said cautiously.

"Oh yes, we do, but many don't seem to be convinced to come."

"So what do you suggest doing?"

"If people don't come here, maybe we should bring the message to them, to the place where they live, so that they'll see we aren't lepers."

"Who do you think can do that?"

"We have cultural attachés at our embassies in Europe," said Hasan. "But they aren't trained in public appearance."

Sure, I thought. *These undercover agents are trained to recruit informers and shoot dissidents; therefore, they have no time to promote cultural events.*

"Why don't you go?" I suggested. That was a bold question, and the answer would define who the lion was and who was the mouse.

He paused. "I would think about it, if I received an invitation."

"From whom?"

"From an academic institution, such as a university. It could assemble hundreds or even thousands of students to listen to an open debate about the true vision of Iran's Islamic Revolution."

"Any university? I can ask some leading Canadian universities if they'd be interested."

"It's important that the inviting entity will be respectable and fair enough to let me voice the truth. It doesn't have to be a university; it could also be a cultural association or a research institute." He paused for a moment to measure my reaction and continued. "It would serve Iran's interests best if an invitation were arranged soon. Some matters need to be brought to the public's attention before things happen for which Iran could be blamed—incorrectly, of course."

If he was sending an unspoken message, I think I got it.

"How soon?"

"A month or so."

"That certainly sounds like a bold and interesting idea. If you'd like, why don't you send me your résumé and a synopsis of your lecture? Upon my return to Canada, I'll be happy to make a few phone calls to cultural and academic institutions and see what they have to say."

"When are you returning?" There was certain urgency to the question.

"I haven't made plans yet. Maybe in two weeks—I have an open ticket."

"Then perhaps you can communicate with the universities while you're still here, and if they have questions, I could answer through you, while you're still here."

"We can do that," I agreed.

"I like your writing," he suddenly said, changing the subject. "I read your article in *European Public Policy* magazine about the liberation movements in Africa and your article on the Indian-Pakistani conflict in *Political Science and Influence*."

It was obvious he had done his homework and had run a search on Ian Pour Laval before coming to meet me. If he wanted to discuss the articles, I was prepared. I had read them all. But why was he mentioning them, other than to hint that he'd checked my background? Though I had no clear answer, I did have ideas. Thus far it seemed that the legend the CIA had built for my new identity as Ian Pour Laval was holding water. We continued eating and talking, but it was clear, at least to me, that the essential messages had already been exchanged, and the rest of the time spent now was just a waste of it.

He drove me back to my hotel. I couldn't stop wondering what it was all about. Was he performing a counterintelligence routine by checking me out to make sure I was a bona fide Canadian author, and not a spy? Was he trying to recruit me to work for him? Given his government position, was he sending me another message I was hesitant to accept as plausible?

Alex, my Mossad Academy instructor, had used a metaphor to illustrate recruitment of a source.

Think of cattle ushered to the slaughter. They're made to approach the chute to the stunning pen area through a narrow gangway that has solid sides. Therefore each animal can only see the rear of the animal in front of it, and will not be distracted by what is happening outside the chute. The chute isn't wide enough for animals to turn around. The animal cannot go back or stop, it must proceed to its ultimate end. Create a situation whereby your source will have no other option than to work for you.

I thought that Hasan followed that rule, although I wasn't sure who was the target. Nonetheless I decided that I needed money, and in case my guess was valid and imminent, I hit the ATM for a quite particular amount. I made several other transactions, but some messages were not included in the short list of commands. I needed to find an alternate manner to convey a very important message that could be urgent, but I had no clue how. I knew it had to be sent immediately; time seemed to be of the essence. I considered several options and discarded them all. The subject was too sensitive to risk apprehension en route. I had to wait until I heard back from the Agency following the messages I'd just sent through the ATM.

After two more days and eight or ten more meetings with alumni, it became more and more boring. How many times did I have to listen to quarter century–old gossip? I decided to travel to Neyshābūr the following day. I was curious to see if the rumors I'd heard had any basis. I could score additional points at home if I were successful. I decided not to think what would happen if I failed. Things were going well, I thought, but I immediately remembered the lesson we'd learned at the Mossad: if things seem to be going well, make sure you haven't overlooked a small detail that will fail you, because only rarely do things go well without a hitch.

Very early that morning, when the only sound heard was of birds just starting to chirp, I dimly heard a persistent tapping on my door. Half asleep, I walked to the door and saw through the viewer a short dark man with a trimmed beard.

"Mr. Ian," he whispered. "Please open up. I came here for the Kāshān carpets you wanted to buy cheap."

It was four A.M. and I wasn't buying any carpets. But he came close to the contact çode, and I sensed the urgency. I opened the door. He entered and I shut the door.

"Padaş sent me. You must leave at once," he said urgently.

"What happened?"

"The VEVAK is rounding up dozens of English-speaking men who've arrived in Tehran during the past two weeks. You fit their profile; we want you to leave immediately."

"Do you know why they're arresting them?"

"The VEVAK caught an American mole in the Iranian president's office in Tehran."

"So what does that have to do with me? I have no connection whatsoever to any mole or to the Iranian President. I'm just an author from Canada." I wasn't going to concede who I really was, even under these circumstances. You could never be too careful.

"I know, I know," he said dismissively, in the same tone I'd last heard from my teacher when I tried to concoct some story about why I hadn't prepared my homework. In plain English it meant, "Don't bullshit me."

"We just heard that Javad Sadegh Kharazi, a senior council member, was arrested. They caught him using a sophisticated, U.S.-made long-distance transmitter during a secret Iranian leadership meeting. The Iranian security forces are trying to discover if it was the Americans who controlled Javad Sadegh Kharazi, or someone else."

"Which meeting was it?"

"The mullahs' secret meeting on Iran's nuclear and terrorist activities. They're furious. It's the most embarrassing espionage case in Iran since the Islamic Revolution began."

"And just because I'm an English-speaking male who arrived here during the past two weeks, I need to leave? Aren't you guys a bit paranoid? I have no connection with these matters. I'm staying. Tell Padaş I said thanks anyway."

"Mr. Ian, there's something else you should consider," he said in the tone of a poker player realizing that no one had noticed him drawing the winning ace from up his sleeve.

"What is it?"

"You met too many people here. That caused some problems."

"Like who?'

"Hasan Lotfi, to begin with."

"Yes, I met him last week and had lunch with him the next day. He's a classmate of my assistant. Why?"

"He disappeared."

I was stunned, but continued with my resistance, though weakened, based on what I'd just heard.

"Why is that any of my concern? Do all people who met him need to flee? What if he took a vacation or locked himself in a room with a young woman who doesn't meticulously observe the Iranian dress and undress behavioral codes for unmarried women? He could be anywhere."

"Do you want to explain that to the VEVAK?" he asked patiently. "They know you met him both times."

"How do you know that?"

"We're always behind you."

"And how do you know that he was a suspect?"

"Lotfi had been under VEVAK surveillance for a few months. Anyone who met with him is also a suspect."

"But you haven't answered my question. How do you know that Lotfi became a suspect?"

"Mr. Ian, we have loyal members everywhere. You also met Mrs. Nazeri."

"So what? Is she a spy too?"

"No. But her son was a very important person who died mysteriously. Any stranger who attempts to talk to Nazeri's family is an immediate suspect."

"Important how?"

"Something very secretive, we don't know exactly. But these things put together are serious enough for you to leave immediately. I'll alert Miss Erikka as well. She'll leave through one border exit and you through another. A person named Sammy will come to your room in thirty minutes. Leave your luggage behind and take just an overnight bag."

There was no point in arguing. My instructions were to take my contact's advice in case of emergency. From what I'd heard, I was convinced that this was an emergency. I wondered how Erikka would react.

"Can I call Erikka and tell her we must leave? She knows nothing about the carpets. She may not believe you."

"Just tell her you have to leave," he said. Apparently he didn't know that Erikka wasn't in the loop.

I couldn't risk using the phone. I went up to her room after making sure the hallway was empty. I knocked lightly on her door. After a few minutes of persistent knocking, she opened the door dressed in a white nightgown. I slipped inside her room before she could resist.

"Erikka, please listen to me," I said in a calm voice, although I wasn't calm inside. "We must leave Iran immediately. A person will come to your room in a few minutes and will instruct you. Please do exactly as he says."

"Ian, what are you talking about?" She sounded frightened.

"It has nothing to do with me or you. But the Iranian VEVAK is very nervous. They think Hasan Lotfi disappeared. Anyone who's been in contact with him will be questioned."

"But we only spoke about our school days."

"I'm sure you did, but I think we should protect ourselves from any forthcoming investigation. Remember how upset you were after the Komiteh stopped you? That was ten minutes. This time it could last weeks or months. Take nothing but your money and documents, and a few things for overnight. The rest can be sent for later. Start packing, and don't call or talk to anyone."

"How do you know all this?" she asked, and for the first time I sensed doubt in her voice.

"The bank called me. They bought an all-risks policy to cover our visit in Iran, a standard procedure of risk management. A security advisory company, hired by the insurance company, just alerted them of these developments and suggested they remove all their insured individuals from Iran. That means you and me, and maybe others."

"But Ian, you aren't working for the bank. I am." Her brow furrowed.

"Right, I asked them the same question. Lucky for me, the insurance policy said 'Erikka Buhler and Ian Pour Laval, companion'—so they called me."

"OK," she said faintly, "I'll be ready."

I returned to my room. "Go ahead," I told the man. "Go to her room. She's in 411. I'll be ready in ten minutes."

"OK, she'll be taken by another member of our team who's waiting outside. I'll bring her over to him."

I quickly filled a small backpack and waited for Sammy. He arrived sooner than I expected, tapping lightly, and when I let him in, he slipped inside like a shadow. His voice was low.

"Please follow me. And make sure you have your documents and your money."

He opened the door cautiously and, after checking the hallway, signaled me to follow him. When the elevator arrived, he ducked in and pressed a series of buttons for higher floors. "We're taking the stairs," he said brusquely, allowing the elevator door to close behind him. We took them all the way to the ground floor. "Where's Erikka?" I asked, catching my breath.

"She's OK. My man is moving her now."

He used a key card to open a ground-level bedroom, and when I followed him in, I saw that it was empty. He strode across the room to a sliding door, which he thrust open, peering out at the swimming pool. Walking out calmly, as if he were the maintenance man, he motioned unobtrusively for me. I followed him through the bushes surrounding the pool area into the parking lot. A sleepy guard didn't even raise his head. Sammy opened a car door and I jumped in.

"Wait a minute," I said. "Isn't this my rental car?"

"Indeed it is. We've left a bunch of brochures in your room suggesting that you left early and drove to Mashhad."

"But I was going to go to Mashhad anyway. How did you know?"

"When you rented the car you told them you were going there. Your shadow was standing right next to you in the line."

I never bothered asking him how he got my car keys.

CHAPTER TWENTY-FOUR

I learned to drive a car in Tel Aviv, where drivers fully believe they're driving tanks, and the Mediterranean hand gestures make steering secondary. I live in New York, where stoplights are informational only, and anarchic taxi drivers set their own traffic rules every minute. But driving in Tehran made those cities look like Des Moines. Nothing had prepared me for the dangers of Tehran traffic in the early-morning hours. Heavy trucks, small cars, motorbikes, and even horse-drawn carts cross through all directions, honking their horns, regardless of any reason or rule. It seemed to be one of the few places in Iran where you could break the law and get away with it. No wonder Tehran ranks at the top of the list of world vehicle-fatality rates. I thought of a saying I'd heard from my driving instructor: "A man who drives like hell is bound to get there."

Sammy glanced at the rearview mirror. "We've got company," he said. "This time they're not our men."

He jerked open the glove compartment and tossed a .38 gun into my lap. I grabbed it between my fingers. Our car suddenly tilted and stopped. We had been broadsided. Heart racing, I swiveled my head to see what had happened. A small car with what looked like two passengers had hit us. I slipped the gun under my windbreaker and took a better look. The other car wasn't badly damaged.

Sammy, swearing under his breath, swung open the door and jumped out to examine the car. I heard the shouting, but understood nothing, staying in the car even as a small crowd quickly assembled to watch. Traffic whizzed by, and the Iranians shook their fists, their voices escalating.

With a shrug and an angry gesture, Sammy turned away from them and jumped back into our car. "They're just con men," he told me, starting the engine. The damage wasn't that bad after all. "They stage accidents and try to blackmail unsuspecting drivers. Let's go." As he accelerated and pushed through, he nearly ran over one of the men, who was still yelling.

"Better to leave before the police get here," Sammy explained tersely. "That'll start a silent bidding war—who's gonna bribe the cop with more money. We can't risk that." He made a left turn into another busy street and maneuvered through commercial areas. After driving for ten minutes in the congested streets, I noticed through the side-view mirror a beige sedan following us. I saw two men in the front seat, but there could have been others in the back seat.

"Sammy, are these guys behind us your men?"

He glanced at his mirror. "Shit. No, they're the VEVAK. I recognize their car."

It was a challenge to get through the thicket of jaywalkers, bike riders, and reckless car drivers, but Sammy found a way. Nonetheless, it was a grotesquely slow chase, at no more than ten or fifteen miles an hour. The VEVAK car was about six or seven car distances behind us. Through a quick and abrupt maneuver Sammy managed to pass a big truck, leaving our followers behind it, blocking their view. He continued passing cars on their right and left, stealing quick glances at the rearview mirror.

"I think we lost them," he said. About two miles later he suddenly turned right into a large unpaved parking lot. "Come on, quick," he said. "We'll leave the car here."

"Are we walking?" I asked, swinging the door closed.

"Not to worry, we won't be overexerting ourselves," he said wryly, pointing to a beat-up blue sedan, Japanese made, parked at the corner of the lot. "Jump in, and keep down." I complied, watching Sammy with head down and eyes raised as he put a hat on and tore off a fake mustache. He started the engine and drove away through the other end of the parking lot, spraying gravel and leaving a cloud of dust behind us.

Keeping my head down, I heard Sammy dial a number and begin speaking in what sounded like Kurdish.

He snapped the phone shut. "They're on to you," he said swiftly. "The VEVAK is looking for you all over, including at the airport and train stations. We'll have to change plans. You can't leave through the airport, and we can't smuggle you through the mountains to Turkey—the roads leading to the border are still blocked by snow. We'll go to Plan B."

I was lying on the back seat, alternately cursing the secret police, the Tehran city engineers who didn't bother to maintain the roads, and the lousy car manufacturer who hadn't managed to engineer a car that didn't lurch over every pebble. I said nothing. What was there to say?

Thirty minutes of driving felt like eternity. Finally, the car stopped. Sammy got out and I heard a metal gate screeching. Sammy opened my door.

"You can come out now. You'll be safe here."

I looked around. We were in an enclosed yard, blocked from the street by a plate-metal gate, surrounded by a high stone wall.

"What is this place?"

"Your hideout until their search cools down or the weather warms up, whichever comes first," said Sammy with a grim smile. I followed him into the dilapidated building. He produced a key to the wooden door from his pocket, and hinges squeaked as we entered into what looked like a deserted factory, perhaps for textiles. Rusty machines stood idle, like statues sculpted by an avant-garde artist. Remnants of textile bales were piled on the floor. Sammy went behind a huge machine and opened an inconspicuous trapdoor just underneath it.

"Come," he said when he saw my hesitation.

I slowly went down wooden stairs. He closed the trapdoor above us and turned on the light inside by pulling a cord. I found myself in a spacious, windowless basement, with simple carpets on the concrete floor, a bed with once-clean linen, and a small kitchen with a table and an ancient refrigerator. I also saw a small radio and an old television set, probably black-and-white.

"What is this place?" I asked again. I was wary.

"Your hiding place," said Sammy. "We use it occasionally to hide people sought by the security services. As you know, Kurds aren't exactly beloved around these parts." He walked into the kitchen area. "There's enough food here." He opened a wall closet that was full of canned food supplies. "You have these"—he pointed at an electric stove and a refrigerator—"and running water." He opened the kitchen faucet, letting water out, adding, "And a toilet, but no shower and no hot water. Sorry."

"Looks good. But it's cold in here," I said.

"Use this." He pointed at an oil radiator on wheels. "I'll come to see how you're doing every three days."

"How do I communicate with you?" I asked.

"Use the cell phone you rented at the hotel, but only if your life is in danger. The police can trace you though the phone's signals. Take the battery out. The phone transmits signals even when you aren't calling anyone."

"I did that when we were leaving the hotel," I said. "One question. How do you get away with using electricity and water? If VEVAK is worth its salt, it knows how to monitor deserted places by checking power use."

"We hooked the power and the water to the next building, where one of our men lives. There's no movement on the factory's electric and water meters. He'll also keep an eye on this building from his apartment, which overlooks the yard. There's a side door between his building and the factory, so the metal gate we just used to enter from the street is rarely opened. Even if this location is observed from the outside, no movement will be detected."

He handed me a torn white cloth. "If you're in distress, display this above the machine on the factory level. Our guy can see it through his window." He paused. "Keep the gun. You may need it here." He reached into his shoulder bag and produced a small box with twenty-four rounds.

After giving me additional technical instructions concerning the toilet, waste disposal, and maintenance, Sammy said his good-byes. "I'll see you in three days. I'll enter the yard through the side door. If you hear the metal gate open, that means trouble."

I sat on the bed. It was only with Sammy gone that I realized how quiet this place was.

I sighed. I had always managed to extricate myself from trouble, and I had an abiding faith that I'd continue to do just that. There was no reason to be sure now, but what the hell. A fall into a ditch makes you wiser. I turned on the TV on low volume—nothing but programs in Farsi. I tried the radio; no luck.

Well, might as well go to sleep.

I curled up on the bed, wondering for a moment what they had done with Erikka, what they had told her.

A few hours later, I stretched awake, hungry. I opened cans of tuna and sardines, and ate them with a few stale crackers. I was bored. I tried the radio again. Nothing. I listened to random noises coming from the outside world. Cars passing and honking, or airplanes approaching. I wished I had something to read.

My thoughts turned toward my kids. Were they worried about me? Probably not. At least not yet. They were used to

me being out of the country for long stretches on assignments. Actually, I was thankful they had no idea what a bind
I'd gotten myself into. It would have worried them, of course,
and that would have meant that I was making my problem
their problem. That was the last thing I would have wanted. I
prided myself in always being able to separate my work life
and my family life.

Three days later Sammy came and brought me three cucum-
bers, two tomatoes, five oranges, and more canned food. To
my delight he also brought English-language newspapers.

"What's up?" I asked. I was glad to see him.

"Things aren't great," he said. "The VEVAK is searching
for you everywhere. They say that you're an American spy.
They posted your picture in public places—train and bus terminals, and even at the bazaar."

My heart sank. My picture? When had it been taken?
When I'd met with Lotfi last week, in Vienna, or even in Pak-
istan? The answer to that could help me build a new legend if
I were caught. But who did I ask?

"God. Well, it looks like I'll be stuck here for a while."

"Unfortunately," said Sammy.

I thought for a moment. "Can you get me one of the wanted
posters?

"I'll try."

"Does anyone know I'm safe here?" I asked. I didn't know
how much Sammy knew about my identity.

"We reported that you're OK. Everyone at home knows
we'll take good care of you. Do you need anything else?"

"Just reading material in English and fresh food. Everything else I already have. Thanks for everything."

"It's nothing," said Sammy. As he was about to climb the
stairs, he turned around and asked, "Did you really want to go
to Mashhad in search of your roots?"

I sensed that the question was loaded. I knew even less
about Sammy than he knew about me, so I had to tread carefully.

"Yes," I said nonchalantly. "I was also planning to stop in Neyshābūr, you know, to see the birthplace of Hakim Omar Khayyám. I think I have a relative there."

"What an interesting coincidence," he said, with an edge I didn't expect. "Neyshābūr is also the ultrasecret future birth-place of the Iranian nuclear bomb."

"Really?" I said, striving to keep my voice level. I didn't know where the conversation was going.

"Yes," he continued. "They are secretly building a low-level enrichment plant with a capacity to supply enough uranium to build three to five nuclear bombs a year."

"I read someplace that their plant is in Naṭanz."

"Naṭanz is for the UN inspectors to visit. Neyshābūr is the real plant. It is built five hundred feet deep into the ground. It's called Shahid Moradian, after some guy who died in the war."

"Interesting," I said, trying to sound uninterested.

"The Neyshābūr plant was built by Russians. Very recently, Bulgarian transport planes brought tens of thousands of cen-trifuges from Belarus and Ukraine. Soon Ukrainian engineers will install them. Some of their families are already there."

"Wow. I know so little about that stuff, since I write fic-tion," I said blandly. "I'm useless on science."

He gave me that look again. "So the only reason VEVAK is looking for you is because you met some people in connec-tion with a book you are writing?"

I shrugged. "I guess so. But who knows what goes through their heads?"

"Maybe VEVAK suspects you had plans to go to Neyshābūr for more than just tourism or family business."

"They would be wrong. I was going to visit Khayyám's tomb. Look at some art."

"You couldn't get near the plant even if you wanted to," said Sammy matter-of-factly. "Neyshābūr plant is protected by the special Revolutionary Guards Corps elite Ansar al-Mahdi unit."

"I had no intention whatsoever to go near any strategic installation I didn't even know existed until you told me," I said firmly. What I didn't say though, was that I had wanted to become friendly with the Ukrainian families. Spouses always talk, regardless of their gender. Promising contacts could be developed by people with money and an agenda with people who come from a poor country like Ukraine and who have no particular allegiance to Iran.

Sammy sighed, realizing that there was no confession forthcoming. "Be well," he said curtly.

Obviously he didn't believe a word I said. On the other hand, I believed every word he said. The news about the Iranian Plan B, created in case the known locations were bombed, had been slowly trickling out. Now, Sammy's words supported it. I had no way of knowing the weight of Sammy's account, nor could I relay the intel home. Maybe Sammy had already done that. Or had he? Had the solitude of the stinking basement made me paranoid? Or maybe my healthy instincts had finally kicked in. Was I really hiding from VEVAK? Did I have proof, other than Sammy's words? How could I be sure and believe him? Something about our recent conversation had jarred me. It had sounded like an interrogation.

Was my escape and hiding a contingency well planned by the CIA in case of an emergency, or rather a well-orchestrated ploy by the Iranian secret services to extricate information from me, using a Kurdish contact to pose as my guardian angel? Perhaps the real Sammy was caught and he'd talked, and the person I was seeing now was an agent of the Iranian services. I quickly made a mental roster of my conversations with Sammy. Had I told him anything revealing? Had I disclosed my true identity? I was sure I hadn't. I decided not to use Sammy's messenger services to relay the messages that were burning in my head. The risk was too high.

I was torn from the inside. The hint Hasan Lotfi had given me left me with no doubt. There was a major terrorist attack on the United States that Hasan, as chief of intelligence of the Revolutionary Guards, was planning, or at least knew about, and now he was using this information as a bargaining chip. Could I trust Sammy to convey the message? What if he was an Iranian agent, and the messages were to be stopped, or worse, altered? What if my assessment of Hasan was accurate, and now his arrest would frustrate a major intelligence achievement, too big to even think of? I had to find a way to send the message. I even toyed with the idea of letting the Iranians intercept my message. Fearing detection of their plan, or even being ambushed perpetrating it, they might abort the mission. The doubts were tearing me from the inside. I was also worried about Erikka and hoped she made a safe departure.

Days went by, and I got used to my daily routine. Wake up at dawn, eat a small breakfast, boil hot water and wash up with makeshift towels I was collecting from the factory's floor, and throughout the day read books Sammy brought me. I tried to exercise—pushups and crunches. At night I ventured outside to the yard to breathe fresh air. I grew a beard out of boredom. I hooked up a loose wire I found on the factory floor to the radio to enhance reception. That helped me tune in to an English-language radio broadcast from the Gulf States. But the news edition was short and general, except for Gulf-area local news. Still, if a major terrorist attack had hit the U.S., they surely would have reported it in their newscasts. So I knew for now that nothing major had unfolded yet.

But that didn't help ease my anxiety about the situation. In fact, it heightened it. It made me feel useless sitting there twiddling my thumbs in my little hole-in-the-ground hideout while the bad guys were probably putting their plot into action. I needed to get the hell out of there, but I was effectively trapped for now.

It was also vital to hear the Tehran local news, and that I got only twice a week from Sammy, who brought me copies of the *Tehran Times* in English. I combed each copy to see if there was a mention of the manhunt for me. But I found nothing. I marked the passing days on the wall with a pencil. Forty-eight days had passed. Sammy never gave me more details on the manhunt and never got me copies of the wanted posters. That didn't help increase my level of trust in him. I said nothing, though; I was completely at his mercy.

CHAPTER TWENTY-FIVE

I stirred awake. I glanced at my watch, but it was too dark to see the time. I turned on the light. It was three thirty A.M. "Shit," I muttered, and turned off the light. Then I heard the same slow screeching metal noise with another muffled sound that woke me up.

The gate? I raised my head from my stinking, lumpy pillow. The noise was too distinct to ignore. I quietly left my bed, climbed the steps to the factory floor, and peeked through the window. It was a crisp-cold and bright night. Other than the occasional noise of a passing car, I heard nothing. The area of the factory yard leading to the metal exit gate was empty. The gate was closed. *Solitude was driving me crazy,* I told myself. I was imagining things. I crawled back into my bed, which was still warm. I fell asleep.

But it didn't last long. I woke up again, unable to ignore a different sound coming from the outside. I decided not to venture to the factory floor again. I might have been going crazy in isolation, but the sounds I was hearing were definitely not a figment of my imagination. They were muffled, but very real. Maybe it wasn't the gate. I couldn't tell whether the sounds were coming from the yard, the factory main floor, or the neighboring houses. As always, I had to hope for the best, but prepare for the worse. I held on to my gun. Other than keeping quiet, like a mouse in danger, there was nothing I could do. I heard steps right above me. They were too obvious to ignore. I wasn't imagining things. Somebody was walking on the factory floor.

I clenched the gun, tiptoed to the kitchen to grab the sharpest knife I had, and hid behind the stairs. I tried to identify the steps. Was it one person, or more? I held my breath. I heard "my" name called.

"Mr. Ian, where are you?"

I didn't answer. It was definitely not Sammy. I never had middle-of-the-night visits from Sammy. Was there an emergency that brought about the sudden visit? This person knew I was somewhere around here and knew my name. Should I venture out? I just sat there with the wheels of my mind racing trying to figure out what to do next. I decided to wait. Eagles may soar, but weasels don't get sucked into jet engines.

Padaş's men knew exactly where I was hiding. There was no need to call out my name. One of them could go directly to the trapdoor and walk down the wooden stairs. I felt the adrenaline rush. This visit was not friendly. The trapdoor was the only way out of my underground shit hole, and venturing out could be devastating. I unplugged the electric power cable feeding the basement and just sat there looking up at the ceiling as if my eyes could see anything other than complete darkness. I measured the location and sound of the steps. They were probably made by one person. I didn't hear talk. Ten minutes later the noises stopped, and a minute later I heard the gate screeching. This person left, or maybe wanted me to think he left. I stayed put, and fell asleep sitting on the floor with my head leaning against the wall.

This time I woke up from the cold. The heat wasn't working—my fault, having unplugged the power—and the temperature was near freezing. I hooked up the power again and the basement slowly warmed up. I still didn't feel like venturing out to peep from the factory floor's window. I vowed to stay in the basement the entire next day. Only during the following night did I quietly climb out to the factory floor. I needed fresh air, even if that air was the stale smell of an abandoned factory. To me it smelled like a field of roses. Under the entry door I saw a handwritten note.

Mr. Ian, I was come to meet you, but you not here. I must to speak to you very important. I come again soon.
Jamal

I put the note back exactly the way I'd found it. Who the hell was Jamal? Obviously he knew I was around, he knew my name, but not my exact hiding place. His visit was out of the ordinary. Sammy came only at agreed-upon times, and never in the predawn hours. Was it a trap or a genuine attempt to communicate with me? The reasons the visitor didn't know exactly where I was could be diverse, from simple forgetfulness to sloppy instructions from his supervisors.

This guy is definitely strumming on my nerves.

I didn't want to think of the possibility that Sammy had been captured and his men had come to warn me, with only a general knowledge where I was hiding. I decided to wait until Sammy's next scheduled visit on the following day. I slipped back to my hideout.

The next day, Sammy didn't show up. I sat tensely, waiting. It was already two P.M., and he had been expected to show up at twelve thirty. This time I wasn't the wife in the jokes waiting for her husband to return from the bar with a fairy tale to tell. I was really worried. Sammy had never missed any of our meetings. I had enough food for another two days, so that wasn't the immediate problem. But what if Sammy had been caught by the security police? What if he'd talked? As much as inaction pained me, I decided to wait another day. To be on the safe side I rationed my food consumption and ate only one can of tuna, one cucumber, and six crackers.

Another day passed. Two more days passed. Sammy hadn't shown up. I was running out of food, and I didn't know what to think. Did his absence show he was an Iranian agent after all? Or maybe on the contrary, it showed he couldn't come because of these security services? Anything could have been true. My food supply would last only one more day.

I had one more option. Resignedly, I took out the white cloth and placed it on the machine facing the eastern window of the factory, my distress sign for the neighbor I had never seen.

But that didn't work either—there was no sign of the neighbor after twenty-four hours. The hollowness of hunger and fear had begun to overtake me. Pessimism was a luxury I couldn't allow myself. I had to leave that place. I had enough Iranian currency to buy food. My overgrown hair and beard would make it difficult for anyone to identify me. For one single second I also entertained the hope that the VEVAK had forgotten about me, but I wasn't that naive. I decided not to use the front metal gate, and went straight to the small door in the wall leading to the neighbor's house. I waited until five thirty P.M. It was already dark.

I tried the door, but found it locked. Damn it. I looked up at the ten feet of wall, took a deep breath, and climbed. It had been years since boot camp or training, but the boredom of solitary confinement had driven me to exercise. I landed on my feet on the other side of the wall. I looked around. I was in the yard of a three-story condominium. It was a dilapidated building with chipping plaster and rusty railings. I quietly walked toward the street, and even the bark of a small dog didn't shake me from my path.

I took a deep breath and enjoyed the cool air. But I wasn't as calm as I wanted to be. Alex, my Mossad Academy instructor, had told us, "In clandestine intelligence work in hostile territory, what you don't do is just as important as what you do."

I walked slowly on the cracked, dirt-encrusted sidewalk, looking for somewhere to buy food. It was a drab area, one that hadn't seen fresh development in decades, a mix of small industry, garages, and a few residential buildings occupied by tenants with no better place to go. There were only a few other people in the street, and nobody seemed to look at me.

Dan, you're blending in, I thought. A bearded man in a country of bearded men attracts no attention.

A few hundred yards down the road was a small grocery, with dusty shelves piled with food. I decided against purchasing a large quantity of goods, fearing I'd attract attention. There was also the problem of crossing the high wall again. I selected a few items, making sure they were all within my reach on the shelves so that I would not have to speak with the owner—I couldn't reveal that I didn't speak Farsi. I paid and left. The owner said something, but my only option was to ignore him. He gave me an odd look as I left the store.

As I approached the factory, I stopped. Two cars were parked right in front of the gate and three men were talking to a woman in her fifties dressed in a black chador. She was waving her hands in excitement. My skin crawled: exactly the type of scenario I had to avoid. I slowly turned back and made a left turn into one of the alleys.

At first I thought of dumping the plastic bags with the food supplies to make my movement easier, but I decided against it. A man carrying groceries was commonplace and would help me seem like a local. I had no idea where I was or what I should do next. I knew one thing for sure: I couldn't go back to the factory. First the unknown visitor in the middle of the night, then the note, and now this. And frankly I was tired of hiding. I was always more defiant than humble. Being meek went against my nature and training. "In hostile circumstances, you don't hide, you maneuver, reposition yourself, and fight if necessary," were the words of my Mossad Academy instructor.

I hailed a cab. "Bazaar," I said, hoping it'd be enough. It was. Twenty minutes later we arrived at the bazaar. When I got out of the cab, I dumped the shopping bags into a trash can. As I started walking up the street looking for a restaurant, I saw a policeman looking at me suspiciously. With my overgrown hair and beard and clothes that, though clean, had not been ironed for two months, little wonder he became suspicious. He approached me, sized me up, and said something in

Farsi. He wasn't impressed with my ignorance and seized my hand.

"Tourist," I said. "Tourist!"

He then repeated the word I could understand: "Passport." My Ian Pour Laval passport was in my pocket, but I had no intention of showing it to him. Such a move was likely to send me into the hands of VEVAK in no time, and I still had use for my fingernails. A few people stopped to watch. My only prayer was that he would not try to frisk me. The gun was strapped to my calf and could be located quickly. I decided to talk in English instead of using body language. An obvious mistake, because a bystander intervened.

"I speak little English, you American?"

"No," I said. "I'm Canadian, and I don't understand what he wants." I broke the rule that a good time to keep your mouth shut is when you're in deep shit.

The bystander, a tall man in his early twenties clad in American-style jeans and a brown leather jacket, turned to the policeman and said something in Farsi. The policeman responded brusquely. The man turned to me. "He want your passport."

"Well, I don't have it here with me, but if he waits here, I'll go to my hotel to get it."

The policeman may have been a low-level cop, but he wasn't stupid. He shook his head. He told something to the bystander.

"He go to your hotel."

I had to isolate myself from the crowd, which was getting bigger by the minute. I tried to think of a hotel's name that would be too far to walk to.

"Esteghlal Grand Hotel," I said, remembering seeing that hotel when passing it on the Chamran Expressway.

"Very far," said the bystander.

I raised my hands in frustration. "I can take a cab with the policeman. I'll pay for the cab." I was hoping that the bystander would not join us. In these circumstances, three is a crowd.

A cab was idling nearby, and I wearily hailed it, getting in it. As the cab pulled away, I considered my next move. The language barrier between me and the cop could serve my purpose. I slowly started looking in my pocket for a piece of paper and a pen, hoping to "accidentally" dig it up with enough money to cloud the cop's judgment, but still protecting my ass if he proved to be the one of the few incorruptible Iranian cops and accused me of trying to bribe him. When I saw his widening eyes as he looked at the wad of Iranian currency I'd "unintentionally" pulled out of my pocket, I knew I'd be OK.

"My wife is asleep at the hotel," I said pointing at my finger where a wedding band should be, and then I made the universal sleeping gesture, resting my head on my hands to one side. Maybe he'd agree to take the money and forget about the whole thing. I slipped him the money wad. He just took it and held it in his hand. He told the cabdriver to stop. I jumped out. The cop didn't move. The cab drove away. Let the cop pay the $2 taxi fare. I'd left him with more than $25. I crossed the street and entered into another road against traffic, in case the cop changed his mind. But there was no sign of him. I found a small hotel two blocks away. I walked inside.

"*Sprechen Sie Deutsch?*" I asked, hoping the man at the reception desk didn't speak German. He shook his head.

"*Francais?*" No.

"English?"

He shook his head again. Good. That solved a lot of problems. I signaled with my hands that I needed a room. I paid in advance in cash for a week. He was so happy to see my cash that he didn't ask for any papers. And even if he had, I could always have pretended I didn't understand. I couldn't show him my Canadian passport. My name was likely to be all over the place courtesy of VEVAK—if indeed anyone was looking for me.

I went up to the modest and so-so-clean room to freshen up. Moments later I went out to the street, entered the first restaurant I saw and ate my first cooked meal in months. I entered an adjacent store and bought a few clothes and toiletries. After a hot shower and limited beard and hair trimming, I was ready to plan my next move.

I needed to communicate with Sammy and get the hell out of there. I took every precaution I could. I'd learned not to mock the crocodile before I finished swimming across the river.

Early in the chilly morning, as the neighborhood slowly awoke, I went to a nearby pay phone and dialed the number I'd received from one of Padas̨'s men when I arrived. There was a busy signal followed by a recording that sounded like an announcement that the number was no longer valid. I tried two more times and got the same recording. How come when I dial a wrong number it's never busy?

I found a nearby bank and made a cash withdrawal through the ATM. I also punched a few additional strokes on the keypad, again frustrated by the short list of coded messages I'd been given. I returned to my hotel. Other than venturing out to eat, I stayed in my room most of the time. I patiently looked through the window to see if my ATM messages had gone through.

It was two days later that a short and stocky mustachioed man approached me in the street, just as I was about to enter the hotel after having dinner.

"I know how to find nice carpets made by hand in Kāshān. Very cheap."

At last.

He signaled me to follow him to a waiting car. Two other men were seated inside. I recoiled for a second. Perhaps it was a trap. But reason took over. It was unlikely that the VEVAK could intercept my communications with the Agency back home. Although there was a slight change in the code words, I wasn't alarmed. If they were VEVAK, they could have arrested me without the introductions. I entered the car.

"Where is Sammy?" I asked.

They didn't answer. "No English," said a tough-looking

guy behind the wheel. I quickly assessed my options to escape. There were none. Two gorilla-size men were blocking the doors. I was in their net. I tried to figure out a good legend, fearing that the author's cover would not hold water. Where had I been during the past six weeks? What did they know about my true identity? Had Hasan Lotfi had me arrested when I failed to deliver? I felt like a trapped animal.

After an hour of driving in utter silence, we entered a small villa on the outskirts of town. Sammy came out of the front door and hugged me.

"What happened?" I asked, still confused. *Should I be happy or suspicious?*

"Your next-door neighbor was apprehended by VEVAK. I couldn't come for you, not knowing how much he'd talked. You know, at the hands of VEVAK everyone talks. I figured you'd identify the danger and leave that place. I'm glad you did."

"What did the neighbor know?"

"Luckily, he only knew that you were hiding at the factory, but didn't know exactly where, because he wasn't supposed to know. His duty was to observe the factory and alert us if there was an emergency. Did the VEVAK try to find you there?"

I told him about the strange noises and the note I found. I had to.

"That means he managed to send somebody to warn you," Sammy said.

"Or maybe he had to tell them about my hideout, and they tried to lure me out."

"Unlikely," said Sammy. "If VEVAK were there, they'd come with full brute force and turn the place upside down. But whatever it was, it's time to move. We think we can whisk you out now. Let me have all your documents; just keep your money." He handed me a used Armenian identity card with my photo. "Use this only in an emergency—some cop may be stupid enough to accept this as genuine." He handed me a hat that smelled bad and an ethnic-looking jacket.

"Put them on."

"What are these?"

"Qashqai clothes," he said. "We'll smuggle you over the mountains to Turkey with the help of our Qashqai friends. You must look like them and blend with the others." Qashqai men wear a typical felt hat with rims considerably raised over the top. The jacket was also typical Qashqai.

I knew from my briefings who the Qashqai were. A semi-nomadic tribe mainly located in Fārs Province in southwestern Iran, they were the second largest Turkic group in the country, after the Azerbaijanis.

"Can I trust them to get me safely to Turkey?"

"Of course, they're very experienced. In the winter they move from the highlands north of Shiraz to the lowlands north of the Persian Gulf, and now they return to the highlands."

"I'm sure about that, but can I trust them not to turn me in?" I knew loyalties in this part of the world could quickly change.

"They don't know who you are, and I don't think they care. They know you're under our protection, and that's all that matters." He smiled. I wasn't sure I could return the smile.

CHAPTER TWENTY-SIX

Sammy drove me to the parking lot next to Tarehbar Square, the wholesale fruit and vegetable market in south Tehran. He stopped next to an old truck and pointed at the driver. "He'll take you across the border to Turkey. Be prepared for a long ride."

"How long?"

"A nonstop trip from Tehran to the crossing point to Turkey would take about twenty-four hours, maybe a little longer depending on road conditions, since the snow is melting. But in this case, your entire trip across the border may take four to six days, including stops, because part of the way will be off-road on horseback."

I looked at the grizzled truck driver standing next to his shabby 1963 Mercedes Benz truck. Its sixteen-foot bed was covered with a canvas tarp with several patches, but new holes were in the making.

"There's no planned route, because if road conditions, police roadblocks, or the weather change, the driver will look for alternative routes." Sammy chuckled. "There's no itinerary of sites to visit or hotel reservations to worry about."

"Who are these people?" I asked when I saw three men climb into the truck.

"Other passengers he's smuggling. In fact, it serves our purpose, because you can blend with them."

"Blend?" I snorted. "I'm fair skinned and six foot four, and they're dark and a foot shorter. I'll be the obvious outsider."

"Not necessarily. We can't do anything about your height, but your beard and these clothes do a good job of masking your appearance." He pointed at a short man with a hat similar to mine. He smiled at me. "This is your driver. His name is Kashkuli Buzurg. He'll take good care of you." Sammy and the driver exchanged a few sentences.

"What language does he speak?"

"A dialect of Turkish. But like most Qashqais, he also speaks Farsi."

"And how do I communicate with him?"

"Let this be the least of your concerns. You'll manage. Use your hands and body language," Sammy answered.

"When you get closer to the Bazargan border crossing to Turkey, police activity will increase. He'll use dirt roads to bring you to a Qashqai camp. From there, they'll take you on horseback across the Zāgros Mountains in western Iran into the vicinity of Doğubayazit, Turkey."

"The Iranian police and military don't supervise that border area?" I asked.

"They know that the nomadic Qashqais move their herds

twice a year in this area, so the police and army aren't expected to immediately suspect such movement. The Qashqais summer location is about ten thousand feet above sea level. It's still cold up there—not all the snow has melted."

The name "Doğubayazit" sounded familiar. Then I remembered: it was the city next to the Ararat mountain range, where the remains of Noah's Ark were alleged to have been found. A strange thought passed through my mind. The *Titanic* was built by professionals, while Noah's Ark was built by an amateur. Some people believe that a symmetrical, streamlined stone structure near there has the right dimensions and interior configuration, and symmetrically arranged traces of metal, consistent with its being the Ark. Also, anchor stones have been found near there. I always wondered, whenever I was scratching my aching skin in summer mornings spent outside the city, why Noah didn't let the pair of mosquitoes stay behind and drown. He probably never experienced having a bloodthirsty mosquito in his bedroom at two in the morning that cannot be smashed or cast out. I looked at Sammy and felt a pang for having suspected him. I took a thick stack of U.S. hundred-dollar bills and offered it to Sammy.

"Here, please take it. I can't thank you enough."

"No," he said firmly, pushing my hand away. "You're very kind, but I can't take it. Your people are helping us in many ways, and helping you is just a duty of honor for us."

Sammy shook my hand. "Good luck." I hugged him. He walked to his car. *Thank you very much,* I wanted to say again, but he was already out of hearing range.

I climbed into the back of the truck. I sat on a pile of old blankets padded with sheep's wool, wrapped myself with one, and offered a broad smile to my new travel companions. They nodded and said something I couldn't understand. So I just nodded back. The engine roared and the truck left the parking lot.

I was troubled by not being able to communicate in any language with the driver or my travel companions. That could be hazardous in case of emergency, when reaction to perils needed to be immediate.

I had to try my best. I blurted out, *"Salaam Aleikum"*—hello, or peace on you.

"Aleikum Salaam," they returned the greeting, without the least look of surprise on their faces. *"Maen kaemi farsi baelaedaem"*—I speak a little Persian. *"Haletun chetoreh?"*—How are you? They burst into laughter; I guess my accent wasn't perfect, or maybe not even close. I thanked Erikka in my heart for teaching me these few sentences. Where was she now?

"Aez ashnai tun khosh baek taem"—Nice to meet you! *"Saelam ba ba! maenaem, adriyan."*

"To bozorgi." I didn't know what he meant until he used his hands to gesture: you're big. His friends burst out laughing. I grinned.

From the position of the rising sun I realized that the truck was going northwest. We left the madness of the city behind and soon found ourselves moving along a busy highway. About an hour's drive out of Tehran, we started to gain steadily in elevation into the mountains. I put my head on a blanket, covered myself with another torn blanket, and thought of my children. It was times like this that I missed them the most. They were used to months going by without word, but still I wondered if they worried.

I must have fallen asleep, because the next time I looked outside I saw nothing but vast, empty land. What always struck me in countries like Iran was how drastically the line between city and country was drawn. One moment you could be risking your life in mad city traffic and the next be in calm country surroundings with no lights, no pollution, but a timeless scenery all around.

Apart from a few stops for fueling, the ride was monotonous and without incident. At about eight P.M. we pulled off to sleep for the night. I couldn't sleep just yet. I'd had my share during the day, so I decided to take a short walk in the moonlight to ease my tension. The hillsides were dotted with trees, and the hills sloped gently down into canyons. It was breathtaking. After my months of indoor living, I relished the outdoors.

On first light the next morning, we continued. The landscape became higher and wilder, until the boulders grew to the size of mountains. The major roads disappeared and gave way to tracks populated by people who cared only about tomorrow's meal, and not about terrorism or international politics. From the looks of it, they were living as their ancestors had lived for hundreds, or even thousands, of years.

The scenery appeared to have been molded by endless earthquakes, with enormous boulders and uneven cliffs coming right to the edge of the road. Occasionally we would catch a quick glimpse of a mud-brick village. I saw several waterways carved in the rocks flowing down the slopes to the village for drinking and irrigating.

An hour later, I felt the truck shudder. A car had rear-ended us. I peered over the side of the truck to see if we'd suffered any damage. Nothing serious. The men near me called to our driver, evidently telling him there was no need to stop. He continued driving, ignoring the impact and leaving the colliding car behind us.

Our next stop was Mākū, an Azeri town along the road close to the Turkish border. It didn't appear to consist of much. The landscape, though, was amazing. Volcanic cliffs rose around the town, giving it an aura of mystery. The small mud shacks ascending the cliff looked fascinating. Our driver had stopped for food. Since the truck couldn't be locked and all of our meager belongings were in the truck bed, someone had to stay behind when the others took off. It was clear I was to be the one, lest I attract attention.

I lay back on the truck bed, letting my eyes range over the signs. SINA BAIRAMZADEH INTERNET CAFÉ. Internet! I was considering running over and sending a message, but I changed my mind when I saw a police squad car parked right across the street. I hadn't come this close to the border to be apprehended. Disappointed, I sat on the dingy blankets until our driver returned with a big plate of pilaf rice with lamb chops and warm naan, the local pita bread.

"*Maem nunaem,*" I said. Thank you.

"*Khahesh mikonaem.*" You're welcome.

We headed out of town and kept on until after dark before camping for the night in an off-road valley. My mind was still on that faraway Internet café. What news was waiting for me in my e-mail account?

The new day began with a bright blue sky. Powerful winds made billowy clouds fly around the surrounding peaks and slide down the mountainsides. As we were still heading northwest towards Turkey, the mountain range that we were crossing seemed to be a slender backbone rising from the flat terrain; its peaks were still covered with snow. I couldn't tell if we were a few hours or a few days away, and my efforts to communicate with our driver beyond basic greetings were to no avail.

The villages in this region made more use of lumber in their buildings, and the terraced villages were abundantly green, making good use of the snowmelt I saw streaming down from the mountains into rivers and streams. I'm always a little disoriented for a short period in a foreign country with a different climate and people.

Toward noon, the air became warmer once again, although the elevation was high. On the left, I saw a tartan green stretch of rice paddies, in terraces up toward the rugged slope of the mountains.

We stopped, and everyone on the truck headed to the nearby stream for the first bath in days. It was bracingly cold, but we were all grateful to wash off the dust and filth of the road. I wondered how I looked to the world. It had been days since I'd seen a mirror. Was the grime helping me blend in?

Three men on horses approached us. I stiffened, sensing trouble. Instinctively I looked for my gun, but it was buried in the pile of clothes I'd left on the water's edge just a few feet away. But our driver spoke with them in a friendly enough manner, and pointed at me. He signaled me to come closer. I put my clothes on and walked shivering from the cold toward them. Our driver waved his hand toward me and then signaled at the horse riders. "Turkey, Turkey," he said nodding his head, signaling me to join them. I retrieved my daypack and shrugged it on. I heard car engine noises. Two military Jeeps were approaching us, signaling with their lights to stay put. I didn't have to look twice to realize that this time it was real trouble, and that I was their target. How had they found me here? I needed to move quickly.

One of the horsemen slipped his foot briefly out of one stirrup so I could use it, gave me his hand, and pulled me up to sit on the blanket behind him. My companions during the past three days waved at me.

"Ba aman-I-Khuda"—May God protect you—they said with their hands over their hearts. "Baerat doa mikonaem"— I'll pray for you—said the eldest man.

I was so tense that I forgot the farewell words I'd toiled so hard to remember. I was too busy thinking how long it'd take before the Jeeps would catch up with us. My guide was cool and undeterred. He quickly steered his horse toward the dense woods up the hill on a narrow pathway. The Jeeps stopped, but not before we heard shots and angry yelling in Farsi.

We galloped away through the woods, the thicket scratching my face and arms. I held the rider tightly. An eternity later, just when I thought that every muscle in my body, even ones I didn't know existed, would never loosen again, we arrived at a simple mud-brick hut. We got off the horses and entered the hut. I felt I was dragging myself along every step. It was clean, with no running water or electricity. There were no beds in the hut, just old blankets on the floor. My hosts gave me pita bread with goat yogurt. No words were spoken, but warm hospitality was abundant.

In the early morning, I shuddered awake, cognizant of light streaming into the hut. There was a smell of burning wood.

One of the men was making coffee on a small fire in the middle of the room. He offered me a small, ornamented, bronze-colored cup with thick, bittersweet coffee. It was no time to be picky. I held the cup in my hands to warm them up and emptied it in one gulp. Slowly, tentatively, I walked outside. Two of the men followed me and when they saw me looking around, they pointed at the huge mountain range ahead of us and said, "Ararat!"

We were in a landscape of jagged stone high up above the timberline. Outside our hut I saw about a hundred tribesmen camping on the grounds.

"Turkey," said my host, pointing toward the ground. "Turkey." That explained why he didn't seem to be worried that the Iranian military Jeeps would continue their manhunt. Although there'd been no checkpoint and no change in the terrain for the past few days, we were in a different country.

I'm out of Iran! I'm in Turkey! I wanted to yell. Thank god.

A pickup truck came through a dirt road to the hut, and my hosts signaled me to enter the truck's cabin. I waved good-bye to them. We had barely exchanged a word, and I had no idea who they were. But they had saved my life, part of a team of anonymous lifesavers.

The truck was driven by a small-framed, chain-smoking man in his late fifties. After a six-hour drive off-road we finally hit a paved road. The first sights that struck me with the reality of having finally left Iran were signs on a roadside gas station and restaurant in the Latin alphabet: KREDI, with the capital *I* dotted. In his quest to modernize Turkey, Kemal Atatürk had made all Turks convert from the ornate Arabic script to the far more efficient Latin in six intense months in the 1920s.

An hour later, the truck stopped in the center of a small town. There was a figure in the distance, with uniformed men on either side of him. I rubbed my eyes. Could it be? At last, a familiar face. Casey Bauer. I heaved a sigh of relief.

The truck came to a stop. *"Khuda hafez."* Good-bye. I used

my Farsi cautiously. I gave the driver my gun. I wouldn't need
it in Turkey—keeping it could even get me into trouble. My
driver smiled in gratitude and drove off, waving his hand
through the open window.

CHAPTER TWENTY-SEVEN

Casey's face split into a grin. "Good to have you in one piece,"
he said, opening his arms for a hug.

I nodded. "Thanks, I'm so glad to be back. Is Erikka OK?"

"She's fine. We managed to spirit her out through the
Tehran airport. She's back in Vienna." He looked at me, at the
traces of truck riding and Jeep-escaping, of horseback riding
and mud huts on my face and clothes. "Let's get you cleaned
up," he said, not unkindly.

A hot shower and a shave in a modest local hotel and a hearty
meal were all I needed.

We drove toward Istanbul. Casey gave me a copy of a Turkish newspaper in English. The headline read,

A SENIOR IRANIAN REVOLUTIONARY GUARDS OFFICIAL
DISAPPEARED.
TEHRAN SUSPECTS DEFECTION.

"Is it today's paper? I asked.

"No, it dates back to about two weeks after your escape
from your hotel."

I devoured the story.

Iranian authorities are deeply concerned at the recent
disappearance of Hasan Lotfi, a key security official of
the Revolutionary Guards. Intelligence sources indicate
that Lotfi, who was privy to Iran's most closely guarded

secrets, was under surveillance by his own subordinates after he held unauthorized meetings with people whom Iran considered enemies of the revolution, and was suspected of disloyalty. A spokesman for the Iranian Ministry of Information said only that the matter is under investigation.

I put down the newspaper. "I knew it!" I said vehemently. "I knew it! Since I couldn't control the wind, I adjusted my sails. My guardian angel in Tehran told me that Lotfi had disappeared, but I couldn't ask for details. Did you get my ATM message about him?"

Casey smiled. "Yes, that's why I brought you this newspaper. We made immediate contact with him through Benny's Kurdish friends, but before we could agree on terms, Javad Sadegh Kharazi, who worked as an aide to President Ahmadinejad's close consultants in chambers, was arrested. Lotfi, who'd had previous contacts with Javad Sadegh Kharazi, was afraid he'd be arrested as well. So he put his faith in our goodwill without an agreement, and we got him across the border into Iraq."

"I'll be damned," I said.

"Do you know why he made the first contact with you?"

"No. When I first met him I felt he was sizing me up, or even suspecting me—natural, given his position. But then, as we talked more, despite all the *taarof* double-talk, I thought he might have been trying to tell me something."

We both knew what *taarof* was—an Iranian custom of engaging in flattery and false humility to make the other person feel good, but still preserving the original agenda, which could be selling you something, or even killing you. A way of suffocating you with compliments—sweet talk and a show of false humility to cloud your judgment.

"What message?" asked Casey, though I suspected he already knew the answer to that question.

"I thought all the talk of speaking in Canada was really about wanting help getting out of Iran. That he was dangling huge bait."

Casey smiled again. I had no doubt he was enjoying this. "And the bait was . . . ?"

"Information on a major terrorist attack on the United States, in addition to all the top-secret stuff he knew."

"But why did he choose you?" Casey repeated with a half smile, ignoring what I'd just said. Clearly Casey was toying with me.

"Because I was a foreigner who was about to leave Iran and could carry a message?"

"The only explanation is that he knew who you were," said Casey evenly.

"How? You mean he knew and still didn't have me arrested? I know he was a classmate of Erikka's and probably didn't want to harm her. But leaving me intact, even though he knew who I was, just for old time's sake, is a bit much, don't you think?"

Casey's tone became serious. "Remember Parviz Morad, the Iranian defector that Benny brought over?"

"What about him? Has he been reevaluated? He was too evasive in answering your questions regarding the identities of Atashbon members."

"Of course neither we nor the Mossad trusted him. But the final verdict came from a completely different source, BND. The German Federal Intelligence Service suspected that the uncle, who posed as a dissident to Iran's regime, was in fact working for it. BND wiretapped his telephone and intercepted the call Parviz Morad placed from the pay phone at the men's room. As it turns out, Parviz Morad knew that his uncle was a turncoat and tried to use the uncle to cut a deal with the regime in Tehran. He'd offer his services as a double agent, reporting on his contacts with the Mossad and CIA in return for a hefty amount of money."

"Yes, he managed to call his uncle, whom he supposedly thought was an Iranian dissident in Germany," I said.

"The uncle turned out to be an agent of the Revolutionary Guards in Europe." He let it sink in for a moment.

"So he double-crossed us?"

"At least he tried. He's in an Israeli prison now."

"And he was reporting to Hasan Lotfi!" I said.

"Right. The uncle, Morteza Mughnia, installed a watch on the safe apartment you were training in, which probably included taking your photo as a souvenir for his album. Two plus two is one suspect."

"The bastard," I said in slight appreciation. "Hasan was playing a mind game with me. I was his insurance policy, just as much he was mine. Either I helped him out of Iran, or he'd turn me in for the brownie points."

"He was damn lucky that the U.S. forces on the Iran-Iraq border didn't shoot him. His American School English came in handy there. Dan, you had good sense and good luck."

"Why did he defect?"

"I suspect he was already working for a foreign power. He wanted to move out of Iran, but his handlers obviously wanted him to stay put. We estimated that he was an extremely valuable asset. But lately he'd been suspecting that his foreign contacts were compromised and he could be arrested soon. The arrest of Javad Sadegh Kharazi left him with no choice or time. He had to take off, or stay behind and get some of the treatment his subordinates at the Revolutionary Guards and their VEVAK colleagues give those who betray them."

"Does he know who he was actually working for?"

"He says NATO, but we checked. No NATO connection."

"Benny?"

"A possibility we can't rule out. I'm sure Hasan would never believe it in a million years if we told him he was probably working for the Israelis. So we haven't discussed it with him yet."

"Was Javad Sadegh Kharazi also working for the Israelis?"

"No." That was a very firm no, and it made me understand that even if I asked, Casey wouldn't tell me who Kharazi actually did work for. I had my own guess.

"What about the potential terrorist attack on the United States? Did he give you details?"

"Yes. As always, the Iranians planned this attack through a proxy organization to distance themselves from any suspicion."

"Who's the proxy this time?" I asked.

"A new name they invented, the Messengers of the Faith. We have arrested twenty-one suspects who planned to bomb six major railway and subway stations throughout the United States, all on one day."

"Any connection to Atashbon?"

"The members of the Messengers of the Faith don't know the specifics of Atashbon, although they confessed to having contacts with individuals in the U.S. whom the FBI is investigating as possible Atashbon members. We suspect that identifying the targets and supplying the logistics was made by Atashbon members who were instructed by Tehran to 'wake up' from their dormant status."

"What did Lotfi have to say about that? Wasn't this the bait he was dangling?"

"So far he has confirmed the basics that led us to the Messengers of the Faith. But we've got a long way to go with Lotfi. He isn't an easy client. His double-talk is driving our interrogators crazy. Even when it's information that assures his ticket to freedom and safety, you can never get a straight answer from him. We must clear a few other things first. Atashbon waited twenty years; we can wait a few more days, or even weeks." I wasn't comfortable with the latter part of that answer, but said nothing.

"Did you identify additional Atashbon members through the reunion?" I was curious if our visit to Tehran was worth it.

"At least one, but we are working on additional names as well."

"Who is the one?"

"Remember the Farshad Shahab you met, the guy who studied at the University of Nebraska? Erikka told us all about the meetings."

"So she knew?"

"No, she thought we were a marketing company working for the bank in connection with the bank's effort to get Iranian business. Well, he was an Atashbon, and was actually arrested in the U.S., but he managed to get away."

"Arrested as an Iranian agent and was let go?" I asked in disbelief.

"No," he sounded apologetic. "We didn't know his true identity then. He assumed the identity of Alec Simmons, a smart and brave young American. When Simmons was captured by Iranian agents, he was interviewed and filmed. Apparently he understood why the personal details were so important to his interrogators. So he changed some of his personal information, hoping that anyone using his identity would be caught. He misspelled the names of his parents and gave his captors a wrong Social Security number."

"And we missed it?"

"Almost. When Farshad enrolled at the university, he had the nerve to ask for a student loan, and gave what he thought were Alec's parents' names and his Social Security number. A routine cross-referencing flagged a problem. He was arrested but released on $2,000 bail. Everybody thought it was just a simple fraud matter. Farshad jumped bail and took off. He soon assumed a different identity and lived in the U.S. for five more years."

"So he never graduated from the University of Nebraska?"

"Of course not. He couldn't even return to Lincoln. Finally, before returning to Iran he pulled off the final scam when he bought an engineer's diploma from one of those diploma mills where the only thing between you and a degree is $5,000 and the week it takes to print and deliver the impressive but bogus certificate."

"Come to think of it, when we met, I was quite amazed to hear bold criticism from him of the Islamic regime. He probably did it to provoke me to say something incriminating, or hint at a recruiting possibility, which would make him a double agent."

"I have no doubt of that," said Casey.

"I suspected him at the time," I said, knowing I sounded like a Monday-morning quarterback. "No Iranian would dare be so critical of his government to a complete stranger. I intended to check him out later. But it didn't occur to me he was dangling bait to make me attempt to recruit him."

"Hindsight is always twenty-twenty," said Casey matter-of-factly.

I tried to think of other people I'd met, but my excitement was impairing my focus.

Two days later I was in New York. After three days of debriefing, spending time with my children, and getting used to civilization again, which included taking three hot showers every day, I felt I had to complete my mission. As if on cue, Benny called.

"Where are you?" I asked.

"In New York," he answered.

"Good," I said. "I need help on the case." I was back in business.

"Is that a way to speak to an old friend? You don't say hello, how are you, and more specifically you don't tell me how it was?"

Jewish guilt games again? Well, he had a point. I hadn't even thanked Benny yet for his role in saving my life.

"Sorry, you're right. First and foremost, thank you for your role in getting me out. I know it was your men who whisked me out."

"A small contribution to the case," he said. "That's nothing among friends."

"Not so small, given the other stuff. Let's have lunch."

I made reservations at a kosher restaurant right off 47th Street in Manhattan that caters to the heavily Jewish Diamond District, and met him there. We spoke for a few minutes on the case. The Chameleon was very much on my mind, and the time I'd spent in the stinking hole underneath the textile factory did help in cracking the mystery to its end. We lapsed into quiet as the waiter placed a plate on the table loaded with cold cuts, rolls, and deli mustard.

Benny smiled. "Let me guess, you'll have a double helping of everything."

I was eager to dig in, but first I said, "Well, it takes quite a bit of this kosher food to fill me up."

"You'll survive," said Benny drily.

"The way I see it," I replied, "I don't smoke, do drugs, gamble . . . so food is my one concession to vice." I got back to business. "Benny, I need your help." I'd had a lot of time to plan my next move while idling in hiding.

"What is it this time?" he said, pretending, just pretending, to be annoyed.

"I need access to Tempelhof Bank's records."

"Access?"

"Yes, I need to look up the bank's contacts with McHanna Associates."

"Who are McHanna Associates?"

"I already mentioned them to you. A New York–based financial corporation run by McHanna, who was the Chameleon's victim in South Dakota."

"What do you expect to find out?"

"I want to see the level of cooperation between McHanna Associates and Tempelhof Bank." I decided not to broaden Benny's horizons yet, nor complicate the request any further by telling him I also wanted to see whether the bank played a role as intermediary between McHanna and Al Taqwa. When I saw Benny's expression I asked, "Is there a problem? You own the bank!"

"Dan. We own it, but management doesn't know it, and obviously the Swiss government doesn't either. I can't just go there and start snooping."

"Then how do you control the bank?"

"Through nominee directors. Distinguished businessmen. Even the instructions concerning the bank's marketing efforts in Iran through the reunion were suggested to management by one of our nominee directors."

"So management doesn't know who they really work for?"

"You got it," said Benny. "They believe oil billionaires from the Gulf States own the bank."

"How did you manage to do that and survive the Swiss regulators' scrutiny?" I asked curiously.

"Don't ask," said Benny. "But it works fine. Now you can understand my difficulty, not to say inability, to let you have access to the bank's records."

"I don't need current records," I said. "I need to go back to 1980 or 1981 through, say, 1995."

"It's possible that the records for the earlier years are archived or even shredded. But that I can find out."

Later on in the afternoon Benny called. "These guys are so meticulous, they never destroy anything. The documents are stored in"—he paused, and I heard pages turning—"Manheim Document Storage, in Bern. Does that help you?"

"In a way. I'd either need to break in or get a court order."

"Get a court order under some pretext," suggested Benny. "We don't need the media attention if a break-in is discovered."

I returned to my office and found in the day's mail Mrs. Nazeri's power of attorney that I had had sent to her earlier, marked *The Law Offices of Dan Gordon, Esq*. She had executed it before the Swiss consul in Tehran and faxed me an advance copy. This was the original. As I instructed my assistant to messenger it to the surrogate's court downtown, I reflected that at last, I was practicing law again. Well, not exactly. I wasn't expecting to be paid, and my motive went beyond the need to serve a client. Also, the pleadings had been drafted and filed by a discreet Agency lawyer, not by me.

No matter. I was the one who'd signed the petition seeking my appointment as the administrator of the estate of the late Philip Montreau, aka Christopher Gonda. Wasn't that enough?

A week later the surrogate's clerk called me. "You have indicated in the petition a Swiss address of the decedent."

"Yes."

"Did the decedent have any assets in Switzerland?"

"I think he just had bank accounts."

"You will most probably need ancillary letters of administration for a Swiss court. The Swiss banks will not honor a New York court's order. You'll have to convert it to become a Swiss court order as well."

Nonetheless, he said, my appointment had been confirmed, and he faxed me a copy. In short order, I dispatched a locksmith to meet me at Nazeri's apartment. The locksmith opened the door, replaced the lock, gave me a key, and left.

I entered the spacious three bedroom apartment. Nazeri had spent a lot of money on decor. Not to my taste, all these pink figurines and lace, but still expensive. I searched the apartment. It was clean. Too clean. I put on plastic gloves and looked around. I opened drawers and closets. Nothing. It was like a model apartment in a development for people of middling taste. There was nothing personal in the apartment, and there were no documents whatsoever, not even an old phone bill. The apartment was neat and tidy, as if the maid had just left, removing everything personal or made of pulp. I sighed. I'd have to send lab people to search for fingerprints.

I returned to my office and wrote a report to the file. Two days later the surrogate's court issued the additional documents to be sent to Switzerland. After we had them approved with an apostille, that antiquated but still-necessary method of authenticating documents for transmission to foreign authorities, I sent them to Switzerland by registered mail. Boring, formal, but necessary.

CHAPTER TWENTY-EIGHT

A week later Dr. Liechtenstein, our Swiss attorney, faxed me the court's decision. It took me some time to decipher the archaic German they used. I read it again and again until I understood that in fact the Swiss court had authorized the request of the New York City Surrogate's Court to

> order Tempelhof Bank to open their archives and provide the New York Surrogate Court's appointed Administrator Herr Dan Gordon with copies of records of deposits and other transactions of the late Philip Montreau, also known as Christopher Gonda, who resided in Wehntalerstr. 215, CH-8057 Zürich, made or occurring between January 1, 1980, and December 31, 2005, at Tempelhof Bank, or for which Tempelhof Bank acted as a banking correspondent.

The order contained additional conditions and details, but I was already celebrating in my heart. I had managed to make another small step forward.

I called Dr. Liechtenstein in Zürich and asked to arrange my visit to inspect the documents.

"I've already talked to them. It will have to be at their storage facility," he said. "I'm sorry—they tell me that the physical conditions there aren't so good."

Five days later I was in Zürich, my court-authorized appointments and travel documents having been fully vetted. "You never know with the Swiss authorities," Bob Holliday had said. "They're extremely fussy when U.S. government agents visit their country, even when the visit complies with a Swiss court's order."

I met Dr. Liechtenstein with the bank's lawyer, and we traveled to Bern's Manheim Document Storage company. There were an hour and a half of formalities, which included my execution of a confidentiality agreement, in case during the course of my search I was exposed to documents unrelated to Mr. Montreau, and therefore not included in the court's order. I signed. Why should I care if I stumbled on secret deposits of this dictator or that thug? I raced through the formalities. I had one agenda: Chameleon and his Atashbon cohorts. I wouldn't be distracted, not even by the bureaucratic hurdles put up by the young blond man who was assigned by the bank to help me. I knew he was in there to make sure I wasn't sidestepping my court-approved gangway, which was like the one used to herd cattle to the slaughter. My gangway here was fitted with virtual sides, railings, and other means of protection, to prevent me from looking at any other documents. Here, I thought, I was the cattle.

I'd come prepared. Before leaving New York I had met with Special Agent Matt Kilburn of the FBI's Counterterrorism Unit, whom I'd first met at the conference in Giverny, France. Matt had been working on the investigation of Nada Management, previously known as Al Taqwa, and provided me with excellent written and oral reports on the methods of its operation.

Heinrich Andrist, my chaperone, appointed by Tempelhof Bank, was a gentle person with a very polite demeanor.

"OK," I said as all the lawyers left. "Let's start with 1981. Can you tell me how these cartons are cataloged?"

"By account number and by our client number index."

"Can I see the index?"

"I'm sorry, you can't. It contains names and details of the bank's customers, and that is protected by Swiss law."

"Of course. Let's look up by name. The decedent's name was Christopher Gonda, and then Philip Montreau. He may have also used Reza Nazeri."

"Of course, Herr Gordon," he said patiently. He went to the third row of the eight-foot-tall heavy metal shelves, climbed a small stepladder, and pulled out a carton case.

"That's Mr. Gonda's file for 1981."

I chose that year to begin my search, although I was almost certain I'd find nothing. But just in case, I wanted to make sure I wouldn't miss anything.

I quickly ran my eyes over the yellowing documents. There were bank statements and deposit slips, telegraphic transfers and other documents. But there was nothing to quench my thirst or satisfy my hunger for pertinent facts. They were just old papers, seemingly irrelevant to my subject of interest. I need to see the buzzword *Al Taqwa*, or other similarly exciting leads telling me where the money went. An hour later I closed the box and shook my head.

"Nothing here," I said. "Please bring the next box."

Heinrich brought me 1982, then every year through 1987. Nothing. The documents represented typical bank accounts of a businessman who liked to travel and buy expensive gifts for himself. There were many transfers or withdrawals, but with all deposits made in cash, it was impossible to trace their origin or the source of his income. I made a record of significant outgoing transfers, all of them to other banks in Europe and the U.S. Hours went by. Heinrich looked at his watch; it was four thirty P.M. But he still said nothing.

"Please get me the 1988 box, and we'll call it a day," I said. He seemed relieved.

That box was bigger than the rest. As the flying dust reached my nose, I sneezed, and then, getting a better look, restrained myself from crying aloud. Lying atop the pile was a printed envelope of Al Taqwa. Inside were copies of seven wire transfers made from an Al Taqwa account in Lugano, Switzerland, through Tempelhof Bank to a McHanna Associates account at Manufacturers Hanover bank in New York. I quickly added up the amounts. They totaled approximately $7 million. The transfer orders were signed by Gonda. That was a strong indication that he had signature rights at Al Taqwa to move funds around.

I frantically leafed though the other documents in the box and felt like Ali Baba in the children's story, breaking into the cave of the forty thieves and finding heaps of silver and gold, bales of silk and fine carpets. An inch deeper into the box, I found additional documents showing wire transfers from Gonda to Al Taqwa and from them to McHanna Associates, using Tempelhof Bank as a correspondent bank. Heinrich made me copies of the documents I selected. I signed a receipt and left.

"I'll see you tomorrow at eleven A.M.," he said.

I returned to my hotel, ordered room service, and concentrated on reading the documents.

An alarm bell sounded. "*Feuer, evakuieren Sie bitte alle Räume. . . .* Fire, please evacuate all rooms." I opened my room door. People were running in the hallway. I didn't see or smell fire or smoke. I looked out the window: there was no fire engine or any special activity in the street.

"Another fire drill," I muttered. I'd already been through one in Islamabad—I should have been considered exempt. I was in shorts and a T-shirt and didn't feel like leaving my room again. I had no intention of playing. I closed the door. Seconds later came a series of strong bangs on my door. I opened it.

A man with a flashlight and fireman's hat said in a thick German accent, "You must to leave now."

"What?" I asked, pretending not to understand.

"You must to leave," he repeated.

Reluctantly I stepped into my pants, took my laptop and my personal documents, and went to the door. I stopped, turned around, and took the copies of the bank documents I'd had made at the storage facility. Maybe I could find a corner to go over them while this stupid, untimely drill was going on. The elevator door was blocked, and I had to use the stairs.

About a hundred people were in the lobby, some in night clothing and some wrapped in blankets. Twenty minutes later I heard, *"Falsche Warnung"*—false alarm, said the guy who had ousted me earlier from my room, as he entered the lobby. "Somebody pressed the alarm button. We shall report this to the police. It's illegal to do that," he announced in German, then repeated it in English. I had no patience or interest to hear the rest of the things he had to say and ran first to the elevator.

I opened my door and took a step back. My room had been ransacked—every drawer thrown open, the suitcase shaken out. I opened the door wide, placed a shoe to stop it from shutting, and gingerly walked inside. If the intruder was still inside my room, I didn't want to be locked in with him. He could be armed, and there could be more than one intruder. I checked the bathroom and the closet. They were empty. I looked around. The bed linens were thrown on the floor, and my clothes in the closet were piled up in the corner. Somebody had pressed the fire-alarm button to get me out of my room.

I called security. The same "fireman" came over. He must have been their jack-of-all-trades. *"Mein Gott,"* he exclaimed when he saw the mess. "Is anything missing?"

"I don't know," I said. I was still holding my laptop computer and the stack of documents. "Please check to see if other guests were victimized as well," I said. If I was the only one, then the conclusion would be clear: I'd been singled out. Someone wanted something I had. And the only things I had were the papers and my laptop. It wasn't my fashionable attire.

"I need another room," I told him. "I can't stay here."

He went to the night table and used the phone. A few minutes later a chambermaid came and gave me a room key for a room on a different floor. I quickly packed and moved there. I left my luggage in my new room and went to the twenty-four-hour business center, still carrying my laptop computer and the documents. I faxed the documents to my New York office and shredded the copies I had, taking the confetti-like pieces with me.

Whoever had broken into my room was either interested in the documents because he didn't have the information they contained, or he wanted to see how much I'd found. I could have been wrong, of course, but so far there was nothing to contradict me. The alarming conclusion was that someone knew to expect me in Switzerland, knew where I had gone that day, knew where I was staying, and had used the alarm-bell button to get me out of my room. Had my talents for identifying followers rusted? I hadn't noticed anything unusual. Frankly, though, I hadn't been paying much attention. For once I'd arrived in Switzerland for something that was so aboveboard that I was relieved to not have to constantly look behind me. And of all my cases, this visit—the perfectly clean one—had to be marred by a hostile entry? I threw the confetti into the fireplace in the lobby and waited to see it blaze.

I called Casey Bauer to report. He was more alarmed than I had been. "Dan, leave the hotel immediately. Cancel tomorrow's meeting at the warehouse. You may have to return to the U.S., but not just yet. We need to arrange security before you can return to the warehouse."

I called Lufthansa Airlines using my room telephone, asking the switchboard operator to connect me. I spoke with the airline representative and bought a one-way ticket to Frankfurt. I asked the desk to prepare my bill and send up a bellman, although all I had was one small suitcase. I told the bellman I was going to Frankfurt and asked him to get me a taxi. I paid the hotel bill and mentioned I needed to fly urgently to Frankfurt.

At the airport, when I'd made sure I wasn't observed, I took the elevator down to the arrival hall, pressing all the buttons to make the elevator stop on every floor. I was alone in the elevator, but anyone looking at the lit numbers above the elevator door wouldn't see on which floor I'd exited. I went to the

taxi line and took a taxi to Zürich, where I checked into the
Hilton hotel using my Anthony P. Blackthorn documents.

I called Casey Bauer, reported my new location, and fell asleep
in front of the television. I was angry and surprised that I'd
been spotted. Field security was lax somewhere. Next time the
consequences could be more serious.

Two hours before my scheduled meeting with Heinrich
Andrist, my chaperon at Tempelhof Bank's warehouse, I
called with my cell phone to apologize. "I had to fly unexpectedly to Frankfurt to meet another client. I'm sorry for
any inconvenience I may have caused you."

"Will you be back?"

Now he misses me? "In a few days. I'll call ahead."

Casey Bauer called my cell phone. "There's no question
there was a security leak," he said. "Did you tell anyone where
you were going?"

Sometimes I feel like kicking the bureaucrats who ask stupid
questions. But Casey didn't qualify—he was a trained CIA officer covering all bases. "Nobody in New York but my office
administrator."

"Weren't you involved with the courts in New York and in
Switzerland?"

"Yes, but they didn't know if and when I was coming to
Switzerland. My contacts at the bank didn't know where I
was staying. That leaves only Dr. Liechtenstein, the Swiss attorney I hired to help me get the Swiss court order. He knew
when I was arriving, and knew where I was staying."

Casey sighed. "Let me check on him," he said grimly. "But
it seems whoever it was wanted something from your room,
and not you personally. Otherwise they'd have been waiting
for you inside your room."

Once stretched on the sofa in my spacious room I was finally able to analyze the documents I had retrieved from the
bank's warehouse. I turned on my laptop and logged into my
New York office. In less than one minute I was connected,
passing through four sets of different username and password

screens. I opened the data files and read the documents I had faxed my office computer earlier.

The conclusion was unavoidable. In 1988 Reza Nazeri, aka Christopher Gonda, aka Philip Montreau, had moved millions of dollars between Switzerland and the U.S., and back. During that time money-laundering laws had been reserved for drug lords and corporate frauds, and the phrase *terror financing* hadn't been coined yet or thought of. Most of the transfers had gone through Al Taqwa in Lugano and Tempelhof Bank in Zürich, and in all of them the name used was Gonda, not the two other names, Nazeri and Montreau. But although I found 1988 records, he'd had an account with Tempelhof Bank at least as early as 1981. Was there an explanation?

Perhaps the answer was simple. Since he'd used the stolen identity of Christopher Gonda to open the account, and Gonda disappeared at about the same time, I assumed that 1981 was in fact the year the account was opened. Why had Nazeri/Gonda needed the account before the banking scams had begun? Since my first quick review of the earlier files at the warehouse didn't reveal anything suspicious, I went on to the next year. I was locked into an assumption connecting Nazeri/Gonda to McHanna. Therefore, I may have overlooked Gonda's activities before his account was used to launder money transferred between McHanna and Al Taqwa. I'd have to go back to the warehouse to look again in the files, including those I'd already reviewed, but definitely those of the years subsequent to 1988.

Casey called me again. "There's no point in your hanging around in Switzerland until we resolve the security issue. We can't get you much protection without drawing unnecessary attention."

I was really eager to return to the warehouse and solve the puzzle, but as instructed, I returned to New York the following morning. I went straight to the office, where Bob Holliday was waiting for an update.

"Did you have a good flight?" he asked, wryly avoiding the crisis at hand.

"Excellent," I replied. I gave him a quick summary of my findings, and the need for more work.

"We have a meeting tomorrow morning with Robert Hodson, assistant director in charge of the FBI field office in New York," he told me.

When I entered Hodson's office, Casey Bauer and Bob Holliday were sitting on the leather sofa opposite Hodson's huge desk. I joined them as Hodson dragged a chair over to sit next to us.

Holliday started. "I went through the documents that Dan brought from Switzerland, and I tend to believe that Reza Nazeri was a member of Atashbon. We don't know exactly what role he played until 1988, but there's no question that in 1988, and perhaps in later years, he moved millions of dollars between the U.S. and Switzerland, mostly through the notorious Al Taqwa, a known terrorist-financing institution."

"I saw the documents and I concur with Holliday," said Casey. "Here's what I think we should do next: send Dan back to Switzerland to get more documents from later years. We also need to look at the transfer of documents from the other end—Al Taqwa, later named Nada Management." He looked at Hodson. "We'll need your staff to help us on that. We must also develop additional information as to what was done with money, or from whom it was received. We've just touched the tip of the iceberg."

"That depends on the Swiss government's willingness to cooperate. Just moving money isn't a crime per se, but under the circumstances, it reeks of money laundering," said Bob.

We continued analyzing the options for how to proceed, when Hodson got up.

"Well," he said. "My legal department just told me that the documents Dan has obtained give us probable cause to seek a search warrant at McHanna Associates. That prick McHanna is in New York, so we don't need to go far. Are we done?"

"Sit down, Bob," suggested Casey in a soft tone. "There are a few more issues we need to cover." Hodson sat down, visibly reluctant.

"There's also a small matter of security leaks," I added. "I had to leave Vienna in a rush because Casey warned me that the safe apartment used for my Iran briefings was compromised. Then the whole operation was put on hold because a Mossad agent wasn't paying attention, and Parviz Morad, the Iranian refugee whom Benny was so proud of getting out of an Iraqi prison, managed to make an unauthorized phone call. Then after I returned from Iran, my room at a Bern hotel was searched."

"You mean you don't know what caused the security breach?" asked Bauer.

"Know what?" I asked, although I did know the cause for at least one security breach. Casey Bauer must have forgotten bringing me up to speed in Turkey after my escape from Iran, giving me details about how Hasan Lotfi had known who I really was.

Casey explained. "Parviz Morad called his uncle, Morteza Mughnia, whom he claimed he believed to be an Iranian dissident. But in fact the uncle was an Iranian agent posing as a dissident. The uncle was regularly reporting to Iran on the dissidents' activities in Europe. Some of them were killed. Morteza Mughnia, who knew about Parviz Morad's escape from the Iraqi prison from letters Parviz sent his family from Israel, asked him where he would be later on that evening, so he could come and see him. Parviz gave his uncle the address of his hotel. Morteza Mughnia suspected that the Israelis would take his nephew out of Israel only if it were an important intelligence matter, and alerted the local operatives of the Iranian security service.

"They staked out the hotel and followed Parviz to the safe house. Our security team in the building opposite the safe apartment took photos of the scouts the uncle had sent. One of the scouts was identified as a member of the Iranian Revolutionary Guards working in the Iranian Embassy as a 'cultural attaché.' Since he had diplomatic immunity, we notified the Austrians, and he was cordially asked to pack and leave."

"Just because of that?" I asked.

"No way. There was a whole file on him concerning undiplomatic activities."

"So this is how I was exposed," I said, letting the information sink in.

"Probably. They must have taken your photograph as you entered the building. Then you went to the Iranian embassy to obtain a visa and were captured by video when you entered the building, and also attached your photo to your application. The counselor, who is no doubt an intelligence officer, made the connection."

"That means I entered Iran already exposed."

Hodson nodded.

"Then why didn't they arrest me immediately?"

"Either because they wanted to know whom you'd be contacting locally or because the information stopped at Hasan Lotfi's desk."

"So, if my identity was known to others in the security services, when Lotfi met me at the hotel and then for lunch, he doomed himself, because he was already under surveillance."

"Exactly. But he was on the alert for a while. When he suspected that he came under suspicion he took off after contacting us, even before we concluded a deal."

"That means I contaminated everyone else I met," I said.

"In a way, but only those that couldn't explain. We believe that the school alumni came clean when they gave a true account of the circumstances leading to their meeting with you. Your Kurdish friends escaped to the Kurdish enclave in the north, where no Iranian policemen dare set a foot, unless they are suicidal."

"One thing isn't solved, though," said Holliday. I knew what he was going to ask, and I had no answer. "Where the hell is the Chameleon? Let me remind you that he's our prime target, and is expected to lead us to the other Atashbon members."

"I don't know yet," I said candidly, "but I'm getting closer. I hope the search of McHanna's records will tell us more. I'm not easing up the chase. Positive identification of Nazeri as Atashbon will probably bring us closer to the Chameleon and his comrades."

I went back to my office and wrote Erikka a personal letter telling her that my publisher had put the book project on hold, and therefore her services were currently no longer needed. I attached a check drawn on a Canadian bank to cover the remainder of the period for which I'd agreed to retain her. I added a $500 bonus.

"It was a pleasure to have worked with you," I wrote. "I hope I can complete the book project one day." I put the letter and the check in an envelope and sent it to her through a mail-forwarding service in Toronto. I didn't include a return address.

My phone buzzed. It was Bob. "A federal magistrate judge signed a search warrant for McHanna Associates; FBI teams are on the scene as we speak. Meet me tonight at Hodson's office."

CHAPTER TWENTY-NINE

I arrived at the federal building in downtown Manhattan at eight P.M., but Hodson's office was still empty. Over an hour later, at nine twenty P.M., as my nerves jangled, five FBI agents finally walked in with Hodson and Casey. Bob Holliday arrived a minute later.

"What's in the crates I saw you carrying?" I asked the agent standing next to me.

"The last of the stuff we seized at McHanna Associates. The bulk of it was brought over a few hours ago."

Hodson, sensing my impatience, said, "Our analysts are already starting to examine the first few cartons. I'm afraid it will take time until we have a hit."

"Can I participate in the analysis of these documents? I know a few things about white-collar crime and money laundering."

Hodson and Holliday exchanged looks and Holliday nodded.

"OK," said Hodson. "Be here tomorrow at nine A.M."

"Tomorrow? I'm not waiting until tomorrow. I want to do it right now."

Hodson smiled and used the intercom to call his assistant. "Tom, let Dan Gordon join our analysts in cracking the material we seized from McHanna Associates."

"Thanks," I said, and before leaving I asked, "Was McHanna taken in?"

"No. Give me a probable cause, and he will be. So far we've got nothing to support an arrest warrant."

I went two floors down. In a big room were six young men and women buried under massive stacks of paper. Open cartons were everywhere.

"It's slow going, but it's going," grunted Mel, a clean-shaven young analyst, when I'd introduced myself.

"Why? Because of the volume?"

"No. We only started three hours ago, but from what we see already, the documents reflect years' worth of international banking activities. Now add the fact that I already counted four or five foreign languages that were used, and you've got a complex audit on your plate."

"Any computer files?" I asked.

"Yes, we seized McHanna's computers. We're waiting for the tech people to hook them up so we can quickly search files electronically."

"Can I take a look at some of the files?" I asked.

"Help yourself," he said, and quickly explained their organization system so that I wouldn't disrupt it.

I went to the mountain of stacked crates and pulled out the top box. I put it on an empty desk. The label was marked *1990*. After going through several hundreds of pages I saw nothing that immediately showed any relevance to our case. I took another box, marked *1993*. A few hours later, I felt a creeping frustration. There was nothing there that could be important to my investigation. I looked around the room at the other analysts; their faces were patient, but unenthused. I decided to change course. Instead of looking for a smoking gun, I decided to understand the business logic of McHanna. How were they transacting business, what was their profit center, and how were they actually making money? That is, if they were making money. And if they weren't, who paid for McHanna's fancy office, and why?

I realized it'd take me more time, but that was a commodity I had. Bob Holliday agreed to ease my caseload, and I immersed myself in my new project: McHanna Associates.

Three days later I began to see a pattern. McHanna Associates was in fact a clearing house for charitable donations. Money in small amounts was collected in certain Islamic centers throughout the United States for various charitable causes and brought or transferred to McHanna Associates. Next, McHanna transferred the funds in batches smaller than $10,000 through a New York bank to banks in several foreign countries, some in Europe and some in the Middle East. One or two days later, the receiving banks would wire similarly sized amounts to McHanna's bank account in New York.

Why were they doing it? I wondered. Why send the money back here? And if there was a reason, why couldn't they simply offset the incoming and outgoing amounts? The back-and-forth transfers made no business sense, other than to the transferring banks, which made hefty commissions off the transfers. And while I understood the reason for transferring amounts to the Middle East to support charities, I couldn't understand why there were incoming money transfers to the United States.

I decided to take it yet another step forward and see what happened to the money received by McHanna from the European banks. It was routed to charities in various states throughout the United States. Several names of the U.S. receiving institutions surfaced repeatedly. There were two in Texas, three in Michigan, five in Brooklyn, and four in Florida. One common denominator of all receiving institutions was that they were Islamic charities. They also had something else in common. The checks made out to them weren't endorsed.

That was a finding that bewildered me. I checked the entire contents of the box. There were many bank statements, but among the attached checks made out to the charities, I couldn't find even one that was endorsed.

I turned on my chair and loudly asked the other analysts, "Guys, has anyone been through any bank statements yet?"

"We all have," said Mel.

"Have you noticed something odd?"

"Like what?"

"All the checks I've seen that were made out by McHanna to charities are stamped as paid, but none carried an endorsement signature on its back or any stamp of a financial institution, and none of the checks appeared on the bank statements with the check number on it as having been cleared."

Three analysts answered at the same time: "I saw that too."

"Do you have any idea how this could have happened?" asked Mel.

"I've seen it before," I said. "That's a trick money launderers use to hide the source or destination of dirty money."

Mel said, "Maybe they just recorded the money as outgoing locally, in cash, but in fact it was sent outside the country."

"Maybe what we could do is select at random a specified period and check all bank accounts managed by McHanna Associates," I suggested. "Then we could see if the wired incoming amounts match with the outgoing amounts at the end of the day. I don't mean literally daily, but over a period of time—say a week."

Two hours later we had interim results. Every single analyst in the room confirmed that the incoming and outgoing amounts roughly matched. The difference was about 5 to 8 percent.

"That's for the administrative costs," I said jokingly, but in fact I was dead serious. I had a hunch that the excessive commissions were in fact a channel to bury even more deeply the fact that the transfer of the money created a profit that could be escrowed by any of the foreign banks and then transferred internally to another account. That other account could accumulate the graft to line someone's pockets, but it could also be used as a terrorist slush fund. A foreign bank account is, of course, immune from audit by a U.S. regulatory or law-enforcement agency.

"OK, I'm going to try to synthesize this in a report for Hodson. I assume you guys will do the same." As I began walking out the door, I stopped. I knew what bothered me—not something I'd seen in the boxes, but something I hadn't.

"Wait a minute," I said. "Have you seen any records containing the transactions with Al Taqwa and Tempelhof Bank? I saw them in Switzerland, but there weren't any here."

They all shook their heads. So McHanna must have cleaned out his office, or he may have had additional records elsewhere.

"I'll be back," I said pensively. I went out to the street, remembering that I was hungry. It was the middle of the night, but I found an all-night deli.

There was no question that we'd hit on a money-laundering operation. But we still had to see how it actually worked, and for what purpose. I sat at the corner table and wrote down on a napkin points to remember. I spilled some mustard on the napkin, painting my comments in yellow. But even without the stained napkin I knew exactly what to do next. I returned to the analysts' room.

"Mel, may I suggest something else?"

"Sure."

"Let's focus for a moment on the route of the money. We've got records telling us that there were small deposits coming from people and small businesses into McHanna Associates' bank accounts. Next, McHanna transfers roughly the same amounts to several banks in Europe. Next, roughly the same amounts—less up to 8 percent return to McHanna Associates—from Europe, not necessarily from the same banks to which McHanna originally sent the money. Now McHanna Associates writes a check, always in an amount smaller than $10,000, to various Islamic charities in America and the Middle East. Let's talk about American charities first: the check made out to them was never cleared through the banking system or even endorsed. Nonetheless, there's a 'paid' stamp on it. How did the charity get the money?"

"In cash," we both answered at the same time.

"Did you see any receipts?" I asked.

"Yes," answered another analyst. "But only a few. In some instances there were receipts signed by individuals with typical Arab names, such as Ahmed or Ibrahim, without a surname or street address. In other instances there were grocery receipts, with a handwritten signature of a purported recipient."

"Do we have any proof that the charities in fact received the money?" I asked.

Most of the analysts shook their heads.

"And even if they did receive some money, who benefited from the 8 percent difference in the funds sent to Europe and returned here?"

"Probably the guys in between," came the answer from one of the analysts.

"So we've got an intricate bidirectional money-laundering operation orchestrated by McHanna, benefiting anonymous entities or even individuals here, and unknown entities or individuals in Europe and the Middle East, not necessarily with charitable causes on their minds," I concluded.

Aha, my friend, I thought. *I'm on my way to get you.*

"And where did the cash come from?" asked one analyst.

"I don't know," I said. "The money went out of McHanna's account, there's no question about it. But did the payments ever make their way to any charity here? Is it possible that McHanna simply churned the accounts by moving money back and forth, each time leaving 8 percent to institutions outside the U.S. and away from our reach? Or that he sent the money out to somebody somewhere for an unknown reason or purpose, but on the books it appeared as if the charities received the money? That's an ingenious plan, whether McHanna planned it or was just used as a facilitator."

"But why?" asked Mel. "They didn't want to leave a paper trail in the U.S.? There couldn't be a tax reason. All these charities are tax-exempt anyway."

"As I said, I don't think these charities ever got the money, or maybe just a fraction of it. But if they did receive cash, we must conclude that its source was meant to be hidden from some eyes, maybe the FBI's counterterrorism unit."

"Just because the receiving institutions have Islamic and Arabic names doesn't automatically mean that they're supporting terrorism," said Mel.

"True . . . " I said in a level tone.

"I'm a Muslim," he went on. "And in my neighborhood in Brooklyn there are several Islamic charities that do holy work for the sick and needy. I don't think they have anything to do with terrorism."

There was no point in arguing with him. Who knew?—these charities' names could have just been used by McHanna without their knowledge. But there were also charities that were raided by the FBI, suspected of being a hub of money laundering for Islamic terrorist groups in the Middle East. So I only added, "What we need to check first is the legitimacy of the institutions listed in McHanna's records. We can check if they received any money from McHanna and if they're for real."

I relayed the same suggestion to Hodson.

Two days later, almost-identical responses came from FBI field offices throughout the country. A typical example read,

The charity in question doesn't maintain a valid office or employ any staff. A principal who was interviewed claimed that they're saving costs and directing all donors' contributions to the needy in their community. There were no organized records showing names of recipients of support from the charity. We didn't identify any records showing they received money through McHanna Associates. We didn't get an answer to our query why money was sent from their communities to McHanna instead of using it locally. We recommend a thorough inquiry and audit. Since donations made to the charity interviewed are tax-exempt, an IRS audit is necessary to ascertain compliance with the rules.

Well, it was time to meet with my old friend Timothy B. McHanna. Would he be happy to see me? I had no doubt I'd give him heartburn—but then again, who cares?

Unannounced, I went to his office. The door was open. I didn't see any staff, and the office was in complete disarray. Empty files and papers were strewn on the floor. Drawers were half open. Not such a clean job by our men, I supposed. With no one to stop me, I went directly through the reception area to McHanna's private office. He was standing looking helplessly at the mess.

"Hello, Mr. McHanna."

"Hi," he said, a bit startled to see me.

"Remember me?"

He nodded hesitantly, looking down at the papers on the floor.

"I need to know only one thing. Where is Albert Ward?" Going straight to the jugular wasn't a friendly approach, but it was justified under the circumstances. McHanna had already lost his "virginity"—the FBI had already raided his office, and there was no time or cause for sweet talk.

"I already told the FBI. I don't know who that is." He nervously walked toward his desk. As he sat down in his chair I heard the familiar hissing sound of a bullet. If I still remembered its unique *shoosh*, it was a 7.62 millimeter. It smashed the window and went just over McHanna's head, hitting the opposite wall. I thought of Dave, my Mossad Academy guns instructor, who'd said with half a smile, "Remember, if the enemy is within range, so are you."

CHAPTER THIRTY

I dove to the floor and yelled at McHanna, "Get down, get down!" He fell on the carpet and crawled under his desk. I edged to the window to peep outside. I saw a gunman on the roof of the adjacent building aiming at our window with his scope-mounted gun.

"Don't get up," I said. "There's a sniper on the roof of the next building."

"Some crazy guy," said McHanna. "This never happens in South Dakota. But then again, South Dakota is much smaller."

What was wrong with him? Somebody shoots at him, and his immediate reaction is a statistical comparison?

"Do you know why he's trying to kill you?" I asked, still lying on the carpet wondering what the sniper would do next.

McHanna didn't answer. He'd just broken the rule I learned during my military service: don't draw fire—it irritates the people around you. I was clearly in the shooter's range, and could take a bullet if I got up.

"Stay where you are," I said. "There could be additional snipers." I crawled toward the entrance door. Another bullet hit the door just inches above my head.

Son of a bitch. I had no gun, no backup, and no idea how many shooters there were. I saw one, but there could have been more. I couldn't risk exiting through the door because it'd put me directly in the line of fire.

I dialed Hodson's office from my mobile phone. After two rings I heard Hodson's secretary announce, "Mr. Hodson's office."

As I responded, "Julie, this is Dan Gordon," she said, "Hold on," and put me on hold. I anxiously looked at the battery bars on my phone. I was left with only a few more minutes of power. I couldn't take the risk. I disconnected and dialed 911. The operator came on.

"What is your emergency?"

"Shots fired at me by a sniper," I said, but realized I was talking to myself. The phone was dead. Battery empty. I crawled toward the desk and tried to reach the telephone. Another shot shattered the mirrored display cabinet next to the desk, covering me and the floor around me with broken glass. I pulled down the telephone cord and grabbed the receiver. There was no dial tone.

"McHanna," I said. "Do I need to dial 9 or something to get an outside line?"

"No, just press any button on the right."

I pulled the phone to the carpet and tried them all, but the phone was dead. I checked the cord. It was still hooked to the wall, but the phone was still dead.

"We should leave immediately," I said. "Is there another exit?"

"You mean from my office?"

"Yes."

"Only the door you came in through."

"How about your office suite? Does it have a back door?"

"Just the one front door."

I crawled back toward the windows, groping for the curtain cords. I managed to close the heavy curtains on two of the three windows. Another bullet went through one of the curtains and into the opposite wall.

Damn. The shooter had time and ammunition, just the things I was hoping he'd be short of. If I identified correctly based on my military training, the sniper was using a U.S.-made USMC-series gun, which has a magazine capacity of five rounds and an effective range of one thousand yards. We were only fifty to seventy-five yards away. He had already used four rounds. I tried to push the heavy desk toward the window to block some of the shooter's view, but even with McHanna pushing from underneath, we couldn't move it. The desk was too heavy.

Rays of sunlight emerged through the one window with open curtains. That gave me an idea. I crawled to the wall on the shattered glass, cutting my arm and knee, and found a largish piece of a mirror, which had fallen from the wall unit. I pushed a guest chair around to face the window and quickly mounted the mirror on its cushion, leaning it against the chair's back. The mirror captured the sun's rays and reflected them in the general direction of the shooter. As I heard the next shot breaking the mirror I jumped to my feet and ran through the door. I tried the phone on the receptionist's desk. It was dead as well.

I needed something to protect myself if I encountered any opposition face-to-face, but the only thing I could find was a metal letter opener on her desk. I cautiously checked the outside door. The hallway was empty. I ran to the emergency exit next to the elevator door and down the stairs to the floor below McHanna's office.

The first office was a dentist's clinic, and the receptionist and two waiting patients were startled as I barged in. I was breathing hard and bleeding from my hand, and my pants had blood stains in the knee area.

"I need to use the phone," I said, and when I saw their hesitation—a small wonder given my bloody and messed-up appearance—I added, "I'm a federal agent."

"Let me take care of that," said a man in a white doctor's gown who emerged from an inside room hearing the commotion. "Are you hurt?"

"I'm OK, thanks, but I really need the phone," I said. Looking uneasy, the receptionist handed me the receiver. Moments later I heard sirens and the building was flooded by SWAT, the Special Weapons Assault Team, wearing black protective gear and carrying high-power guns. A neighbor must have called the police after hearing the shots. One SWAT member entered the dentist's office and approached me.

I flashed my DOJ ID. "There's a shooter on the roof of the next building. There could be more than one."

"Were you the target?" he asked.

"I may have been, but more likely they wanted to get Timothy McHanna. He's on the twelfth floor, in McHanna Associates. Don't let him out of your sight. He's the subject of a federal investigation."

He radioed to his team, and we ran to the twelfth floor. McHanna was still cowering under his desk. But police were already everywhere, and no one was shooting. The officer answered his radio. "Got you."

"OK," he said. "There was just one shooter, and he got away, leaving empty shells behind him."

"I'm getting the hell out of here," said McHanna as he emerged from under the desk.

"I think we need to talk first," I said.

"I have nothing to tell you," he said dismissively.

"Who wanted to kill you? He may try again."

"How do you know I was the target? Could have been for you. From what I hear, you've got your own enemies."

He had a point, but I wasn't about to concede it.

"I'll look into the list of people who want me dead. But I suggest you do the same. I suspect the bullets were meant for you."

"Why?" he asked faintly, although I suspected he knew the answer already.

"Because nobody knew I was coming to see you."

"Not even in your own office?"

"No. I was in the neighborhood and thought I'd pay a visit to an old friend. Just a spur-of-the-moment thing."

"Mr. Gordon, I hardly think this is funny. My life is in danger."

Now he was admitting it. *That's some progress,* I thought.

"Were any threats made against you?"

"No."

"Tell me, who wants you dead?"

"I really don't know."

"Obviously the shooter knows, but he's currently unavailable. I don't have his e-mail or phone number, so I can't ask him. That leaves only you to answer my question. Who wants you dead?"

"I said I don't know."

"Why are your phones dead?"

"Dead? All of them?"

"Yes."

"I don't know. Maybe a power failure."

"Where is your staff? I didn't see anyone when I came in."

"I told them not to come in for now. We can't operate our business when all our files and computers are gone."

"Do you have any new employees?"

"No, they've all been with me for quite some time."

"So nobody came in today?"

"Just the receptionist. She came in this morning as usual, but I sent her home."

"Did she leave immediately?"

"I don't really know."

"Did she say anything about the mess in the office?"

"No. She was here yesterday during the search."

"What's her name?"

"Saida Rhaman."

"What's her address and phone number?"

"I only have a number. She told me she recently moved to a new apartment, and I don't have the address." He removed an address book from his inside jacket pocket. "Her number is 718-555-9878."

I told the SWAT agent quietly, "Don't let him out of your sight."

I went outside and called Hodson from a pay phone. "I think the attempted hit is directly connected to our search yesterday," I told him. "Somebody is trying to silence McHanna. It's also possible that the sniper was just sending him a warning.

A shooter with a sniper's rifle with a scope doesn't miss from such a short distance unless he's totally clumsy."

"That means that, whoever they are, they don't trust McHanna to keep quiet voluntarily," said Hodson. "Maybe it's time. I'll send agents to pick him up for questioning."

"I thought you'd do that, so I asked the SWAT team's commander to keep an eye on McHanna."

I called the duty FBI agent. "I need to locate Saida Rhaman, telephone 718-555-9878."

"Hold on."

"The last known address we have is on Atlantic Avenue, Brooklyn, New York." He gave me the house number.

"What's the cross street?"

"Third Avenue."

"Did you check the phone listing?"

"Yes, it's listed under Nikoukar Jafarzadeh."

"Please run a check on that person," I requested.

"OK. Call me in an hour."

"Sure, and once you're done with him, I need background on Saida Rhaman, a receptionist at McHanna Associates. Her boss gave me the number listed as Jafarzadeh's."

The name Jafarzadeh sounded Iranian, and Saida Rhaman sounded Arabic. But maybe it was a coincidence. Or not. An hour later I called the agent again.

"Nikoukar Jafarzadeh, a male born in Tehran, Iran, in 1970, applied for a student visa in 1988 sponsored by a language-learning institute in Virginia. An F-1 student visa was issued on 2/88. The visa expired on 2/90 and there's no record of his leaving the country. On 7 November 1992 he was stopped in Arlington, Virginia, on a minor traffic violation. He carried a Virginia driver's license, number 099889004334. Virginia's DMV records show his address as 1528 North 16th Road, Arlington, Virginia 22209. There's no telephone listing for that address. No connection to Saida Rhaman was found. Additional information is forthcoming."

"Do I understand from the immigration info you've just mentioned that he's an illegal alien?"

"Probably, since we presume he's still in the U.S. There's no Social Security number attached to his name, nor an INS 'A' number indicating he received permanent residence, a green card, or that one is pending."

I called Hodson and reported. "Let our people in Virginia handle this," said Hodson when he heard my suspicions. I was entering his turf.

Mel, the analyst, called me. "You'd better come down here," he said. "We found something interesting."

CHAPTER THIRTY-ONE

As I walked into the analysts' room, Mel gave me a document and exclaimed, "Look at this!" It was a one-page form. "This is a money-transfer order of $7,900 to Niarchos Alexander Papadimitriou, International Bank of Hellas, Athens, Greece, account GF 8873554."

I gave him a wondering look. "And?"

"We also found this," he said and flashed a red-cover Greek passport. I opened the bio page and saw our dear friend Timothy McHanna's picture. The name on the passport was Niarchos Alexander Papadimitriou, nationality Hellenic, valid for five years. I leafed through the pages. There were a few entry and exit stamps, all from European countries.

So multiple identities weren't the Chameleon's exclusive domain. I returned to the office and ran a check on Niarchos Alexander Papadimitriou. Nothing came out. I quickly sent a query to Interpol, U.S. National Central Bureau to seek Greek police assistance in identifying Niarchos Alexander Papadimitriou, and to ask whether the passport was genuine. I attached a copy. I didn't have much hope from that end. I suspected that the genuine-looking passport was homemade.

Although the passport appeared to have been used for travel

outside the U.S., I assumed McHanna used it for additional purposes. The money-transfer order, though in the modest amount of $7,900, could indicate that McHanna didn't trust the pension plan the true owners of his company had prepared for him and was building his own nest, padded with somebody else's money. If there was one transfer, there could be more.

"I suggest you ask your team to keep looking. I think the strategy should be to look for all money transfers to individuals."

"That's easy," said Mel. "We have their computers up and running."

Within moments the printer spewed out a report of all outgoing money transfers during the preceding seven years, sorted and grouped by recipient.

"That's fantastic," I said. "Can we sort the data by date? That way we can see when money went out and to whom. Next we should do the same with incoming transfers, and finally do the same when the sending or receiving party was a corporation or a trust." I had just brought upon myself weeks of tedious paperwork. Next, we'd compare the accounting with the records I'd brought from Switzerland.

Within an hour we started to see a clear pattern. McHanna was moving small amounts, usually $2,000 or $3,000 at a time, to his Niarchos Alexander Papadimitriou bank account in Greece. In just one year the transfers totaled $215,080. I searched the files for the name Nikoukar Jafarzadeh—just a wild guess—but there was nothing for that name.

The FBI duty agent called. He'd contacted the Bureau of Alcohol, Tobacco, Firearms, and Explosives and learned that Nikoukar Jafarzadeh's name had come up following a query on his name at the National Tracing Center, Crime Gun Analysis Branch. It brought up his gun purchases: two sniper rifles and a handgun from one dealer at a gun show in Virginia. The dealer had filled out a form for ATF. That information, combined with the other evidence we already had, was too strong to ignore. First McHanna said that he'd told the receptionist not to come to work on the day following the FBI search, but she had. Next, the phones weren't working and the receptionist had disappeared. Then came the discovery that her home phone was actually listed under Nikoukar Jafarzadeh, a man with a fondness for sniper guns.

I called Hodson. "I may have a direction for you," I said. "The shooter may have had inside help." I gave him the details. "I'll be back in the office tomorrow," I said. "Is McHanna there already?"

"Yes, we are working on him now."

When I returned to the federal building on the next day, I saw Hodson with his aides. "Made progress with McHanna?"

"No. He isn't talking," said Hodson. "A dead fish is more talkative."

"First-degree interrogation?" I asked, thinking how aggressive FBI interrogators can be.

"Second, as well," he said. "He's been under interrogation for the past twenty hours, but he isn't saying anything meaningful."

I entered the interrogation room. McHanna was rattled when he saw me. He looked bad, really bad, with black circles under his eyes, which were shifting from one side to the other.

"Can I be alone with him?" I asked.

The FBI agent left the room.

"McHanna, look at me. I'm your chance to live through this."

He raised his head with a contemptuous look that said it all.

"I know what you did during the past two decades, or for an even longer period. No question you're looking at a prison term. But we can pretend there's nothing against you and let you walk right now."

"You mean I can go?"

"There's some paperwork to complete, but yes, I'll recommend letting you go."

"What's the catch?" he asked suspiciously.

"No trick. You refuse to cooperate. It will be a while until all the documents seized in your office will be analyzed. We may not have a probable cause to hold you any longer, so I think you're about to leave this place soon. We have patience, though, and I'm sure you'll be back."

He gave me a doubtful look.

"Of course, your employers will not be so patient. Do you know why?"

He looked at me, waiting for me to continue.

"Because they'll understand you talked. Of course, an inadvertent leak from a 'knowledgeable government source that spoke on condition of anonymity' could appear in the media saying that you're cooperating, and therefore were released on your own recognizance."

That got to him. "Are you crazy?" he yelled. "They'll kill me."

"Why? You have been serving them loyally for such a long time, they'll probably try to smuggle you out of the country."

It didn't seem to be an option that McHanna had even considered viable. And we had not yet said who "they" were.

"It's a good thing that you understand reality," I said, and sat on a chair opposite him. "They'll have no such plans. They don't believe in protracted justice."

He didn't react.

"Of course, the fact that you were stealing them blind isn't going to help, if they find out."

He was too shaken to say anything. "Mr. Niarchos Alexander Papadimitriou," I said in a theatrical solemnity. "Do you have additional names and passports leading to bank accounts with money you skimmed?"

"What do you want to know?" he asked faintly.

"Where is Kourosh Alireza Farhadi?"

"Who?"

"Kourosh Alireza Farhadi."

"Never heard that name."

"Kourosh Alireza Farhadi, aka Albert Ward III."

"Really? Is that Albert's name? I didn't know that. I told you, Albert's in Australia. He's retired."

Aha, I said to myself, *McHanna forgot when he lied, when he told the truth, or when he'd said anything.*

He supposedly knew him only as Whitney-Davis. He had just confirmed knowledge of Albert Ward, although he'd previously denied it.

"And where is Harrington T. Whitney-Davis?"

"They're all the same person. Retired in Australia."

Bingo! But I didn't want to show him my joy, and moved on. "Retired? What do you mean?"

"He told me that he decided to retire in Australia."

"When was that?"

"I think a few months ago."

"While he was in the U.S.?"

"He called me from Australia. I last saw him a few years ago."

"Who owns McHanna Associates?"

"I do."

"Formally?"

"Yes."

"And informally?"

He hesitated. "I have silent investors."

"Who are they?"

"Foreign institutions."

"I need names."

"I can't give you any."

"Why?"

He didn't answer.

"Mr. McHanna, I know who your investors are."

"You do?"

"Yes. You're the paymaster of an Iranian covert operation in the U.S., which moved millions of dollars to and from the U.S. to finance secret operations of Iranian intelligence services, and to support terrorist organizations."

He became so pale that I though he'd faint immediately. I leaned toward him. "Mr. McHanna, I hope you realize that under the Patriot Act, what you did could get you the death penalty by lethal injection in a federal prison."

Before I could move, McHanna vomited on me and on his own clothes. It smelled terrible—he must have eaten the carcass of a skunk after he was brought in. Was that the kind of food they served there? I calmly took a tissue from my pocket and wiped the slime off my face and clothes, remaining in my seat.

"Look at me," I said. "I'm the only one who can help you out of this mess. Tell me where our guy is."

"I want a lawyer," he suddenly said. "I've got rights."

"Do you know what is going to happen if your Iranian bosses discover you were skimming off the top? I hardly think they'll like it."

"I didn't steal anything."

"Right," I said. "It was actually Papadimitriou who transferred money to his personal bank account in Greece, and it so happens that Niarchos Alexander Papadimitriou looks exactly like you."

"This was money I was entitled to."

"Don't expect me to believe that," I said. "Your Iranian friends will like even less the fact that you killed their agent who suspected you. U.S. prisons are safe places, but you know, anyone really determined could get to you even there. Shit happens.

"Look, I know you killed Christopher Gonda—that is, Reza Nazeri," I suddenly said.

McHanna didn't answer. He was as pale as a sheet of paper. I took a step back. I wasn't going to let him vomit on me again.

"The man you are looking for is in Sydney, Australia," said McHanna faintly. "During recent years he used the name Herbert Goldman."

"Where can I find him?"

McHanna hesitated.

"If you don't tell me, then I'll assume it's just another lie. Or maybe you had him killed?"

"No, no," he protested. "Look in my personal address book. Your men seized it when I was brought here."

I remembered looking through it and not seeing any reference to Goldman. "Under what name did you list his number?"

"Norman McAllister."

"And the number is in the address book? Is there an address as well?"

"No, just the phone number. It's in code. You have to add numbers to get the correct telephone number."

"What's the code?"

"Add one to the first number, two to the second number, three to the third, and so on."

"Tell me when you spoke with him last."

"A week ago."

"What did he tell you?"

"He wanted me to send him money and a passport."

"Did you?"

"Yes, I wired him $3,000 through Western Union. I had no way of getting him a passport." McHanna buried his head between his soiled hands. "I want a lawyer," he repeated faintly.

"Do you want to make a deal? Is that it?"

"Maybe."

"I'll get you a lawyer." I left the room, and asked the agent to assume control. I went to the men's room to wash up. There wasn't much I could do. I used the industrial-strength soap and water to wash my hands and my face and the stains off my clothes, but the soap smell just got mixed with the sour smell of McHanna's vomit.

I returned to Hodson's office. They were still sitting there when I entered, together with the jet stream of smell, courtesy of McHanna.

"What happened? You smell like shit," said Holliday, stepping a safe distance away from me.

"McHanna doesn't seem to like the menu here," I said wryly. "And I took his complaint." I went on, "He wants a lawyer, probably to make a deal."

"What does he have to offer?"

"You'd better watch the video. For one thing, he didn't flat-out deny my theory that he was heading the financial arm of an Iranian clandestine operation here, moving millions to finance terror. Next, he conceded that Ward, Farhadi, Whitney-Davis and Goldman—our Chameleon—were the same person. Look in his address book under Norman McAllister for the Chameleon's number." I gave them the code.

"I'm sure more details will come in McHanna's full account," I continued. "It's looking like he wants a plea bargain. Between all this and Reza's statements, he'll be locked up forever."

"What statements?" Hodson sounded surprised.

"Reza sent his mother three letters and asked her to keep them in a safe place. She kept the letters in an envelope together with other personal stuff he had left behind. She showed me the envelope, and there I found the first lead to Reza's connection to Al Taqwa. I borrowed the letters and had them translated."

"Borrowed?" asked Holliday, catching the word immediately. "You said they were personal. Did his mother let you take them?"

He knew me well. "Well, she showed them to me, and I borrowed them."

"Without letting her know?" asked Bob.

"I'll return them," I promised. "But anyway, Reza wrote to his mother that McHanna, the head of a financial institution in New York where Reza had been working, was stealing from the company, and when Reza confronted him, McHanna threatened his life. Apparently McHanna kept his promise, although he didn't confess doing it yet."

Holliday told me what they'd learned after sending "Dan Gordon's law partner" to look for additional documents in the Swiss bank archives. "We found documents establishing that Nazeri was a member of Atashbon. He'd first used Christopher Gonda's name, and as of 1988 used the name Philip Manteau. He was actually functioning as McHanna's boss, but disguised as an employee."

"Were all three letters saying the same thing?" asked Hodson.

"Only two. The third one hinted about the possible fate of the Chameleon. It only said that McHanna was nervous about recent developments, and that he even told his employees that if they ever reported on him, he would get them. I think Reza sent these letters to his mother as an insurance policy. Maybe he didn't trust Atashbon command's protection that much."

I got up. "I'm going home to wash up. Even I can't stand myself any longer."

Back home, my happiness at the developments couldn't distract me from how ill I felt. Was it the vomit that McHanna dribbled on me? I checked my temperature—it was 101.9°F. I took two Tylenols and fell on my bed. I slept on and off for eighteen hours until the fever subsided, but I was still aching. All of the travel and adventure was catching up to me. I remembered my mother saying that after a certain age, if you don't wake up aching in every joint, you are probably dead.

CHAPTER THIRTY-TWO

Two days later I was asked to attend a meeting at Hodson's office. Casey and Holliday were there as well. Hodson pulled out a white envelope. "This is for you."

I put it in my pocket.

"No," said Hodson. "Read it now."

I opened the envelope. It contained a letter from the assistant secretary of defense.

Dear Dan,

On behalf of the United States, I wish to thank you for your contribution in unveiling the sale of long-range cruise missiles to Iran. Maintaining the military supremacy of the United States and disarming rogue nations guarantees our national security. Your efforts were an important step towards fulfilling that goal.

"What the hell is he talking about?" I was really surprised. "I had no connection to any information on Iranian missiles."

"You missed a lot while you were in isolation," said Casey. "The pieces are all falling together. Ukraine has confirmed that twelve of its cruise missiles were sold to Iran and six to China. However, when it became public, the Ukrainians claimed that the sales were unauthorized. They also claim that private businessmen sold Iran twelve X-55 cruise missiles, which are known better as Kh-55s or AS-15s."

"With nuclear warheads?" I asked.

"No. But that's no consolation. They have a range of eighteen hundred miles, which covers most of Russia, Japan, and of course Israel."

"I heard that Iran was developing long-range missiles," I said. "And that their ultimate goal is to develop transcontinental missiles with a sixty-five hundred mile range that can get to the United States. But they aren't there yet, so that's why they purchased ready-made ones. But what have I got to do with it?"

Hodson ignored my question and continued. "Even now, after that sale, Iran is already the third country in the world, after the U.S. and Russia, to have cruise missiles. This type has a sophisticated navigational system that corrects itself after launch by comparing the terrain it passes with photos of the target programmed into its computer."

"But you didn't answer my question. What have I done in this matter to deserve the letter?" I persisted.

Casey finally spelled it out. "You identified Hasan Lotfi as a potential defector. We made contact with him. He brought in the information. The Pentagon is pretty pleased. Pressure put on the Ukrainian government led to the dealers' indictment, and the Iranians will have a difficult time getting spare parts and tech support. Without that, the missiles won't be operational too soon."

I folded the letter and put it back in the envelope. "My grandchildren will be proud of me," I said with half a smile. "What about McHanna? I was sick like a dog for two days."

Hodson briefed me on McHanna's interrogation.

"What about the sniper?" I asked.

"Staged," said Hodson. "We suspected from the beginning that the event was odd. A pro using a scope missed from fifty-seven yards? No sniper would miss from four times that short distance using such sophisticated equipment. The conclusion was that the shooter didn't intend to hit McHanna."

"He only wanted to frighten him?"

"We thought of that too. But your initial suspicion of Saida Rhaman, the receptionist, was right. We got to her, and from her to her uncle, Nikoukar Jafarzadeh. Corroborative evidence was found when we discovered that the gun was purchased in Virginia by Nikoukar Jafarzadeh. He and his niece told us that McHanna had asked them to arrange the mock shooting."

"Did he give them a reason?"

"Yes. According to them, McHanna said that his management didn't appreciate him and was about to fire him, which could lead to Saida's losing her job as well. Therefore he thought that an attempt on his life would make it difficult for the company's owners to get rid of him."

"Did you buy that story? It doesn't make sense."

"Do I look like I just fell off the turnip truck?" grunted Hodson. "We've leads suggesting that Nikoukar Jafarzadeh was the Atashbon's local muscle, and the shooting came as a warning to McHanna."

"Why didn't he take McHanna out?"

"We'll investigate that. But personally I think that McHanna misread the Iranians. He was too valuable to them, his stealing notwithstanding. Money was not their problem at that point—you'll soon hear why. McHanna was the only non-Iranian in the operation, and they didn't trust him completely, but still needed a Yankee in the operation."

"I guess they were right." I scratched my head. "What

about Reza Nazeri? He was pushed from the platform of a train to his death. Was McHanna involved?"

"McHanna confessed that he ordered his death as self-defense. Reza discovered that McHanna was stealing and threatened to turn him in."

I wondered why Reza hadn't just had McHanna quietly eliminated. Had he tried and failed?

"What about Nazeri's apartment? I found it too clean."

"We haven't gotten to it yet, but I'm sure McHanna went there personally or sent Jafarzadeh."

"So if we have sufficient evidence, why strike a deal?"

"McHanna told us these details in a proffer, with the understanding that there will be a plea bargain. Life without the possibility of parole. That's a worse punishment than death."

"What about the remaining members of Atashbon?"

"He said he has details on only six members."

"Did he name them?"

"Yes. Kourosh, our Chameleon; Reza, aka Gonda, now deceased; and Arthur Jenkins, Timothy Williamson, Alec Simmons, Kevin DiAngelo, and Frank Gonzales. These names match the names of American men who went missing in the eighties. These six suspects changed these names to other American-sounding names immediately after they completed the first round of the scam operations. They simply used the good old throwaway cover: one alias was layered on top of another alias. That's why we couldn't find them—the string of aliases was abandoned, but the operatives remained here. They are all in custody. They claimed that they had severed their relationship with Iran a long time ago, and are now law-abiding citizens."

"Though not, of course, of the U.S." I said. "Do you believe them?"

He chuckled. "They'll be indicted, and tried. If convicted, they'll be deported after serving their sentences—that is, if they're still living forty to sixty years from now. Oddly, or not so oddly, some of them claimed to be employees of a legitimate printing-press company. When we checked their story an interesting thing happened. In addition to their racket-eering activity in defrauding banks and being covert operatives of Iran, they were operating a much bigger operation, which dwarfed the $300 million stolen from U.S. banks. We're talking billions of dollars here. Three hundred million is a lot of money, but it cannot collapse the U.S. economy. But hundreds of bil-lions could cause serious damage."

"Billions? I saw no reference to it in the files."

"There was no reference there," said Hodson. "Together with U.S. Secret Service we discovered that Atashbon members in the United States were running a printing press of counter-feit U.S. dollars. Iranian agents bought the printing machines from Germany and smuggled them to the U.S. in several ship-ments, using a front company run by Atashbon members. The sad thing is that Americans trained the Iranians to use these high-end printing presses."

"You mean we trained them to print dollars?" asked Bob Holliday.

"Of course not," said Hodson. "In the early 1970s the Shah of Iran asked the U.S. to help solve counterfeiting problems that threatened to undermine Iran's currency. So we sent technical people from the Bureau of Engraving and Printing to Tehran to improve the safety of the Iranian currency."

"The balls on them!" said Casey Bauer. "We trained them. Now we discover that they had an incredible audacity. Years later these motherfuckers were intending to collapse the U.S. economy."

"Good thing the hundred-dollar bill was redesigned," I said.

"There are three types of forged dollars," explained Hodson. "Two are rather primitive and easy to detect, but the third is a real piece of art. Common forgers use offset lithography, which prints dollars that lack the feel of real currency because the ink is flat, unlike the raised ink of genuine bills. Digital forgeries are very common because anyone with a scanner and high-quality printer or a copier can become a forger. But again, unless you use the fabric of genuine dollars, the notes printed are in fact

Monopoly money, particularly when they all have the same serial number. But the Iranians managed to produce high-quality
notes, using the same intaglio printing presses that the Bureau of
Engraving does."

"What's intaglio?" asked Bob.

"A press that creates miniscule ridges on cotton-linen paper by forcing it at high pressure into the ink-filled grooves
of an engraved plate. Now the outcome looks—and better
yet, feels—like real currency," answered Hodson, looking at
his notes.

"How did they get over the biggest obstacle, the material
used for U.S. currency?" asked Holliday.

"It's difficult but not impossible," said Hodson. "Currency
paper is composed of 25 percent linen and 75 percent cotton.
Red and blue synthetic fibers of various lengths are distributed evenly throughout the paper. Governments can buy it
freely, and we assume Iran had no problem acquiring it. We
think they decided to print the currency in the U.S. because
it'd be much easier to smuggle the fabric into the U.S. than
the final product—bales of billions of forged U.S. dollars.
Nonetheless, the Secret Service is still investigating how the
fabric entered the U.S. for the Iranians' local printing needs."

"The printing operation here was seized, and that's what's
important," concluded Casey.

Hodson nodded. "I must concede that we knew about
the Iranian effort, but never made the connection to the
Chameleon cases until we cracked them. As early as 1996 the
General Accounting Office reported that a foreign government was sponsoring production of the 'Superdollar'—a
high-quality bill."

"How did they distribute that volume?" asked Holliday.
"You can get away with a few millions, not billions."

"The operative word is *slowly*. We have evidence that bills
printed in the U.S. were introduced into the circulation
through their bogus charities and using criminal enterprises that
usually launder drug money, to launder much bigger amounts.
Some of the money printed in Iran was given to Hezbollah and

Islamic Jihad to finance their operations, and they distributed it from Lebanon's Bekaa Valley. Soon enough, the money turned up in Hong Kong, Macao, South Korea, Russia, and Latin America."

"Has anyone assessed the actual or potential damage to the U.S. economy?" I asked.

"There are only estimates," said Hodson. "We have no numbers to measure the impact, but this counterfeiting is a clear form of economic warfare that could cause serious inflation in the U.S., and undermine the world market's confidence in U.S. currency. Now we put the lid on it."

I was curious to hear more about the ploy we used to infiltrate me into Iran. "Did the alumni hold the reunion after all?"

"Yes, we sent Erikka back to complete the arrangements. If the reunion plans were scrapped, a suspicion could arise about whether the plan was just a cover for your activities. We wanted to keep that part of your mission clean."

Why would we care? I thought, although I knew the answer. The reunion helped recruit new assets.

"Was the event successful?"

"From our perspective, yes. We had to close the circle." He'd tacitly confirmed my assumption.

"Any progress in the investigation regarding my Bern hotel-room search? Do you know whodunit?" I touched my head. I'd had enough of unpleasant encounters with strangers in European hotel rooms. Couldn't my rivals just for once send somebody nice? How come in the thriller movies there's an attractive woman who is gently confronting the good guy, while in reality I collide with burly men with body odors?

"We have incomplete results."

I sensed that Casey wasn't telling me everything, but CIA guys tend to be like that.

"We didn't clean up the world from all sorts of bad guys, but we're trying," he said. "The job at your hotel was carried out by people working for the Iranian security services. We think they were local burglars hired for that onetime job. The Swiss police already have a suspect. Our assumption is that they

wanted to know what you found out at the bank. When we realized that, we asked Benny Friedman to find a way to alert
Tempelhof Bank to increase security at its warehouse. They
could attempt to destroy the evidence."

I paused. "I hate to dwell on this, but how did they find
out I was coming to Switzerland and where I was staying?"

"Benny has investigated it from the direction of the bank
personnel. The Mossad found a bad apple in the bank's staff,
whose duty was to alert Iran whenever there was any outside
interest in their clandestine financial activities passing through
the bank. That was a very smart move on the Iranians' part, in-
stalling security on both sides of the money-laundering ring."

"How did Benny catch the mole, without having any official or formal connection to the bank?"

"Benny never said it in so many words, but I think he pulled
out an old trick for smoking out your enemy. He spread a
rumor at the bank that on that very day the Swiss police were
about to raid the bank seeking evidence of 'private' deposits
made at the bank by members of the current Iranian regime.
One employee was monitored leaving the bank in haste during
office hours and was photographed making a call from a pay
phone just outside the bank. Benny had anticipated it and
bugged all public phones in the area."

"Shrewd move," I said in appreciation.

Just as I thought we were done, Hodson gave me a folder.

"Pack your bags, you are going to Australia to get the
Chameleon."

"Again? Why? Hasn't the telephone number in McHanna's
address book been decoded? The Australian Federal Police can
find him easily." I just didn't feel like leaving again.

"It was decoded. It belongs to an Australian woman. She told
the police that Norman McAllister has rented a small apartment
from her but took off just about the same time you gave us the
number. He still owes her two months' rent. So far, the Australian Federal Police have no clue. Since you know what the
Chameleon looks like and you have the most 'Chameleon
hours,' we thought that your presence there could help."

"Did you try to trace the Chameleon through the $3,000 wire transfer McHanna said he made?" I asked. Maybe not all bases were covered, and I'd be spared that long haul.

"It was just another lie. There was no such transfer to anyone by that name in the past month. McHanna was bullshitting you."

I thought it was strange. McHanna didn't lie regarding the Chameleon's phone number, but lied on the money transfer. I wondered why. But said nothing.

"When am I leaving?" I asked, accepting the travel folder.

"Tonight."

Two days later I landed at Sydney's airport and Peter Maxwell, the curly-haired Australian federal agent, picked me up.

"Any news?" I asked anxiously as he escorted me through immigration.

"Nothing yet," he said. "We searched his rented apartment, but nothing was found. His landlady said he was a quiet tenant and had no visitors, but he was always behind on his rent. She said he left a few short days ago without any luggage, together with two men who came with a late-model Japanese car."

"Any more details?"

"Nothing, she just saw them from the back. All she could say was that the car was white."

"Did you get his phone records?" I was hoping for a clue there.

"He never used the apartment's phone for outgoing calls, only incoming. She said he had a cell phone, but she doesn't know the number."

"Did you trace it through other means?"

"No," said Maxwell apologetically. "There were no listings for any of the names we had."

"Including Norman McAllister?" I asked with a shred of hope.

"Yes, but there's nothing. It's quite possible he used a stolen phone or one of these 'pay as you go' phones that require no registration."

I was exhausted, but after only a few hours of sleep I forced myself to start working. *I'll rest in my old age,* I promised myself. I had a hunch where to start looking for the Chameleon.

I called Sheila Levi, the legal secretary that the Chameleon almost managed to marry.

She sounded very surprised, but glad to hear my voice. "I was hoping you'd call," she said in a soft voice. "In fact I wanted to call you, but I didn't have your number."

"I'm here now. Is there something you wanted to tell me?"

"Yes. I told you last time we met that I gave Herb Goldman jewelry I'd inherited from my grandmother."

"Yes." I remembered how disgusted I'd been to hear how the Chameleon, posing as Herbert Goldman, had used Sheila.

"Well. He sold them to a jewelry shop near the Rocks. About two weeks ago I looked at the window of that shop and was happy to see on display a necklace and a ring that I gave Goldman. They were not sold yet."

"If you want to get them back, you'll probably need a good lawyer." I said.

"No, I didn't mean that. I entered the shop. I know the owner. He's a member of the Jewish community—he's a nice person. I asked him if I could pay him over time for the necklace, hoping to retrieve at least one piece from my grandmother's gifts to me."

"And what did he say?"

"He agreed immediately. I'm paying him $10 a week for sixty-five weeks, and it will be mine again. He was kind to let me have the necklace immediately. The interesting thing is that he said that Goldman came by his shop last week to sell him more jewelry."

If I was still tired, I forgot all about it. "Tell me more."

"The reason I wanted to call you was that I knew you were looking for him. You see, the shopkeeper told me that he refused Goldman's offer to sell him that jewelry until Goldman could prove ownership. He became suspicious."

"Why?"

"Because Goldman asked for $500 for jewelry worth at least $1,500."

"Did Goldman tell the shopkeeper he'd be back with proof?"

"I don't know."

I called Maxwell and gave him the information.

"It's a start," he said. "We have an additional lead. A person answering Goldman's description has attempted to purchase a forged passport."

"Any leads from there?"

"No, it was an anonymous tip to our hotline. We assumed he was unable to leave Australia because his Goldman passport became useless ever since you exposed his Goldman identity."

I ran the facts through my mind. It was possible that the Chameleon had unilaterally severed his relationship with the Iranian intelligence services and had no way of getting another passport. Otherwise he'd have been out of there a long time ago. The fact that he'd tried to get a passport independently both locally and from McHanna only supported my hunch. Active agents of foreign countries can be sure that in time of distress, their handlers will extricate them. When that didn't happen, the only conclusion was that the Chameleon didn't contact the Iranians.

"The Chameleon must still be around," I said.

"The Chameleon?" asked Maxwell in surprise.

"Yes, that's the name I gave him." I went on to give him the limited scope of information about the Chameleon's ties to Iran I was authorized by Holliday to divulge to the Australians. "I think that even while still in the U.S., the Chameleon panicked and was sure that the FBI was on to him. He needed to escape. Of course, if he'd asked to be returned to Tehran, they would have smuggled him back. But since he didn't, and based on our interrogation of another suspect in the U.S., I think the Chameleon had decided on going independent, without telling the Iranians. He simply obtained a false passport under the name of Herbert Goldman, a thirteenth alias, and decided to go to Australia, hoping that the FBI wouldn't trace him and that Tehran would ultimately forget about him. That by itself is a cause for concern for any intelligence service, because independents try to market the goods they have to anyone that will buy them—in this case, information about his previous employer."

"We know about the Iranians' reaction in these instances," said Maxwell without elaborating.

"I'm sure the Chameleon obviously knew of the Iranian intelligence services' policy to save on pension payments to self-declared retirees, by moving to entitle their families to some death benefits instead. We suspect he went independent in Australia, because he called a contact in New York seeking a passport and money. The man who'd conned millions out of banks and investors remained penniless. He had to resort to petty crime and defrauded Sheila Levi, that poor secretary he'd promised to marry. He hinted to his New York contact that the FBI may have received information from the Australian Federal Police that had traced him in Australia."

"It could be just disinformation the Chameleon was giving that person in New York, probably to obtain his cooperation," said Maxwell dismissively.

"You are right," I answered. I couldn't tell Maxwell that McHanna had a direct interest in keeping the Chameleon quiet. Temporarily or permanently.

I felt tired. The twenty-four-hour travel between the U.S. and Australia had taken it's toll on me. I returned to my hotel. When I woke up there was a coded message from Hodson on my laptop.

The following is additional information obtained from McHanna during his interrogation; be aware that it has not been corroborated. McHanna alleged that the Chameleon had told him during the telephone conversation that was earlier disclosed to you, that he (the Chameleon) had a lot of money hidden in Switzerland, probably a commission he paid himself each time he stole on behalf of the Iranians. McHanna also said that the Chameleon couldn't get to his money, because it was kept in cash in safe-deposit boxes in Switzerland. That made wiring the money impossible.

That's very interesting, I thought. McHanna lied to me regarding the wire transfer to the Chameleon and now he tells the FBI that the Chameleon has a safe-deposit box in Switzerland? That wasn't earth-shattering news. The Chameleon had to keep his money somewhere. For me, the things that the Chameleon didn't say in that connection were far more interesting. My conclusion from McHanna's statement was that the Chameleon was totally dependent on him. I was sure that McHanna couldn't risk the Chameleon talking. That would endanger McHanna's freedom if the FBI found out what he did, or his life, if the Iranians discovered he'd betrayed them and killed their agent. No, I concluded. McHanna doesn't want us to find the Chameleon alive.

I called Peter Maxwell and discussed my conclusion with him. "Can you get your people in the street to listen to vibrations? I think the Chameleon's life is in danger."

"We already have all our intelligence sniffers on the alert," he said.

I sent Hodson a coded message.

I have a problem with McHanna's story. Did he really have that conversation with the Chameleon? And if he did talk to him, did the Chameleon request help? If so, did he give McHanna his location? How was McHanna supposed to send money or a passport without an address? The Chameleon obviously knew that McHanna also worked for the Iranians. Wasn't he afraid that McHanna would turn him in?

A few hours later I received Hodson's coded answer.

We asked him these questions. McHanna said the Chameleon threatened him that if he went down, he'd take McHanna with him. Apparently the Chameleon knew about the private nest McHanna was building for himself using the Iranians' money. But we don't know if the call actually happened.

I sent Hodson another coded message.

Please interrogate McHanna regarding an attempt on the Chameleon's life. My suspicion is that if the Chameleon betrayed the Iranians and killed Nazeri, he'd have no qualms in betraying McHanna. Therefore, I think McHanna would have him killed before we could get to him. McHanna's giving us the Chameleon's telephone number was probably meant to be used as a future alibi. If accused of arranging the Chameleon's assassination, he could deny it by asking why would he give us a clue where the Chameleon was hiding, if he wanted him dead rather than alive and talking?

One minute later, I received another coded message written and sent before my last message to Hodson went out.

Dan, we have another development. McHanna has confessed to ordering Ms. Otis clipped. He said that Otis was married to the Chameleon and he may have told her something damaging. McHanna confessed that he knew that she had already exposed the Chameleon as Ward and Goldman to the Sydney rabbi. That was enough, even if she didn't know about the Chameleon's Whitney-Davis identity or the Chameleon's covert activities and his real name. If the Chameleon were apprehended, then the shit would hit the fan and the way to McHanna would be short. The Chameleon's identity exposure was not just a matter between the rabbi in Australia and Loretta Otis in the United States, two private individuals. McHanna told us that the Chameleon called months ago telling him that his identity as Goldman was blown. No further security infraction was necessary to convince anyone in the loop that Otis had to be eliminated.

So Hodson had reached the same conclusion as I had. The Chameleon's life was short unless we got to him first.

I deleted the messages.

I went to meet Peter Maxwell. He came with a tall, slim, blonde woman in her midtwenties. "This is Gilian Caldwell. She's a member of my team." We shook hands. "Tell him," urged Peter.

"There's word on the street that anyone identifying Norman McAllister could make $1,000," said Gilian.

"Any credence?" I asked.

"Yes, pretty much. We spread that rumor." She chuckled. "A petty thief came forward and told us that Mr. McAllister has bought stolen jewelry from him for $150."

"The same jewelry the Chameleon tried to sell to the jewelry shop?"

"Probably. The thief became scared when he heard there was a bounty on McAllister's head. He told us he was afraid of getting accused or involved in this matter. He was out of his league."

"Of course the $1,000 reward was also a consideration," said Maxwell.

"Did he tell you where to find McAllister?" I asked.

Peter's phone vibrated. "Maxwell," he answered. He listened for a minute and told us in a hurried voice, "Let's go, a contact has been made."

When Gilian heard the address from Maxwell she said coolly, "That's the same address the petty thief gave us."

We jumped into their unmarked police car and Maxwell drove us to Bondi Junction, an eastern suburb of Sydney four miles east of the Sydney central business district. When we arrived, the area was buzzing with police activity. A uniformed officer approached Peter. "Sir, there's a person who has barricaded himself on the second floor of the house." He pointed his hand toward a two-story apartment building.

"Any demands?"

"No. We think he was probably held hostage, but his captors escaped when we arrived. The neighbors called us when they heard screams coming out of the house."

"If the captors left, why is the person barricading himself?" asked Peter, and my hope that we were going to find the Chameleon died. This didn't seem to be related to our case, so I just stood there letting Peter and Gilian do their job.

A few minutes later Peter came over to me. "We think the Chameleon is inside the house. A next-door neighbor gave us a description that meets the Chameleon's physical description. We need to convince him that we are the police and that he can leave safely."

"Is he armed?" I asked, wondering why the police didn't storm the house.

"No, but he shouted that he's holding a can of benzene and a lighter. He promised to burn anyone getting close. We want to resolve this without anyone getting hurt."

A policeman came over. "Mr. Maxwell?"

Peter turned to him. "We have a visual from another building. We can see that he's holding a tin can that is normally used to store petrol, but we don't know if it's full or not. His face seems burned or injured. His demeanor seems as if he is badly shaken; his hands are trembling and his speech is blurred. He could be deranged."

"For how long did the neighbors hear the screaming?"

"A whole night. At the beginning they thought it was just a domestic quarrel, but then realized they were screams of pain, so they called the police."

"Maybe someone was torturing him," I suggested, and Peter didn't seem to reject the idea.

"There's a crisis-management psychologist on the way," he said. "Maybe he can talk him out of it."

The next thing I saw and then heard was the sound of a bullet, followed by a fiery explosion that shattered windows in our vicinity, then sent a shock wave. A black cloud of smoke emerged from the house where the Chameleon had barricaded himself.

"Shit," said Maxwell, expressing my thoughts as well.

Police forces rushed into the building together with firemen and medics. I stayed behind. I knew already what they'd discover when they entered the house. The Chameleon had perished.

Maxwell joined me twenty minutes later. "The petrol tank held by the Chameleon was directly hit by a bullet and exploded. The Chameleon died instantly."

McHanna or the Iranians got him first, I thought. *That means that the Australians have an Atashbon of their own.*

After hearing more details from Maxwell, I returned to my hotel.

As I took off my clothes, I smelled the smoke, although I was standing two hundred feet away. I sent a message to Hodson, Casey, and Holliday reporting the Chameleon's demise. Then I crashed.

When I woke up I received a one sentence response. "Return home."

On the plane ride home, I was thinking what Goldilocks once said referring to that bowl of porridge: *This is just right.* After thumbing his nose at the law for so long, pay time for the Chameleon had come.

After getting over the jet lag, I went to see Hodson. Holliday and Casey were there as well.

"Did McHanna say anything about the Chameleon's death?" I asked.

Hodson smiled. "We forgot to tell him. Instead, we suggested that the Chameleon was arrested and was cooperating, putting all the blame on McHanna."

"And what was McHanna's reaction?" I asked in an amused tone.

"He threw everything back at the Chameleon and, in fact, filled in all the missing blanks."

"Didn't he suspect that you were pulling an interrogation trick on him? After all, he's a sly fox."

"We thought of that. But when we gave him details of where the Chameleon was hiding, he was convinced that we got him," said Casey.

"Does he know the truth now?" I was curious.

"Yes. Under the same plea we reached earlier, he confessed to sending a hit man to kill the Chameleon. He will be locked up forever."

"Was terminating the Chameleon McHanna's idea or Iran's order?"

"McHanna says Iran told him. Obviously we can't ask Tehran for comment. That leaves us with McHanna to face murder charges. As a lawyer, you know it makes no difference if he had him killed under orders from Tehran or on his own initiative. It's still murder," concluded Casey.

"It's all over but for the shouting," Hodson said. "Iran's most dangerous spy ring operating in the U.S. has been eliminated."

"Are you sure?" I insisted. I had the clear impression that Bauer, Hodson, and maybe even Holliday were looking to wind it down. But I still had unanswered questions.

"I am."

"Well, I'm not. If I were you I wouldn't ring the gong. I think we should continue digging. There were about eighteen members of Atashbon, and we've accounted for only eleven."

"We have accounted for all of them," Hodson said, beginning to lose his patience. He looked at Holliday and Casey, who shrugged their shoulders.

"That's Dan Gordon," said Bob Holliday. "You have to take him the way he is."

Hodson smiled. "You may not know this, but Dan and I have worked together before. I've had enough 'Dan hours' to teach me that he's relentless and cannot be stopped."

Holliday said in an amused tone, "My predecessor, David Stone, called him a pit bull who never lets go."

"I'm blushing," I said. "Stop." But in my heart I hoped they wouldn't. Admissions of imperfection? Not right now, and not from yours truly.

"I have to admit I was wrong," I said suddenly in a futile effort to improve off my image.

"That's a first," said Casey. "Enlighten us."

"I labeled him a chameleon because he caught his prey with his tongue and changed his skin each time he changed location. But apparently in nature, chameleons don't change their color to blend in with their environment. In fact, they mostly change their color when faced with imminent danger, or when their mood changes."

So the lid was finally put on the Chameleon and his comrades, although belatedly, I thought as I walked out the door. The forces of karma might have a good sense of justice, maybe even a sense of humor, but certainly a bad sense of timing.

ACKNOWLEDGMENTS

I inherited the love of writing from my father, Yehiel Carmon. Like me, he had a "day job" and a "night job." During the day, he was a stern CEO of an Israeli bank. But come evening, he was sequestered in his library, which had a huge collection of books squeezed on wall-to-wall shelves. There, he was glued to his noisy typewriter typing books and articles with two fingers. His library was his shelter from the high-pressure banking world, and there he immersed himself in the mysteries of Far East philosophies and Jewish wisdom. Little wonder that when I turned thirteen, my father's gift was his first published book, *The Decanter and the Goblet*.

My intelligence thrillers were inspired by my Israeli professional background, as well as by my twenty years of service for the United States government. Like my father before me, I also had a publicly known "daytime" activity as well as a "nighttime" covert activity. Since 1985 I have been representing the United States government in its Israeli civil litigation, appearing in Israeli courts in lawsuits to which the U.S. is a party. But away from the public eye, I was also engaged by the U.S. government to perform intelligence gathering in multimillion-dollar white-collar crime cases that required sensitive undercover work in more than thirty countries. Obviously, in my years working for the U.S. Department of Justice and other federal agencies, I could not share the hair-raising aspects of my work with anyone but my supervisors, and some adventures not even with them. Sadly, these events, which are sometimes more fascinating and breathtaking than the best fiction I have ever read, will never see the light of day. The story of Dan Gordon and his battle against the invisible FOE—forces of evil—is my idea of the next-best thing.

The Chameleon Conspiracy is the third installment in the Dan Gordon Intelligence Thriller series, preceded by Triple Identity and The Red Syndrome. More thrillers in the series are to follow. In my professional life, first in Israel and then working for the United States government, I have had enough adventures, frequently dangerous, to fill at least ten books, and those are just the ones I can talk about. The others I can't even fictionalize.

Many friends and family members helped me with this novel, to avoid pitfalls that loom when fiction and reality intertwine. Although The Chameleon Conspiracy was inspired by my work, it is not an autobiography, but rather a work of fiction brought closer to reality with every passing day. Apart from historical events, all names, characters, personal history, and events described in this book have never existed.

Many of my friends, after reading the barrage of my literary-related announcements and realizing I wrote four books in several years, asked me whether I switched careers again. My answer is always the same: my love for law and my passion for writing intelligence thrillers exist side by side. My novels, though fictional, carry a real-life message: read the writing on the wall! Terror, terrorists, and their state sponsors threaten the Free World and must be stopped. Unless we learn from the mistakes of others, we are doomed to repeat them.

Sarah McKee, former Justice Department general counsel of Interpol's U.S. Central Bureau, read the manuscript and helped me avoid pitfalls while describing Interpol's work. She also made suggestions based on her distinguished career as a federal prosecutor prior to her top role at Interpol. I am grateful for the special efforts she made, and for her unfailing grace and professionalism. My former supervisor and mentor,

David Epstein, is now retired, but in eighteen years of guidance he helped achieve that which inspired my novels, and I am forever grateful to him for that.

Lee Harounian was very helpful steering me off potential mistakes writing about Iranian customs and using short conversations in Farsi; visiting Iran was an unforgettable experience, but memory fades. Michael Valentino made important editing comments; Dr. Ariel Blumenthal reviewed the manuscript and made helpful suggestions. My anonymous Mossad friend used his computer to apply more "cut" than "paste" in his comments, and Jo Anne Shaw put an order into my otherwise erratic writing. Andre Le Gallo, a former CIA senior officer, made important observations and wrote the introduction. I'm grateful for his professionalism and friendly help. Don D'Auria, my editor, was encouraging and patient. I'm thankful for his efforts. My daughters Daria and Irin spent many hours reading drafts and making suggestions, although it was difficult for them to be introduced to the far and dark side of my work. Irin, my journalist daughter, applied to the manuscript her excellent editorial skills, and I'm thankful to her for that. My wife also endured the nonfictional tension of my long absences. Many of the hours I spent writing this book were taken away from my family, and my gratitude for their sacrifice is eternal.

Join the Dan Gordon Spy Club to receive free Spy Club Newsletters *and* get a chance to name a key character in a Dan Gordon Intelligence Thriller®!

Sign up for the Dan Gordon Spy Club and you'll get periodic updates on the gripping world of international espionage, with highlights on clandestine operations and spy gadgets. You'll also be entered in a contest to name a key character in a future Dan Gordon Intelligence Thriller®. Name the character after yourself, or give a loved one the special gift of being a part of the wildly popular series. You'll even be mentioned in the acknowledgments!

Please note: We respect your privacy. Your information is never shared with anyone other than for delivery of the newsletter. You can unsubscribe at any time.

By entering your e-mail address, you agree to receive a periodic Dan Gordon Spy Newsletter and other announcements concerning the author's thrillers. If your entry wins the random drawing, the name that you suggest shall become a character in a Dan Gordon Intelligence Thriller®, and all copyright to the name you suggest shall become the sole property of the author, without any further remuneration for the submitter. Additional restrictions apply.

No purchase necessary. One entry per e-mail address. Offer ends 12/31/09.

www.SleepWithOneEyeOpen.com

A CEECEE GALLAGHER THRILLER

STACY DITTRICH

AUTHOR OF *THE DEVIL'S CLOSET*

According to legend, Mary Jane was hanged as a witch and still haunts her grave. But when a teenage girl is found brutally murdered there, Detective CeeCee Gallagher knows no ghost is responsible. It's up to her to hunt down the very real killer before he strikes again. Her investigation will take her across the country and land her deep in the middle of a secret so shocking the locals have kept it hidden for a hundred years. With her career—and her life—on the line, CeeCee will have to face her darkest fears if she wants to uncover the truth about…

MARY JANE'S GRAVE

ISBN 13: 978-0-8439-6160-7

Against All Enemies

Like most wars, it started small. When the South American country of San Selva began burning Amazon rain forests, Washington applied pressure to appease popular opinion. But pressure led to attack, and attack led to counter-attack, and soon America found itself in a full-fledged war—against an enemy it was not prepared to fight. Now the stakes are raised and the U.S. sends Special Forces and Navy SEALs to try to regain the upper hand. As the fires in the rain forests rage out of control, ground troops prepare to go in. What started as politics will have to end on the battlefield. But is this a war anyone can win? And at what cost?

Maj. James B. Woulfe, USMC

ISBN 13: 978-0-8439-5140-0

DAVID ROBBINS

Doomsday. The end of all things.

Dreaded by many, scoffed at by skeptics.

And now it has come to pass.

At a remote site in Minnesota, filmmaker Kurt Carpenter has built a secure compound and invited a select group of people to bunker down until the worst is over. The world into which they reemerge is like nothing they've ever seen. At first they think they're the only ones left. But they soon find out how wrong they are. In the wasteland of what used to be America, their battle to survive is only just beginning...

ENDWORLD
DOOMSDAY

ISBN 13: 978-0-8439-6232-1

From the towers of Manhattan to the jungles of South America, from the sands of the Sahara to the frozen crags of Antarctica, one man finds adventure everywhere he goes:

GABRIEL HUNT

Backed by the resources of the $100 million Hunt Foundation and armed with his trusty Colt revolver, Gabriel Hunt has always been ready for anything—but is he prepared to dive into . . .

The adventures of a lifetime.

Coming soon to a bookstore near you...

HUNT *At the Well of Eternity*
Available May 2009

HUNT *Through the Cradle of Fear*
Available August 2009

HUNT *At World's End*
Available November 2009

☐ YES!

Sign me up for the Leisure Thriller Book Club and send
my FREE BOOKS! If I choose to stay in the club, I will
pay only $4.25* each month, a savings of $3.74!

NAME: _____

ADDRESS: _____

TELEPHONE: _____

EMAIL: _____

☐ I want to pay by credit card.

☐ VISA   ☐ MasterCard.   ☐ DISCOVER

ACCOUNT #: _____

EXPIRATION DATE: _____

SIGNATURE: _____

Mail this page along with $2.00 shipping and handling to:

Leisure Thriller Book Club
PO Box 6640
Wayne, PA 19087

Or fax (must include credit card information) to:

610-995-9274

You can also sign up online at **www.dorchesterpub.com**.

*Plus $2.00 for shipping. Offer open to residents of the U.S. and Canada only.
Canadian residents please call 1-800-481-9191 for pricing information.
If under 18, a parent or guardian must sign. Terms, prices and conditions subject to
change. Subscription subject to acceptance. Dorchester Publishing reserves the right
to reject any order or cancel any subscription.